THE SECOND NATURE OF INDIGO

AUBIN ELISE

KNIGHT KING PRESS

THE SECOND NATURE OF INDIGO

A rush to the head,
is it blood or ink?
My pen flowing black,
thoughts spilled on the page.

Are my words ink or thought?
I dare not answer.
Not in whisper or shout,
for fear the shadow
of doubt come nigh.

—Æ

PROLOGUE

Night of June 2nd, 1888
England

heodora is walking through her house, hand trailing the wall. Shadows cover the dark blue hallway like a collection of so many paintings. It must be after midnight, yet she will not rest. Why is she looking for The Girl? Theodora doesn't know, but she must find her.

After some time with only the sound of her own footsteps, she hears a scuff on the hardwood. Turning a corner, she finds her quarry. Grey, unblinking eyes stare up at her.

"Why are you here?" Theodora's voice comes out harsher than she expects.

"I came here to see you." The tone is light-hearted. A loving smile spreads over The Girl's face to match.

This is *not* her stillborn daughter.

"You would never do that."

"You're right." The eyes turn to the floor, an ebony ringlet framing the young face. Just as quickly, a mischievous glint lights up her gaze. "But you can't be right every time."

Turning, The Girl runs into the black hall and disappears. Theodora sprints after her, emerging onto a moonlit roof. She can barely hear The Girl falling to the slate over the beating of her own heart. Theodora tries not to look down. She knows how this will unfold.

Even as she attempts to resist, her hand guides the silver blade over The Girl's neck. Beneath her sword, those eyes hold nothing but pity and heartbreak.

With her next blink, she sees *herself* through the eyes of The Girl, cold and unfeeling. Empty. The roof presses into her spine. She wants to reach out and help that poor creature, but in this moment, the sharp embrace of the cold metal cuts through.

Theodora screams and the nightmare dissolves.

Through the rest of her dreams, she weeps. Bitter tears stream down her face, sliding into her mouth. As the sun rises, she wakes, trying to ignore her plans for the day.

What am I going to do? She doesn't know in this moment. For that is what this is: a single moment, the dusty collection of seconds in which one must choose their next steps. A choice that can change everything. Opportunity.

And then… it's gone.

CHAPTER 1

Forty-Two Days Earlier
Afternoon of April 21st, 1888
England

"Indigo!"

The word echoes up to me. I know it will come again.

"Indigo, heavens! Where are you?"

Phoebe could try to find me, but that would be impossible.

"Indigo! It's time to get ready. Don't make your mother regret letting you go to the circus."

It's technically *not* a circus, it's a theatre furnished to look like a circus. Alas, she's right. I don't want Mother or Father to question their decision any more than they already do. I drop from the rafter, my bare feet thudding softly on a beam. I retrace my steps to the hole in the ceiling. My feet poke into the closet first, the rest of me following.

Phoebe's back is to the door when I find her; she's busy looking for me under cushions and behind curtains. Honestly, who does she think I am? My sister? Only *she* would think of such an obvious place to hide – somewhere free of dust and with enough room for that big bustle of hers. Olive Patience Taylor and I, Indigo Arabella Taylor, are quite different people. Many comment that our voices sound similar, a fact that has infuriated Olive since the age of seven, but what we say is quite different.

"Here I am."

Phoebe starts, spinning towards me. She is thirty-one years old and half a foot taller than my five feet and four inches. With her chocolate-brown hair up in a bun, she seems quite imposing, unless you know her.

"Indigo! You have to stop that. You walk too quietly." She frowns. "Look at you! You're covered in dust. We must get you dressed. There are only two hours before you have to go. Olive's already begun."

My room is dark blue, with one wall papered in a pattern of bronze suns. Next to my bed, tucked under the windows, is a bookshelf overflowing with notebooks, all full; novels, all types, excepting romance; dictionaries, each in a different language; a well-loved book on gymnastics, which is in German and a monstrosity to translate; and finally, a large, discoloured atlas of the world. Some of the pages are wrinkled from a misadventure I had when I tried to use a glass of water as a magnifying glass.

The dressing table Mother forced upon me sits against the wall beside the door. Inside the third drawer down is a false bottom; when I found it, it held a small bag of abandoned coins. I added a few other things, and now the drawer is put to good use. On the opposite wall is a set of French doors to a second-floor balcony. My rope ladder gives me a quick route to the gardens. Mother makes me take it up when we have guests.

I take a bath down the hall, finishing quickly. Phoebe isn't in the room when I return, so I sit in my chair in front of the dressing table. For a second I'm startled to see myself in the mirror, as I often am. My eyes are the exact shade of grey as my grandmother's. It's rather jarring.

In a moment, the sound of Phoebe's chatelaine announces her arrival and she pulls my long, black ringlets into the mandatory excruciating bun. Her silver Luna moth necklace peeks through the gap in her collar. We resume a conversation we've been having over the past few days about the hiding spots throughout the house, and how best to go from one to the other. Phoebe's adamant that from the washroom I'd go down the hallway and then into the linen closet, but on this point I disagree. It's far better to avoid the open corridor.

Just as we're done, a knock at the door resounds.

"Come in, Olive." I'd recognise her gait anywhere. She shortens her strides to a minuscule length and each step is accented with those ridiculous heels she insists on. Olive has already finished dressing, of course, and in the latest fashion.

"Are you ready, Indigo? We have dinner in less than an hour!"

Had it been my choice, I would only have started getting ready now. I've never understood why it takes two hours when anyone *helps* me get dressed, when I take only a fraction of that time to do it myself.

Olive looks me over, searching for something amiss. Phoebe and I just finished, so she shouldn't find anything. As if she can hear my thoughts she arches an eyebrow and points to my feet. From beneath my dress peek my stockinged toes. I walk to the wardrobe and quickly reach for my boots in the vain hope that Olive won't notice. Before I can pull one on, she shoves a pair of fashionable – and horribly uncomfortable – slippers into my hands, returning my boots to their original position.

Dinner is the regular affair, but afterwards Mother and Father lead us out to the drive. It takes what seems a lifetime to reach the Cirque du la Reine Theatre, though my count is only twenty-six minutes and nine seconds. Paper lanterns of all shapes and colours line the entry. Inside, electric lights hang from the ceiling high above our heads, illuminating a grand foyer. To the left is a sweeping staircase with a black railing curving and curling, leading to a circular doorway ringed in the same flowing pattern. Under our feet is a scarlet carpet with a pattern of teal wisps weaving in and out.

A man dressed in the same colours approaches us. "Tickets, please."

Father extracts slips of paper pressed with the emblem of Cirque du la Reine: a honeysuckle vine growing around a red hoop. Inside, the cream letter "R" interrupts a blue-green background. We're given directions to our seats and ascend the stairs.

After a climb, which my poorly clad feet sorely protest, we find our box. The auditorium is extensive. A sea of vivid red velvet stretches out beneath us, leading to a teal-and-gold curtain, drawn closed. Behind me, Mother, Father, and Olive are arranging themselves, but we have a quarter-hour before the show starts and I like to watch the room filling below.

Someone else joins me at the rail: a boy standing on tiptoes, gaping at the stage. Following his gaze, I find what he's wondering at – caged lights cast figures onto the curtain. As they rotate, couples appear to dance across the fabric, while children run in a blue-green field.

I must stare for a long time. Next thing I know, the house lights dim and the orchestra hums. I take my seat just as the curtain begins to rise.

* * *

As I open my eyes, the thought strikes me that I had no nightmares last night. Not one. My room – dark blue wallpaper, wardrobe, and the rest – greets me as I throw off sleep. The dress I wore last night reposes on Phoebe's chair opposite my bed.

Last night! The circus!

The thought lifts me out of bed and spins me around. The quilt, still around my shoulders, flares out behind me like some empress's cape. It brushes the dress off the chair and falls away from my shoulders. Laughter tickles me as I retrieve the dress from the floor and dance it around the room. My feet find no particular rhythm but that of ecstasy. I hum the anthem of the show and repeat the parts I can remember.

The silver dress has quite some difficulty in keeping up. I stop spinning and the world tilts far too much. The mattress catches my calves and I land on the bed. Dust flies out of the sheet into the stream of daylight coming in through the window.

The circus!

Sunlight touches my face and hair. Its warmth graces my skin as I close my eyes. This dress means last night wasn't some wonderful dream. It was real.

"Indigo?" Phoebe calls through the door. "Are you awake?"

Phoebe!

The dress is left behind as I leap to the door and open it. "Phoebe, oh, Phoebe! It was amazing! There was a woman – she was so strong – she was on a crescent moon made of metal – at least fifty feet in the air and she… I don't know how she did it. But then the moon came down to the stage. He started throwing knives at this other man, who was on a tightrope."

Phoebe's eyes grow wider and wider.

I unclasp the door handle to pull her into the room. "And

the man on the tightrope tried to get away, but the moon followed him. He ran to a maypole with ribbons on it and he just spun and spun until I thought he was going to fly out into the audience." I suck in a breath to add, "But he didn't. Of course. But the moon —"

"Wait, wait." She holds her hands out. "The woman on the moon was chasing the man on the tightrope? Why?"

I chuckle. "No, no. There was a festival and the woman on the moon was one of the villagers celebrating, but when night fell the moon came out and asked her to come up with him."

"The moon is a man?"

"Yes, the man in the moon." I grin, waiting for her to smile back, but Phoebe is still processing my last remark.

"And one of the village women… climbed up to him?" She squints. "The moon?"

"Well, not *immediately*. First they danced around the maypole, to string it up, you know, and then they played Ring a Ring o' Roses. Rather, it started like that; eventually the children —" I sigh wistfully. "*Children* were doing all sorts of tricks: no-handed cartwheels, flips. Oh!" I grip her arm. "And they made a human pyramid. Children and adults together."

Phoebe's mouth falls open. "Is that how the woman got up to the moon?"

"No, she climbed the roof and jumped. The moon was low in the sky at the time. He caught her. Oh, how they danced!"

"They danced on the moon?"

"Well, of course, it wasn't traditional dancing. It was… something else entirely. It felt like dancing. Eventually the woman wanted to go back down to the village, but the Moon didn't want to let her go."

"What did she do?"

I widen my eyes. "She jumped."

Phoebe gasps. "No!"

"The villagers caught her in a sheet and flung her back up into the air. She flipped and spun herself somehow." I close my eyes and the theatre comes back all in a rush: the lights, the stage, the curtain drawn back. "It was perfect. But when they finally stopped tossing her she didn't move." I lower my voice to a hoarse whisper. "She was stiff as a board." This isn't *particularly* true, but it *is* a delightfully chilling statement. "A little redheaded girl got a magician and he raised the woman up so she was floating four feet off the ground and brought her back to life."

Phoebe clutches her chest. "He did?"

"Yes! And then her family —" A sudden fit of giggles takes me. "Her family was wearing the most ridiculous clothes. The two women were wearing massive hoops like Mother when she was a girl, and powdered wigs that were at least this tall." I hold my hand as high as my arm will stretch. "And the two others, men, had top hats that must have been attached somehow, because they were taller than the wigs. One of them, the older one, pulled a watch chain out of his pocket end over end until it dragged all over the floor. When he finally got the time he ran off without a goodbye."

She shakes her head with a grin.

"Her family tried to convince her to go back with them, but she wouldn't. She wanted to stay in the village. So the other man stayed behind with her while the women left."

Phoebe's expression softens. "Poor girl."

"That's when the man, the one who stayed, got on the tightrope."

"Oh, he's the one on the tightrope."

"Yes. That's him. At first, he pretended to struggle with his balance, but when the Moon also got on the rope he steadied." I raise my eyebrows menacingly. "That's when the Moon drew the knife."

"And he threw it? It wasn't fake?"

"It was real." I nod sagely. "I saw the blade sink into the side of one of the houses."

I continue regaling the adventure. When I finish the climax, Phoebe breaks in before I can describe the set in too much detail.

"What was your favourite part?"

"I don't know!" I wriggle my shoulders into a dress, a much simpler affair than the one from last night. "Maybe when the Maiden was on the moon. And when they caught her in the sheet. But… The end was so impressive, and everything leading up to the end… Maybe…"

Phoebe waits patiently as she loops the buttons at my back.

My hands fall to my sides. "I suppose I'll have to say all of it."

She pokes me lightly with a finger. "You can't pick all of it. There must be one moment in particular. Maybe just *one* of your favourites?"

She steps away and I retrieve my boots. "Then I'll just say…"

I can't say the pyramid was my favourite, but it certainly was *amazing*. And the magician making the woman float was quite a feat. Then again, so was the finale. Maybe I'll just say the finale and… I tilt my head. I suppose the human pyramid *was* one of my favourite things…

I groan. "It's too hard."

Phoebe sees my agony and shows some mercy. "Alright. Never mind. What did Olive think? She must have a favourite part."

I roll my eyes and shove my foot through the chimney of my boot. "Her favourite part was the handsome face in the box across from us."

"What?"

"She stared at him through her opera glasses the entire time. She tried to hide it by gasping loudly at the exciting parts, but she was always late." I knot the laces with an extra tug. "He must have looked over in her direction once, because she dropped the glasses and smiled demurely at the stage. Can you imagine? She's in one of the most incredible theatres, watching the most brilliant show, and all she can do is smile *demurely*?"

I stand and run my fingers through my hair wearily, wrapping my curls into a bun.

"I'll never understand her."

CHAPTER 2

"*I*ndigo, pay attention!"

I whip my head around to face the blackboard in front of me. Mrs Millicent Wood, my tutor, stares down at me.

"Indigo, what did I just say?" She enunciates each word crisply.

"That I should pay attention."

"Before that."

"Before that, you said that my copies of poems are due in two months."

She lifts her gaze to the ceiling with a sigh.

* * *

A HEADACHE BEATS my brain with a poetry book – one from Mrs Wood's endless collection. She made me read the thing for two hours. One hundred and twenty minutes! I want to scrub my mind of the rhymes. It takes conscious effort not to think in couplets. I place the modest book of poems on the desk and slap my pencil on the cover.

Flat, boring prose is the cure. *Emma* is perfect.

I ask Mother if I can go to read at the bakers. It's been weeks since I visited Mrs Perkins. Mother consents and, after gathering a few things from the kitchen, I return to my room to stow them in my satchel. Through her door, I can just hear Phoebe humming a lullaby she used to sing to me.

"Phoebe, I finished my work. I'm going out. I'll be back for dinner."

Her voice comes in through the open door of my bedroom. "Don't make promises you can't keep."

"I never said I'd be on time."

A snort of laughter. "Don't do anything foolish."

"Never."

* * *

I GO to saddle my horse. Quest and I have known each other since I was nine, when I learned to ride. I'd like to believe we share a strong bond, but she doesn't seem to think so.

As I open the stable door, Quest nickers at me, tossing her head. She is about as patient as I am. "I know. You don't have to tell me." My footfalls disturb some loose strands of hay from her stall. "Hello, Murray."

Murray, the stableman, dips his head in greeting. His gnarled hands never stop brushing Whinney. "Afternoon, miss. Finish with your schoolin'?"

"For today, at least." I pull a blanket down from a shelf. "Going to the Tray for some reading."

He returns to Whinney, shaking his head. "Say hello to Mr and Mrs Perkins for me. Take care of yourself."

"I will." I let myself into Quest's stall and run my fingers along her muzzle. "My poetry copies are due in two months. That means in only four months I have to turn in my own poem."

At the mention of my poem, Quest shakes her head. I've written many versions of my verse and have recited most of them to Quest, though she has politely ignored them all. I have a deepening suspicion she loathes my poetry.

"Fine, then. I won't tell you."

An audible sigh escapes her.

* * *

THE BAKER'S is not our only stop. There is something that needs seeing to first. I don't even have to ask Quest to stop; she knows exactly where we are.

The building is made of light brown stone, roughly cut. Around the top, a line of embellishment wreaths the granite in a stately pattern. Overall, it has the air of a bank, though that isn't its function.

After sliding down, I make sure my dress isn't rumpled and my hair isn't windswept. My bag is hitched up on my shoulder, and butcher's paper crackles inside as I pat the canvas.

The interior of the building could also be mistaken for a bank, with a single line of counters occasionally barred by glass and wood. The immaculately polished floors reflect the intricate plaster ceiling. The sole middle-aged attendant looks up when the door shuts behind me. His chipper look sloughs off, punctuated by the click of his pen in an inkwell.

"Hello, Miss Taylor." It's more a sigh than a greeting.

"Hello, Mr Gillman." My tone makes up for his lack of enthusiasm.

Mr Gillman's thin lips and even thinner moustache curve downward. "I hope you haven't come to ask again, because I cannot give you a business licence —"

I wave him off. "No, of course not. Asking to start a detective agency was totally ridiculous of me. I'm far too young and haven't the funds to keep one running."

He draws a fortifying breath and uses the counter to support himself. "Then why are you here?"

"No reason in particular." The waxed paper shrieks objections as I slide it across the counter. "I just came to drop these off."

He arches an eyebrow.

I lean against the counter, one elbow propping me up. "How are things back home?"

He doesn't look at me, instead lifting the fold of the paper between the tips of his thumb and middle finger. "Fine."

"That's nice."

He pulls out a green envelope, holding it up while still looking at me. "What's this?"

"A note." I point to the brown paper. "There are also some sweets."

"Yes, I see that, but why did you give me this note?" He flips it around to squint at the seal.

"It's not a bribe, if that's what you're asking." My polite, conversational tone slips a bit.

He bounces the note in his hand. "So, I'm to believe this is just to my good health?"

"Why else would I give it to you?" I ask, tracing the pattern in the countertop.

Mr Gillman looks to the ceiling. "Never mind. Good day, Miss Taylor."

"Good day!"

I wave goodbye. He raises a limp hand.

Outside, I rub my hands together. Though the building may not be a bank, I'm certainly investing in my future.

* * *

IN A MATTER OF MINUTES, the sight of The Empty Tray welcomes us. I leave Quest next to a tea-coloured horse. After passing her a smuggled carrot, I push open the door to the sound of the small bell above. I helped Mr Perkins replace it once. The screws had become loose and the bell had fallen. Mrs Perkins was grateful and told me that I could come in any time, even if I didn't buy anything.

All the tables are full. It's Friday afternoon and this is a popular spot. Most of the patrons will leave soon, but for now I pick my way to the far window seat, sun washing the worn cushions. The view shows the constant coming and going of people, horses, hackneys, hansoms, bicycles, and the occasional dog. I had intended to read, but with the warm sun, the comforting smells of flour and vanilla, and the blanketing hum of the bakery… I drift off to sleep.

In my dream, I'm on a trapeze, but it's made of a baguette. It breaks and I fall onto the torso of a reclining giant. The titan rears its head to reveal Mrs Wood, wearing the wig of the Maiden's mother from the circus and an unfortunate amount of face paint. My tutor plucks me up and holds me at eye level. Her thumb and forefinger wrap around my middle as I struggle against her grasp. The smell of my baguette – which, it appears, Mrs Wood has eaten – hits me as she opens her immense mouth. The possibility of Mrs Wood eating me seems to be growing more and more likely – but instead, she opens her mouth to say…

"Miss? Wake up, miss."

I sit up, almost smacking into the person standing over me. Blinking, I try to see who it is; it doesn't sound like anyone I know. In my current state I can only note a few details: dark, wavy hair, light green eyes, and an olive complexion.

"Sorry to wake you, but you started to fall off."

I prop myself up on my elbow. "No, no, it's alright. I hadn't meant to fall asleep. Thanks." Outside, the light is weakening, and rain speckles the ground. How long have I been asleep?

He gives an easy smile. "You're welcome. Have a nice evening."

"You as well."

With a tip of his flat cap, the boy shoulders a large canvas bag of bread. It's just possible to hear the small bell ring as he goes out the door.

Now, what could he be doing with all that bread? Perhaps he's feeding a small army: a growing multitude of rebels following in the footsteps of Guy Fawkes to replicate the Gunpowder Plot. Perhaps I should've asked a few questions. Maybe I could've figured out where they're going to meet.

Oh well. He's already gone.

The clock over the counter reads a little after four, plenty of time before I must ride home. Perhaps it could be called procrastination, but instead of reading *Emma*, I veer towards the counter to say hello to Mrs Perkins. She notices me after the customer at the counter bids her a good evening.

"Indigo! How lovely to see you. It's been some time." Mrs Perkins doesn't try to suppress a naughty smile. "Been up to much trouble lately, dear?"

"Not really, no."

Mrs Perkins wipes her hands down the sides of her apron and rests the left on her hip. "How's Phoebe?"

"Well. She got another letter from her sister on Saturday. She's doing fine too."

"And school?" She nods encouragingly.

I rein in the impulse to snort. "I learn almost nothing of actual import."

"Keep at it." The sly grin returns. "I'm sure you're usin' some of all that for your own purposes?"

"No escapades at the moment. I did hollow out an etiquette book two weeks ago and filled it with sweets. I thought I was done with it, but apparently Mrs Wood thinks otherwise."

Mrs Perkins puts a hand to her chest, quaking with mirth.

"That sounds jus' like you." She shakes her head, the giggles still bubbling. "Every word." She takes in just enough breath to continue, "What did Phoebe say?"

"She said I shouldn't have done it… after she finished laughing."

This sends Mrs Perkins off again. When at last she exhales a final chuckle, she says, breathless, "Oh, Phee. Dear Phee."

I feel the presence of a body behind me – something about the air's movement, and the slight notes of a breath being taken in.

Mrs Perkins runs short fingers through her hair, ordering the flaxen strands. Her voice becomes measured. "Mr Landsleigh. I'll be with you in a moment."

The older man looks down at me, his confusion bordering on disapproval.

Mrs Perkins pastes a smile on and leans a bit further over the counter. "Tell Phoebe I miss her. And be careful when getting into trouble." She puts a hand on mine for a brief second and returns to keeping shop. I step out of the way, towards the tables.

"Hullo, Mr Landsleigh —"

Before she can continue, the man puts both hands on the counter to lean over and whisper something. I can't catch it, but Mrs Perkin's eyes become more shielded and her jovial expression stiff. The only thing I can hear is her reply: "You don't know that none of these other customers *aren't* her chaperone."

Ah. Of course. That's why he was staring. Phoebe gave up chaperoning me long ago. I always run off somewhere and return in an hour or so, unharmed. Well, there are the occasional scrapes and bruises, but always my own doing.

Now, to what I really came for. Back in the window seat, I pull out my copy of *Emma*. The book was given to me by my friend Myra, before she left for Scotland. It's one of her favourites, and she made me swear to read it before she came back. I read the last few pages to see if there would be any action in the book. There isn't. It's painfully long.

Many arduous pages later, I glance out at Quest, now next to a rusty-brown mare. She shakes her mane, obviously irritated by her neighbour. Behind her, of all people, *Phoebe* hastens towards the shop on the back of Julius, our Friesian. I don't think I've committed any recent transgressions, so why is she here?

I push out the door, meeting Phoebe on the other side.

She speaks in one breath, the colour high in her cheeks. "Indigo! You shouldn't be out at this time, not when it's getting dark." She and I both know that it's only on the edge of twilight, and dinner isn't until six o'clock. "You must come home. Now!"

Phoebe grips my hand, pulling me towards Quest. She watches the passersby as I mount, then practically shoos me up the street.

* * *

I CHANGE for dinner quickly as Phoebe makes certain the balcony door is bolted. She moves on to the curtains, which I usually close just before I go to sleep, peering out of each before snapping them shut.

"Phoebe, what's wrong? Am I in trouble?"

"Trouble? No, no." She fiddles with the window latch, though it's perfectly fine.

"Then what is it?"

She doesn't look at me. "Nothing."

"It's certainly not nothing."

She closes the last curtain and looks around for something else to do.

"Phoebe?"

She finally looks at me, arms crossed close to her chest. Despite her official position in our house, Phoebe has always confided in me. I hold her gaze, waiting for an explanation. All in a rush, it tumbles out of her.

"There's been a death. A murder. A man in the Fieldcroft neighbourhood. It was in the papers this morning. Mr Edmond Smith – you remember, yes? – was his next-door neighbour and is suspected, and your father has been asked to prosecute. It's all a very bad business, but please don't fear, Indigo. Your father will sort it out."

Mr Edmond Smith? I thought he moved out to the country to get away from all the publicity. About a year ago, he was brought to court for stealing large amounts of money from his business partner. From what Father says, he got off on a technicality. Father was very upset about it for weeks, as was almost everyone. That explains why Phoebe is upset, too. The baker's is only a ten-minute walk from Fieldcroft, and Mr Smith probably has friends. It's no secret who my father is.

However, she neglected to mention *how* the neighbour died. Was there a witness? Did the dead man have any known enemies? Was he a gambler, perhaps? A gambler with debts he couldn't pay? If not a gambler, perhaps he had irrefutable evidence on Smith? Who is investigating? And when exactly —

Phoebe raises her hands. "No questions. I don't know anything, but it's a great mystery and your father is involved. Now, let's get you down to dinner."

* * *

I SCOUR the news for days, searching for anything about the murder, but tedious blather allows it less space than it deserves. All I find is speculation and opinions on the politics of it all. But what's a mystery without details? *Facts?*

Phoebe made me promise not to go anywhere near The

Empty Tray or Fieldcroft, but it's been difficult to get away at all. Today, though, I convince her to let me go.

I don't want to ring up any of the pampered stuffed-shirts I'm expected to call friends. My real friends – Leo Luckford, Poppy Gentz, and Myra Merryweather – are all busy. Poppy's away in France, and Leo's at boarding school. Myra's off in Edinburgh, probably sketching some ancient castle. Myra is Scottish, but her family moved here when she was born. They go back every spring and stay for a few months. I tried to stow away this year in Myra's trunk. Our plan would have worked, too, if her father hadn't been so suspicious of the weight of her luggage.

I decide to practise my crosshatching in the park. When Myra gets back, she'll expect me to show her my progress. I naively asked her to teach me to draw, but quickly realised that was a mistake. Myra threw herself into the task with such fervour that it soon became exhausting.

I ride a tram to the park, leaving Quest to preen in the stable. In my shoulder bag are a charcoal stick, a pencil, and a blank notebook. I choose a shady tree to sit under, drawing the old oak across from me. Light lines form the general shape; then, in darker strokes, the interesting edges of the bark come into focus. I add a bird's nest and the little girl of about four or five playing with her doll. She wasn't there when I began the drawing, but she's so charming. I get her dress down quickly enough: pleats with buttons down the top half. However, she's sitting cross-legged, and I misjudge the perspective of her knee *three* times before it's correct enough.

The girl's face is a bit harder; she rarely stays still for more than a moment. Faces have never been easy for me, and I've never tried a portrait when the subject is moving. Glancing up again, I notice she's staring at me. Her eyes are wide and her mouth opens in a small "o". Hesitantly, she stands, shuffling toward me. Her hair is a wild bob of fiery red curls poking out at odd angles. When she's close enough, I see that her hazel eyes sink to blue near the pupils.

"Miss, are you a princess? Is it a secret? I won't tell anyone," she whispers, covering her mouth the second she finishes, as if trying not to spoil something.

"Why, no," I whisper back. "Are you?"

She laughs. "No, silly. I'm learning to fly on the trapeze! Cicely is teaching me. Do you want me to show you? I'm getting better." Her entire face lights up at the prospect.

She must be the redheaded girl from the circus! It's been over a week, but I remember every moment of it. I slide the notebook back into my bag. "How far is it?" It's not as if I have a timetable; I just need more information.

"It's the big house with green doors." She points to a house just down the street.

"It's beautiful." I put the pencil to my bottom lip. "But —"

"Louise! There you are! You didn't tell me where you were going." A young woman hurries up the path. She looks to be the same age as Olive, about seventeen. She has stunning dark skin and hair and her smile is just as bright as Louise's. "Thank you for finding her…"

"Oh, she found me." I switch my bag to my other shoulder. "A pleasure to meet you. I'm Indigo Taylor."

The young woman inclines her head. "I'm Cicely Jaros. Nice to meet you." Her voice is melodic.

The redhead tilts her head to the side, gravity pulling her springy locks back to earth. "Indigo is a funny name."

I'm often met with this reaction when I introduce myself. Even still, I wouldn't trade it for any other.

The girl rolls the name around on her tongue. "I like it. It's the name of a princess. See you tomorrow!" She starts to turn, waving a hand back at me.

"Tomorrow?"

"Oh, yes. Louise wants me to see her on the trapeze."

After a moment of surprise, Cicely recovers. "We often have guests. Visiting hours are between one and five."

"I'll see if my parents will allow it. Good day."

"Wait!"

I turn.

The girl holds up her hands. "You don't know my name yet! I'm Louise Brickwade – I mean, Trinter."

And with that she skips off in front of the tall woman named Cicely. They head to a knot of children between some alders. The group sees her coming, and a boy separates from the others and scoops her up.

CHAPTER 3

As I start home, my thoughts begin to head in a new direction and there's no time to waste. Little Louise gave me an idea.

I gather all the newspapers I can find with anything relating to the murder case. I don't know why I'm so interested. Perhaps it's because my studies are almost finished.

Alone in my room, with all my finds on the floor, I take off my boots and quietly slip down the stairs. Father keeps a pair of scissors in his study. The hallway is empty, and all of the doors are shut. The murmurs of a conversation sound in the drawing room. The soft *sush* of my covered feet seems deafening now.

"Indigo is too wild. She needs to learn how to behave properly, as a lady of quality should. I hear that Poppy is going to Mrs Moring's Finishing School. It's an hour away, and I don't like the idea of her being so far, but…" Mother trails off.

Father replies, but he's farther from the door, so I miss his words.

Finishing school! What a death sentence. I *cannot* go to finishing school. It would be the end of me. Shaking my head, I clear my thoughts. It's not decided yet. Now that I've overheard their schemes, I can prepare countermeasures.

Back in my room, scissors in hand, I set to work. It's time to see why the papers suspect Mr Edmond Smith.

I arrange the clippings before me in chronological order. The earliest report sensibly opens with a description of the body when it was discovered. Details stitch themselves together in my mind, forming the scene. Tobias Walker, age 42, was found to have died peacefully in his armchair. According to neighbours and colleagues, he was a polite but unremarkable man, who kept to himself. There were no marks on the body and Walker appeared to be in excellent physical health, making it improbable that he died of natural causes.

As I reach the most recent article, my eyes are drawn to one word: *SOLVED*.

Wait just a moment. They can't have solved my mystery. Not yet. I just started investigating! And now I have to keep my thoughts off finishing school.

WALKER MYSTERY SOLVED BY INSPECTOR WALLACE

As of last night, the recent murder of Mr Tobias J. Walker – accountant, bachelor, aged forty-two – was the mystery of the decade. Some of the best minds in the county have been looking over the case ever since the tragic occurrence Thursday last. It was just today that Insp. Absalom B. Wallace stepped in and solved the enigma. Yesterday evening Inspector Wallace went to the crime scene at 340 Bridges Street. After inspecting the area thoroughly, he discovered an almost empty bottle of a yellow liquid, which has been determined to be arsenic. It appears the nefarious poison, with such illustrious history we know all too well, has claimed yet another life. The

Inspector has filed a report, and the court trial of the infamous neighbour, Mr Edmond Smith, will begin on the 21st of May. More news on the details of this chilling case will be forthcoming in the following days.

ON THE FOURTH OF MAY, *at five o'clock, pictures will be taken of the scene of the crime. Inspector Wallace will attend and answer questions from the press.*

ARSENIC! The reports state that Walker seems to have died peacefully in his armchair by the fireplace. That can't be arsenic. Father's book said that arsenic leads to convulsions and vomiting. And, because of the Marsh test of 1836, arsenic can be traced in the body, so they must know by now it can't be that. But why would they pin it on arsenic if it was obviously something else?

Unless… there isn't anything else to be found.

No, perhaps they don't know for *certain* what the substance was. They must've tested the bottle and found arsenic, and decided the entire case on that. But why would the murderer – especially the neighbour – leave the bottle?

This case is not solved! But if the trial of Mr Smith is on the twenty-first… that means that Father may prosecute an innocent man! This cannot happen.

I have to get into Walker's house.

A headache begins to set in, and I rub the spot in vain. I don't have much time to smooth out all the details of my plan, but I'll have to make do.

* * *

FOR THIS TO WORK, I have to convince Mother and Father to

release me from the luncheon with whomever is invited tomorrow, so I'll attempt to hit two birds with one stone.

Phoebe helps me choose a dark green dress with a high collar and small buttons down the front. I grimace as I wriggle my feet into those terrible slippers I wore to Cirque du la Reine. It's just the sort of thing Olive and Mother will be wearing.

When I enter the dining room, I find Mother, Father, and Olive already seated.

"Indigo! You look wonderful, dear," Mother says. "Why don't you sit down?"

I take my customary place across from Olive. Though there are only four of us, Mother and Father insist we sit at a table large enough for a small army.

"I hope I am not late." I know I'm not. I just want them to notice.

"No, dear, you're perfectly on time."

I do my best to remember all the manners Phoebe and Mrs Wood have taught me. Throughout dinner, Mother and Father keep surreptitiously glancing at me. They share a hopeful look while I catch the smallest amount of broth I can in my soup spoon.

My chance comes when Father asks me a question after the dishes have been taken away.

"Indigo, you look lovely tonight, and your manners have been impeccable. Why this sudden change?"

For full effect, I fold my hands in my lap. "I just thought that since I turned fourteen a few months ago, I should start acting like a young lady. It hit me today that I am not a child anymore, and I should not hold on to such foolishness."

By the end of this *highly* scripted speech, Mother and Father are beaming. Even Olive looks hesitantly relieved.

"That is wonderful," Mother puts in, turning to look at Father. "Your father and I have been talking about the possibility of allowing you to go to finishing school. How does that sound?"

I almost gag, but I must stick to the plan.

"Oh, this is so sudden! May I think about it... *all* day tomorrow?"

Mother glances at Father, seeming to have her answer already. Father nods, first at Mother, then at me. "Yes, you may."

The first phase of my plan is complete. Now for the hard part.

* * *

I spot the redheaded girl and the tall woman from yesterday, even though I'm early to the rendezvous point. I didn't ask my parents if I could come, but I never intended to.

The moment Louise sees me she breaks into a huge grin, hopping impatiently from foot to foot. "Can I show you my trapeze now?"

I nod, and Louise takes my hand in one of hers and Cicely's in the other. As we walk, the little girl keeps up a steady stream of conversation, talking about whatever crosses her mind. By the time the house comes into view she's practically running in front of us, talking over her shoulder.

Reaching the house, Louise grips the silver doorhandle – a starling in flight – and pushes it inward. A woman steps forward to meet us. Not much taller than me, she'd be the beauty at any ball, but doesn't seem to care for that kind of attention. She doesn't wear any sort of cosmetics or jewellery, aside from a blue-and-silver wedding band. The ring brings out a bit of her fading hair, though most is still honey-blonde. The silver only makes her look more graceful.

"Hello, dears. How was the walk?" She kneels down and Louise kisses her on the cheek.

"Perfect! Mama, this is the princess." Louise holds her hand out to me.

The woman stands and takes my hand in both of hers. "I'm Helen Trinter. And you must be Indigo Taylor…" A smile tugs at one corner of her lips. "The princess." Mrs Trinter steps toward Cicely, bringing one of her hands to the young woman's arm. "Cicely has been teaching Louise trapeze. Louise, are you ready to show our guest what you've been learning?"

"Yes!" Louise says with more than a hint of exasperation. She turns to go through a doorway, but something halts her.

I hadn't taken in the room and now its details overwhelm me. The foyer floor is white marble with threads of honey and grey. Above, a bronze chandelier drips with crystals, sending light into the reaches of the room. In the back left corner is a staircase, curving slightly and reaching upwards. Beside the staircase is an arched doorway – which Louise almost went through – leading to a hall. Open doors to my right lead to a library; inside are two green velvet chairs, dark wood book-shelves, and a sliding ladder. A door across from the library leads to what must be a sitting room. Dividing the foyer from the library is a wall with two rows of small rectangular doors, each labelled with a number from one to twenty, rather like a wall of oversized post-boxes.

Sitting, her dress pluming around her, Louise takes off her shoes and places them in the cupboard labelled with the bronze number one.

"You should take off your shoes," she pipes up. "You can put them in number nineteen."

Mrs Trinter quickly spins to me. "Oh, we never *make* guests take off their shoes. You can take them off if you feel more comfortable that way."

"I think I will, if it's all the same to you."

The lady nods, and I set my shoes and bag behind the door

of box number nineteen. The moment I'm done, Louise grabs my hand, dragging me down a hallway and around a few turns. When we stop, she dramatically throws open the doors.

"Ta-da!" Dancing into the room, she gestures grandly at the space around her.

I stop not two steps into the room, dumbfounded. It's a large, circular space, about ninety feet in diameter. The walls are glass and wrought iron formed into a botanical pattern. Periodically, white planters grip the wall with vines or colourful flowers peeking out. From the ceiling hangs a hoop, trapezes, ropes, and three hammocks. On the ground there are weights, a tightrope, a balance beam, and large mats everywhere. A net above our heads divides us and the aerial apparatuses, etching fascinating shadows on the floor.

Above me, there's a couple on the hoop. Across the room, a pair of men are lifting weights. In the corner, four people are practising handstands. A single laugh burbles out of me before I can stop it: a breathy, unbelieving, awe-inspired sound.

"We started building it onto the house when we moved in. It took so long, but when it was finally done..." Mrs Trinter looks at the glass overhead and closes her eyes, breathing in a smile. "It was better than I ever pictured." She turns back to me. "Do you like the circus?"

"How could I not?"

Mrs Trinter laughs – a beautiful music that memory could never capture. "My, dear. Many people have told me otherwise."

The door behind us shuts; a tall man in black trousers and a cutaway jacket appears.

"There you are! Indigo, this is my husband, Edgar Trinter."

"Pleasure to make your acquaintance."

Mr Trinter's brown hair is streaked with grey. His bright white teeth shine in an ever-present, jovial smile. There's something about his eyes that expresses intense enjoyment of life. The actor and playwright has had even more press than his wife. It made quite a stir when he and Mrs Trinter brought circus acts to the stage. That was years ago, now.

"So, you must be Indigo, the girl we've heard so much about?" He offers me his hand and I take it.

"Well, I suppose that depends on what you have heard, sir."

Mrs Trinter's eyes spark at this. "Very clever. What kind of person are you?"

"I would hardly have an unbiased answer."

She tilts her head to the side. "But you know yourself better than any of us."

"That doesn't mean I'm wise enough to examine myself and give an honest answer. Even if I could, I'd be unable to give a *simple* answer."

Mr Trinter grins. "Well, I'm happy to meet you, whoever you may be. I'm very sorry no one else came with you; I would have liked to meet the king and queen."

"Oh. They…" What excuse is plausible yet unmemorable? That certainly crosses out sudden death in the family. And a house fire. And being summoned to court. "Ah…"

I'm saved by the pitter-patter of Louise's feet. "You're back!" She runs to her father and he catches her up in his arms.

"I've only been gone since this morning, little bird."

Louise hugs his neck. "I know." In a second, she lets go, looking at me. "Can I show you my trapeze now?"

"Yes! Please."

Louise has changed into a vivid green leotard and a pair of pale pink tights. Cicely is already walking to a ladder in the corner. It's easy to see the rungs when she rests her hands or feet on them, but they're wrought in almost the same pattern as the wall, so after she moves it's hard to pick them out again.

From the net, Cicely climbs another ladder to a small platform and uses a sort of shepherd's crook to bring the trapeze to her. Louise follows eagerly, her little body spidering up the wall. When she joins Cicely, the pair in the hoop stop their routine and move to a hammock.

Cicely gestures to the other side of the room and back. Louise nods excitedly and rolls her hands in the air. The woman makes a halting gesture. Now that they're next to one another, it's plain they are wearing the same shade of green.

"She wants to be like Cicely. So, for a surprise, Cicely asked if Louise's leotard could be the same colour," Mrs Trinter says, addressing my unasked question.

"What did she think?"

Mrs Trinter's eyes break away from her daughter. "Oh, she loved it! She said it was one of the best surprises in the world."

Mr Trinter tilts his head. "And of all time, I believe. Of course, then we could hardly get it off her. She spilled milk down the front before she consented to only wear it for practice."

Cicely rubs the little girl's shoulders, then Louise climbs up onto a box to grasp the bar of the trapeze. She seems so small, standing at the edge of the platform – breakable and delicate as a little green bird. She squares her shoulders, heaves a breath, and jumps.

My hands instantly begin to sweat and I clasp them together in front of me.

Bringing her legs over the bar, Louise pulls herself up so she's sitting. She gives a bright little wave, and I can see her smile even from far below. At the high point of her arc, at the far end of the rope's length, she drops again to hang by her knees. As she approaches the centre, she drops into the net below. Louise stands, bows, then turns to Cicely expectantly. The woman nods encouragingly.

The young boy in the hammock flips off, landing in the net with a bounce. Louise bounds over to him, words tumbling out of her. He gives her a quick embrace before approaching the edge of the net. Hanging down, he lets go and tucks into a roll, popping back up on the mat below.

Cicely seems to be critiquing Louise's performance, so we wait at the foot of the rungs.

"She's getting stronger. She pulled herself up much more easily this time," Mr Trinter remarks to his wife.

"I think so too. Her momentum was excellent until she turned back upside down – I think she started a bit too late. But that's the best she's done yet."

How could they be talking so calmly about this? A tiny slip of a girl just flew through the air on a metal twig.

Two taps on my right shoulder. It's the boy who came down from the net. He seems to recognise me, though I… Wait – he's the boy from the Tray. Those green eyes are unmistakable.

"So you're the princess?" His tone holds a laugh.

"I don't know about 'princess'. I'm Indigo Taylor. A pleasure to make your acquaintance. Again."

Mr Trinter turns towards us. "You've already met Atlas?"

"We met at The Empty Tray a few days ago, but I've seen her often when I go for bread," Atlas explains.

He's been there before? He must've been buying bread for all the people here, not starting a revolt. I knew I was being ridiculous.

Mr Trinter's eyebrow twitches upward. Mrs Trinter glances between Atlas and me, a mysterious look coming over her face.

"Are you Louise's brother? She said her name was Trinter, but only after another name… Brickwade?"

Atlas nods with only the slightest hesitation. "She's my adopted sister. She brought you here, didn't she?"

"Yes. She asked me quite seriously if I was a princess yesterday, but I told her I wasn't."

He shrugs a shoulder. "She has an active imagination. Louise figured you *couldn't* tell her you're a princess."

"I also have an active imagination, so I cannot fault her."

He blinks, the light green of his eyes disappearing for a shaved second. "Have you ever seen the trapeze before?"

"No, but I've read about them. I went to a show at Cirque du la Reine for the first time last week. It was incredible."

Mr Trinter has a blank look for two seconds. "Was that the Festival, Playing Games, or Twenty Knights?"

"The Festival. I loved it! I recognised Louise in the park."

Mrs Trinter looks surprised. "You did? I suppose it was the hair?"

I nod. "Are you in the shows?" I put the question to everyone.

Mrs Trinter puts a hand to her chest. "Edgar and I haven't performed for years now, but we create them. We always attend on opening night. Atlas is in them sometimes."

His eyes light up. "I just finished with Playing Games. Right now, I'm preparing for the July shows. So is Louise. She loves it." Atlas looks over my shoulder to his sister. She has her hands folded behind her back as she listens to Cicely. The light filling the room makes her hair look as if it were a living flame.

"That comes as little surprise. You should have seen the way she lit up when she mentioned the trapeze."

A proud half-smile spreads across his face. "Oh, I know what that looks like. I get to see it every morning at breakfast. Sometimes, she'll be halfway through porridge and look up, having just remembered that after school she gets to practise."

"That must be nice. I hardly ever see my sister Olive get excited. Except when she'll be spending time with her friends or..." I stop myself from saying "whoever the handsomest boy at the time is". Even then, Olive never lets it show too much. "I wish I could run away to the circus."

I thought I only said it in my head, but no. Atlas laughs, but Mr and Mrs Trinter only give me quizzical looks. Atlas notices they didn't join in. "Most of us did – that's why we're here. Others didn't have anywhere else to go. Or no other *good* place." His features cloud over, darkening for a brief second.

Before I have much time to think about what he means, Louise and Cicely stride over.

"How many of us do you know, Indigo? I see you've already met Atlas." Cicely asks.

"I believe just two – well, now five. I suppose I'd have to see everyone to know for certain." The wild notion sends my hands to my pockets.

Louise is ready to get back to the important things. "What did you think of my trapeze?"

I kneel down to look her in the eyes. "That was amazing. You were incredible."

She looks down with a shy grin. She bumps into Atlas's knees and he lets her climb onto his back. Craneing his head around, he asks. "Are you going to practise more or do you need to change?"

Change! I still have to go to Walker's house! I can't be late.

"What time is it?" I say abruptly, and everyone's attention snaps back to me. I hold up a hand, then put it to my forehead. "Excuse me, that was impolite – it's just that I have to be somewhere at five." Atlas looks at me quizzically as I twist a stray lock of hair away.

Mr Trinter consults a pocket watch. "It's twenty minutes to five."

"I'm so sorry to interrupt."

Mrs Trinter brushes away my apology. "It's fine. Do you need to change? There's a bathroom down the hall."

"Do you need a ride?" Atlas offers. "It's no trouble."

Mr Trinter shares a look with his wife, the beginning of a smile at the corner of his mouth.

I hesitate. "I hate to take you away from your work, but I took a tram to the park." This isn't *exactly* true. I took a tram to scout out the area around Walker's house on foot and then I *walked* to the park. I planned on leaving earlier, but time moves far too quickly here. It would take too long to walk now.

After saying a reluctant goodbye, I find the bathroom and change quickly. The boots are by far the most cumbersome part of the disguise. They were Olive's when she was younger, and the heels, in my opinion, are much too large to be practical. Desperate times, I suppose. I trip on my own feet four times before I find Atlas at the end of the hallway with Mrs Trinter and Louise. They say one more adieu before I sling my bag, my own boots inside, over my shoulder.

Atlas glances at me sidelong as he takes a flat cap from the hat stand on the way out. I walk slightly behind him so he can't see me trip occasionally; even so, it's difficult to hide my struggle. To the left of the house is the stable. Three horses, each in a comfortable stall with plenty of hay, greet us as we enter.

Atlas leads out a tea-coloured horse and starts putting on the basic tack. "Where are we going?"

I know he has to have some idea of our destination, but there seems to be another layer to his curiosity. Nothing for it, I suppose.

"Bridges Street."

He looks over his shoulder to stare incredulously. "Bridges Street? Where the murder was? The Inspector is there right now; it'll be mayhem." He looks for a sign that I am serious. I already have my story.

"Oh, really? How awful. No wonder Mother looked so grave when Grandmother asked for me to come to tea today."

If Atlas knew anything about me he'd know that my only living grandmother, on Mother's side, lives hours away from here. His eyes narrow slightly, and he waits a moment before turning around. "Do you know the way to Bridges Street? I think I can find it, but I'm not sure."

I look out past the gate, a mental map unfurling. "Yes, it's not so far when you ride."

Atlas *hmms* to himself. "Right." He gently tightens a strap and runs his hands over the buckles. When he's checked everything he lifts his head, his expression clear. "Ready?"

After an uneventful ride, we sight the swarm of activity from two streets away: officers, journalists, and bystanders jostling for space. Above it all is the Inspector, explaining how he found the bottle of arsenic under a few logs in the fireplace. In front of me, Atlas sighs, shaking his head the tiniest bit.

After we stop, I hop down, my heel buckling under me as I land. I look at a house down the street. That will serve as "Grandmother's". Atlas is about to dismount when I raise my hands to stop him.

"Thanks so much for helping me this far. I've got it from here." The words tumble out in a way that could never be mistaken as natural.

His eyes dart to the growing crowd, then to the infamous house. "Are you sure that your grandmother asked you to visit *today?*"

"Yes, I'm sure. Goodbye."

He looks intently at my face one more time, then gives a slight shrug.

"Good day, Miss Taylor."

Before I can ask him to call me Indigo, he's gone.

I let out the breath I didn't know I'd been holding and walk toward the house I chose at random. When my heel meets the grit of the brick entry I turn, neglecting to knock, venturing into the herd of people. Immediately, I have to duck to avoid a flying newspaper.

"Read the bloody paper and you'll see," someone bellows.

"Decided to come outta your hole for once?"

"Alright, alright. Nothin' to get excited about. I know now." A man I pass reaches down to pick up the morning's edition.

"Excuse me! Sorry! Mind the grease. Sorry!" Many people don't acknowledge me, so I'm forced to elbow my way through.

When the door comes into view it's blocked by two imposing officers and the Inspector himself standing between them. He gestures grandly to the house next door. "Edmond Smith, the fraud and thief, has sunk even lower…" A dramatic pause. "To murder his own neighbour."

A general muttering is sprinkled with a few shouted obscenities.

Perhaps there's another way around the back? This is going nowhere. Slipping through more people, I make my way around the row. These infernal boots are still uncooperative beneath me. Pedestrians walk by, noses in the papers. Some lean from windows to see what the commotion is about. All their attention is drawn to the front of the house.

The back door is flanked by two more officers, but this, of course, is to be expected. With a prim cough, I step up to the door.

"Excuse me – I am Rosana Wallace, the Inspector's daughter. I need to speak with my father, but there's a mob at the other door. May I go in? I know not to touch anything."

The two guards share a look; one has a rough beard the colour of watery soup and the other has a slicked moustache and wire-rimmed spectacles. The one with the spectacles tilts his head back, examining me down his nose.

What if he's seen the real Rosana? I saw her once at a party years ago. At the time we looked similar enough that a few people asked if we were sisters. I have no idea what she looks like now, but I'm sure she's taller than me. Perhaps if I'd had time I could have come up with a more convincing costume…

The officer opens the door, nodding respectfully. "Be quick, Miss Wallace. Your father and Mr Stout will be taking pictures soon. Good evening, miss."

Before he can change his mind I nod and pass into the house, the door shutting quickly behind me.

CHAPTER 4

I lean against the door as I close my eyes and clear my mind. I must start the case again, as though no conclusions have ever been drawn. I won't have this opportunity a second time.

A bird call rings clearly through the house – no trill I've ever heard. Did Mr Walker have a pet bird? He lived alone, so it's likely that he would have some sort of pet, though it wasn't mentioned in the papers. It's possible that the journalists would deem something like that unimportant.

The stairway is narrow, with faded and stained green wallpaper, and there's an awful creak on the third step from the bottom. At the top of the stairs is a sitting room with two large windows, fairly clean, offering a prime view of the flats across the road – perfect for spying. Perhaps Mr Walker discovered something he shouldn't have? In front of the windows are two armchairs, both wingback and badly worn. The wooden armrests bear no tell-tale marks or odd dust formations. The feet of the chair closest to the window are wrapped in fabric. Are they damaged? Or was he worried about the legs of the chair picking the carpet?

Between the chairs is a low table with an empty teacup, an old journal, and an ornate cage with a bird. Its plumage is orange and black, its eyes like polished jet. Is it a bullfinch? No, it's too large. The bird cocks its head at me questioningly, letting out another call. Hopefully that's normal and the officers outside won't think anything of it.

"Who's been feeding you?" The trapped creature tucks its head against its breast, letting out a call. "I'm sorry, I don't have anything for you." Its wings ruffle and its small clawed feet shift on their perch. "I wish you could answer my questions."

Moving over the oriental rug, I cross to the fireplace. This would be where the supposed bottle of arsenic was found. The logs are charred on the underside, as if there'd been a fire but the one watching gave up on it. Finger marks show exactly how the log was picked up, seemingly with the whole of the… left hand. Left hand? Is the Inspector left-handed? It is possible that he left these marks, though even *I* would be surprised at that level of carelessness. It's not out of the realm of reason to suppose that the one who left this obvious little bottle in the fireplace was in a state – or that it was planted.

No *competent* poisoner would throw a bottle of arsenic into the fireplace, even in liquid form. If powdered arsenic comes into contact with flame it can release arsine gas, as I recently learned in *The Thirty-six Deadly Sins: An Alphabetised Account of Common Poisons.* I was honestly surprised to find it in our library at home. Or I was, until I found an entry Father had circled for a case a few years ago.

Faintly, the noise of the crowd outside rises. What could the Inspector have said? I can't help an eye-roll.

Moving on to a closet to the right of the staircase, I find a tan lounge suit hanging neatly from an otherwise empty rod. A shelf above it houses an old top hat, a knitted scarf, and two pairs of shoes: one scuffed dress pair and one caked in mud.

When was the last time we had rain before the man died? It must have been that very day, because the murder occurred on the twenty-sixth of April...

Down the stairwell there's a soft click and the groan of the step – most definitely a footstep.

How many stairs was that one from the bottom? Fourth? No, third. That gives me about ten seconds at *most* to find a suitable hiding place. I shut the closet door behind me as quietly as I can.

The closet reminds me of one of my hiding spots at home, though severely lacking in protection. Even so, I press myself against its wall. It's better than sitting in Walker's armchair pretending to be dead.

The seconds tick by slowly, even in my head. Four... Five... Six... Seven... Hopefully they won't think to take pictures inside the closet. The alternative is the Inspector finding me and asking the guards why they let me in.

"Indigo Taylor? I know you're in here. Where are you hiding?" The whisper is rather loud, making the silence before seem overwhelming.

It can't be.

Another step is betrayed by the whimpering floor. "Miss Taylor?"

I must tell him to stop calling me "Miss Taylor".

With the opening of my closet door comes an increasing wedge of light, carved out by the silhouette of a boy wearing a fraying flat cap. The figure turns and I pinch my eyes closed, bracing for him to see me.

"I knew you'd be in here."

With a sigh, I open my eyes. "I promise I'm not always this predictable."

Atlas crosses his arms. His whisper-shout is paired with an almost scandalised look. "I would call this *far* from predictable.

Honestly, what are you doing here? You're not Rosana Wallace. And why are you dressed like that? It is a disguise, isn't it? Do you do this often?"

"You followed me?" is all the answer I give.

"Of course I followed you. I have a feeling you'd have done the same. You're dodging my questions."

No, he's dodging mine. I'll circle back around to my answers later.

"Why are you here?" I ask him.

"You first."

I can't gauge his expression, though it might not matter anyway. I hold up my hand, pinky finger extended. "One, I am here because this case is *not* closed, despite popular opinion. There is more to it than arsenic in the teacup." I raise my ring finger. "Two, I am dressed like this to get into the building. I guess you *could* call it a disguise." My middle finger joins the first two in presenting my case. "As to how often I do this, you may not believe me, but I do *try* to keep it to once a month. It's just sometimes…"

Atlas puts a finger to his lips.

"I was joking."

The door closes at the bottom of the stairs. "Need any help with that?" a voice sounds.

"No, no, quite alright. I've got it. Delicate equipment, this."

Atlas steps inside the closet. The second the light disappears, the footsteps reach the second floor. One tread is heavier while the other is distinguished by a shorter gait. The lighter must belong to the Inspector; the other to the photographer, Mr Stout.

"Where do we start, then?" The voice is gravelly, but the words are spoken with professional steadiness.

"Both bedrooms and the sitting room. Make sure you get the fireplace. You can still see where the bottle rested in the ashes. Try to get that from every angle. Every angle."

"Yes. I know my job, sir – I have been with the force nigh on seventeen years."

Footsteps, heavy and shorter together, come towards us.

"This way to the bedroom?" A hand rests on the closet door handle, ready to turn it. I hold my breath.

"No, no, that's only the coat closet. Unimportant, really. I checked it myself. The bedroom is this way."

The Inspector's footsteps retreat and Mr Stout follows after a second. The pair go down the hallway and into another room. It's impossible to hear what they're saying.

"Why did you think it was a disguise?" I whisper.

"I wouldn't have thought much of it, but you wore ill-fitting boots. The only reason to do so would be to make yourself taller."

I keep my voice low. "How did you know I was lying?"

"Knowing what people are thinking or feeling has never been especially difficult for me. I do it without thinking. Also, it helps that you're an awful liar."

Before I get the chance to respond to this slight, the Inspector moves into the hallway, probably trying to stay out of the way of the camera. His voice travels easily: "Yes, wasn't it clever? A little trick I discovered during a case a few years back." Never mind – not worth listening to.

"Even still, why would you follow me?" I ask Atlas.

"I followed you because you were going to a murder scene – without, I assume, the knowledge of your parents or anyone else. How could I leave? And…" He hesitates. "I figured out the flaw in the case. I guess you did too?"

"Of course. Had I actually gone into that house down the street, would you have left the crime scene?"

"Yes. Well, probably. I'd have to be completely mad to come in here without permission." He sounds as if he's trying to convince himself.

"And yet, following a complete stranger into the house isn't mad at all?"

He starts to say something, but the words are halted.

"You wanted to come in here and solve the mystery," I go on. "I was just your excuse. You're welcome."

"You... I..."

"How did *you* get in, by the way?" I interrupt.

"I tried convincing the policemen at the door that I was a courier with an urgent message for the Inspector."

I put my head against the wall behind me. "I wish I'd thought of that."

"Oh, no, it didn't work. They thought I was playing some sort of trick. The crowd got out of hand, so the guards were called away. I just slipped in."

That must've been the rowdy noise from outside.

The muffled voice from the hallway drones on and on. After five minutes and fifty-eight seconds, they move on to the second bedroom, where the tones of a very one-sided conversation continue, with occasional interruptions from the bird. Eight minutes and twelve seconds later they move on to the sitting room. Now every word is crystal.

"So you see, Mr Stout, after Rosana finishes her studies, we're sending her to either Mrs Moring's Finishing School or St Anne's."

St Anne's. I must remember that to make certain I'll never be incarcerated there. I should take a look at the plans of the building on the off chance that I'll have to escape. And those of Mrs Moring's Finishing School as well, for that matter.

"Pretty little oriole. Always wanted a bird for myself. As a boy, I tried coaxing a blue one with apple seeds from my lunch. The bird never came."

Does he really think you can feed apple seeds to a bird?

"Aren't you a pretty thing? Yes? You think so too?"

A vision of the poor bird being patted by the Inspector's careless hands is all too vivid in my mind.

"Ah! The thing pecked me! The little beast pecked me!"

From the sucking noise sneaking under the door, it sounds as though the Inspector is now holding his finger in his mouth.

"Well, I think we're done here, Mr Stout. You will see to it that these are developed, yes?"

Mr Stout makes a grunt of assent.

"Thank you. I'll see you tomorrow. I have to take this naughty bird to the station or it'll starve."

The sound of jangling metal mingles with the protests of the bird. As the Inspector breezes past our hiding spot he mumbles about how his pecked finger has begun to burn. Mr Stout packs away his gear, quietly humming to himself.

It seems like ages before the exterior door closes below. I reach out to gently turn the knob. Atlas puts his hand over mine.

"Don't! If they forget anything, they'll come back for it in the next few minutes."

Reluctantly, I dig my own boots from my bag to pass the time.

One, two, three, four, five, six, seven…

The third step creaks lightly. I freeze with only one boot on, the laces still half-tied in my hand. Padded footsteps glide over the floorboards into the drawing room. Something is slid off what sounds like wood. The mantle, perhaps? A thick silence reigns until the back door clicks below; the stranger must have skipped the third step on their way down. That couldn't have been either the Inspector or the photographer. The pacing was all wrong. And neither the Inspector nor Mr Stout would have been so quiet.

We wait a few minutes more. When no other sound comes, I slowly crack open the door. The room is empty. I tie the lace of my second boot in the light. The room appears identical to before, and yet… something is different. The birdcage is gone, revealing a wear mark on the table. The windows remain unchanged, the fireplace untouched, and the logs exactly as they were.

Wait. Something glints in the fading light coming from the window. It's only a small screw; probably fell from the photographer's bag. Atlas crosses the rug to stand at my elbow. He whispers something, though I'm not listening.

"Atlas. Where did you just step?"

He looks from the screw to me. The half-light makes his eyes an even paler shade of green. "I was just standing by the chairs. Where do you think the screw came from?"

I pass it to him. "I think it goes with the camera, but where did you just walk? Over the rug?" I take a guess as to where Atlas would have set his feet. He crouches to set the screw on the rug again.

"Did you hear something?"

"Yes. Did you walk this way?"

He watches my boots, a crease appearing between his eyes.

"No, it was more like this… I wanted to examine the chairs." He walks by the wingback closest to the window. His third step sounds unlike the rest.

"Should we move the chair?" He looks uncomfortable at the prospect. To tell the truth, I'm a bit hesitant; but the possibility of not finding evidence is worse than rearranging a dead man's furniture.

"Definitely."

The wingback is surprisingly light and makes almost no sound as we set it against the wall. The material tied around the feet silences the bulk of the noise. Kneeling, I peel back a corner of the fibres, revealing a thin rug pad and the outline of a small door. I take the edge of the rough felt and lay it over the rug. This part of the floor has been shielded from the sun for so long that the wood grain is noticeably darker.

The trapdoor has no handle, but there's enough of a gap for me to get my fingers under the edge. The heavy wood is completely smooth, and though it's difficult to find leverage, no splinters force their way underneath my skin.

Atlas helps and we lift the trapdoor up and off to the side.

He draws a sharp breath. "I'll grab a light."

CHAPTER 5

While Atlas finds a candle, I poke my head into the darkness. I block most of my own light, but the cavity can't be larger than six feet long and three feet wide. The floor isn't far below, so I lower myself through the opening. Standing in the cavity, my elbows rest on the drawing room floor.

"What are you doing?"

I turn. Atlas holds a tall candle, trimmed and lit.

"I'm searching for evidence." I crouch down and disappear under the rim of the opening. I reach my hand up and wiggle my fingers. "Pass me the light and come down."

Solid wax fits nicely into my palm, and as I bring down the halo of light, illuminating the tiny room. Two boots are followed by Atlas's body. He crouches and turns his head to give the close ceiling a wary glance.

Covering one entire wall are what must be hundreds of papers thrown up any way possible: pasted, tacked, folded. There's even a small notebook hung by a string. Its contents appear to be a ledger of some sort. Small lines of nondescript dates, names, numbers, and mentions of "The Creation" march across the thin pages. A few clipped newspaper articles display headlines of "Unsolved Mystery", "What Killed Mrs Jacobson?", and "Police Baffled by Poisoning". The details of the cases from all over Britain span five years.

The layer of literature is so thick that hardly any of the walls can be seen.

A square sheet of black paper stands out among its beige, white, and brown comrades. Deep creases indicate that it was once folded as an envelope. In the centre of what would have been the back panel is a seal the same shade as the paper. In the centre is an uppercase blackletter "I" with rose vines choking it. When I tilt the paper, the light catches words written around the seal in dark ink: "Regards from the new Phantom. *Denuo natus invisibilia.*"

The paper makes a satisfying *rip* as I tear it from the wall. Atlas's flat cap snaps in my direction. "What was that?"

"That was this." I hand the paper over.

He takes it hesitantly. His stunned look morphs into concentration. "This reminds me of something… but I don't remember what…" Trailing off, he looks blankly at a brass pin. With an intake of breath, he sits up, opening his mouth – then closes it again, slumping. "I can't think of it. Perhaps it'll come to me later."

He hands the square sheet back and I fold the empty edges around the seal. As an extra precaution, I wrap the specimen in my handkerchief and nestle it in my pocket. Something small brushes my other hand. I stifle a scream, but it turns out to be only a note that slipped from its tack. Two torn holes near the top of the cheap paper crown the scrawled words: "One bottle of your creation at the seventh park. Red scarf. Payment as usual." I let the slip ghost to the ground and return my attention to the wall.

A realistic drawing in an odd, line-filled style shows the swarthy features of a man in red ink. Thin script with long flourishes titles the page: "Do it yourself". Almost as an afterthought, a line at the bottom reads, "Your re-initiation fee. *Denuo natus invisibilia.*"

Pictures, orders, tiny slips with nearly nothing on them; but never any mention of places or names.

And still, all of it was hidden just underneath everyone's noses… But not —

"Atlas, the journal! The journal was sitting on the end table, next to the bird. Did you see it after we came out of the closet?"

What better place to keep an even greater stash of evidence than in a book hiding in plain sight? If I had any secrets, that's where I'd keep them… in code, of course.

Atlas's eyes continue over a cramped line of the suspended notebook, waiting a moment to meet mine. When they do, they seem much calmer than I feel, but he confirms my fears. "No. It wasn't there."

Why hadn't I taken even a moment to look at the journal? Why? The photographer couldn't carry it, not with all the equipment. The Inspector, then? It isn't likely, but…

"If it wasn't the Inspector, the stranger who came in must have been —" He waves generally at the wall. "One of these people. Walker must have been aligned with some sort of… cult, or secret society. And they turned on him."

The laces of my boots become hopelessly tangled by my nervous, meddling fingers. "We don't know that. I do have to agree that it seems unlikely now that it was the neighbour. Unless…"

Atlas straightens, his head dangerously close to the ceiling.

"…the neighbour was one of them!" we say at the same time.

It's a possibility.

"They're keeping him in the city jail until the trial. If I could just…" It would be difficult, far more so than dressing up as Rosana Wallace. If only I were a *real* Inspector.

"I'm coming too."

The possibilities of getting myself arrested or slipping in with the laundry fly from my head.

"What?"

"I want to help."

"Why?"

Atlas crosses his arms. "For the same reasons as you, I suspect."

That's hardly an answer and he knows it. We'll have to shelve the issue for now.

"First, we have to get out of here. Do you think they'll be watching the house?

Atlas is quiet for a moment, but he lowers the notebook, saying, "I guess we'll have to find out. Should we look out the windows?"

"No. If they're watching the house, it'd look suspicious. Even if the police aren't, the secret society might be."

I plant my hands on either side of the trapdoor opening and hoist myself out. I offer my hand to Atlas, and he puts the candle in it. The journal that was on the table is gone, and the last flicker of hope that Atlas could have been wrong is snuffed out.

After a quick sweep of the house, finding nothing more interesting than cobwebs, we plan our way out. "Should we go out the windows?" I propose.

Atlas walks over to the glass. He stands on tiptoes to see as much as he can of the building between the curtains. "There aren't hand or footholds, and it's a twenty-foot drop. Why don't we try the back door?"

He slinks down the stairs but returns almost immediately.

"The police are outside. I heard them talking."

"How about a fire escape?"

"I can't imagine there being any trustworthy fire escape, and if there were, we wouldn't have anyone to tie down the slide at the bottom. That might be the most dramatic way out possible."

"It isn't," I say, matter-of-factly.

His eyebrows lift. "You can think of another one?"

"Of course! But that isn't the point. The roof?"

Atlas looks out through the mullions, blinking a few times. After a moment he exhales.

"I guess the roof it is."

I clap my hands too eagerly, startling him. "I'll find a way up."

* * *

CLOUDS THROW a red-and-pink shroud over the horizon. Warm light from house windows grows stark against the greying facades. On one end of the row, just barely peeking above the edge of the flat roof, are the branches of a tree.

I point over the low ridges dividing the flats. "We could get onto the tree and climb down."

"Perfect."

The noise of the crowd is gone, and only a faint breeze rustles our clothing. The temperature is cooler but still pleasant. The poor tree is far past its golden years. It would be a majestic thing if it resided in some field, but here it has barely enough ground to stand on. The bark has a cracked, rough texture on the thicker branches and trunk. Leaves obscure much of the tree, but there is one promising branch that's clear. Unfortunately, it's about seven feet below the edge of the roof.

I've never liked heights. Well, not heights themselves, I suppose, but falling from them. I try not to look down, but I can't help it. Bile climbs up my throat and I snap my eyes from the ground.

One – two – three – four —

No, no. I'm counting too quickly. Breathing in through my nose, I roll out my shoulders and count extra slowly. Atlas steps closer to the end of the roof, puts both hands on the edge, and lowers himself. Even before I can start worrying for him, there's a rustle of leaves as he lands on the branch.

My turn. I crouch, grip the lip of the roof, let one leg down. Then the next. Before I can question myself, I let go. Instinctively, my knees bend at the moment of impact and one hand reaches for the wall while the other goes out to the side.

That wasn't too bad. I use the wall to negotiate a half-turn to face Atlas. He's poised behind me, ready to stop my fall.

He lowers his hands and nods. "Good landing."

"Thanks."

The branch leads back to the heart of the tree, where another limb reaches out. If we go from this one to that and drop from the smaller bough, we'll be on the ground. Or I could just jump from here. I check the strap of my canvas bag before I crouch, reaching one foot into the air below. I let my other foot down, release my grip, and drop to the ground.

It's about the same height from the roof to the branch. The only noise I make is the sound of my boots hitting the packed dirt. A stripe of pain shoots up my legs, lingering in my ankles and knees. The contents of my bag are shaken up, but nothing's broken.

Atlas lands next to me. He brushes hair out of his eyes. "Alright?"

"Fine. You?"

He shrugs. "You may not believe me, but I do try to keep jumping from rooftops to once a month."

I match his smile.

The sky, now hemmed by buildings, is fading fast. I hadn't

thought to bring a light. The streetlamps are flickering to life. Ominous clouds mutter to one another above, conversing about the weather and the price of good tea. Few people walk along the pavement, but those who do grace us with glares.

After escaping the neighbourhood, we find Atlas's horse, Emil, tied to a post outside a small medical practice.

"Which way is your house?"

"Oh, I can find my way back. It's alright." I inject some jaunty confidence into my tone.

"I insist."

I thread a finger through the straps of my bag and swing it over my shoulder. "I can take a tram back."

"At night?"

Oh! They've all closed; or if not, they won't be accepting any more passengers. I hoped to catch the last ride towards home half an hour ago. I should have kept a closer watch on the time.

Atlas takes my silence as acceptance. "Can you tell me how to get to your house? Is it very far?"

I sigh. "It isn't too bad. Go past the Tray and turn left at the clock repair shop."

"Then...?"

"I'll give you the rest of the directions as you need them."

He sighs. "If you say so."

He stretches out his hand.

I squint. "What's that for?"

"For getting up."

I can't help a quiet laugh as I put a foot in the stirrup and grip the saddle with one hand. I push off the ground and mount easily. Atlas only shrugs and does the same, but I catch the hint of a smile as he settles. After a moment, we're riding off into the gathering gloom.

* * *

RAIN SHOWERS down on us as we ride through the city. The streetlamps create golden crowns of ricocheting drops. As we leave the tight streets, the drizzle lessens.

At home, we leave Emil outside the gate and approach the house on foot. Skirting just inside the garden, we pass moonlit flower beds full of stems pinned with buds.

"How long has this been here? The garden, I mean." Atlas turns his head to me.

"When Mother married Father, he asked her to fix up the house as she'd like it. He'd just bought the place, and it needed someone to help it along. Mother pored over the plans for a long time before showing them to Father. The rest of the house was cleaned up and polished gradually. In her plans, she included two swings, saying they would be for their two children. They hadn't decided together about having any children, but that's when Father changed his mind. Olive and I used to play here for hours."

We trudge on for a few more steps. The sprinkle of rain has made the grass glossy and fat drops slip onto our heads from the trees. Birds trill evening melodies overhead, and the night air is soothing.

"You have a sister? Older or younger than you?"

"Older." I turn. "Why do you ask?"

Atlas shrugs. "I thought you were an only child."

"What would give you that impression?"

He puts a finger to his mouth. "Hmm. Something about you running around by yourself. My second guess would have been middle."

I'm usually asked if I'm the middle child after someone hears of one of my escapades. "Never the oldest?"

"No, you don't remind me of any of the oldest siblings I know."

"So, you're the middle, then?"

Atlas shoves his hands into his pockets. "Yes, I have an older brother."

Our conversation trails off, leaving only the sound of wet grass beneath our feet. The house comes into view. Most of the windows are glowing behind the curtains, and the gas lamps by the front doors are flickering eagerly. A shadow paces in Phoebe's room.

"Let me guess." Atlas inclines his head to the house. "Your room is the one with the ladder to the balcony?"

"Precisely. I used it earlier today, and I'll be using it now. Goodbye, Atlas. Perhaps we shall meet again."

"Perhaps?" he repeats. "We're both solving the case. I'm sure our paths will cross. Goodnight, Indigo." With a nod, he walks off towards the gate.

* * *

I DRY my boots and return them to their customary spot in the wardrobe. The black paper, still wrapped in my handkerchief, fits neatly in the false-bottom drawer. I sneak down the hall to the bathroom, locking the door behind me. In the basin I soak a singed napkin that Mother was going to throw out. (I didn't *mean* to burn it, but it's useful.) The warm water feels heavenly on my face, but I have things to do – calming Phoebe, for one.

If she isn't looking for me now, she will check on me in a few minutes. It's not uncommon for me to disappear for a few hours. Usually it's only because no one can find me, but it is extraordinary for me to miss dinner, and she'll be worried. To combat her fear, I have come up with another story, hopefully one more convincing than my last. My plan was to tell her what really happened, but I suppose I didn't account for finding anything of true importance.

I wring out the small square of fabric, the water now dripping clean, and drape the damp napkin over the washstand. As

I turn, I instinctively jerk my arm away from a nail sticking out of the window frame. How long until Father finds a competent craftsman to fix this? It's been weeks since the workman left this hazard in his attempt to repair the water damage.

By now, Atlas is probably halfway home, back to the house with the bright green doors. If only I could find a plausible excuse to go back there. "I think I left my gloves in the glass room, on the trapeze", or "Here is a basket of sweets I made – I can go set them down in the kitchen".

A wry laugh twists itself from me. I'm not going back. I'm not that lucky.

By the time Phoebe knocks, I've changed into my night-dress and am in bed reading *Emma*. I'm relieved to have an excuse to stop reading.

"Indigo, are you in there?"

"Yes. Come in."

If doors can slam open, this one does. "I looked everywhere for you!"

I have strong feelings about the phrase "looked every-where", because if the seeker had indeed "looked everywhere", they would have found me. To be fair, I did make it extra hard this time.

"Well, I hid in the attic and fell asleep. I think I may have bruised my back." Perhaps details will make my story more believable?

"Oh, Indigo!" she sighs. "A scarecrow could lie better than that. You'd best tell me what you were really up to today."

"You don't understand. I was just so tired, and the next thing I knew, I was awake and stiff as a board."

She stares at me, hands on her hips. Is she trying to hold back a laugh? I must be mistaken. Oh, no, I'm not.

"Indigo, really now." Phoebe wipes her eyes. "You're good at finding mischief, but you are the worst liar I've ever known."

I give a contrived sigh and explain that I really went to the bakery to read. I'm met with a cold glare. There's no hope for me.

"I met a little girl in the park yesterday who works for the circus and she invited me to see her on the trapeze. I couldn't refuse!" I stop biting my lip when pain flags the unconscious tic.

"You wouldn't hide that from me. Out with it."

I cross my arms and sit on the edge of my bed. "Is this an interrogation?"

Phoebe mirrors my stance. "It can be, if it needs to."

I throw my hands into the air. "Fine. After I left the little girl's house – and I *did* go – I disguised myself as Rosana Wallace and took a peek around 340 Bridges Street. A boy from the circus house followed me. Apparently, he thought I was lying when I said I was going to my grandmother's house. After a look around, he escorted me home." I shrug. "That's all."

Phoebe's face hardens. In an instant she's kneeling in front of me, grabbing my shoulders. "You went to the scene of a homicide? Alone? No, worse – with a strange boy? And you didn't tell me?" She blinks a few times quickly as her voice grows thick. "Indigo, I've turned a blind eye to your investigation of petty crime in the past... But this is different. This isn't a stolen ring or a broken window. This is murder. This is death. Whoever did it – because I find it difficult to believe it's Edmond Smith – is still out there and might be watching. You have no idea what you could get pulled into, no idea what it may do to you. Indigo..."

She relaxes her grip enough to slide her hands down to meet mine.

"I think you will be a wonderful detective. I think, if that's what you want to do, you'll find a way to do it. But if you throw it all away with this case, you may not get the chance. And you have no clue what your death or disappearance would do to me." A single tear drips from her dark eyelashes onto my knee. She sniffs and runs her sleeve over her cheek. "Or your mother and father. Or Olive. I know you don't think she loves you, and she may not even know herself. But she does." She chokes out a laugh. "And let's not forget your grandmother."

I laugh too, the tears in my own eyes almost spilling over. Phoebe sits heavily on my bed, still looking at me.

"I was so worried. You didn't come down for *hours*. And then it was time for dinner and you were still gone." She puts on a warning look. "Which your mother and father are not pleased about. I went out to the gardens about an hour ago to see if you fell asleep out there, or... I don't know. And still I didn't find you."

I straighten, laying my head on her shoulder. "I'm so sorry."

"I know you are." She leans her head against mine. "Just don't do it again. Do you understand?"

I swallow painfully and nod against her shoulder.

Phoebe exhales shakily, wrapping her arm around me – more for her sake than mine, I think. After a moment, she lifts her head. "I saved food for you. Do you want me to bring it up?"

"Let's go down to the kitchen together. Unless you'd rather go to bed?"

She waves a hand. "No, that sounds like a wonderful idea."

* * *

I CLIMB INTO BED, and stare up at the ceiling. A snake of guilt writhes inside my gut. I suppose I never really expected to find anything. But now... now I know something the police don't. Something that changes the tone of the case entirely. This was no fed-up neighbour with murder in his veins. This is a network of... I don't even know. Thieves? Assassins?

And as I follow this to its end – because it seems no one else will – I won't have Phoebe to confess to or lean on. She's never acted like my nurse or ladies' maid. She was always different; even when we argued, I knew she'd still listen to me. Still want to believe me. What if, at the end of this, that can never happen again?

No, that's preposterous.

Isn't it?

It's a long, long time before I eventually fall asleep.

CHAPTER 6

Mondays are so trying. The clock chimes four by the time I'm free from school. It's getting more difficult to avoid my parents looking for my decision on finishing school, so I hide in my room. I reread my notes from three nights ago at Walker's house. I wrote the experience down in a casebook, dedicating a full fifteen pages to the subject. By the time I'm through reading it again, and no new thought strikes me, only forty-five minutes have passed.

I guess I'll take a nap. Dinner is in two hours; I should be awake before then. Beside my bed, small raindrops fall against the window, providing music to the beginnings of a dream.

I'm in a building that's laid out like Mr Walker's house, but with all of my family's furniture. I'm about to tell my parents that I don't want to go to finishing school when I find myself in the sitting room and see Olive bent over, sniffling.

"Where are Mother and Father? I have to tell them something."

Olive looks up at me, her eyes red with tears. "They ran away to the circus, to go dress up in tutus and train bears. They said that I had to stay here to keep the house. Will you stay with me?"

A knocking from somewhere snaps me from my stunned stillness. Opening the nearest doors, I see nothing but call out, "Come in!"

Still the knocking continues. Slowly I wake to realise that, first, Mother and Father did not leave me to go to the circus, nor does Olive want me to stay with her; and second, the knocking is real.

My hair sticks to the side of my face as I raise my head. "Come in." But no door opens. "Phoebe?"

"Indigo!"

The call is slightly muffled, but I recognise the voice immediately. In a flash, I am at the balcony doors. Atlas stands on the other side. I furrow my brow questioningly at him.

"I remembered."

I unlock the door and join him in the rain. Drops fall from the brim of his cap and trace their way down his sleeves, but in his excitement he hardly notices.

"There's a crumbling mansion on the edge of the city. The building is nearly covered in climbing roses, and above the front doors is a blackletter "I" that is identical to the one in the seal. People say it's haunted and don't go near it. It's been empty for years."

It is possible that if there *were* a secret society, they would hide out in an abandoned building. *They* may even have spread rumours about it being haunted. Perhaps a reconnaissance mission is in order? I should go now, before it gets any later and I lose the advantage of daylight.

"Where is it?" I ask.

Atlas jerks his head vaguely. "I'll show you."

I try to sound reasonable, as if I am letting him out of some terrible chore. "Atlas, you don't have to join me. All I need are directions. I have a map too; you can just show me on that."

"I want to help. And without me, you won't know where to go."

I lift my chin an inch. "I can find it without you."

He shakes his head. "That would take too long; the trial is too close."

Well played. I could search for weeks without finding anything. Perhaps it's not a real lead anyway. I can find something else. But Mr Walker's house is constantly watched, and getting in *again* would be a miracle. "Alright, but we have to hurry. We can be back in an hour and a half, right?"

He squints a fraction. "If we're quick."

"Good. Then I'll just put on a quick disguise and we'll get going."

I have a black shirt that I wore to my father's sister's husband's great aunt's funeral. (I can't say I was very attached, and I spent most of the ceremony trying to remember her connection to Father.) With the addition of a black skirt, bonnet, and gloves, it will be the perfect mourning front. Oh! And I will add some darkness under my eyes as well – my favourite uncle died, and I've been haunted by nightmares since.

Atlas's gaze flicks past me into my room. In a second he's on the ladder again. I spin around to find Phoebe.

Phoebe! She isn't supposed to know! She turns a full circle before noticing me on the balcony. I shut the door behind me a little too hard.

"Well." I clear my throat. "It's certainly raining out there."

I brush off my shoulder and run a hand through my hair. Some strands still stick to my face. I tuck them behind my ears.

"What are you doing, Indigo?"

Heat creeps up my neck until the flaming colour covers my cheeks. "Doing? Oh. Um. I was… looking at a bird."

Phoebe's eyes narrow. She brushes past me and out the door.

"I think it may've been a starling." Even I notice the strangled timbre of that remark.

"You went out in the rain to see a starling?"

"They're very pretty birds, you know."

Phoebe surveys the ground around the balcony, then the garden. Discreetly, I peek over the side. Atlas is still on the ladder. He looks up at me with wide, panicked eyes.

I casually position myself in front of the ladder, my hands placed on the railing to either side.

"I am aware of the starling's beauty." Phoebe turns towards me, noticing my posture.

My voice ranges dangerously higher. "Though it may have been some other bird. I only saw it for a second – oh, Phoebe, you don't have to —"

She leans over the edge to look straight down the ladder.

"Phoebe, I can —"

But Atlas is gone.

Affecting a laugh is harder than it sounds, and my attempt falls miserably short of genuine. "Oh. I guess the bird flew off – I was going to point it out. We should head inside, you're getting wet." I start heading to the door.

Phoebe puts a hand on my shoulder. It's hard to look up at her.

"Indigo…" She stares down at me, but I only see this in my peripheral vision. She heaves a sigh. "You can tell me anything."

"I know." I look up at her eyes – brown with flares of golden hazel. The only other eyes I know so well are my grandmother's.

Phoebe waits a second longer, then marches back into my room, heels clicking. "Don't be late for dinner."

The ire in her words jams a hot poker into my resolve.

"Wait, Phoebe!" I have no story to tell, but there has to be something I can say to soothe her doubt, something that will partially make amends. The door shuts, leaving only the sound of rain. In the reflection of the glass, I see Atlas climb back onto the balcony. He hangs back, one hand still on the rope ladder.

"Should we go another day?"

"It won't change anything." I jerk a shrug. "I'll leave the disguise off today. Did you bring Emil?"

"Oh no!" He claps his hands to his mouth. "I forgot that the trams close at night! I'll need a lift home."

I lift a hand towards the stables, hidden behind trees. "Oh, that's alri—"

He stops me. "I was teasing."

I chortle. It surprises me that it isn't forced. Atlas smiles a bit too.

"I'll meet you at the street in ten minutes."

* * *

I TAKE Quest while Atlas rides Emil. We go at a brisk pace, not fast enough to attract attention but quicker than an evening ride. We reach the outskirts of the city in seventeen minutes, leaving the rain behind us.

The mansion looks more romantic than haunted. It's a grandiose building with large, curved windows. Numerous panes of glass are missing. Two crumbling brick towers remind me of an illustration from *Saint George and the Dragon*. Rose vines crawl up almost the entire front of the house. The double doors are mostly gone, and there is indeed a blackletter "I" chiselled in stone above the entryway.

Atlas was riding ahead of me, but now he hangs back. "What do you think?"

"It's beautiful. It looks like something from a storybook. An abandoned castle, perhaps. But how did you know about it?"

"The children's home Louise came from is down the street. I've been here many times, and this place always caught my attention."

I reappraise the buildings around me. The once-elegant three and four storey houses have now become nothing more than shells, only standing out by their architecture and wild lawns. All that remains is for some enterprising factory owner to snatch up the lot of them and forge a smoke-belching monstrosity.

Before we can pass the abandoned mansion, Atlas urges his horse closer to mine and whispers, "Ready to head back?"

I consider for a second. "Why don't we take a quick peek inside…?"

"We shouldn't."

"We'd just take a quick look and get out. Or we could come back at nightfall, and we would have a better chance of seeing candlelight." He must see the flaws in this plan, and that will make him more likely to agree to my first proposition.

"Do you really believe that a band of thieves and murderers would use candles in a building without blackout curtains? It's more likely that *we* would be caught."

"Then we should go inside now."

He gives the mansion a hard stare, then turns to me. "Promise that you'll be careful?"

"Of course. I would like to go home tonight."

"Do you think we should go in through a window?"

I can't help the mischievous smile that begins to show. "How about the front door?"

* * *

WE STEP over the remains of the double doors, quiet as death. I suck in a breath – which I should *not* have done, because I get a throatful of dust, and it's difficult to cough quietly. The entry hall's ceiling is three storeys high, windows going all the way to the top. The thorny vines outside steal sunlight from the room, shifting it into a nest of snakelike shadows. The ceiling itself is highly decorated and has a chandelier hanging, rather precariously, in the centre of the foyer. In front of us is a grand staircase with sweeping bannisters and marble steps. The marble is cracked in some places, and everything is blanketed in pollen. At the top of the staircase are two pillars of the same marble as the stairs, inlaid with gold and silver. Floating everywhere, adding an ambience of fantasy, nebulae of dust parade in the streams of early evening sunlight.

Atlas shakes me from my reverie. "Where do you want to go? Up or down?"

I'd nearly forgotten. "Up. There is a boot mark in the pollen on the stairs. Also, the crystals that fell from the chandelier are gone – they must have been taken. Someone's been here."

Going up the main staircase seems hazardous, and the pollen will record our tracks, so instead we find a door behind the pillar on the left. I assumed it was a cloakroom, but it's a hidden corridor. It can't be more than three feet wide, and the wooden floor is raked with scratches and pockmarks. The doors on either side have splintered fragments ready to stab errant fingers.

Atlas peeks into all the rooms on the left and I the ones on the right. The first door I open leads to a forgotten parlour with silhouettes of furniture under ghostly sheets. Across the room, the moulding on the dark wall forms vertical rectangles. Assuming my door follows that pattern, it would be nearly impossible to tell which section of the wall is the secret entrance.

The second room is a library, with built-in bookshelves lining the walls. The books are so coated in dust that their titles are impossible to make out. This time, I step into the room to see how my door appears from inside. It is also a bookcase, though this one holds old family portraits. The slightly textured paint is dusted with grey. I tug gently at the gaudy frame of the portrait. It doesn't budge.

"Indigo?" Atlas's whisper is the epitome of calm.

"I'm in here." But even as I say it I slip back into the hallway and shut the door gently behind me.

"What did you see?"

"A library. I was just curious to see how the secret door fit into the wall."

He nods, opening the door beside him. I put my hand on the dull handle of the next door. As I twist it, the handle drops to the ground and thuds against the floor. We freeze. I turn my head to Atlas, but he remains still as a statue. There is no alarm, no stomping footsteps, only the nearly inaudible sound of our shallow breathing.

Slowly, Atlas reaches toward the next handle. It swings open quietly. In fact, every door we've tried opens smoothly. If the mansion were truly abandoned, the hinges would have grown rusty.

A hand covers my mouth. Atlas pulls me through a door on the left just as a door ahead of us opens, and a shiny boot steps into the corridor. When the door is almost closed behind us – closing it fully would be too loud – he removes his hand from my lips.

"Is our client ready for me to deliver the package?" The voice has the pressed syllables of a member of high society.

"Not yet. He's still deciding what to use," a second man responds in a heavy cockney accent. "He wants the one from Walker, but we're saving that for higher-paying customers. The client should let us know within the next day or two and then you can make the drop."

"Why can't we just make more? Didn't Walker have an assistant? We could just force them to show us the process."

"Walker?" The man scoffs. "He'd never teach anyone the secret. Probably thought that'd be enough to save him. Real shame we had to kill him; he was a master of his craft."

"We don't even know what it's made of?"

"That was his bargaining chip – if he died, so would the formula. He must not have known the new Phantom."

The two men are silent for a moment. Then the first asks, "Do you think the Phantom would give up the society if caught?"

The cockney voice takes on a sharp edge. "The Phantom is smart. Smart enough to know when the fight is over and when it isn't. Smart enough *not* to get in those situations. So don't you worry about us. You can't catch what you can't see. *Denuo natus invisibilia.*"

"*Denuo natus invisibilia.*"

"There's another delivery ready to be dropped off that we need your expertise on…"

The voice is muted as a door, just a few feet down the hall, closes softly behind them.

"Well, that answers a lot of questions," I whisper.

Atlas's eyes are as wide as mine. "But now we may have more. Who is the Phantom? What were they saying when they said '*Denuo natus invisibilia*'? I'm not very good at Latin."

My eyebrows furrow. "That's easy enough – it's something about being 'again invisible.' I can double-check my Latin grammar."

He nods. "Can you bring what you find to my house tomorrow? I'm not sure how long I can avoid meeting your parents or…" He averts his eyes. "Anyone else."

Phoebe. A tightness pulls at my chest. "When do you want me to arrive?" I could take Quest and be there within a half-hour.

"When do you finish school?"

"Four o'clock, usually."

He nods once. "After school. Don't be suspicious."

"When would I ever be suspicious?"

Atlas decides not to answer.

We slip quietly out the door and down the hallway. We keep

out of the dust and pollen as much as possible, smudging our prints when we're forced to wade across a large patch. By the time we make it outside, the sky is beginning to smoulder with brilliant colours. The temperature is just on the edge of cold, but the minute's walk to the horses helps to warm me up. The streets beside us are almost completely silent; the only people travelling are us and a man hobbling along with a cane.

When we come into view, Quest shakes her head at me. "I know, sorry." I pat her flank, her body heat welcome on my hands.

We mount our horses and ride toward the main part of town. I can't help feeling a little smug. We just infiltrated a den of thieves and escaped with not a hair out of place. Even so, I occasionally glance back to see if anyone is following us, which no one is. We weave through a few back alleys just in case we didn't see the pursuer. We separate at the main road, going opposite ways.

At last, I pass the wrought iron gates of home and lead Quest to the stables. Sometimes I wish I could live somewhere else – somewhere not so grand, so obvious.

There is light under Phoebe's door as I navigate around it to enter my room. I can make out the sound of paper rustling – probably a letter from her sister. Should I ask her about it later? I throw on a new dress and go down to dinner.

When I return, Phoebe's light is still on, her shadow journeying across it. The door seems a much more imposing barrier than yesterday morning. I breathe in and tap lightly on the wood with a knuckle. "Goodnight, Phoebe."

There's a pause on the other side of the door. Seconds drag on; one by one they pass me by. Just as I'm turning away, it opens.

"Goodnight, Indigo." She wraps me in a warm hug for a moment. It's a bit more stiff than usual, but it's an embrace nonetheless.

CHAPTER 7

I knock at the house with the green double doors, otherwise known as 416 Old Twinings Road. A tall, brown-haired man wearing black work trousers and a plain shirt opens the door. "And who might you be?" he asks politely, looking down at me with quiet eyes.

"My name is Indigo Taylor. I'm here to speak with Atlas Trinter."

The man, who introduces himself as Arlo, seems to know this already and welcomes me in. This time, I keep my bag and shoes with me as I'm led into the drawing room and told Atlas will be here in a moment. The room is gorgeous. The walls are decorated with white-and-blue wallpaper. Natural light pours in through a bay window on the front wall. Bright green bookshelves line another wall, with a large map of the city in the corner. Facing me are a few plush grey velvet couches with elegant wooden end tables, lamps perched on each. On the wall to my right are more bookshelves, also bright green, with framed pictures among the volumes. Some are architectural drawings of the Cirque du la Reine Theatre, while others are photographs of performers themselves. There's a dated picture of the theatre's opening day. A crowd is gathered; a few wealthy-looking gentlemen and ladies – who I assume are the donors to the building fund – stand in the front with Mr and Mrs Trinter.

"Mama and Papa started Cirque du la Reine when they were first married. But it wasn't always like it is now."

Flinching, I almost knock a framed stage plan across the room, but pull back my elbow just in time.

"Atlas! Don't scare me like that. I see now why Phoebe hates it."

He laughs. "Do you really do that to her? I'm sorry, I thought you heard me."

I glare at him, and he smiles a little more apologetically.

"This room is amazing! Is every room in the house this incredible?"

"Not every room, but most. When Cirque du la Reine started, we performed at events. As it became more popular, my parents bought this house and renovated some of the rooms to host performances here. Eventually, they outgrew the house, and the theatre was built. Some of the performers travelled from far away, and others had nowhere at all to go; everyone who needed to stayed here. Now only a few of us live in this house. We all do our best to keep it nice." His eyes wander the room, fondly remembering things I'll never see. His gaze sharpens. "Do you have the translation?"

I pull out my notebook, flipping through the pages until I have the right one. "*Denuo natus invisibilia* translates to 'Born again invisible'."

We stand there for a moment. It doesn't clear up as much as I'd hoped, but it isn't nothing, either.

"That would explain the blackletter 'I,'" Atlas says.

"Do you think *denuo natus invisibilia* is some sort of password or signal?"

"It could probably be used as one. I doubt they say it in public."

I will commit it to memory; it could be important. I may need to use it to gain entry into a secret room, or to disturb my sister by chanting it over toast.

"I don't know what to think of this yet." Atlas folds his hands and dons a serious expression. "But I have a proposition."

I place the notebook into its pocket in my bag. "What is this proposition?"

"First, are you fascinated by the circus?"

Is he mad? "Yes. Of course." How does this relate to the mystery?

"And are you willing to work hard?"

I cross my arms. "Depends."

"Do you mind if I bring in my parents to talk with you?"

"Why would they need to —"

"You'll see."

Despite the belief – shared by more than a few – that I am quite the risk-taker, I don't throw myself into every situation hoping it'll turn out well. If I need a quick escape, the window should only be a few feet off the ground.

Atlas comes back in twenty-five seconds with the couple.

"Hello, hello. Lovely to see you again, Indigo," Mrs Trinter greets me.

"You as well, though I'm not certain why I have the pleasure."

Mr Trinter is more ebullient than usual. "Well, we are prepared to offer you a position of importance."

I shift the strap of my bag on my shoulder. "What would that be?"

"The highly esteemed position of daughter-in-law."

He lets that hang in the air, looking perfectly serious.

Atlas turns very red. "Papa…" He clears his throat with some difficulty. "That is not what we discussed."

Mr Trinter appears to remember something. "Oh, yes! I had quite forgotten! Sorry, not a proposal of marriage just yet." He tents his fingers. "For now, we'd like to offer you instruction on circus arts. You and your parents can decide how frequently you'd join us. We would like to meet them to discuss it, but we wanted to make sure the idea appealed to you."

They seem perfectly genuine, all three of them. But how? There must be some mistake. They can't want me. I'm the girl who spends her nights under the covers reading mystery novels. I'm the girl who gets distracted in manners class. The girl who forgets to do her assignments – though only on occasion, and with good reason. I'm the girl haunted by nightmares and plagued by impossible daydreams. I am strikingly, inescapably… human.

"But I am just… me," I say. "What you do seems so perfect."

Mrs Trinter laughs, Mr Trinter smiles, and Atlas looks mildly confused.

"No one is perfect, dear," The woman says between laughs. "Especially not us."

Mr Trinter leans forward. "I can vouch for that. This one" – he directs a finger at his laughing wife – "is a load of trouble. And that one" – this time he points at Atlas – "has far too much talent for practical jokes, and impractical ones."

Mrs Trinter stops chuckling enough to add, "Indigo, we don't require perfection. We only need you to be willing to *learn*."

"So, you're serious? This seems too good to be true."

Mr Trinter looks aghast. "How could you say such a thing? When would I ever jest?" He raises his right hand. "I swear that this is no trick. We just want to know if you're willing to try."

It's not much of a question. "I must ask my parents, but I am. Can I ask why?"

"Of course. For quite some time we've had the idea to bring on a student who is young and interested in what we do. I've never seen anyone with your curiosity about the circus outside of this house," Mr Trinter says plainly.

"You may think it means little, but that and resolve are essential," Mrs Trinter adds knowingly. "Do you think it would be possible for us to meet your parents? Or would you like to talk to them yourself?"

"My parents will be hesitant. It would help if you could present the idea to them."

"We'll send a letter telling them about the idea and inviting them to join us for tea."

My insides hollow with excitement. "Is there anything else I should know?"

"Just that your parents may not comply," Atlas reminds me.

I set my jaw, determined. "I'll convince them."

* * *

"THE CIRCUS? Is this a joke? Indigo, we thought you were becoming a lady of refinement. Gallivanting at the circus is not ladylike."

Father holds the Trinters' letter in hand, shaking it slightly with each sentence. It arrived earlier today, but he waited until after dinner to question me about it. Mother presses her hands to her face, while Father's arm rests protectively around her shoulders.

"It's no joke, Father." I stand in front of our couch in the drawing room, like a witness before the jury.

"Why you?"

The question stings. Father knows just the ones to ask to pick apart a testimony.

"I met two of their performers: one at The Empty Tray and the other at the park. I told them I was fascinated with the circus. We met again, and they asked me if I wanted to learn."

"When have you been meeting these strangers?"

"Well, I went to The Empty Tray after school one day, and then on a Saturday in the park."

"And the other time?"

There's no hope for it. My fingers start fidgeting of their own accord.

"At their studio on Old Twinings Street."

Father's face turns red, and I can just picture the ends of his combed moustache curling. "With no chaperone! Why did you not tell us? You went alone into a house full of strangers?"

It sounds terrible if you say it out loud.

"There were children." It's a weak argument, I know, and now that I think of it, perhaps blindly going into the house was naive. "And they're so friendly." I mentally wince; I'm not helping anything.

Father's voice goes low and almost gravelly. "The best actors are very convincing; often their true selves are completely invisible. I know Cirque du la Reine has a reputation to keep, and most of what they do may be honest, but every organisation is made of individuals. Not all of them are scrutinised. Don't ever do this again. Ever. Do you hear me?" He pinches the bridge of his nose. "At the very least, you should have taken Phoebe with you."

"Yes, Father."

He waves the letter in the air. It bends, forming a crease in an instant. "I'd like to meet these Trinters just to know what kind of people you have been exposed to." Father stands, as if to storm the gates of 416 this very moment. What a stroke of luck.

I knit my fingers together. "When are you available?"

He extracts a pocket calendar, eyes scanning for a moment before he snaps the booklet shut. "Saturday the thirteenth. I'll send a message at once. Until then, Indigo Arabella, you may not leave the grounds. And you may *never* go into a house of strangers – or anywhere with strangers – without a chaperone *and* our express permission."

"Yes, Father."

He storms out of the room, stowing his pocketbook. Success! All I have to do now is pretend to regret refusing all social calls. Ha! This couldn't have gone any better.

"Indigo, why would you do such a thing?"

I turn to see my mother wiping at the corners of her eyes with a handkerchief.

"I don't agree with your father's punishment. I think you need more time at social functions. The rules and manners will do you good. These may be good people, but they are also entertainers. Entertainers, Indigo!" Here she pauses to wave the handkerchief to-and-fro in front of her face. "Indigo… Oh, Indigo! You will *not* be an entertainer of that variety. We have been invited to the Luckfords' dinner party on Thursday. And on Friday a group of us are going to see an opera. I'll see to it that you join us on both occasions." She rises and puts a hand to her cheek, shaking her head. After a moment she raises that hand to my face. "Goodnight, Indigo. I love you."

I put my hand on hers. "I love you too, Mother."

She leaves the room, still dabbing at her eyes.

Oh, I hate long operas. The circus is much better. And, worst of all, I'll have to see Violet Luckford, my archenemy.

CHAPTER 8

I find myself thinking of caged birds, which comes as little surprise. Phoebe has imprisoned me in a sunny yellow dress – not her choice, of course; it was all Mother's idea. I can't help feeling that she chose this one *particularly* because I am so averse to it. What dress could possibly need a bow the size of the Oxford English Dictionary on the back?

Phoebe puts my hair into a plait, which she mercilessly nails to my head. I offered to do it myself, but to no avail. I wish I'd only been forced to stay in my room. Then, at least, I could read or work on more important things.

Father has agreed to meet with the Trinters on Saturday at one o'clock. (I haven't been told this, but a glass against a door can be very informative. Besides, I know they meant to tell me sometime.) Two days seems too long to wait, so I preoccupy myself with strategies. How to avoid Violet all night? We are *sworn* enemies, engaged in a fierce battle of politeness, though most of the time we each pretend the other does not exist. As a secondary plan, I'm compiling a list of excuses to leave the party altogether.

* * *

OUR CARRIAGE PULLS UP to a large house near the centre of the city. I visited so frequently when I was younger that it seems as if I'm stepping into an odd dream: a familiar place, but a very different scenario. As children, Leo, Poppy, and I were the best of friends. Violet was older and altogether meaner, so while she and Olive played with dolls, our threesome played hide-and-seek and practised fencing. But that was before Leo left for boarding school and Poppy travelled abroad.

Violet meets Olive the second we enter the house; clasping hands, they rush off together. Mother's hand rests on my shoulder for a moment, her brow forming tiny valleys on her forehead. "Indigo, run along now. I believe the young people are meeting in the parlour. You know where that is, don't you?"

Of course I know where it is; I just don't want to go.

"Oh, yes, Mother. I can find it."

She nods and strolls off arm-in-arm with Father. I'm left at the top of the stairs, looking into a sea of people. Nowhere do I see Poppy's face or Leo's blond hair. What if I have to make conversation with one of Mother's friends? Mrs Cantona only ever wants to talk about Crown gossip. I tried bringing up recent crime once, but her lips bent into a demoralising frown and she immediately denounced my choice of topic.

"Indigo?"

I turn. "Poppy! Leo!"

They are waiting in the corner, away from the rest of the group. Poppy has a lively face with large upturned hazel eyes. The colour pairs well with her dark brown hair, which is so thin and silky it always slips out of its fastenings. Leo has a narrow frame, sandy blond hair, brown eyes, and a posture that would make Mrs Wood snap to attention. He's the younger brother of my archenemy, though if I didn't know, I'd never suspect. He's *far* too nice.

"Mother said that we would meet in the parlour…"

"We came to greet you and keep an eye on Violet." Leo casts a glance into the crowd.

Violet has never been afraid to show her true colours with an audience before, but I appreciate the gesture.

"Though I'm sure we'd have *loads* of fun up here, why don't we practise fencing downstairs?" Leo looks at Poppy, then me. I thought it would have been too much to ask for them both to remember our favourite pastime, but I suppose I'm not the only one who missed our "lessons".

We make our way across the room, passing other guests, slipping between canes and bustles. It reminds me of the espionage games we used to play. I taught them how to find the best hiding places.

We creep past the parlour and down a set of stairs to a room dedicated to the art of fencing. I can't imagine many houses having a fencing piste, so we're lucky. For months, I used chalk to draw a piste outside my house, but the rain washed it away so many times that my resolve slowly eroded. Here, there are dressing rooms as well as a permanent piste and tall windows almost reaching the ceiling that make the room feel larger than it is. Poppy and I are changed in minutes, exchanging our party clothes for fencing attire.

Leo has the best technique, Poppy the most grace, and I am the most daring. We are about equal, though. Leo is the only one who has ever had professional training and wins slightly more often, though there have been many intense matches over the years.

Leo demonstrates what he's learned recently. The lesson is informative, and we begin. Poppy against me: I win. She attributes some of her closest fencing losses to a stray piece of hair, and this time is no exception. Next: she wins. One more time: I win. Now Leo against me: he wins twice in a row. Finally, we catch up with each other while we stand in a circle, exchanging points.

"How was France, Poppy?" I beat her foil.

She blocks my second intention. "Oh, it was wonderful! I wish we could all go together one day."

"What was your favourite part?" Leo asks as he disengages from my lunge.

"I loved the train ride, but I wouldn't call it my favourite. We spent a morning near the Seine, and then we rode a boat down the river the rest of the day."

I score a point on Leo after going in for a remise. It goes on like this until we have to change back into our dinner attire. Poppy's purple dress sweeps the floor a bit. Her brown hair is plaited at the back of her head, and she's wearing —

"Wait, you're allowed to wear boots? I'm forced to wear *these*." I lift my skirt a few inches to show off my slippers.

She smiles. "Mama insisted I wear a corset. I was determined to wear boots. We both got something we wanted." Poppy's preferred method of doing *anything* is by compromising, though she prefers to call it "negotiating".

Leo comes out of another hallway to join us. He's wearing a dinner jacket over a white dress shirt with a green cravat. "Shall we go up, then?"

Poppy and I each link arms with him. He looks mildly uncomfortable for a moment, then remembers it's just us. We used to do this all the time when we imitated our siblings, mocking their gossipy tones. Poppy and I smile at each other behind Leo's back. I suppose these parties are more enjoyable than I thought.

We march upstairs and into the dining room, detaching ourselves from Leo as we walk in. The table is laid with elegant cutlery and china, all in a silver floral pattern. The chandelier overhead glows radiantly and there are candelabras along the table. Dessert fruit, water, wine, and extra cutlery are spread periodically between spaces reserved for the food. I find my place between Leo and Poppy. Among the din of the others finding their seats, it is impossible to have a conversation, so I look down the line of guests.

Many I recognise, though a few are new to me: two men with trimmed, greying beards, who appear to be brothers. I believe they were recently in the paper for funding something important. Another newcomer is a lady who has yet to be seated. She's dressed in a high-collared shirt with a sparkling black brooch and a black jacket with brass buttons down both sides. Her skirt is the latest fashion from Paris. (Olive forced me to study the fashion plates from America, France, and our dear ol' England one afternoon under the guise of "sisterly bonding".)

The woman's iron-straight hair is pinned into a tight bun at the nape of her neck. Strange, when the thing to do now is to wear it up. Her face could rival Aphrodite's. Above her prominent cheekbones, she has brown eyes, so dark they are nearly black. Her gaze is penetrating, dissecting almost, as it sweeps over the guests.

Leo follows my gaze and leans over to whisper, "Her name is Mrs Theodora Thwite. She's a widow. Her husband died of heart failure eight months ago. All she ever wears now is black. Rumour is that she never leaves the house unless it is to attend a social function."

I nod absentmindedly. A gold ring on Mrs Thwite's left thumb catches the light. It's an odd ring, much too big for her. Ink stains her fingernails and the blade of her left hand.

Leo and Poppy start talking about hot air balloons. I believe they ask me a question, but I'm not listening.

Why is the ring too large for her? And without a stone? Perhaps it fell out? No, she had to sell it to a pawn shop, for money to bribe the undertaker to... What? Oh! To make him turn a blind eye to her digging up her husband's body to talk to his corpse. The truth of her husband's death never really set in. That must be awful for her.

Over dinner, Mrs Thwite speaks little, preferring to listen to her neighbours' stories. When asked, she answers questions briefly with subtle wit the others don't understand. After dessert – which I saved much of my stomach for – the ladies retire to the sitting room. I walk behind Mrs Thwite to get a closer look at her ring, but she keeps her left hand in her pocket. Consciously or not, it's impossible to tell.

When we arrive in the sitting room I secure a spot to her left. Tea is served. The woman takes her hand out of her pocket to hold the cup and saucer. It's a signet ring with a pattern the size of a small coin. From this distance, it's impossible to pick out the image.

I need a closer look. Before the conversation has gone on too long, I reach for my cup on the end table between Mrs Thwite and myself, knocking it over.

"Oh, sorry!" I lean over and right the teacup, which is still perfectly intact. Mrs Thwite does nothing to help me clean it up before a maid brings a towel. I must think of something else. Mother glares at me. I try to look apologetic.

When the cups are drained, some of the men rejoin our group, Leo among them. He chooses the seat next to Poppy, who flushes.

The talk gets around to women's rights, and Mrs Thwite suddenly throws herself into the discussion. She's a suffragist, and as she finishes a speech, she rests her hand on the arm of her chair. I place a hand on hers, as if to suggest my sympathies. She twists in her seat to smile at me, her face rosey with passion.

"Do you agree?" She was just explaining why women should get the vote.

I don't even have to lie. "Of course." I remove my hand to

place it over my heart, the ring falling into my dress. I let the conversation go on a bit longer, then excuse myself.

I don't go to the bathroom as I implied, instead detouring to the nearest candle. I extract the ring from my dress. Tipping the candle, I watch as the flame licks the wax. A single drip forms and lands in the base of the holder. I rotate the candle so the wax is melted evenly. A second drop joins the first. I've forgotten how long it takes. One, two, three, four, five. Ten seconds turn to thirty. The small pool grows slowly.

"You could always come to my house for the afternoon. You know I enjoy your company." Two pairs of footsteps tap down the hall.

"Thank you, Elizabeth. Very kind of you. You're always welcome here as well."

That's Mrs Luckford and her friend, Elizabeth Williams, coming towards me. This should be just enough wax, but can I leave the ring and hide? I can't stand here and get caught with Mrs Thwite's ring. I press it into the opaque wax.

"How is Leo? I feel as though it's been such a long time since I saw him last. He has grown so tall!"

"He has. And he's been doing so well at school, I only wish he'd come home more often. Hendrik thinks he'll be a wonderful successor."

I have about ten seconds before they turn the corner and see me. I frantically blow on the mould. Their footsteps are approaching quickly. I slide my fingers under the cooling wax. It separates from the metal in one piece. Three seconds later, it's wrapped in my handkerchief.

"Indigo, what a surprise. Are you lost?"

"Oh, yes. Sorry. I was just… I got… turned around."

Mrs Luckford looks me over for a second. Her posture melts a bit. "I'm sorry, Indigo. It has been quite some time since you've been here. Mrs Williams and I were going to see the library, but I am sure we could go back for a moment. Mrs Williams?"

The lady in question nods vigorously, never taking her pitying gaze off me. Her pupils are unnaturally dilated, probably from lemon juice. She must carry a dropper with her. Her wispy blonde hair is spun up into a bun and she looks older than I expected, with wrinkles around her mouth and eyes.

"Of course! Indigo Taylor, isn't it?"

"Yes, madam." I brush the fabric of my right pocket. The bulge of my handkerchief is not terribly noticeable.

"How polite! I don't mind going back." Mrs Williams takes my right hand. "I had a girl like you once." She sighs heavily. "She's all grown up and married now."

I seriously doubt that she had a girl like me.

Mrs Luckford walks to my other side. I'm surrounded and there's no chance to look at the seal.

"How are Mary and Talmadge?" Mrs Luckford asks.

"Oh, they're doing well, I think. Mary just sent news that they are expecting!"

It is a very long walk, but eventually we arrive at the sitting room. Now for the last bit: returning the ring.

I turn to my escorts outside the doorway. "Thank you both."

"You're entirely welcome, Indigo." Mrs Luckford clasps my hand briefly for one last time and then they're gone.

Poppy and Leo give me curious looks, but I only shrug in response as I walk to my seat. After dropping into my chair, I let go of the ring, allowing it to fall to the rug below.

It's torture waiting another hour for the conversation to end, especially after the topic strays to more mundane things. Finally, Mother says we must go. I stand up, letting one of the hairpins I've extracted fall into the floor. I shake Mrs Thwite's hand cordially. Poppy and Leo wish me a good evening and I do the same. Pretending to notice that a hairpin is missing, I turn back to the chair. As I bend over to pick up the pin, I retrieve the ring as well.

"Is this yours, Mrs Thwite? I found it on the floor when I was searching for my hairpin."

Her complexion pales, but she coolly plucks the ring from my hand, sliding it back on her thumb. "It is mine. Thank you. I would hate to leave this. It was my late husband's."

I let my face carry some of the sympathy I feel towards her. "Goodnight, Mrs Thwite. I hope we'll meet again – at the ballot box, perhaps?"

She brightens, a little of her natural colour returning.

Mother and I meet Father and Olive in the hallway, and we're off. As we get into the carriage, Father remarks that it's nearly eleven. At this hour, I would usually be sleeping or else drifting off, but tonight I don't feel tired.

It takes *ages* for Mother and Father to hang up their cloaks, talking about so-and-so's neighbours, and whose son is off to Cambridge. When they're finally done, I bid them each a good night and try not to run to the privacy of my room. After shutting the door firmly behind me and securing all the windows, I thrust my hand into my pocket to find… nothing.

I suck in a breath as I search my left side, but it rushes back out as I extract the wax imprint. During a tedious discussion of fashion – for which Mrs Thwite was absent – I'd switched it to my left pocket so that the bulge would be more difficult for her to spot.

The fabric falls away easily and the fragment is left bare in my hand. In the pale wax is a blackletter "I" choked with rose vines.

It seems that I have found a lead.

CHAPTER 9

'm being chased through a forest. I know my pursuer is Mr Walker's murderer. Once I get far enough ahead, I try to hide and see who it is. About twenty paces away, a polished wooden door with a crystal handle stands alone in the woods.

Ducking behind it, I wait, suppressing my gasps for air. After a few seconds, a twig snaps not four feet from my hiding spot, but then silence. It becomes easier and easier to inhale as I catch my breath, but still nothing comes. I peek out from behind the door.

There's no one.

Without warning, the door opens and a hand pulls me over the threshold – a hand wearing a large signet ring. Then, somehow, I'm sitting in the room Atlas led me into at the mansion to hide from the men in the hallway. There's a toppled couch in the corner, under which I wedge myself. Opera music warbles from a phonograph.

Above the aria, muffled footsteps in the hall make their way to me through the layers of dusty velvet. I become aware of a slithering noise coming from behind me. Turning to see what it is – and getting a splinter in the process – I spot a rose vine snaking its way toward me.

Its long stem is armoured with prickles, and the delicate tips of the petals are sharp as stiletto knives. The vine rears up and strikes my arm, which has somehow become pinned beneath the sofa. I scream.

The footsteps in the hallway stroll into the room. It's Mrs Thwite, the ring on her finger. She wears a crown made of crystals from the chandelier and swings a hangman's noose lazily in one hand.

Shoving the couch away, she kneels down to look directly into my eyes. "This is either for you… or for the neighbour." Her voice sinks to a caressing whisper. "You or the neighbour?"

Her eyes are no longer brown; they are purely black. She pulls the noose down over my head with the air of awarding a medal.

Like a light being switched on, I wake from the nightmare. Around me are all the familiar objects of my room. Phoebe is messing with something in my wardrobe. Tremors rack my body, and hard as I try, I can't stop shaking.

"Phoebe?"

She looks over her shoulder and immediately comes to wrap her arms around me. "What was it this time?" she asks gently.

My dreams are so real, they catch me in their claws and hold me fast until they've said their piece. Phoebe sitting beside me, stroking my hair, comforts me more than I thought possible. She's done this almost since I can remember. It was one of the main reasons Mother and Father found her. They were exhausted from being awakened at all hours by my screams. Phoebe became the one to sit with me in the dark and ward off terror. Now, mostly, I startle awake to breathe slowly and count the seconds.

"I was looking for someone, but they found me, and…"

It's the sixty-seventh time I wish I could talk to Phoebe about the case. But the fact is, she'd tell Father. Then Father would tell the police, and the knowledge of the secret society would get out, and everyone would know. The society would scatter, only to regroup. Then they'd find me for certain. The crime has become so sensational, the media wants a decisive conclusion. With no other reasonable suspects, the blame will still be pinned on Edmund Smith. If he hangs, this horrible guilt will always be present: that I might have saved his life. Whatever nightmares I'm having now would pale in comparison.

"…and they wanted to hang me."

Though my shaking has stopped, Phoebe holds me closer. "That's awful, Indigo."

We sit there in silence, my heartbeat gradually slowing and my breath steadying. Despite the horror of the nightmare, it's nice to have this moment with Phoebe.

After a time, the distant noises of the house reach our sanctuary.

"I should get dressed."

"Of course." Phoebe kisses the top of my head and leaves the room.

I throw on whatever is at hand, which happens to be a shirt with bishop sleeves, a maroon skirt, and my boots. After eating a few mouthfuls of food, I dash back to my room. My messenger bag conceals the wax imprint in my handkerchief. In a moment, I'm out the French doors and heading down the ladder.

It shouldn't take long to ride to 416 and back. I have to tell Atlas about the seal. Perhaps he will have some idea about how to proceed.

The ladder swings a bit at my clambering, so I jump down past the last few rungs. The grass kindly muffles my landing. Instead of springing back up to walk, I stay bent beneath the windowsills, following the hedges until the slate-coloured gravel drive forces me to leave my protection.

Just as I'm about to follow a branching path to the stable, a voice stops me.

"Indigo? What are you doing?"

Gravel shifts beneath me as I freeze. "Only getting a breath of fresh air on this fine morning."

"What are you really doing?"

I spin on my heel, little rocks scrambling away from my boots. Olive stands by the front door, hands on her hips.

"Mrs Wood won't arrive for another hour, and I just wanted to see Quest."

"Indigo, I can tell you're lying. What are you really doing?"

A torn envelope and folded paper are clasped in her hand. "Who's the letter from?" I ask.

Olive hides it behind her back. "No one. It doesn't matter." She lifts her nose in the air haughtily, but that only reveals the colour creeping up her neck.

Instead of heading back in the direction of the stables, I advance towards Olive. She takes a half-step back.

"It's none of your business."

"Why?" I thrust my hand around her back, jumping to the side a bit.

"No! Stop it!" She lifts the letter up and tries to push my shoulder away. My right hand is free, and with her arm busy, I easily pluck the paper from her hand. I lift it up to my face and dance away as Olive tries to grapple it from me. She fails miserably.

"Thomas Evans? He's new."

"Give that to me!"

I turn the paper over, reading a few lines. "This poetry is absolute rot. It's even worse than mine. You may have to consider his taste, Olive, dear."

I let her snatch it back this time. Her face is truly red now. "How dare you?"

The gate whines as it's opened, and up drives Mrs Wood's hackney.

"Hide the letter!" I hiss between my teeth. Olive blinks twice, then shoves it into her pocket.

"Swear not to tell?" she whispers.

"Promise not to tell I was heading for the stables?"

She jerks her head up and down. "Promise."

"I swear."

"Indigo. Olive. What are you two doing?" Mrs Wood steps out and offers a few coins to the driver. He ducks his head respectfully and flicks his whip.

"We were getting some fresh air," Olive twitters quickly.

"Very invigorating," I add sagely.

"Well, Indigo, you must come with me. Your mother told me to come early today because you are going to an opera tonight and must get ready." She hoists a groomed eyebrow. "Did she not tell you?"

"She must've forgotten to mention it. But I'm ready now."

Mrs Wood strides past both of us. "Good. Shall we begin with how to properly greet one's tutor?"

Olive gives me a sympathetic look before I trudge in Mrs Wood's wake.

"Only if you think it would be informative," I mumble.

* * *

"Phoebe?"

"Yes, Indigo, come in."

I twist the handle. On the wall across from me are a bank of windows and her bed. Glass panes reveal a trimmed emerald lawn and, further back, ancient trees that must've seen Queen Elizabeth raise her ring. By the door is her mother's writing table. Phoebe smooths a stamp onto the envelope of her newest letter. She looks up at me and I speak before I lose my nerve.

"I'm going to clear my head in the gardens. I'll be back soon."

Phoebe spends a few seconds focusing on my face, smiling a little sadly. "I understand. Don't forget you still have to get ready for the opera." She raises her eyebrows teasingly. "I don't want to go looking for you again."

"I'll be back in plenty of time."

* * *

Quest and I ride swiftly until number 416 comes into view. Cicely answers the door, looking mildly alarmed. Admittedly, my knocking had been enthusiastic.

"Good afternoon, Indigo. What —"

"I need to speak to Atlas immediately. It's very important."

She leads me to a familiar room, where I wait four minutes and forty-seven seconds.

"Indigo, what's wrong? Cicely said it was important?" Atlas closes the door behind him quietly.

"I found a lead last night." I pull the evidence from my bag and lay it on the table. "This is the imprint of a signet ring in the possession of one Mrs Theodora Thwite. She said it was her deceased husband's."

Atlas stares at the impression with hesitation. "Do you still have the black seal from Mr Walker's room?"

I hadn't thought of it, but thankfully it's still in my bag. I lay them side by side.

Atlas leans over them. "They're identical in every way. Is there a date on the envelope?"

He picks up the black copy without waiting for an answer. Having already checked, I shake my head. "There isn't."

Atlas lays the paper down. "When did her husband die?"

"Eight months ago."

He straightens and crosses his arms. "Who told you that?"

"My friend Leo."

An indecipherable expression passes over Atlas' face. "I think I'll head to the

library to check the newspapers. Though it may be difficult to get permission from Mama and Papa. They're asking questions, Indigo."

"Have you thought of telling them?"

"Every day." He glances out the window, arms still crossed.

"Would they understand?"

"They'd be worried." He sighs. "They'd probably just call the police."

"I'm sorry."

He shrugs with obvious effort. "It's better they don't know."

"Should we go now? Do you have any more school?"

Atlas looks down, partially obscuring a growing half-smile. "I'll meet you there?"

"You never know, I may find another case on my way."

He laughs. "I won't wait, then."

* * *

I DO WAIT PATIENTLY for thirty-seven seconds, then I wait impatiently for four minutes. By the time Atlas arrives at the library I've discovered that Mrs Thwite's full name is Theodora Ember Florence Thwite – Florence being her maiden name – and that her husband died of heart failure on September seventeenth. The page in front of me starts to fade as I think of another way to dig up some information. Ideas flit and slip through my mind, but each is implausible.

Another minute sneaks past. I slap my hands down on the paper. "I haven't found any more clues. You?"

93

Atlas gives his own paper a glare before putting it down. "No. Nothing."

"Right, so I think we should try to find a way to question Edmond Smith ourselves."

"Are you suggesting we try to sneak into the *city jail?*"

"It's not so bad as breaking *out*. We're not criminals, you know."

He expels a short breath. "We might be if you intend on breaking into a jail."

"You're being melodramatic. Even if we get caught – which, according to my plan, won't happen – to say that we would then be criminals is an overstatement."

"I am *not* being dramatic. Indigo, we wouldn't find a way inside, much less out. It's a prison, for heaven's sake. Perhaps by tomorrow, one of us will have thought of something else."

A warm shiver runs a finger up my spine. I'm going to 416 tomorrow with Mother and Father. It might be difficult to talk inconspicuously, but some opportunity may present itself.

"Right. See you tomorrow, then?"

Some of the weariness slides from Atlas's shoulders. "Tomorrow."

CHAPTER 10

A knock sounds at the door as I kick my boots off and throw my capelet on the bed. Phoebe bustles in, giving me a once-over. "I hope you haven't forgotten about going to the opera tonight. Your mother wants you to be ready."

The opera! When will my life be governed by more than an opera?

"I was afraid of that. Well, we still have time. Your mother told me Mrs Wood expects you to give her five sheets of *excellent* hand lettering, recording all the manners you've learned over the past year." Phoebe raises her eyebrows expectantly.

"What? Why? She didn't tell me!"

Phoebe shakes her head. "She just had a meeting with your mother. It seems to her that it's the best way to prepare you for finishing school."

I haven't told my parents I don't *want* to go to finishing school. They must've assumed that I do. Or decided for me. The handwriting will take hours. Not only will I have to look up all the manners I should have learned, I'll need to find a place where no one can hear my wrathful grunts directed at the inkwell.

"Right. I suppose I can fit it in somewhere. What time is it?"

Phoebe peruses my wardrobe. "Time to start getting dressed."

"That's a non-answer."

"That's because you'll think it is far too early." Before I have a breath to object, she adds, "I think tonight you should wear the dark green dress. And what if I plait your hair around your head in a crown?"

I sit in my chair as Phoebe continues asking questions she knows I won't answer.

"Whatever you think is best."

* * *

COLD – frigid, really – and much too bright. I salvage what little warmth is left as I curl into a ball.

"Good morning, Indigo. It's time to get up. You're going to the Trinters' for tea, remember?" Phoebe stands over me, my precious blanket in hand. "It's eleven."

Little wonder I slept so long when we only got home at midnight. Phoebe throws open the curtains. I find what solace I can under the shade of my pillow.

"Shall I fetch some water?"

As much as I don't want to endorse the effectiveness of this threat, she did douse me once. It was horrible. My pillow harrumphs into place as I slide out of bed.

Now that I'm out of the warm sheets, excitement takes over. I'll be going back to 416 in a matter of hours!

"Food is in the kitchen, and your sister is still in the dining room if you want to eat with her."

Downstairs, Olive is sitting at the dining room table, looking far too awake.

"You aren't even dressed? Indigo, you have to leave in only three hours!" She sounds scandalised, as if Mother and Father are racing out the door this minute. Of course, she's already dressed in her current favourite gown: cream with yellow inside the pleats of the skirt and leg-of-mutton sleeves. At least, I think that's what they're called – my mind is consumed with food at the moment, so I could be remembering incorrectly.

"I am dressed."

Olive almost flinches. "Oh… yes, I see."

What could possibly be the problem? Phoebe picked Olive's old dress; she loved this one when it fit her. But she can't take her horrified gaze off me.

"I hope you haven't finished with your hair."

I reach up and feel a snarl of knots and twists. This will take some time to sort it out. "Just finished with it, actually. Don't you like it?"

Olive insults her toast with a poisonous glare.

* * *

COUNTING seconds is not a productive thing to do while waiting for something more than fifteen minutes in the future, unless I'm doing something else simultaneously, like riding or hiding. To start, I finger out all the knots in my hair and plait it up before Phoebe can get to it. It's not as pretty as when she does it, but it's much less painful.

There's about an hour before it's time to go, so I pull out embroidery floss: purple and three shades of green. One of my favourite things to do when I was younger was to make little embroidered flowers. I put them on everything. It's calming to do it again.

My first subject is an old handkerchief with samples of previous work, but I want something bigger. Taking a simple dress – charcoal grey with a straight skirt and three-quarter-length sleeves – I put my embroidery knowledge to use. The work is quick, and soon I have a garden blooming from the hem of my dress.

Phoebe knocks, coming in a second later. "Time to go. Are you ready?"

"I think so."

"Did you finish your handwriting?"

"Ah." I cough. How could I have forgotten? "Right. I'll get it done after we come back." The last stitch pulls tight with a tug and I knot the remaining length of thread. Since I don't have scissors with me, I use my teeth.

"Don't let your mother see you doing that."

"She'd probably make me take up embroidery again. But just now, I haven't the time. Are you coming?"

"No, I'm staying here with Olive. I'll hear all about it when you get back?" she finishes curiously.

"Of course!"

After a quick hug, Phoebe disappears into the hallway, the door of her room closing softly. I hoped that she would come, had even expected it. But at least Olive won't be coming.

I try to run quietly down the stairs. Technically I'm not allowed to run in the house, but I'm not allowed to be late, either. I only slow when I pass through the front door to walk to the carriage.

Father is just helping Mother inside as I cross the gravel.

"Good afternoon, Mother, Father."

Father takes my hand as I ascend the step and duck into the seat opposite my parents. It shouldn't make a difference that they're coming to 416 with me, but it does. What will they think? Will they be impressed? What if they blame Mr and Mrs Trinter for me not telling them about visiting? What if Father decides to sue them? Father would make sure to win. Then where would Cirque du la Reine be? Out of the theatre. And what of 416? Where would the Trinters live? Poor Louise would watch as everything her parents built was stripped away. Atlas would have to move to some distant country town where he'd forget all about Mr Walker and his murder. How could Father do such a thing? He won't. I'll make sure of it.

My fingers play with a stray ringlet at my ear. One. Two. Three. Four. I settle my counting to the rhythm of horse hooves striking the street. Mother starts on the subject of Olive's debut next year and her birthday plans. I shut their voices out and soak in the passing view.

As we draw closer to our destination, Mother and Father turn from guest lists to questions directed at me.

"Who did you meet when you came here last?" Father sits straight as a rail.

"Mrs Helen and Mr Edgar Trinter," I begin hesitantly.

Father raises an eyebrow. "And? Surely you met others?"

"Yes, sir. They introduced me to their children, Louise and Atlas. Also, a woman named Cicely. She's a trapeze artist."

Father flicks his eyes to the ceiling. "There are no trapeze *artists*. Artists are painters, sculptors – composers, as well, but…" He grimaces. "Not most of them —"

"Cicely, the trapeze artist." I enunciate, "I don't believe I had the chance to talk to anyone else."

Father looks plaintively at Mother. She gives me a chiding look. We all sway in our seats as we come to a stop.

"Is this it?" Father leans into the window of the hackney. "It's massive."

The bright green doors are set off wonderfully by the red brick. The windows glint without a smudge, the yard has not an inch untrimmed, and the silver door knocker and starling handles look freshly polished. Mother practically climbs over Father to get a closer look.

"Remember your manners, Indigo," Father reminds me before I follow Mother onto the path.

Mr Trinter opens the door before we can even knock. I'd

forgotten how cheerful he looks. Mrs Trinter stands by his side, looking beatific.

Mr Trinter raises a hand. "I saw you coming up the lane. What a pleasure to meet you. Come in." Inside, he introduces himself. "I'm Edgar, and this is my wife, Helen."

Father cordially shakes our hosts' hands. "A pleasure to meet you, Mr Trinter. I'm John Taylor; this is my wife, Amethyst." He gestures to me. "And you've already met Indigo."

"We have!" Mrs Trinter says, as if it's the most wonderful thing. "How good to see you again."

I dip my head. "You as well."

"Shall we —" Mrs Trinter starts to say, but little feet pattering down the stairs interrupt her. Strands of fiery red curls appear behind the balusters. A blue-green eye peeks between hands gripping the wood.

"Louise!"

"Indigo! You came back!" She bounds down the rest of the stairs and I kneel down to catch her.

Atlas appears on the stairs, looking harried. "Beg your pardon. I told her not to run down here."

Louise pulls away to gesture at me. "Atlas, Indigo is here!"

"It's alright, Atlas," Mrs Trinter reassures her son. "Mr and Mrs Taylor, this is our daughter, Louise, and our son, Atlas. Louise has been impatiently waiting to see Indigo again. Darling, say hello to Mr and Mrs Taylor."

Hesitance returns to the little girl's expression. "Hello." Her shy gaze drops to the floor. She rubs the toe of one shoe into her ankle. "I'm Louise. I'm five."

"She just had her birthday about a month ago," Mr Trinter adds.

Louise stands up straighter. "That's when Cicely started teaching me trapeze."

"After tea, would you like to show our guests the studio?" her father offers.

Louise clasps her hands together. "Yes! Oh, yes please."

"You have a studio? For painting?" Mother turns curiously to Mrs Trinter.

"Our studio is for practising circus acts. Would you like to see?"

Father looks at Mother. She turns slightly towards him, meeting his gaze and pursing her lips together almost imperceptibly. Father blinks slowly, then breaks Mother's gaze.

"I think that would be a wonderful idea."

Louise skips out of the room and into the hallway, leading the charge. Father, Mother, and Mr and Mrs Trinter disappear after her, passing Atlas where he waits on the last step. He joins me as I follow the others.

"How are you?" I ask him.

"I'm fine. How are you, Miss Indigo?" He lowers his head and whispers so quietly I barely catch it. "I had some thoughts on the case." He puts his lithe hands out in front of him for emphasis. "We know that Walker was killed by the guild. We know that he made an efficient poison, and we know that he has a secret room full of evidence. You saw Mrs Thwite wearing a signet ring, the exact impression from Walker's house. She claims it was her husband's. Her husband died, according to the paper, of a heart attack. I went back and checked another paper after you left. It says that he didn't die of heart failure. He died of 'an unknown cause'. He was reportedly in perfect health. So, why did he die? What if it was because of Walker's poison? Theodora's husband must have been working with the group, and he might have known Walker personally."

Everything fits, but... I lean closer, keeping my voice down. "Then the question is... Does Mrs Thwite know?"

Atlas rubs his jaw. "The ring might have been found on his dead body? She could have just recognised it in his things."

As we turn into another hallway, a terrible idea pops into

my head. I quickly shove it away. It wouldn't be safe. In fact, it may be *the* most dangerous option.

"What is it?"

"Nothing." Not even I would attempt this plan… probably. But, on the off chance I *did*, I wouldn't need to visit dear Edmond Smith in jail.

"Something is rarely ever nothing," Atlas presses. "You had a thought, didn't you? But you don't like it?"

I try to forget the idea, but thinking about forgetting is counterproductive. More reasons and details emerge, quickly forming into a plan.

"What is it?"

I shake my head to dislodge the scheme. "It is too dangerous."

I could never ask him to do it, but maybe I could do it myself.

Atlas's eyes widen. "No, Indigo," he whispers too loudly, causing Father to glance back at us. Atlas moves away a few inches, shoving his hands into his pockets and adding at a normal volume, "No, I have *two* siblings. My brother is much older." How does he recover so effortlessly?

Mr Trinter asks Father a question, drawing his attention. Atlas wheels back on me.

"I see you thinking about doing it yourself. That's out of the question. What's your idea?"

"Can't you turn off reading people's minds?"

"I'm not sure. I'd certainly never do it when it comes to you." He adds the last with particular emphasis.

"Why?"

He raises an accusatory eyebrow. "You'd probably come up with some dangerous plan, which you'd attempt alone, despite stating otherwise. Besides, even if I did, you're still a terrible liar."

This plan is even worse than going to the jail tonight, but it might be *far* more effective. To balance risk and reward, Atlas must stay out of it.

We cross into the heavenly wide-open studio. Sunlight showers down, spotlighting the acrobats on the tightrope. Mother drifts, as if in a daze, to the iron vine pattern in the glass, reverently fingering a leaf. Father surveys the apparatuses above us.

"How are those anchored to the ceiling? Is it safe?"

Mr Trinter slides one hand into his pocket, while the other points out areas of pattern without light passing through. "If you look closely, you can see that behind the wrought iron are beams of commercial steel. This holds up the iron and anything we attach to the ceiling. The net is threaded through loops welded to the beams. We change the net every year, and have it professionally tested every six months. It was checked last week."

Father's about to ask another dissecting question, but the sound of mirth cuts him off.

"I'll be right back with them." Mrs Trinter stifles another laugh as she exits the room. Mother covers her mouth with the tips of her fingers, still giggling.

"What was that, Mother?"

"Helen's going to show me the costume drawings for one of the shows. She designs them with Mr Trinter. Isn't that amazing?" Mother shakes her head. "Where do they keep all their extra costumes?"

"Our seasonal ones are stored here, while most of them are at the theatre," Atlas replies.

Mother gives him a look of surprise. "You perform as well?"

"I do," my compatriot assents.

"Me, too!" Louise chirps as she springs up beside me. She proves her statement by arching over backward until her hands touch the floor.

Mother lets her Mona Lisa smile part – her equivalent of a gasp. "You do?"

Louise nods vigorously.

Atlas beams. "Louise was in The Festival, which I believe you attended."

Mother cants her head to the side. "How often do children perform?"

"It's rare that more than a few of us are in a show at once. The Festival is the biggest exception so far," Atlas assures her.

"What do you do?"

Atlas hums and looks up at the ceiling. "I suppose I do whatever I'm needed to do. I've learned different things over the years."

"Like what?"

"Tumbling, juggling, tightrope..." He pauses to shrug. "Lots of things."

Ha! I know he's hiding something. Perhaps it's just because I'm getting to know him, though; Mother doesn't seem to notice.

The door glides open and Mrs Trinter returns with a sealed metal cylinder. She brushes a strand of blonde hair back. "There's no table in here, so we'll go back to the parlour to look at these. Atlas, would you mind bringing the tea? It's on the kitchen table."

He nods. Just before he turns away, he looks at me for a second.

"Indigo, are you going to join us?" his mother asks sweetly.

The promise of costume drawings is tantalising, but if I go now, I may be able to meet Atlas in the hall.

"Certainly, but..." How to escape for the moment? "I need to use the facilities."

* * *

THE HALL IS DARKER than the glass room, and it takes my eyes a moment to adjust.

"What's your plan?"

I blink rapidly a few more times and Atlas appears in front of me.

"What did you hide from my mother?" I ask. "You left something out, didn't you?"

He strides beside me, shaking his head. "Yes, but only because I thought she wouldn't approve of learning to throw knives. I started a few weeks ago, so I'm still not very good. But that's not important. What are you thinking?"

Why is he so insistent? A hallway branches to the left, but I keep straight. "We should come up with other ways to figure this out. Forget I thought anything."

"Um, Indigo, the kitchen is this way." Atlas waits, leaning against the wall of the path I just missed. The doors are open, and light lies on the wood floor like a rug, one of the rectangles covering his shoes.

"Right."

We continue down the hall in silence. Atlas glances at me expectantly as our footsteps fall in sync. I walk faster just to break the pattern. The corner of his mouth lifts.

"Alright," I huff. I explain my plan to him in basic strokes. He's slightly horrified, but as I go on, he masters himself. I finish as we enter the kitchen, and Atlas waits a few seconds, looking at the tabletop.

The kitchen may be my favourite of the rooms I've seen. A long wooden table stands parallel to two ovens and the largest icebox I have ever seen. Five burners gather together on the counter, without a single smudge on them. Several large windows run the whole length of the room; pushed aside are the same cheerful curtains that decorate the other windows in the house.

Atlas taps the wood thoughtfully, speaking slowly. "That is… risky. And even if we try it soon, Edmond Smith goes on trial in ten days." He slides the teapot away from the table's edge and rests his elbows in its stead. We're probably late for bringing tea, but perhaps they won't notice. "We need to get the police to realise that they don't know the whole story. We need to lead them to the evidence."

I lean forward, mirroring his planted elbows and crossed arms. "We can't just skip to Walker's house and nail up a sign."

"I know, but if we hand it over, they might say we planted evidence in the trapdoor room."

I pull out a stool and sit on it. "I see what you mean."

"Perhaps… Oh!" Atlas snaps his fingers and stands straight. "What if it wasn't *us* who gave them the information? What if we left a breadcrumb trail for the Inspector, and *he* found it? He would be more reliable than us in court."

Then I'd never have to deal with Mother and Father finding out. Or Phoebe. "Brilliant idea, but how would we do it inconspicuously?"

"We could spread rumours about the trapdoor until he had to look for himself? No, that would take too long." His expression falls only for a second. "We could suggest that you

smelled gas in the house next door, when we were delivering an advertisement or some such thing. The police would check the house."

"They've already gone through the house and didn't find it. It's unlikely they'll look more closely the second time."

Atlas nods, looking at the space next to my head, biting the inside of his lip. "What if… What if we sent him an anonymous note?"

An intriguing proposition, but… "What if the Inspector is suspicious of the information?"

"It's evidence, and if they're worthy of their positions,

they'll test to see if it's genuine. When they realise it is, they'll present it in court." Atlas speaks quickly, getting more and more excited. "We'll have to use a typewriter, to make sure the handwriting can't be traced. And we should buy envelopes from a common store, to make sure those can't be traced either."

I walk around the edge of the table to him. "I can do that. How will it be delivered?"

"I don't think we should try disguises." He must have seen the thought in my posture, or perhaps the sudden hopefulness in my eyes. I need to try a different tactic.

"What about a courier?"

He nods slowly. "That could work, but —"

"Perfect! I'll disguise myself as a courier, deliver the letter, Wallace finds the evidence, and, at the very least, the trial is postponed."

He frowns. "I thought you meant we'd send a *real* courier."

My nose wrinkles. "Why would we do that when I charge a much better rate? I don't mind doing it at all."

Atlas looks down at the tabletop, laughing. "I know you don't *mind* doing it. But I think the Inspector would recognise you."

"Oh, alright. It's not such a bad idea, though."

"We could just send it by mail – leave off the return address – and he should get it within a day or so."

"Then I'll just drop it in a post box. And this case will be on its way to being stalled."

As we make our way back to the parlour, we decide that I should enter first. Atlas waits outside the door while I go in. The sound of laughter floats to my ears – Father and Mother's *genuine* laughs.

Though it's the same room I was in yesterday, the early afternoon light gives it a new aspect. The rays of sunshine are a natural decoration. Mrs Trinter and Mother sit on the grey velvet sofa and pore over some papers on the table, while Mr Trinter and Father joke about horse races. I start to walk over to the women, but they see me coming and shield whatever they were looking at. My eyebrows rise.

"Your mother has been giving me some wonderful costume suggestions for one of our shows, but we're still keeping them a secret. I hope you understand, Indigo." Mrs Trinter's expression cannot contain her excitement. "Mrs Taylor, do you think you could help me with mock-ups for these while Indigo is practising?"

"I may not be able to come as frequently as she does, but —"

The meaning of Mrs Trinter's words sinks in. I squeeze Mother in a hug.

"Oohf." She pats my back. "You also have your father to thank."

I fling my arms around him. He looks down at me with a surprised smile.

"Yes, yes, we're allowing it. Mr and Mrs Trinter will teach you well. You must listen to them and pay attention during sessions. They will alert us if you ever lose your focus in class."

Well, that is quite the turnabout.

"Yes, Father. I'll do my best."

"Did I miss anything?" Atlas enters, balancing a mirrored tea tray on his arm and managing to keep an innocent expression.

"Mr and Mrs Taylor have decided to allow Indigo to practise with us," his father answers.

"Wonderful!" Delicate silver-rimmed teacups lightly clink their saucers as Atlas lands the tray.

Mr Trinter lifts a cup. "This calls for a toast!"

"Can you toast with tea?" Mother asks, eyeing the saucers dubiously.

"Of course!" Mrs Trinter rises from her seat, graceful as a ballerina. "I wouldn't have it any other way. Now Atlas and Indigo can join in."

Atlas and I each choose a cup and Mr Trinter pronounces, "To general health… and quickly healing bruises."

CHAPTER 11

*A*tlas and I will enact the main part of the plan in two days – exactly eight days before the trial of Mr Smith is scheduled to begin. However, the first half must be set up now, or it may be too late.

At home, I can hardly find a gap in the conversation to propose my idea. Mother and Father wander into his office, still chatting about the Trinters. It's a utilitarian room, with nothing to interrupt the oak panelling except a portrait of Mother and two windows looking out on an old English oak. Father's simple desk sits in the middle of the room, supporting his typewriter.

I trail them to the doorway but entering Father's office is an unforgivable sin. I align the tips of my boots with the boundary of the private room, hands hanging down by my sides. That feels stiff. I fold them in front, but my fingers are sticky with a cold sweat. Finally I curl my hands into fists and stuff them in my pockets.

"Well, Mrs Trinter is marvellous. I must have her over sometime soon," Mother gushes as she stands by the window.

Father sorts the post, tossing a few envelopes onto his desk.

"Yes, we must invite them all over soon." He sounds surprisingly genuine.

Mother laughs, the honey-coloured light making her look ten years younger. "Not all of them, dear, didn't you hear? Seventeen people live in that house."

Father drops three letters into the bin by his chair. "Seventeen? Where do they fit them all?"

"It is a large house."

Father joins Mother at the window. "I had no idea that Edgar was the son of Maxwell Trinter. He's one of the most successful businessmen in all of England."

They stand together for a moment, simply looking out over the front yard. My best chance is now.

"Mother… Father…" I clear my throat. "I have been thinking. It might be nice to… to have a…" Why is this so difficult? I force the words out before they lodge in my throat. "A masquerade ball for the end of spring."

Mother spins around, one hand on Father's shoulder. "Oh, Indigo! I'm so happy you asked! When do you want it to be? Who will we invite?"

"How about June second?" In my pockets, my crossed fingers must be turning white. I don't actually believe this will give me luck; it just keeps my hands still when I'm nervous.

"We should write down all of the people you wish to invite, and send invitations first thing tomorrow. Darling," she squeezes Father's shoulder, "we need a few sheets of paper. Indigo, you and I can work in the boudoir."

* * *

AFTER BREAKFAST THE NEXT MORNING, I shut the door to my room, grab the notebook I've dedicated to this case, and sit at my desk. A pencil already waits for me on the tabletop. How to write an anonymous letter? I suppose most of the rules still stand, though I won't sign with my name. Perhaps:

Dear Sir,

In the case that your moustache was too large and you missed the trapdoor in Mr Walker's house, here is your second chance. There is a secret room under a certain oriental rug in the deceased's living room, in which you will find much that may be useful to you.

Faithfully

No, that would probably be too suspicious. My pencil lead breaks as I cross the message out. I resharpen it. This time I try:

Dear Inspector,

I understand that you have been assigned the case that concerns a certain Mr Edmond Smith and Mr Tobias Walker. I have reason to believe that there may be something more to this case than you have discovered. Have you checked under the deceased's rug?

Obviously, you haven't. If you had, then might've have stopped all this nonsense about Mr Smith days ago and tried to

I scribble it out, the words becoming unreadable. An exasperated breath scatters flecks of graphite across the page. I use the blunt end of the pencil to scratch under my eye. What should the tone be? Perhaps simplicity is best.

In Walker's house, under the oriental rug, is a trapdoor. You will find a new perspective.

Faithfully

Not quite as spicy as I would like, but at least Atlas cannot accuse me of being too obvious. I slide my hands under the covers of the notebook and slap them together. Father should be out for the next few hours at least. For now, his office is empty.

* * *

THE GLOSSY GREEN typewriter sits on his desk, basking in its place of honour. A stack of paper sits in a shallow box, the edges aligned precisely. I take the first and thread it into the machine. The wheel is newly lubricated and it takes little effort to position the sheet.

I spread my notebook out on the desk and hold it open with my left hand. I don't know how Father types so quickly on one of these. The letters are randomly scattered. How are you supposed to find anything? My fingers hover over the keys. D is neighbours with E, and A… isn't too far from there. Where's the "R"? It has to be somewhere! You can't write a paper without one of the letters of the alpha— Oh, there it is.

The sound of the keys slapping the paper is unbelievably satisfying. As I type, the letters get easier to find. My pointer finger locates them in a second or two. When the message is done, I pause. There are no steps in the hall, so I go ahead and type the Inspector's address on a second sheet. I'll trim it later.

I slide the typewriter arm over, as Father does, and it rings loud enough to wake the dead. My hands dart out and grab my notebook in a flinch. Why is it so loud? I snatch the paper from the typewriter. Hot, nervous needles prick the back of my neck until I'm safely in my room again.

* * *

AFTER SCHOOL THE NEXT DAY, Mother summons me to the dining room. In front of her are all the invitations, but only a few are tucked in envelopes. She returns the fountain pen to its well and massages her palm with a thumb. "We've run out of envelopes. I'll ask your father if he'll purchase more on his way home from work tomorrow. Do you have any special requests for the decoration?"

My heart speeds. "Envelopes? I can get envelopes. Today! We don't want to wait." I shake my head. "It would be rude to send invitations too late."

Mother considers the papers on the dining room table and

nods. "Yes, you're absolutely right. Perhaps Phoebe should go with you? She can help you choose the ones you want."

"Yes, Mother."

* * *

QUEST SETTLES into a brisk pace even before the black gate closes behind us. I told Phoebe that I was going to get envelopes for Mother and I'd be back soon. She didn't raise an eyebrow.

A light rain starts, not much more than a heavy mist, but the chill seeps into my clothes. Not many people are out, but about halfway along my winding route I spot the Luckfords' coach. The driver cracks his whip over the horses' heads and the thunderous roar of the carriage wheels passes me. Inside, Mr Luckford is glaring down something in his lap.

Following the path of the coach, I look behind me. Three adults on safety bicycles pedal past a hackney driver, who raises his hat to them. A man on horseback, closest behind me, looks downcast compared to the cheerful driver behind him.

The rain gradually comes down harder. Small drops now speckle the cobbles, mixing with grit and making them slick. Perhaps I should have worn a cloak instead of a knitted shawl.

A storefront with dresses in the window reads: Madame Resselin's Outerwear for All Occasions. It's Mother's favourite place to bring me when she's upset with me. It seems to make her feel better, dragging me through that store.

I'm only a few streets away now. In the reflection of another passing window, I catch a glimpse of the same rider I saw earlier. Odd that he's still behind me. His horse is beautiful: chestnut brown with a glossy black mane. I've seen a horse like that before, only grey, when one of Father's distant relatives stayed with us on his way to London. I wasn't allowed near it at the time, being only five, but I still remember the power that seemed to emanate from the beast. He had such a commanding presence about him.

It's probably only my fancy, but just to make certain, I guide Quest to slow. The man slows too.

Quest can sense my agitation now and speeds to a canter. I have to wait a moment before I can use another reflection. When my next chance comes, I only look at his face. His features are hidden by a wide-brimmed hat and his overcoat collar. He's probably just gotten away from the graveyard where he went to see his sister's headstone. Not that she's actually there, of course. She faked her death. He just hasn't figured it out yet. Or… possibly he's trailing me?

Branching Lane would take me to Ethelridge only a few minutes later. I can make up that time on the way back, but I need to see if this rider will follow me. A stray curl blows into my mouth as we make the turn, but I can't reach to remove it.

This time, I check over my shoulder. The road remains empty.

My imagination almost ran away with me.

As we cross over to Ellington Street, a hansom cuts me off and Quest is forced to stop. A young man helps a blushing woman out and we start again… slowly. A cart full of sheep blocks my passage around the carriage. For reasons unknown, no one is moving with any sense of urgency.

A booming voice behind us calls out, "What's the hold-up?" The gentleman's head pokes out of a hansom behind me. His blond moustache stands out against his face, which is pink from shouting. He bellows some more, now arguing with someone further ahead in the traffic.

Beyond him is the man who was following me.

I bend down, closer to the warmth of Quest's neck. "Quest… we've got to make a run for it."

She snorts, tosses her head, and breaks into a gallop. Dodging between the cart full of sheep and the hansom, with only a finger's width to spare, Quest leaves them behind. All except one.

People shout complaints behind me, but we fly past. Other riders and carts of all shapes and sizes fall away. As we pass a corner, frightening a mother and child about to cross the road, I risk another glimpse. The rider seems to be gaining on me. I only need to make it a bit further, then I may have a chance of losing them.

"Ey!" a driver shouts at my back. We're far past him before I can apologise. Streets fly by, each one closer to the one I need. Larring, Sommerhurst, Empty Lane – two more to go. Shops and parks transition to houses and flats with smaller alleys between them. Just ahead is the one I am looking for.

I tighten my grip on the reins and lean closely into Quest. "Now!"

She makes the turn into the narrow space with incredible speed. Clotheslines are strung everywhere, stretching from the windows and roof, just high enough for Quest and me to fly under them.

"Easy. Good girl. That's it." A shirt brushes her ear, but I rub her sides. "Easy. Easy."

Behind us, I hear the *twang* as a wire catches the rider in the chest. His cry of pain is cut short when he hits the ground. Quest's shoes clatter around the edge of the building, and my pursuer disappears from view.

"Yes!" I put my cheek against Quest's neck and kiss the top of her head. "That was perfect! Well done, darling."

We take the smaller street back to the main byway. The coaches and sheep carts from before are gone, replaced by others of that ilk. Nowhere do I see my pursuer.

* * *

ENTERING the safety of Ethelridge Corner Shop, I watch the street for a moment before turning my attention to a table with a variety of stationery. The card and envelope selection features a host of colours. For the masquerade, I select cream with gold filigree to match the ones Mother ran out of. I'm tempted to get the green ones for the Inspector, but we are going for a sterile look. A brown envelope with a string-and-button catch should do the job, but best to get a few extra.

I take both stacks and walk to the front desk. It's vacant. I tap the stem of the polished silver bell, summoning a clear ring. Something bangs the underside of the counter.

"Oh. Ow. Oh." A young woman appears, rubbing her blonde hair with a hand whose fingers still mark her place in a novel. She quickly hides the book behind her back. "Sorry! I was just – Indigo, it's you! Oh, what a relief, I thought you were Mr Jackson. He caught me reading last week and complained to Mr Schwartz. He threatened to give my position to the Robinson boy! Can you believe that?" She blows a strand of her hair contemptuously out of her eyes. "As if he would be any better! Now, what do you have for me?" She leans her elbows on the counter, resting her chin in her hands.

"Oh, just this for today." I slide the packs of envelopes over. "How are you, Eliza?"

"I'm fine." She clacks away on the keys of the register. "Mum is fine, Da too. Maggie started school. She's a bit intimidated by the other kids, but I think she'll be fine. Here you go."

I take the envelopes from her outstretched hand.

She draws a red sweet from her pocket, but it slips her grip, landing on the floor with a crack. "Oops." Eliza bends down to scoop it up, popping back up to give the wrapper a little dust-off. "Still good." She unwraps the red foil and the sweet disappears into her mouth. I can hear it clack against her teeth as she rolls it around. "If you're ever looking for someone to talk to, I'll be here."

"Thank you, Eliza. Oh! Do you have any glue? I brought the address on a piece of paper so I wouldn't forget."

She nods vigorously. "Yes, there's some under here. I accidentally put my elbow in it when I left it open yesterday." She keeps talking even after having disappeared beneath the counter again. "Reynolds came in here yesterday. Do you remember Reynolds?"

"I don't think we've met."

A wistful sigh rises from under the counter. "He comes to the store sometimes. He works down the street also, as a clerk. His real name's Jacob, but I call him Reynolds just to tease him." She appears again. "Here."

I take the glue from her.

"I can't remember anyone's address. I'd likely forget my hair one day if it wasn't stuck here." She puts a hand to her head, touching the spot where she struck the underside of the counter with a grimace. "I don't know how some people do it. Reynolds, the one I was telling you about, he can remember all sorts of things. Of course, he has to for his job and all…"

I finish with the glue and blow on the strips of paper. "Thanks again, Eliza. Tell Maggie I say hello."

"I will, and thank you!"

Outside, I slide the letter into the brown envelope with the pasted address, smooth a stamp on one corner, and drop it into a post box.

* * *

Thursday morning dawns gloomy, but it feels like Christmas. Today, I practise at 416.

"Good morning, Phoebe!" I call as I finish buttoning my charcoal dress.

"You're awake!" Everyone always states the obvious when they're surprised. "It's so early."

I give her a hug. "Today we go to four-sixteen!"

"Yes, but that's not for hours!" She swirls her finger in the air, and I turn a hundred and eighty degrees. Phoebe fastens the first brass button at my back. She always starts at the top.

"Hours." The word tastes horrible. "Hours and hours."

The next button pulls taut. "I'm sure that handwriting assignment will take a while. Then it'll practically be time to go."

"Oh, right." Good thing I'm up early.

I eat breakfast slowly in an effort to make more seconds pass, in the puerile hope that I won't have time to write my assignment. It is, in the end, a vain wish. Two hours and a thousand pages later, I complete my task.

* * *

JUST AS THE CARRIAGE STOPS, Mrs Trinter opens the door of 416 Old Twinings Road. I am out in half a second, and Phoebe joins me in three.

"Come in!" Mrs Trinter welcomes us into the foyer. "You must be Ms Adgate. A pleasure to make your acquaintance."

Phoebe bobs her head. She stands a full six inches above Mrs Trinter. "You as well."

After leaving my shoes behind, we follow Mrs Trinter into a dressing room. Two screened-in areas sit opposite a table and two chairs. Directly in front of the door is an open wardrobe with a few items on the rack and six small drawers below that.

"Here is your formal uniform. You may leave it here, if you wish. We only wear them occasionally." Mrs Trinter holds out a simple teal skirt with a sweep of fabric in the front, and a grey shirt with red accents around the collar and buttons.

"I think I'll leave them here. I wouldn't want to forget them at home."

"Good idea." She folds everything and places a slip of paper on top of the shirt, setting the whole pile into one of the drawers. "And this" – she lifts the lid off a brown box and hands it to me – "will be your uniform when you're practising. Ms Adgate, you are welcome to stay here or go to the studio. It's the door at the end of the hall."

"I'll help Indigo with her dress." Behind the screen, Phoebe frees the buttons. Once finished, she leaves to ask questions about the circus.

After a few moments, Mrs Trinter calls out, "Let me know if you need any help."

"I've got it." I step out from behind the curtain.

Phoebe breaks into a smile. I look down at the cream tights and blue-green leotard. It's a bit strange, but not in a bad way.

"Are you ready?" Mrs Trinter asks.

I flick my eyes up to her for a second. "I think so."

For the first time, I feel nervous. Why should I be nervous? Phoebe's here, and I'm inside the walls of 416.

Mrs Trinter smiles knowingly. "Well, let's get you warmed up."

Phoebe and I follow her to the studio. I watch as childlike fascination brightens Phoebe's face as she turns to see everything. "It's beautiful," she breathes.

It's more crowded than the last time I came here. I count fourteen people, excluding our group. Most are warming up in clusters while Mr Trinter sets up a hoop on the lower level. A man I don't recognise directs the installation of a third trapeze upstairs, separate from the first pair. Mrs Trinter stops, inhaling sharply. She holds the breath for a second and lets it go in a tight exhale.

Atlas, who had been sitting on a long wooden bench, comes over. Mrs Trinter glances at the new apparatus being lifted. "Atlas, would you mind helping Indigo warm up? I should help with that trapeze."

She rushes off, climbing up the ladder faster than I thought possible.

"Is she worried it might fall?"

Atlas shakes his head, tracking his mother with his eyes. "That was the first trapeze my parents bought together. She's quite attached." He turns to Phoebe. "You are Ms Adgate? I'm Atlas."

"Yes. Pleasure to meet you." She gestures to me. "You know Indigo?"

Atlas looks at me as if I were some casual acquaintance. "Yes, she was here Saturday."

"Hmm." Phoebe eyes me. I smile innocently.

"Are you ready?" Atlas asks.

"For...?"

"Practice?"

For some reason, being asked if I am ready brings on the feeling that I am *not*. But I *am* ready, am I not? I cross my arms. "Is there something I should be worried about?"

"No. Just a few bruises."

A bruise never killed anyone. Well, actually... I'll look in Father's books when I get home.

Atlas waves in the direction from which he came. "Come on, there are a few people I want you to meet."

Any anxiety that had been laid to rest stirs again.

"Indigo, meet Alice, Nora, and Abbott."

The three stand only a few feet away. The girl introduced as Alice steps forward. She has brown hair with red undertones and eyes the colour of honey. A birthmark covers most of her left shoulder, and her nose and cheeks are flecked with freckles.

"I love your name, Indigo! It's so unique! I can help you with balancing acts. Don't worry about not getting it right off, it takes a lot of practice."

Abbott nods. "I'm Abbott, and Nora is my twin sister."

The pair have the same light brown hair and dark brown eyes. Nora ducks her head a bit, speaking almost too quietly for me to hear.

"Hello. It's nice to meet you." She clears her throat. "If you need any help with the hoop, I can help you."

"She is the most flexible person I've ever seen," Alice adds. Nora blushes scarlet.

"Louise wanted to be here too, but she has to finish her reading lesson," Atlas says. "I told her you had to warm up first anyway."

The knot in my chest loosens.

"Can we show her the hammocks first?" Alice bounces on her toes. "They're my favourite."

The hammocks as in the ones above us? High in the air? I feel sick at the thought. Atlas notices my reaction, and suggests I warm up first. The three go back to their conversation.

As we step away, Atlas whispers, "Did you read the papers this morning?"

"What did they say?"

"Smith's trial has been postponed. The letter worked!"

I can hardly keep my voice down. "What's the new court date?"

"All they mentioned is that 'new evidence has been found'. The trial is on June the eighteenth. Now we have plenty of time."

"That couldn't have gone much better."

He shakes his head. "Not by much. Everything is set into motion. Now, we can focus on warming up."

"Warming up" takes longer than I expected, and I'm ready to move on. Just as we finish the last exercise, a small streak of bright red barrels in my direction. Louise jumps around me in a circle, singing, "You came! You came!" She takes my hands in her tiny ones and makes me dance with her. She only lets go of one hand to drag me towards the ladder woven into the pattern of the room. "Let's do trapeze!"

Panic makes my knees lock up – an unexpected response, considering that I have imagined flying on the trapeze too many times to count.

Atlas steps in front of his sister. "No, Louise. Indigo isn't doing trapeze today, remember?"

The little girl halts, an angelic look of disappointment on her features. Her narrow shoulders slump. "Oh."

"Do you want to help her with rolling instead?" Atlas turns his face away from Louise slightly. "I hope you don't mind – she needs to work on this too. All she ever wants to do is trapeze."

Rolls are mostly painless, until one of my hairpins is driven into my scalp. A spot of blood appears, but Phoebe diagnoses it beneath treatment. We move onto a low balance beam that's not much harder than walking on the floor. As I cross successfully for the fourth time, Louise suddenly remembers something and runs off to tell her mother.

Atlas whirls back towards me, clearly trying not to sound too eager. "Ready to go up to the second floor?"

The new trapeze is hung, and no one else is using any of the equipment, so that excuse won't work.

"What will we – never mind, don't tell me." I look to Phoebe for help, but she only raises an eyebrow and makes a shooing motion with her hands.

Atlas and I climb the wrought iron ladder to the second level. The shifting net is difficult to stand on, but Atlas crosses easily to a rope leading up to a group of three hammocks. He isn't going to climb it, is he?

He makes a curious motion with his feet while using his arms, and magically hangs a few feet into the air. "What are you waiting for?"

I haven't moved. Mustn't hesitate, I guess. Then I'll get to *thinking* about this.

Atlas climbs up the rope easily and steps into one of the hammocks. It shifts, rocking slightly from left to right. Perching on the edge, feet swinging gently, he looks down at me. His face is framed by dark tresses.

"Um… I can't do that."

"Oh, right. It's not as hard as it looks. I'll show you."

He slides down the rope to stand next to me. He demonstrates how to climb the rope with his feet, using the technique to make his way to the top again. It's much harder than he made it look. The ceiling is high, maybe twenty feet above me. The hammock is about fifteen feet off the net. Though using my feet does make it easier, the muscles in my arms burn only halfway to the hammock. When I finally do reach level with my goal, I pick the easiest one to get in, breathing heavily. Atlas sits in the hammock across from mine.

"That was good, but try pinching the rope more with your feet; that will keep your arms from getting so tired. Look down and see how far you've come."

I do, without thinking, and nearly fall out of the hammock. Like a helpless boat on a violent sea, my hammock starts swinging erratically. It's all I can do to twine the thin strands around my hands. It seems so much higher when I'm in a flimsy hammock. Oh, so much worse.

"It's been a long time since I was afraid of heights, but I still remember it," Atlas continues.

"You were afraid of heights?"

He looks confused. "I wouldn't even come up here for a whole year. I got really good at balancing acts and fencing."

I sit up in the hammock too quickly and it sways dangerously again. "Fencing?"

"Yes, I was fascinated by it, and it was a good excuse for not coming up here."

"I love fencing." How has this not come up before?

"Really?" He looks surprised, but the expression transitions to a self-deprecating smile. "I should've known. We can try some after this conditioning."

"Conditioning?"

"Yes." His devilish grin does not bode well for me. "Would you rather I push you out or would you prefer to jump?"

My voice comes out in a strangled cry. "What?"

He can't be serious. Oh, but he is. Atlas grabs the rope between us and uses it as a stepping stone.

"You'll be fine, just close your eyes on the way down. I'm going to flip the hammock in five seconds. One, two, three —"

I grab the edge of the hammock, then I take his wrist, which is already positioned to pull the precious net from beneath me.

"Do *not* flip this hammock over. Do not!"

How can he look so innocent when he is about to send me to the hereafter?

"Then you'll jump?"

I'll do just about anything to avoid getting dumped from this hammock.

"Yes. I'll jump."

"Good."

Atlas returns to his own hammock and jumps from it. Not only does he jump, he flips. After landing on his back with a bounce, he gets out of the way, only to lie down on the net again, looking up at me. "Your turn."

My turn? What if I break my neck? What about all the mysteries I'll never solve? I'll never even get to finish my first real case.

"Do you need me to flip it?" he says, as if offering to help me with some difficult task.

Is this training really all that useful? Its educational value must be negligible. I don't think this is what Mother and Father had in mind when they said I had to pay attention.

I step off the edge.

I'm falling, falling. I hold in a scream. It takes forever and no time at all. I land on my back with a bounce.

Lying still, I make sure I can feel every part of me. My head, arms, back, and hipbones are all intact. Atlas's face appears over me, grinning widely. I frown at him.

"That was great, Indigo. Ready to do it again?"

"What?" He cannot possibly think I want to do that again. That would be completely mad… Wouldn't it?

"Yes."

I jump again and again, eventually keeping my eyes open during the fall. After about twenty minutes, I'm only slightly nauseous when I look down.

When I've jumped for the umpteenth time, Atlas suggests we try something else. He's unsurprised when I choose fencing, and brings out two sabres, two masks, and two jackets. My jacket buttons up the side and covers my arms to the wrist. It's a bit big, but not enough to hinder any combination I might try. We roll out a piste of teal ribbons sewn to a large red rug. It's the most elegant piste I've ever seen. Why didn't I think of a rug? Mother would probably notice if one of hers were doctored, but there must be another old one up in the attic that she doesn't care about.

Atlas rolls out his shoulders. "Who will call the matches?"

Phoebe sits in her same spot, fingers piloting knitting needles of their own accord. She catches me looking at her. "You know I can't keep up with the points, Indigo."

It's true. Phoebe has tried many times to officiate my matches with Poppy and Leo, and the rounds always end up in unclear draws.

"Oh, it's finally come to a duel, has it? I had hoped it would take a bit longer than this." Mr Trinter sits on the bench, pulling trapeze boots from a canvas bag. Mrs Trinter joins him, donning her boots as well.

"Are you going to practise your trapeze?" Atlas asks hopefully.

"Yes, but go on. Don't mind us," his mother answers.

"I'll keep score for a round, if you'd like," his father offers.

I've never done this in front of a grown-up other than Phoebe, but I stand in a ready position.

"En garde," Mr Trinter warns.

I adjust my feet and tip my sword up and slightly in front.

"Go."

I lunge first, taking advantage. In less than two seconds, I score on Atlas's arm and we restart.

"Go."

Atlas lunges, I parry, he hits my guard. I try for his torso, but he catches my sabre. He tries for my shoulder, but I parry and riposte and touch his hand, scoring my second point. He should not have given me a sabre. It's my favourite.

When Mr Trinter starts our third round, Atlas and I lunge at the same time. I try to get his torso, but hit his upper thigh. It's not a legal point. His sabre touches my left arm: his first point. We restart. It's an impressive battle; Atlas and I get to fifteen almost at the same time. I win, mostly due to those first two rounds.

Atlas takes off his mask, his dark hair tumbling into place. "Excellent match." The excitement of the sparring is still in his eyes. He sticks out his hand to shake and I take it.

Mrs Trinter rises from her seat. "Would you care for a second match, Indigo? This time against me?"

"Why not?"

Atlas offers his sabre to his mother, but she's walking to the closet. When she returns she carries two foils.

"I'm not as good with the foil."

She *tsks*. "I'm sure you'll do fine."

On "go", she lures me into striking after beating my foil, and is ready with her own parry and strike. Next we get a double tap – it looks like we hit at the exact same time. I thrust after she parries and retreats; she gets a point. I take the blade of the foil and bend it back and forth. I'll try something different this time.

"En garde."

The second the word "go" is out of Mr Trinter's mouth, I launch into a feint and follow it with my second intention, bringing the tip up and hitting just below Mrs Trinter's ribs. A point for me. This is a much better strategy.

It's a close match, but in the end, I win again. Mrs Trinter lifts her mask, slightly out of breath.

"How long have you been fencing?"

"Since I was ten – about four years. I've had a lot of practice."

"Who do you fence with?" she asks, surprised.

"My friends, Leo and Poppy. Leo's the only one with formal training, so he teaches us what he can. How long have *you* been fencing?"

"I was on a team, but that was years ago. I am a bit rough around the edges, I'm afraid. For now, though, I want to go practise trapeze with my husband." She smiles at Mr Trinter as she walks towards him. He smiles back and wraps an arm around her waist. Atlas coughs.

"Oh, yes. Let's go, Helen. We are embarrassing our son." They laugh as they walk to the ladder.

By now, Nora is gone, so Atlas steps in and teaches me a few basics on the aerial hoop. It is, by far, the most painful thing I have ever done in my life. And it's brilliant.

CHAPTER 12

After about thirty minutes, Atlas says I should stop. "You'll have plenty of bruises as it is."

I ease myself onto the floor and touch the backs of my knees. I fear he's right. "Atlas, let's practise hiding."

He looks confused. "I know how to hide."

"I'm sure, but I still know a few tricks. The best way to show you is to play hide-and-seek. Would your parents be alright with us playing in the house?"

He considers this for a moment, then nods. "I'll ask."

Atlas waits patiently for a chance to propose our idea to his mother, who's currently talking with Phoebe. As Mrs Trinter speaks, she absentmindedly tucks her son against her. I gingerly touch the inside of my feet. A blunt pain answers my prodding.

Atlas comes back. "She says that we can, but not to go into any bedrooms. And that we should only invite a few more people."

"How about Nora, Alice, and Abbott?"

He looks pleased with my suggestion and we seek them out.

Alice is doing a handstand by the wall. When she sees us she starts walking our way, still in the handstand. She smiles at my surprise.

"It isn't as hard as it looks."

"No, I'm sure it's harder…" I mumble.

"Alice, we're going to play a game of hide-and-seek, would you like to join?" Atlas offers.

Alice tries to stand on one hand, but doesn't quite manage it. She turns her mistake into a roll. "Sure. Who else is playing?"

"Just Indigo and me, but we were also going to ask Nora and Abbott."

Alice beams. "Nora's practising her splits over there." She points to a figure on the other side of the room. "Abbott has to be here somewhere."

After gathering the other two, we stand in a circle. Atlas explains the rules his mother laid out.

"What are the boundaries?" Alice asks.

"We should stay in the house," Nora suggests quietly, twining a lock of her curly hair around and around her finger. We all agree, and Nora volunteers to be the seeker first. She will give us two minutes because I'm new to the house.

Alice climbs up the ladder – to hide in one of the hammocks, I suppose. I don't keep track of Abbott because I'm describing to Atlas why the hammock is such a bad hiding place. I lead the way out of the room and down a hallway. "It's best to hide when the light is on, so you'll see everything the seeker will see. If you hide in the dark you have no idea how the shadows will fall."

I stop before the bathroom and open a narrow door. Just what I'm looking for: a small closet with shelves.

"Do you mind if I hide in here?"

Atlas looks inside. "No, it's just our linen closet."

I climb by bracing my hands and feet against the doorjamb and shimmying up. With my feet still braced against the wall, I gently grab a few large towels, placing them on the shelf above. The closet is deeper than I anticipated. Even better. I slide onto the shelf and arrange the towels in front of me so that I'm not seen.

"Oh, and make sure you have a proper source of air."

"I can't see you at all!"

Why does he sound surprised?

"Should I go find another hiding spot?" he asks.

"No, just hide on the shelf below me."

I hear him situate himself on the ledge. "How long will it take them to find us?"

"I've no idea. I often just come out after everyone else is found. Most of the time I use the same spot over and over to see if any of them can find me."

"Who do you usually play with?"

"When I was younger I played with Leo, Poppy, Leo's sister Violet, my sister Olive, and anyone else who wanted to play. Now, I mostly just find hiding places and Phoebe tries to find me, but that's not exactly a game."

Silence stretches out. The stillness of hide-and-seek. It's a quiet that has become familiar, comforting even.

Phoebe's the one who taught me to hide. No one else had ever thought to teach me before she came along. The first time we played, she was the seeker. After she finished counting to thirty, she checked under my bed. Then behind the door. Then behind her rocking chair. All the waiting made me impatient and I jumped out of the closet and shouted, "I'm here!"

Phoebe was genuinely startled, but she turned her fright to laughter.

She knelt down, her chest still heaving. "Indigo, you have to let me find you."

I dropped my hands to my sides. "But how long do I have to wait?"

Phoebe thought for a moment, the side of her mouth

ticking up. "Try counting, just like I do while you're hiding. How high can you count?"

"One thousand!" It was the highest number I'd heard of. I had no idea how to count that high.

The memory of her face is so clear to me, even now. She smiled, her eyes lighting up as she looked at me. "Wonderful."

A few nights later, I woke from a night terror, screaming. Phoebe slept in my room then, and she was stroking my hair in a second. "What was it?"

"Father. He was gone. And Mother. And Olive ran away." I buried my face in her chest. "And you weren't there. And, and..." I dissolved into tears again, the horror of what came next too paralysing to tell.

"Well," Phoebe said, cradling me against her, "I'm here. It was just a dream."

"But he's still looking for me."

"Let's count!" she said suddenly. "One, two, three, four, five..."

I joined in. "Six, seven, eight, nine..." Together we counted the seconds; each one felt invaluable, like a second I'd stolen from my pursuer. We started back at one after about a minute. (I still hadn't learned to count to one thousand.)

I played with her luna moth necklace until I fell asleep in Phoebe's arms. In the morning, she said that whenever I was scared or impatient, I should count, even if she wasn't with me.

* * *

IN THE CLOSET, forty seconds go by. Then another twenty. I listen to my breath in the close space between the shelves and towels. It's warm, and it'll soon be uncomfortable. Distant voices sound down the hall. This is my favourite part: waiting to see if it works. The more times it works, the more fun it is.

The door flies open. "I think they could be in here… Nora, come and see." It's Alice.

There are soft footsteps, and Nora speaks. "They can't be here, it's just our linens." Her voice is stronger than when I heard it downstairs. "Why would they hide together at all?"

"I know it sounds odd, but I think I heard them."

"It was probably Meridith and Henrietta going on about something."

Alice's voice takes on a tinge of annoyance. "You might be right. Let's go."

Six minutes and fifty-two seconds later, three voices begin shouting for us to come out. Atlas and I extricate ourselves from the linens. Alice, Nora, and Abbott are about to turn a corner at the end of the hallway when we burst out of the door.

"Wait, you were in the closet? Both of you?" Alice asks incredulously. She and the other two walk back.

"Yes. I was so worried you had us there," I say, wiping sweat from my brow. I hadn't realised how oppressive it was until I got out of the enclosed space. Alice laughs to herself, but Nora looks embarrassed.

"Let's play one more round! I found Alice first, so she can be seeker," she suggests, her bright red blush calming.

As Alice goes to count, our group splits up. Well, mostly.

"Your turn," I say to Atlas.

He points to himself – as if I could be talking to anyone else. "Me?"

"Your turn to find us a hiding spot."

He looks up and down the hall, then opens the door to the closet with a flourish. "Done. I bet not even you have found a hiding spot so quickly."

"You can't use mine!" I smirk. "And you would be wrong about that."

He frowns, leading me down the hallway and into a large

dining room. The ceiling is two storeys high, and the red wall-paper is flocked to create a damask pattern. The dark hard-wood has a pattern inlaid around the perimeter. A stage poses on the far side of the room, with an opulent facade. The platform is raised about five feet off the ground, with small staircases built on either side. We slip behind a curtain, much like the one at the Cirque du la Reine Theatre, only green and gold.

Backstage, I scan the room. There are many spots in here; I wonder which he'll pick. Atlas chooses a hooked ladder leaning against the wall and rests it on one of the exposed rafters. He starts climbing. He just *had* to pick this spot, didn't he? Seems my "conditioning" is being tested sooner than I thought.

We climb onto the square beam and sit. My feet dangle on either side of the trunk-thick wood as I stare at the smooth grain in front of me. With a few motions Atlas secures his wrist to a rope hanging from the ceiling.

"You should hang on. We don't want to fall." He guides my wrist around the cord, looping the end over my hand. "Hold on to the main strand. It's called a wrist-lock."

As an experiment, I tug at the woven fibres.

Up here, Atlas is only an outline against the shadowed timbers. "This is where the first shows of Cirque du la Reine were held. We still eat dinner here on occasion, and we usually practise here before the rehearsals at the theatre."

The sound of Alice and Abbott's footsteps come from a door to the backstage area, so I don't ask the question that comes to my mind. Abbott looks behind a crate. Alice puts a finger to her lips and points to the heavy curtains. Alice takes the stage right curtain, Abbott the left. They count to three together on their fingers.

"Aha!" Alice says, flinging the heavy material. The movement ripples through the velvet like a wave. "Hmm. I thought they'd be here." She puts her hands on her hips.

"Maybe Atlas hid in the library?"

"Probably."

Their footsteps echo until the door closes behind them.

* * *

WE WIN HIDE-AND-SEEK AGAIN, and I give my student a passing grade. Alice, Nora, and Abbott decide to go to the park. Atlas and I head back to the studio. When the others have gone, I apologise.

"What for?" he asks.

"That I'm keeping you from going with them."

He turns back, coming to a stop. "Oh, that – don't worry about it. Did your parents send out the invitations?"

"They did. You should get yours soon."

"What should we take with us? Tomorrow night, I mean."

Several years ago I wrote an imaginary list of all the things to bring on an espionage mission. "A medical kit, two candles, matches, a small knife, one working compass, a wound time-piece, garden wire, a few disguises, extra provisions, and —"

Atlas wears an incredulous look. "Indigo."

"Yes?"

"We can't carry *a few disguises* with us. And extra provisions?"

"You know… water and… I don't know." What food doesn't easily spoil and is small enough to hide on my person? "Prunes."

He drops his head a few degrees so he's looking at me through his dark lashes. "Prunes? You want to bring *prunes?*" He pauses a second before speaking through a suppressed laugh. "Where will you keep them?"

"In my bag, and… other places, in case that gets taken." I shoot him a look. "And you don't have to say it like that. It's a good idea."

"Why not almonds or something dry?"

"Where would I hide almonds?" They might be a good secondary food to bring. Best to vary nutrition.

Atlas's laugh escapes. "Same place you'd hide the prunes, I guess."

He opens a door just down the hall from the studio. Phoebe should still be in there. She probably thinks the game of hide-and-seek is still going.

The room is painted robin's egg blue and a blackboard is hung on the wall next to us. Daylight filters in through three windows, blanketing a semicircle of desks facing the blackboard. Dark wooden bookcases stand sentry on the wall opposite the board. Books, picture frames, jars full of feathers and leaves, extra paper, and writing utensils each claim a spot on the shelves.

"This is where you go to school?" It feels like a place I would go to curl up with a book when no one's around.

"It was one of the first rooms Mama and Papa fixed up. Oddly enough, when they met, they were both studying to become teachers. So this is an important room to them. That one's my desk." Atlas points to a table and chair on the very end.

"Who else is here?"

He points to each desk in turn as he speaks, starting from the left.

"Daniel, Cicely, Henrietta, Abbott, Alice, Marc, Meridith, Everly, Louise, Nora, and me." He walks to a shelf, sliding a volume down and fanning the pages. "Yes, here it is… Wait… Here." He passes me the fabric-bound book and unfolds the second panel of a page. "I found a map including the edge of the city. This is where the abandoned mansion is."

A squarish building sits on the very edge of the page. Warehouses line the river to the north. Other landmarks that I can easily follow are plentiful. If we come down the street with the

Lonely Inn, then we'll see the mansion. We'll know we've gone too far if we pass the orphanage.

"Got it memorised. Anything else we need to go over?"

Atlas looks up from the book, astonished. "Memorised already?"

"Of course. Haven't you?"

"Only because we've been there and I've pored over this map for days."

I shrug.

After going over the details of the plan, we head back to the studio. The light has changed dramatically. Now, shadows invade the room, crawling over the mats and balance beam.

"Ready to leave, Indigo?" Phoebe stands behind the door – we must've just passed her.

How can it be time to go? "Already?"

"Yes. Where were you two? You were gone for quite some time." She looks between us.

"Playing hide-and-seek," Atlas answers automatically. His nonchalant manner puts whatever idea Phoebe had to bed.

"How was the game?"

I tent my fingers and nod in a professional manner. "My student did very well. I say we graduate him as soon as possible."

Phoebe reappraises Atlas. "You *must* have done well. Indigo's picky with her graduates." She gives me a secret smile. "I still haven't passed."

"Only because you were trying to scare me that time. Your suspension will end in a matter of weeks."

She had been hiding behind the door, and just as I was checking under my bed, she jumped out and grabbed my shoulders. We both died laughing, still I had no choice but to suspend her.

"Ah, good. I may finally sleep at night," she chortles.

Atlas looks between us, which reminds Phoebe where we are.

"Hurry, now. We can't keep your mother waiting."

In the privacy of the dressing room, I take off my uniform and change into my charcoal dress. No one passes us as we walk down the halls. Mr and Mrs Trinter meet me at the door.

"Oh! Before we go, Mrs Taylor wanted me to give you this." Phoebe hands Mr Trinter a crisp envelope with "Trinter" written in Mother's effortless hand.

Mr Trinter looks down at the note. "What's this?"

"I believe it's an invitation to join the Taylors at their house on the twenty-seventh."

Atlas looks at me from behind Phoebe's back. I shake my head the tiniest bit. When did Mother decide to invite the Trinters over, and how did I not know about it? I should be keeping up my eavesdropping efforts; it seems I've grown lax.

"Thank you so much for bringing this to us!" Mrs Trinter beams at Phoebe. "I will write to Mrs Taylor as soon as I can. We'll see you next Thursday for your lesson, Indigo."

* * *

WHEN PHOEBE and I are in the carriage alone, she gets that curious look again.

"Indgio..." She folds her hands and speaks delicately. "Is there any reason you didn't tell me about... anyone you've met for reasons other than that you thought that I wouldn't approve?"

"Come again?"

"You know..." She casts about for words. "Is there any particular *person* who... you may not understand your feelings for?"

What is she going on about? I'm usually very decisive about

my feelings for people. They may not always be correct at first, but… "I don't know what you're implying."

She narrows her eyes. "Alright, then. But you never need to hide things from me. I want you to know that. Especially about… more than amicable feelings for someone."

More than amicable? What could be *more* than amicable? I give her such a lost expression that she sighs.

"How was your game?"

CHAPTER 13

The next day, Mrs Wood seems to take ever so long giving her lectures. The seconds flow like treacle even more so than usual. It's not that I'm eager to test my plan. No, that would be ridiculous. I'm just nervous.

That's not completely true. As well as being uneasy, I'm also excited. Ever since I was seven and three quarters, I've wanted to be a detective. At the time, I thought that was what Father was, but I soon found that he solves his cases in a different way.

I was told by Olive, to whom I foolishly confessed my dream, that I'd be destined to work for little pay and die alone in some back alley with a knife between my ribs. For a day, my dream was crushed. I was afraid of the danger and afraid that Olive wouldn't love me anymore if I became a detective. But the next morning, I woke with new passion. Never mind the challenges of doing it professionally, or the danger. Olive didn't seem to love me anyway. This was what I wanted to do. This is what I am going to do.

When Mrs Wood finally releases me, it's as if I'm spring-loaded. Dinner is a blur, and the nightly routine with Phoebe slips by. When she's gone, I sit up in bed. Moonlight pushes its way up through the folds of my curtains.

Everything is so quiet and peaceful.

I have a few hours before I need to meet Atlas at one. I set an alarm clock, stuff it under my pillow, and try to get some sleep.

The dream begins. I fall off of a lyra hoop, high above the alleyway that I rode through on the way to Ethelridge. A voice at the mouth of the alley sings, "Time is running out. You have to solve the mystery before it is too late."

An invisible force presses me against the cobbles so hard I can barely breathe. I try to shout for help, but without air, I can't make a sound.

The ground gives way beneath me and I tumble into the clock shop that Mother took me to many years ago, when Father's watch broke. This used to be the place where all my nightmares were staged. I was so scared of all the noises the clocks made and all the cuckoos jumping out at me. As I fall, though, the room is silent. The ticking that has been the score of my terrors is gone. I don't hear Mother or the clerk, Mr Gerald, but that means nothing.

I'm short enough that I can't look over the tables. When I crouch down to peer beneath them, I can't see any legs besides those of the tables.

Mother?

I can only mouth the word.

Mother?

All the air in my lungs bursts out in a silent scream.

Mama! Phoebe! Where are you?

Suddenly the hour turns, and all the clocks silently set free their mechanical birds. They come off their perches and fly at me, diving, pecking every inch of my skin. Blood wells on my face, arms, back, and fingers. I try to slap the birds away, but with each one I swipe, more take its place.

Something cold slithers up my leg, winding its way around my waist. It's the vine-snake. It rears up, looks me in the eye with its white petals, strikes my neck, and disappears. I raise a hand to my neck; ruby liquid comes away on my fingers. My heartbeat is silent. Everything is silent.

* * *

I SIT UP IN BED, my breaths coming in desperate gasps. My panicked inhales and exhales are blissfully loud. I throw the curtains open, the whoosh of material deafening. The stars in the sky glisten. Instinct tells me to press myself into the corner and cover myself with the sheets. But I'm no stranger to late-night fear.

"One. Two. Three. Four. Five. Six. Seven. Eight. Nine. Ten." I breathe in slowly, holding it for five seconds, and let it go for another ten. I press my forehead to the window, the cool contact mollifying. I dig the alarm clock from under the pillow. It's only eleven forty-six.

I might as well start getting ready. When it comes to dispelling terror, I've found focusing on my fears doesn't help as much as concentrating on basic tasks or needs.

I pack all the things I'll need and think of nothing else. Into my satchel goes a candle, three matches, a small compass that one of Father's guests left behind, a medical kit, leather gloves, a spyglass, an apple, a package of prunes, some almonds, my homemade lock picks, a notebook, and a red cedar pencil sharpened to a fine point. I decide against the pocket watch because it ticks so loudly.

Next, I need the black long-sleeved shirt I wore to Father's sister's friend's daughter's funeral. I lift my wardrobe doors the tiniest bit and pull them out. The hinges glide without a sound and I snatch the shirt and a purple skirt from the rack. This particular skirt has black ribbons sewn into it. The ties were Phoebe's idea, and it's a stroke of genius. The fabric tangled around my legs when I raced Leo a few years ago. I fell, and was scraped up for days. Since then, I've always had one skirt with ties ready for me to use in case I need to run or climb something. Mother hasn't found out yet. For now, I leave the ties down.

I tie my hair back in a single plait and mould one wire into my hair ribbon and another to the back of my ear. Thick socks, personally tested for sneaking, fit snugly into my boots. The clock reads eleven fifty-eight. I'll be early, but there's not much else to do.

Quest is not happy to see me when I wake her. She snorts and pulls her ears back as I arrange her tack. As I put it on, she whinnies in frustration. Her temper cools somewhat with the gift of an apple. A few of the other horses stir, but once I quiet Quest's complaining, they journey back to Nod.

I WAIT OUTSIDE 416. No lights are on inside; only the gasoliers outside the double doors help the streetlamps lift the darkness. Quest shuffles impatiently. By now it must be twelve twenty-seven. I'm over thirty-three minutes early.

A bird coos in the distance and I flinch. A gust strolls down the lane, tickling the back of my neck. Twenty-two, twenty-three, twenty-four, twenty-five. A creaking sound bruises the quiet. It's coming from the stables of 416. A glowing orange light peeks between the slats of wood.

I slide from Quest and slink over to the fence. I see, in a gap, Atlas rousing Emil.

"Atlas!" I hiss.

He turns, a lantern swinging out. "Indigo?"

"Yes. Why are you out early?"

He finds my eye through its peeky-hole. "Why are *you* out early? You're the one who had to ride over here."

"I woke up before my alarm. I knew I wouldn't be able to go back to sleep."

He nods. "I couldn't set an alarm because I share a room with Abbott and Marc. I was so paranoid about sleeping late that I woke up too soon. Do you want to go now?"

"I think that'd be best."

Atlas chooses to ride bareback, so in a minute, we're off. At first we're alone on semi-lit streets with the occasional leaf or scrap of paper lost to the wind. As we get further out, the night grows darker. Couples cross the street on sea legs. Screams of laughter ring through the air, with rowdy music for accompaniment. Another horse gallops past us. Atlas and I ride closer than before.

"Oi!" A man walks down the side of the road, one hand steadying him on the wall. He points the other in my direction. "Goin' so soon?"

I hold my breath to keep from panicking. My fingers knot themselves in Quest's mane. Atlas remains calm, neither speeding nor turning. We pass without saying anything. The drunkard swears something nasty at us and starts singing about "unmentionables". I let out a long breath.

Eventually, the ruckus of nightlife dies, leaving only a baby's muffled wail. The silence is almost soothing. But not quite.

We easily find the abandoned mansion; the silhouette of its towers is unique among the row. A perfect half-moon glows overhead as we tie our horses to an old gatepost by a dilapidated building around the corner. I bend at the waist. It takes nineteen seconds to adjust my skirt, the laces requiring a little extra coaxing from my shaky hands.

"Ready. Are you?"

Atlas looks up. "Yes." He swallows. "Scared, but yes."

We begin by circling the house. The corner seems to have

been severely damaged years ago, and never quite fixed. A heap of loose bricks from the cavity is left behind. The rose vines found their way around the edge of the front corner, but halted their advance after a few feet. Bushes, grown to the height of trees, huddle beside the wall. A breeze brushes their leaves against the mortar, making a rough scraping sound. Extending behind the mansion is a deserted garden. The beds are nothing but a dismal tangle of dead branches. The grass waves lengthy fingers along the overgrown paths, which are difficult to pick out amid the sea of dark grey.

Most of the windows at the back of the house are still intact. No light emanates from within. A door is set a few feet into the house, creating an alcove. As I get closer, the wood and tarnished handle become clearer. Moss creeps over the edges where rot hasn't already gnawed the door away. The recess shelters me from the wind, but its low whistle sounds even more pining here.

The cold metal shocks my skin as I twist the handle and my suspicions are confirmed. The knob meets resistance and grates against something – either some improvised bar or a second door. Even this first lock is secured. I could use my lock picks, but this is probably the door they use, especially because it's more shielded from prying eyes. I let go of the handle and step back. The skin at the back of my neck tingles.

"What is it?" Atlas murmurs as I walk quickly back to him. His hair falls into his face as he looks from the height of the tower to my face. The odd light makes his skin paler than I know it is.

"The door is locked."

We make our way back to the front and step over the jagged threshold. The moonlight can hardly find passage through the screen of vines. Even with my eyes accustomed to the dark, I can barely spot the outline of the stairs and columns beside.

The space feels so much larger in the dark. Our footsteps echo, sounding like someone following us.

We enter the parlour I peeked into the first time Atlas and I came here. The covered furniture looks like contorted albino animals. The moulding on the wall is iced with dust and there is a handprint on the window, near the sill – someone tried to force it up from the inside. We search the room, but find nothing.

The next room appears to have once been an office. It'd be mildly humorous if a secret society of criminals kept their files in a desk drawer. All the locks on the mahogany desk are mangled and the wood has been splintered in multiple places. The other furniture in the room, including an elephantine bookshelf and harpsichord, have been equally vandalised.

The library has no windows, and all but one of the walls are taken up by shelves filled with antique volumes. These, for some reason, have been left intact. We search for the dusty spines for any that have been taken down recently. None have been.

The floor creaks unbearably as we make our way from room to room. We check everywhere, finding nothing but old broken furniture, dust, and rotting wallpaper. There's nothing on the second floor either, but it'd be suspicious if it was easy. Our footsteps tap hollowly against the snow-coloured marble. At the top of the main staircase, a large hallway stretches on with doors to either side.

The third floor contains all the staff bedrooms. The ceilings of this floor are in much worse shape, the best being severely water-stained and the worst having little roof to speak of. There is no furniture or safe place to hide documents.

Out in the hallway again, we spy a paper resting on the floor. It wasn't there before. Atlas bends to pick it up. I look over his shoulder as he flattens it.

The only thing on it is a realistic drawing of an eye in black ink. When Atlas takes his thumb away, the drawing is smeared and his thumb is black. This is new, freshly drawn, maybe minutes old. I spin around, looking for who could have dropped it.

Atlas whispers, "Indigo… look at me."

I turn to him and he holds the paper next to my temple.

"This is your eye."

I look more closely at the drawing. I had thought it was just in ink, but no. The artist used graphite as well, making the iris grey. Exactly like my grandmother's.

I take a shaky breath. Atlas holds his head high and together we noiselessly descend the stairs. This is the part where things could start going wrong.

I stuff my hands in my pockets to keep them from shaking. I will not let them know they scare me. Following the plan, Atlas is next to me as my boot hits the floor of the entry hall.

The only warning is the hint of clothing and a short step. A strong arm wraps around my neck from behind. As it tightens, the abandoned mansion quickly fades to black.

So plan B begins.

CHAPTER 14

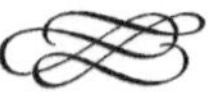

I wake slowly, my neck and head throbbing. I'm still alive and have been captured, so that's step two checked off. I'm tied to a chair, with a gag in my mouth and hands bound behind my back. Yet I don't feel stiff, so I can't have been tied to this chair for long. That still allows Atlas and me to escape in plenty of time to make a punctual appearance back home tonight. Good news all around.

The room is square, its high ceiling forming a pyramid. The windows are shrouded in black fabric. Craning my neck to look behind, I see, in the centre of the room, a raised circular platform supporting a grand piano with baroque candelabras sitting atop it. There are elegant carvings in the piano's body; some of the rotting grain is hidden by peeling dark blue paint.

Atlas isn't here.

I must keep my head. I cannot think clearly if I lose my wits. I know talking will be useless, so I start humming a duet. I hear humming in return from the other side of the raised platform. That must be Atlas. My whole body releases a bit of tension, and I try spitting my gag out, but am interrupted by slow clapping.

"Oh, very good. Very good. No one's ever tried that one before. I'm impressed."

A man wearing a long, dark coat buttoned to his throat steps lithely into view from a deep doorway in my peripheral vision. He wears a grey mask; the candlelight flickers in his eyes. I try talking very loudly. It isn't quite as loud as humming, but it should do the trick.

"Come now, that won't work. That's why I was so impressed by your little humming trick," he condescends.

I, ever the lady, dip my head in acknowledgement and keep talking. Atlas must see what I am getting at and joins in. We are just making noise, in a conversational tone, going back and forth. But the Mask can't know that for certain.

He looks between us. I add a touch of mockery to my sense-less grunting. Atlas affects a laugh, a very convincing one. The Mask must either choose to keep our gags on or take them off to hear what we are trying to communicate.

"Remove their gags." Then, turning to us, "Don't you want to know who I am?"

I shrug and shake my head as two men – also in coats and masks – enter the room, one going towards Atlas and one to me. Their masks are different: pure white. I bow my head so the man can undo the knot at my neck. When his task is done he exits with the other white-masked man.

I work my jaw and try to speak confidently. "I don't need to know who you are."

The grey-mask lists to the side. "So you already know I'm the Phantom."

I smile, pityingly. "No, you aren't."

"What would give you that idea?"

"Because I know the size of the ring with which the Phantom seals their letters. That ring wouldn't fit your fingers. And if you *were* the Phantom, why would you ask me if I knew who you were? You are supposed to be the Invisibles. I assume that is what you call yourselves – *born again invisible* and all that. You're never to be seen, never known. Your leader would hide their identity."

Atlas snickers.

"How do you know what we seal our letters with? Describe it."

I have him on the run.

"It is a blackletter capital 'I' being choked by rose vines. Your hideout, of which I am in the room on the top floor, has the same insignia carved above the door." I raise my voice. "When may I meet the *real* Phantom?"

He flings his hands wide, fingers spread out. "You have met him."

Oh, this is interesting. I hope Atlas is using this time wisely – I'm running out of information to throw at him. I'm about to add to my previous statement, but the door behind me opens with a deep groan.

A female voice, much calmer than the man's, rings through the room. "You may leave us."

The Pretender fists his hands to his side. "You're right, Violet, or whatever your name is. I'm not the Phantom."

I've never been so insulted in my entire life. "My name is *Indigo*."

"It doesn't matter to me what your name is." His words carry an unnecessary bite as he stalks off.

I put together obvious information and exposed his falsehood. No need to get so upset. The door closes behind me.

"Don't be rude to our guest. Pleasure to meet you, Indigo. Welcome to my house."

I still can't see the woman speaking. She might not be the real Phantom, either.

"This is a poor welcome," I say. "Being tied up and conned by this man, who's probably wearing your mask."

A tall figure, also in a black coat, hood raised over a black mask, steps coolly into my field of vision. "I wondered when you would be coming to see me, after you came here the first time. And then your escape from my rider – that was impressive."

"Thank you." I incline my head graciously. "May I ask a question?"

"Why, yes, of course."

"I've not been able to review the official evidence against Mr Smith, but I don't believe what was presented in the papers."

"Oh, no?" The Phantom comes closer, placing her hands on the arms of my chair. Unlike the first man's mask, this one has black fabric over the eyes, so I cannot see them. I swallow.

"I think you planted the bottle of arsenic."

The figure steps back. "That is one of the things we did. You're doing well. You even guessed the name of our society. Let's see if the boy has anything to say."

The Phantom walks around the dais.

"So, you're the boy who has been playing hero with Indigo? Pleasure to finally meet you."

Atlas says something too quiet to hear.

The Phantom suddenly storms out from behind the dais, calling out quickly and with suppressed anger.

"Take the girl to the holding cell. Thirteen will help you. I'll deal with the boy."

The intimidating figure of the Pretender comes towards me. A man slightly below average height follows on his tail; he's wearing a white mask. Together they undo my ropes. The short one – Thirteen – holds me still while the Pretender reties my hands behind my back. I hadn't counted on them using ropes – my lockpicks won't work in freeing my hands. I'll have to figure something else out.

"We're taking her to the hold," the Pretender explains. Thirteen nods once, gripping my arm like a vice. They march me towards the door and into a spiralling stairwell.

On the seventh step, I hear it.

A gunshot.

CHAPTER 15

I scream, not as a conscious action but instinct, and twist my body, throwing my shoulder into Thirteen. He takes a step back to regain his balance, but his heel catches on the step. His hold on my arm lessens for a moment. I tear it free. The man catches himself just before landing on his backside. I try to jump over him, but the Pretender grabs my arm, pinching some nerve so hard that little spots appear in my vision. I kick his knee, making his left leg buckle. Thirteen scrambles to his feet.

Something hard collides with my head and all goes black once more.

* * *

I WAKE up in a room with no windows or door. My eyes adjust and there, high above me, is the faint outline of a hatch. My hands are free. I reach for the wire at my ear, hoping against hope… but no, they found it. Standing, I find my boots gone. The floor beneath my bare feet is made up of wide flagstones, dirt hiding in the cracks.

I try not to think about the loss as I grab the wall. It's lined with some sort of metal. My finger catches a nail, slicing it. I stick it in my mouth. Hopefully I won't catch some awful sickness. Perhaps Atlas is finding a way out of his cell. Maybe he'll find me and we can get out. If he leaned over the edge of the trapdoor I could…

Atlas. The gunshot.

Atlas is dead.

I crumble against the wall. He's dead. I've never felt this before. I've never lost someone I know. Knew.

My plan failed. I failed. We were supposed to find evidence or, if not, get captured, learn what we could and… escape.

I choke and a fit of coughing overtakes me. I hear footsteps above. I quickly wipe my eyes – I'll never let them use his death against me. I will get out of this cell and get out of here.

I take deep breaths. In. One, two, three. Out. Three, two, one. I stand and dust myself off. The trapdoor opens and a ladder unfurls, clattering down into the room. In the dark it was hard to tell how high above me the ceiling is, but now I see that it's at least fifteen feet.

"Come up."

I fold my arms across my chest. "And why should I? For you to kill me?" My voice is still pinched.

"You are to be questioned by the Phantom. Come up."

I retie my skirt and start up the ladder. At the top, the guard grabs my shoulder and ties my hands behind my back before I have time to fully stand. My wrists are becoming raw from the coarse rope. As I'm spun around, I catch a glimpse of my bag and everything that was inside – even the prunes – spread out on a low table, my boots underneath.

I try to get a good look at… her. This guard is a woman. Her eyes are distinct. Her movements are unrushed as she pulls a sack over my head. I'll never understand why people do this; I can still measure distance and keep the number of turns in my head. There aren't many to remember: left, right, right, left, stairs, and a door. My guard sits me down, forcing my hands over the back of the chair before tying my waist. She exits, taking the sack with her.

This time I'm in a wine cellar. The walls are exposed red brick, only covered by a cabinet against the far wall. Before me is a metal table, the same material as my cell. Across from me sits the Phantom, hands folded, expressionless mask staring. Between us is a tarnished candelabra with a few stunted candles.

"How did you find us?"

I hate that mask. "I didn't. I stumbled upon the house."

"Enough games. I killed the boy; I can kill whomever I wish. And I may want to kill your other friends if you choose to be uncooperative."

"Why would you do that?" I try to sound completely innocent. Or naive.

"Why wouldn't I?"

I lean forward until the rope digs into my ribs. "That isn't what I asked. Answer the question."

"I'm not the one being interrogated," the Phantom replies coolly.

"Oh, maybe I missed something? I came here to question you. You have only given me what I want: a meeting with the Phantom. So answer the question: why are you doing this?"

"That isn't what you asked the first time."

I glare at the fabric-covered eye holes. "You're stalling."

"No, that is what *you're* doing." The Phantom leans forward, mirroring me. "How did you find us?"

I raise one eyebrow. "Why are you doing this?"

It's a battle of wills… and possibly a staring contest, but that would be terribly unfair.

"Why should I answer your question? What do I gain from it? Nothing. You gain everything."

"I could say the same thing. Either way, I die. And you're incorrect. You will get yourself a willing prisoner."

"What is that to me? I already took your friend's life. I can take yours."

I rise from my chair, or try to. The coarse bonds pull me back down. I settle for clenching my jaw tightly.

I can hear the smile in the Phantom's voice. "You will just let me kill you if I give you this precious piece of information? I see through you."

"Perhaps *I* am invisible, then? That's exactly what I mean."

"That's not logical at all. I tell you what you want, and then you die with the answer? You couldn't even pass it along."

A grim smile stretches across my face. "It's not likely that I'll get out of here at all. If you give me this then I will die knowing some of the pieces of the puzzle."

"You are tipping your king?"

I nod. "Precisely. Why are you doing this?"

The Phantom waits a few moments, steepling her fingers on the tabletop.

"Take your time."

The black mask had been looking off into the distance, but now rounds back to me.

"Someone was taken from me. Someone I loved. They were brilliant. Strong. A true leader. And yet, for that very reason, their life was taken by Walker's poison. I knew there was foul play, so I followed the trail here. I found the society and overthrew the Phantom, taking control of the people who took what I loved most."

She adds quietly, "I wasn't always like this." As the woman draws up to her full height, her voice hardens again. "But when Walker stepped out of line, I saw my chance. I murdered him myself, using his own poison and framing a petty criminal for it. They should've known never to lay a hand against..."

Here she stops, taking a deep, shuddering breath. The

sound is like a child calming themself after a scrape, almost on the verge of tears.

I let out a breath myself.

She was *so close* to giving away a name.

"My position is tenuous and your actions have done nothing but make all this harder." Something like hurt seems to prick her and she clasps her hands together tightly.

For my next move, I begin: "I know a woman whose husband died of heart failure. She only wears black now and rarely leaves the house. Her name is Mrs Theodora Thwite. She is a kind woman, though she can look severe at times. When I first saw her, I thought she was cold; but I learned I was wrong. You should meet her. Even after her husband's death…"

The Phantom rips off the black mask, slamming it on the table, pieces of black porcelain flying everywhere. Face streaked with tears, her lip quavers as she whispers the words, "I am Theodora."

CHAPTER 16

Theodora Thwite is sobbing now, hands over her face, tears slipping through the seams between her fingers. She bows her head until her chin is tucked to her chest. Her bun, previously hidden by the hood of her cloak, is dishevelled.

A large fragment of porcelain rests not far from my chair. I extend my foot as far as I can. It's not enough. I slouch in my seat. The ropes around my waist make it hard to breathe as I wriggle the coils up my body. I reach my foot out again. The very tip of my toe rests on the shard of mask. The scrape of porcelain on stone is hidden by Theodora's sobs. Slowly, I pinch the shard between my toes. The knife-like edge is a breath away from cutting my foot. Navigating around the front leg of the chair, I arch my foot to lift the tool closer to my hands. The edge of the chair grates against my thigh. I reach my fingers as far as I can and take the fragment.

The shard cuts through the rope quickly enough. I feel little strands spray up. The heart of the cord is tougher than the outer fibres. I saw back and forth with more force. Sweat makes the porcelain slick in my hand, but soon I'm through the rope at my wrists.

Theodora is shaking now; it's like she's experiencing an earthquake all her own. Her world falling apart all over again. She's sobbing so hard she can barely breathe. Letting out a pitiful scream, she collapses to the floor. I have the sudden urge to comfort her, to dry her tears and tell her it'll be alright. To help her wake up from her nightmare. But that's foolish. I'm almost through the bonds at my waist.

"Phantom? Do you need assistance? Shall I come in?" The guard on the other side knocks frantically. "Phantom?"

She bursts in and rushes to Theodora's side. The rope at my middle slumps into my lap. I stand. As the guard's head turns, the cheekbones of her mask catch the low light. Her eyes are livid.

In a second she's up and after me. But I'm closer to the door and make it through. It stops before it can latch closed. A boot-toe is wedging it open. An arm, covered from shoulder to fingertip in black, reaches through and gropes for my neck, fingers straining for my jugular.

I throw my body weight into the door. It smashes into the Invisible, knocking her off balance into the room. I pull the door shut and ram the bolt into its housing, locking her in.

The hallway seems shorter than I remember it, but I count each step and the turns: left, right, right, left. I find the room they had me in. The trapdoor is still open in the middle of the floor. I don my stockings and boots first, then grab my bag from a table, sweeping all my things off the edge and into the main pocket. Its familiar weight is comforting on my shoulder. A cloak hangs on a rusty hook. Lifting it down, I latch the clasp at my throat. The neck is too big and the hem drags on the ground, but it'll have to do.

I crack the door open. The dim hall is clear and silent. The corridor has a plethora of doors to hide behind, but I don't know what I'll be getting into.

A shout comes from the other end of the hall. My heart skitters in my ribcage. Do I hide or run? I run. Thankfully, the dusty carpet cushions each stride. Without it my sprint would sound like cannons firing.

Footsteps resound up ahead. I duck into a little nook probably once meant to shelter a lamp. The excess fabric of the cloak combined with my size makes it easy for me to curl into a ball and look like a heap of cloth.

Invisibles march down the dark hall, getting closer and closer to me. My heart thumps in my ears so loudly I can barely hear them pass. One, two, three, four, five, six, seven... They have to be past.

I uncover my head, the air on my skin now bitterly cold. They're gone.

Assuming I'm on a subterranean level, I must find a staircase to the main floor. Then I can escape from any window. I walk faster, slipping in and out of shadows. None of the rooms I pass are connected to the outside.

Finally! The hallway dead-ends at a cramped servants' stairway. The treads lack carpet, and my footfalls make more noise than I'd like.

As I reach the main floor landing, a pair of feet come in my direction from the hallway. They're probably going to head down to the scuffle. My only option is to go up. This leads to another, shorter hallway with a few rooms branching off.

I hear nothing aside from footsteps in the stairwell, so I try the last door of the bunch. It's unlocked, and there is no one in the room. I quickly see why. The space is full of discarded items and in the corner a massive part of the floor is missing, leaving a gaping hole to the level below.

Something moves to my right. I spin to see a face staring at me. I step back, covering a sharp gasp with my hand. So does the figure.

Wait a minute…

I touch my hair; so does the stranger. It's just a mirror, so dirty in the dim light I couldn't see it clearly.

In the room over, the sound of scraping furniture and footsteps resounds. I drop to my knees and crawl behind the massive looking glass, tucking my legs to my chest. I'm just barely too wide and move so carelessly that the infernal thing starts to slip. No, no, no —

The door to the room shudders open. The mirror slides even further, scraping across the floor. Another floorboard complains softly, closer to my mirror. The immense weight of the looking glass is lifted – and a white mask stands over me.

He leans the hulking glass against the adjacent wall. I kick at his knees; the Invisible drop to the floor. I start to run, but he seizes my wrist and pulls me back to him. I try to score another hit, but he grabs my fist.

"Indigo, stop."

I do stop. I take a step back. He lets me go this time, to reach for the mask. He lifts it, revealing his face.

I retreat again. My throat burns. "This is a *cruel* trick. Stop it. Just kill me now." A tear tracks down my cheek, and the imposter steps towards me. I dart to the door. I have to get out. I have to run.

"Indigo, it's me."

"No. Atlas…" More tears escape as I reach for the door, fumbling with the handle. "I brought Atlas to this place. It's my fault he's dead. I killed him. He's…"

"I am not dead. I thought *you* were dead." He gently pries my hands from the doorknob.

"I heard the gunshot," we say in unison.

I remove my hand to touch his shoulder – a real shoulder. "Atlas?"

He catches me in his arms, speaking over my shoulder. "They told me you were dead. The Phantom was taking me to be questioned when I heard the shot, then they knocked me out so I couldn't get to you. I tried to."

For a second I just stand, stunned. This *is* Atlas. Hesitantly, I put my forehead against his shoulder. His collarbone stands out above his chest, even under his borrowed cloak. My temple rests against it. I look at the wall with cracks running through it.

"I'm sorry I kicked you."

He shakes his head once, leaning it against mine. "Don't be. I'd be worried if you didn't try."

A tear soaks into the material of his cloak. I sniff. "Thanks."

Voices in the hall. I crouch behind a wooden bench. Atlas follows. I grab a dusty curtain and pull it over us.

"How did *both* of them escape? Wasn't one of them being questioned by the Phantom when it happened?" The first man speaks in a Bristol accent, like my grandmother's.

"The Phantom says the girl lept at her. Thirty-One must not have tied her properly. The Phantom should never have allowed women to join. Anyway, when the mask broke, the Phantom hid her face to protect her identity." The second man pauses. "If it got out who the Phantom was..." He clears his throat. "Well, then the little brat knocked the Phantom in the head."

Ha. I single-handedly took down the Phantom and escaped into thin air.

"Nasty little thing. What about the boy?" the first one asks.

"I dunno. I went to the Phantom first. I only just heard to keep an eye out for the second one. I think he was secured in the waiting room. They aren't here – let's go."

Their boots head down the hallway. I start breathing again. So does Atlas. I step out from behind the curtain, a layer of dust covering me from head to foot.

"How do we get out of here?" Atlas rises, craning his neck to see down the chasm in the corner. "If we could get out of one of the windows on the first floor, we wouldn't have to drop so far down."

"But the Invisibles are likely patrolling the halls down there even more than up here. We could tie curtains together and make a rope and climb down."

He draws in a long, long breath. "That might be best. I could go check the other rooms for material while you plan our route?"

"Absolutely not. We're sticking together."

Six minutes and forty-two seconds later, we've created Frankenstein's rope.

"Are you sure this will hold?"

Atlas pulls on the knot again. "I think so. What are we going to tie it to, though?"

My eyes are drawn to the enormous wooden bench, almost like a chapel pew. "What if we tied it to that? The length won't fit through the window, and it looks heavy enough on its own."

Atlas stands from his crouched position and tests the weight of the bench. "We'll have to move it closer to the window, otherwise our rope won't be long enough."

I take one side, and on the count of three we lift. The bench is much heavier than it looks. My already sweaty hands begin to slip. I take a step backwards, keenly aware of the hole in the floor.

"Careful," Atlas whispers. The word is distorted through his mask, which he put back on.

I'm awfully close to the compromised floor. I adjust my grip, but immediately my hands slide to the exact same place as before. I don't think I can hold much longer.

"Set it down on three," I say quickly. "One, two —"

The heavy wood finally leaves my hands, falling an inch to

the hardwood. Despite the minuscule height it sounds like someone beat a massive drum.

"Sorry! Sorry!"

"It's fine, just help me tie the rope." Panic quickens his words. Atlas snatches a part of the fabric and tosses the length to me. I drop the tail out of the window as he kneels to pass it under. I bring it back up and hand it off to Atlas. He ties a complicated knot in a few seconds.

"You go first," we say simultaneously.

I glare at him, but then realise that he's right. If he's found, his mask will buy him a few seconds. Me, on the other hand…

"Fine, but come down right after me."

He nods.

"Hey! There she is. What are you doing?" An Invisible wearing a white mask is pointing up at us through the hole in the floor. "Don't just stand there. Grab her!"

Atlas hisses, "Go, go, go!"

I step from the bench to the sill. I have to duck my head to get through the open window. Securing my hands around the curtain, I take the first step down. Then another. Right foot, left foot. Left hand, right hand. Through the window, I can see the Invisible pulling a revolver from the dark folds of his coat.

Above me, Atlas starts out the window. The gun reports, startling me. I get my feet under me and take another step. Between our combined weight and movement, the bench is lifted from the floor, but catches quickly as it's too wide to fit through. The sudden lurch makes my hands lose their purchase.

For a second my body feels weightless, floating in mid-air. The image of Atlas rolling out of a fall the first time I visited 416 comes to my mind. Everything slows. I stretch out my arms and brace for the impact. The moment my fingers make contact with the ground, I twist and roll over my shoulder. My momentum is greater than I expect, carrying me to my feet with surprising force. I stumble forward a few steps but stay upright.

Another gunshot is accompanied by glass shattering.

Atlas lands on the sod behind me, also tucking into a roll. We start running just as a third gunshot fires from the window. Atlas doesn't stagger, so it must have missed. We run towards our horses. Two more shots ring false as we cross the street and careen around the corner.

Emil whinnies in the distance, about two hundred feet from us. I can see Quest's flank in the moonlight. Just as we reach them, dirt and pottery scatter across at our feet. What remains of a potted plant is strewn across the road.

Back down the street, cloaked men in white masks manage to extend pistols while running full tilt. Atlas sets the horses free and they bolt in opposite directions. We'd have been too easy a target if we tried to mount. Something slices my arm, possibly a shard of pottery.

Atlas and I turn down a side street. In the dark, I can barely see him point down a lane running parallel. We split off the straight path and follow the cobbles. The buildings seem to press closer and closer in on us. I can't hear footsteps behind us over the cacophony of our own. Still, no more shots resound; we must be out of sight and range at least. We double back, then stick to alleyways, staying out of sight.

"We have to hide until they pass us," Atlas pants as we cross another street. "We should have at least another few hours before Mother and Father call the police." A closed-off alley branches out to the left. All the windows above us are dark and shuttered.

"Where'll we go?" My voice is slurred. My arm feels like it's on fire. Bright, white-hot pain. If only I had a bucket of cool water to rest it in. Maybe some ice.

Atlas turns to say something, and freezes.

"What?"

"Your arm."

What could he possibly… Oh.

I've never seen so much blood in my entire life, all put together.

"God." My knees give way and I slump to the ground, beads of my blood falling into a puddle, turning it crimson.

Atlas kneels beside me, lifting my limb. "Let me see. Oh. You'll be fine. I'm going to put pressure on it. This might hurt."

He rips the hood off his cloak and tears it into a strip. The ripping sound is so loud. He peels part of my sleeve away, wiping the blood with the line of cloth. It wells up immediately, but it's clear I only have a deep graze. Atlas ties the scrap of his hood around my upper arm just enough to hold itself.

"Ready?"

I grit my teeth and nod. He presses the whole of his hand over the laceration. I feel the woven canvas on the open wound like a thousand needles.

"How long will this go on?" I try to focus on my words.

He shifts his hand slightly, so the pressure is more even. "Until the bleeding slows, or it becomes clear I need to tie a tourniquet."

"One, two, three, four…"

Atlas looks at me, confused, but joins in, "Five, six, seven, eight, nine…"

My entire body is completely cold. My clothing does nothing to warm me. Distant running sounds down the street, hastening closer. Atlas curses under his breath.

I stop counting. "Is that…"

"Shh. They might still pass us. I'll help you. One, two, three." He grabs my elbows and hauls me to my feet. In the next second, we slump behind a soggy pile of trash spilled across the space between two run-down flats. A trail of scarlet follows behind us.

"Atlas, the blood!"

He puts a finger to his lips. There's nothing to do now but wait and see. He still holds my arm, though the pressure is not quite so even as it was. The stone wall at my back is freezing cold. Between the wound and the heat from Atlas's hand, my upper arm is the only warm part of my body.

The horses' metal shoes are deafening. The sound bounces off the alley walls, making it seem as though a thousand horses are in the street – a wild stampede about to trample us. In a moment, though, they've passed. Atlas hoists me up, without warning this time, and I try to stifle the screech that claws the back of my throat.

"We've got to go now before they circle back, or another group of them come. But first I have to put another layer on your arm. Can you hold it tight?"

He takes his hand away. One, then two drops fall from his palm; in the dark, they look black. Atlas makes a new bandage from the hem of the cloak. When I close my hand around my arm, a squelch of blood pushes between my fingers. I shudder.

"I'm going to have to tie the bandage a bit more tightly. Neither of us can hold it properly while we run."

I pry my fingers away and wipe my hand on my shirt. Atlas wraps the bandage quickly, tying it off with a sharp tug.

"I can fix it when we get home – for now that'll have to do. Come on. I know the way from here."

As Atlas and I stumble through the streets, he pretends not to be worried, but I catch him glancing at me a number of times. I can't think of what number, though. It should be a nice, round number. Like two. Wait, that's not round… Ten, perhaps. Ten times two… That's quite high.

Eventually, 416 looms in the distance. Emil found his way home; we pass him in the stable. A bright light blinds me. A wave of pins and needles charges through my arm all the way to my fingertips. The weight of my shoulder bag, which I'd forgotten about, is lifted and the fabric that was pressed into my wound is taken away. A wet slapping sound echoes close at hand. A hot, sudsy cloth is dabbed against my arm. It's as if someone's squeezed lemon juice, peppermint, and cayenne pepper into my cut.

"Ow! Let me do it." I swat at Atlas's hand.

He jerks the washcloth back, a trickle of soapy water dripping onto his forearm and sliding down. "You'll have to wake up to do that."

The stinging summons some instinct in me, and I register the water closet by the circus room. A cabinet is open, revealing a stash of medical supplies. I'm standing halfway out into the hall. When did we get here? How did we get in?

"Alright, alright. I can get it."

Atlas hands over a bleached cloth with a cloud of bubbles. "Here."

"Thanks. Is there something I can eat?"

He looks from my face to the knot. "After you clean and I bandage that" – he nods down at my arm – "I'll sneak into the kitchen and see what I can find."

"I can bandage it."

He narrows his eyes. "Have you ever done it before?"

"Yes. Have you?"

"We do basic medical training once every year, so yes."

I've always just wrapped the cloth strip around my limb a few times. "I'll clean. You bandage."

He nods and starts washing his hands.

A dot of crimson soaks into the sleeve of my shirt. The top edge of the tear has crusted to a maroon colour. When the soap touches the slash, a suppressed scream whistles between my teeth. After drying his hands, Atlas finds a small tin of safety pins next to a bottle of laudanum.

"You're lucky it didn't go any more to the right, or we'd be waking up a doctor to pull out the bullet." He selects a roll of cloth from the lowest shelf, setting it on the marble countertop.

For some reason, his statement is extremely annoying. I channel my anger into cleaning my arm and manage, "I'm so glad."

My hand shakes as I dip the cloth down to dab my wound.

My breath is strangled by pain on its way out. "One. Two. Three." I drag the cloth against the length of the bullet-trail. "Four." I lift it away, but the glassy bubbles still sting. "Is that good?" I ask desperately.

Atlas bites his lip and looks up from the wound. "Do that a few more times."

I press all the air out of my lungs and fold the now red cloth over, bringing it just above the new flow of blood. I start at the far end of my arm and bring the cloth across before I can anticipate the pain anymore. It's done by the time my brain recognises the fresh wave of agony.

"If you wash your hands, you can clean it without using the cloth." He turns the water on.

I clench my jaw and cup my hands under the deluge. I concentrate on the feel of the water: its warmth slipping through my fingers. Atlas drips soap into my palms and pearlescent domes spring up. I scrub between each of my fingers and around my thumbs. When Atlas says it's sufficient, I bend at the waist and hang the elbow of my compromised arm over the sink. My finger lightly touches the wound. I can feel the absence of skin, the trough that's left. The soap doesn't hit as hard this time. I rub a bit more deeply and the sharp bite returns. In a second the pain washes away. By the time the water trickles off the crook of my arm, I can almost believe it's pure blood.

After a few more repetitions, the pain only rears its head when I touch the graze too roughly. I rinse until the water runs clear, then wash my hands. My sleeve is drenched, along with part of my torso, and all around the sink are miniature lakes.

"Sorry," I mumble.

"You don't need to be." Atlas washes his hands again. When he's done, he pulls another towel from the cabinet under the sink. "Here."

I take the edge and soak up the water on the counter.

Atlas takes the fabric back. "Not for the sink. Your arm." He hides both hands under the towel and wraps them around my upper arm.

"It'll get dirty."

He shakes his head, but there's a laughing grin. "As long as I'm alive to wash a few towels, I don't mind. What's more important is that you and I escaped."

"That's true."

The cold water that had been clinging to my skin is soaked up in the wake of the towel. When it reaches the cuff of my sleeve, Atlas puts his thumb to the vein at the base of my hand on the uninjured arm.

"Your heart is beating far too quickly." In a sudden motion he hands the damp towel to me. "Dry whatever's wet." He starts fumbling at the cloak he borrowed from the Invisibles. "Put this on. You need to stay warm."

The clasp clicks open and he casts the cloak out in a wide arc around me. He refastens it at my neck and lays it over my shoulders. While I press the towel over my midriff and arm, Atlas unwinds a few inches of bandage.

"Indigo, you're going to be fine." His green eyes look so calm. "After I bandage that cut, I'm going to find a blanket, and then you can lie down and rest."

He winds the bandage as he did in the alley, except instead of tying a knot he threads a small safety pin through the cloth and fastens it.

"I'll be right back. Don't move."

I try to think of some clever remark, but nothing comes to me. "Thank you."

He's already gone. I dry off the sink with the damp towel

and sit on the counter. The light floating down from above is soothing. The mirrored cabinet reflects my profile from behind bottles, bandages, a syringe, and other odds and ends I can't name. I wrap my arms around my waist under the cloaks. It's much warmer beneath them.

My throat is so dry. If only I had a glass of water. Then I could sleep. I could sleep for ages. Just sleep, and sleep, and sleep, and…

"Indigo?"

"What!" I open my eyes and the light returns.

"Don't fall asleep yet. Come on, I brought you a blanket." Atlas holds up a light throw under his chin.

I slide from the counter and sit on the floor of the hallway. It's a struggle to pull my boots off after tugging the laces loose. A tiny, paper-wrapped package tumbles out into view.

"What's this?" Atlas kneels down to probe the parcel.

"Provisions. I figured you weren't going to bring any."

Atlas throws his head back, but catches the laugh with a hand. "You actually brought prunes?" His shoulders shake with a fit of suppressed chortling. "And put them in your boot?"

"Yes. I also brought some almonds in my bag. I took your advice." This starts him off again. I sigh. "Clearly, you didn't take mine."

"I did." He gasps with another chuckle. "I have almonds in my pocket."

"Then why are you laughing?"

"Because…" He takes a breath to try to stop, but something about my face must strike him as hysterical and he bursts into laughter again. "Why would you put them in your boot? Don't you have pockets?"

"Yes, but that's so *obvious*. They could have stolen them."

"They searched both of us and took everything. Clearly, it didn't matter."

"It *might* have! Maybe someday it will. You never know."

Atlas just smiles. I can barely tell the colour of his eyes in the light from the open door. "If you say so. Do you still want this?" He holds up the blanket.

"Yes. Can I eat anything?"

Atlas tucks the folds around me.

"How do you feel about almonds and prunes?"

"Perfect."

He pulls out his own paper bag and unrolls the top. I reach my hand in. The flaky skin of the almonds makes my mouth water. Atlas draws his knees up to his chest and tosses a few nuts back. We eat in silence, passing the bag between us, until my fingers find the bottom. My breath comes more easily now.

Atlas closes his eyes and puts a hand to his forehead. Abruptly he turns to me. "I should check your pulse again."

"I'm sure it's fine."

"Give me your wrist." He puts out his hand.

"I just checked. It's normal."

He raises an eyebrow. "Why do I not believe you?"

"I don't know. Because you never do?" My voice goes higher at the end.

He gives me an exasperated look. "I only don't believe you when you lie to me. Give me your wrist."

I let out a sigh and roll my eyes at the ceiling. My poor hand is banished to the cold world outside the blanket yet again. Atlas's first and second finger find my vein.

"Will you count in your head and tell me when you get to thirty?"

"One, two, three…" I continue in my head.

He stares at my wrist, unblinking. The hall is so quiet without people coming and going. In different circumstances, it might even be peaceful.

"Stop," I say, before thirty-one can pass.

"You did lie to me." He doesn't sound surprised.

"It's not *quite* normal. But it's close enough."

"Close enough?" He scoffs. "I counted sixty-eight beats in thirty seconds. That's one hundred and thirty-six per minute."

"But isn't that normal?" I read something about the average heart rate for adults, but what did the book say, exactly? The numbers slip out of my mind before I can pin them down.

"You should be somewhere around eighty beats per minute, considering your age and lifestyle."

"Lifestyle?"

"Well…" Atlas draws the word out. "Most people don't fence and skulk around the city like you do."

"Skulk? I don't *skulk*. And visiting Walker's house was my first time actually *entering* a house illegally. But *I* was let into the house by a police officer. That's just as good as a warrant."

"Is it?" He leans his head against the wall, blinking down at me.

"Certainly. Everyone knows that."

He closes his eyes. "I'll have to remember that."

"Atlas!" My sudden exclamation startles his eyes open. "I forgot to tell you! Theodora *is* the Phantom. We were right!"

His chest expands with an intake of air. "I don't know if that's good news or bad."

"Good, of course! That means that our plan for the masquerade will work."

Atlas looks back at me, his expression a mix of emotions. "Or that now, she may run and we'll miss our chance. She could also try to get you before the masquerade. She knows where you live, who your parents are, everything!"

I frown. "That is unfortunate." But at least she doesn't know anything about Atlas. She can't even know his name, because I never mentioned it, and she's never met him. "You didn't tell her your name, did you?"

"She asked, but I told her it was William Smith. What'd she ask you?"

William Smith! Well played.

"Theodora asked me how I found them, but I didn't tell her anything. How did you escape?"

"One of the guards outside my door left when people started shouting down the hall. I just turned the ropes until the knot was in front of me. Then all I had to do was untie it, which took longer than I expected. Using the door, I knocked the other Invisible unconscious. From there, I took the mask and cloak. How did you manage to break Theodora's mask?"

"She smashed her mask on the table. I didn't do anything."

He casts me a look. "Sounds like you did *something*."

The memory of Theodora lying on the floor of the cellar, shards of mask arrayed around her, replays in my mind. What happened to make her so fragile?

"Indigo? Are you alright? Did she hurt you?"

"No, no. That's not it. I got her to tell me why she was doing this. Her husband was killed by Walker's poison. She murdered Walker herself by the same. Telling me made her so unstable that when I probed she... went over the edge. She started crying. She screamed—" I break off. "Well, then the Invisible outside came to see what was wrong, but I'd already used a shard of porcelain to cut the ropes. I got out and locked them both inside."

"I guess my guards left to find you, so that gave me my chance. Thanks."

"You're welcome."

We sit in silence for a few minutes. Atlas's chin drops to his chest, and his breathing becomes slow and even.

"Atlas?" I whisper.

He doesn't say anything. There's no light under the training room door, so I must have a few hours to get home. Atlas can sleep. If I drift off, who knows when I'll wake up? The image of Mrs Trinter's surprise flashes briefly before me.

I check my pulse every few minutes. It's a challenge to count the seconds and beats, but the rhythm lends itself to my efforts. The thumping gradually slows down to one hundred beats a minute, then ninety, then eighty.

"Atlas?" I whisper again.

Against his skin, his dark eyelashes look like the pen strokes of a master artist.

"Atlas."

I could just leave a note. There's got to be paper and a pencil around here somewhere. I'm sure I could find some. Or I could just leave a message in almonds. What would I spell? *Left? Not captured?* He'd figure that, though. *Home?* That's probably best. Quest will be waiting outside, and I'll just ride back. Atlas can wake up in a few hours and try to explain his strange predicament.

Ah. Except Quest isn't here. If I start walking now, I can make it back before dawn fully breaks. That'll give me just enough time to change and fall into bed for Phoebe to find me. What if the Invisibles are still out there, though? I'll have to be extra cautious.

I take the blanket off all at once and the cold slaps me. Not a bone chill this time, just skin-deep. My feet tingle slightly as they rest on the floor. For a moment, as the prickly feeling passes, I just stare up at the wall. Slipping my parcel of uneaten prunes into my pocket, I bring my boots towards me. The quick way home is taking the main street north for a mile or so, but that way is probably patrolled by a policeman or two. If I stay near the main street, but never go on it, I can go unnoticed or have the ear of an officer if I need it. That will be the safest way.

I put a hand to the wall and slide it up as I stand. The vague silhouette of my satchel slouches in the corner of the bathroom. Miraculously, there is no blood on it that I can see, it must have been on my left shoulder. Snatching the bag, I put it on and replace all the items on the counter back in the cupboard. The tin of safety pins clinks lightly against the glass shelves.

Atlas lifts his head up an inch. "What? Indigo?" He pushes away from the wall.

"I'm here. I didn't want to wake you. I'm starting out for home."

"You were going to leave? Did you check your heart rate?"

"I'm somewhere around eighty now."

Atlas runs a hand through his hair. "That should be right, I think. You shouldn't walk. We can ride Emil."

"Do you have something to wrap his shoes?"

Atlas blinks sleepily. "I can find something. Just… don't go anywhere."

"I won't."

* * *

I've never seen the city so quiet. Not a soul walks down the street or looks out a window. It's hard to imagine that the Phantom herself might walk these peaceful avenues during the day.

The clatter of Emil's feet is greatly lessened by the cloth Atlas found, but what about Quest? She had nothing to muffle her racket. She could have been found by a constable or even one of the Invisibles. What if Quest has woken the house and now Mother and Father are out in their undergarments looking for me? What if they've woken the neighbours? They could be tearing the house apart, or summoning the Inspector.

As we approach the house, no torches are lit at the gate. The iron bars are still closed and bolted. No one calls my name and no lights appear in the windows. Was Quest utterly silent, or is no one looking for me? A small sliver of ice pricks my chest. Did they find me missing and heave a sigh of relief? Not Phoebe. She'd look for me in her nightcap. Wouldn't she?

But no, there – Quest paws the ground underneath the ladder to my balcony. "Quest," I breathe, slipping off of Emil's back.

She trots forward, her head bobbing with each step. Her hair is soft beneath my chin as I rub her neck.

"You didn't miss me, did you?" She snorts into my ear, as if my inference would make a stuffed bird laugh. "Oh, I'm sure not." I shake my head, sighing.

Atlas is waiting a few feet away. I look out over the garden, in the direction of the city.

"If you hurry, you should have enough time to get back and still get some sleep."

He smiles wearily. "I already got some, but I will."

I watch him until he finally disappears behind the trees.

CHAPTER 17

$\mathcal{I}$ blink my eyes open to see Phoebe standing over me, practically nose-to-nose.

"What happened to your arm?"

"Ah!" I work my startlement into something less suspicious. "Ah. Good morning, Phoebe. Nice to see you up early."

She narrows her eyes, the surrounding skin forming little creases. "It's not early. In fact, I thought you'd gotten dressed an hour ago. What happened to your arm!" It's a demanding exclamation rather than a question. "Did something happen in the night?"

"No… Oh, yes! I scraped my arm on the…" I look around my room. "The…"

Her worry mixes with suspicion. "The…?"

"The…" It comes to me: "A nail! *The* nail. In the bathroom. On the trim." Even better for me, it's almost the right height.

Phoebe closes her eyes, sighing. "We need to get that fixed. I'm so sorry, Indigo." She stands, motioning to a dress at the end of the bed. "You should wear long sleeves, if you don't want your mother worrying about that cut. I'll be out today, so no more injuries."

My smile contains a bit of ruefulness. "I'll try to break the habit."

When she leaves the room, I sit up. It takes a moment to get the world into focus. My arm feels sore, but more than that, I'm hungry. However, feeling hungry in one's own house is much better than being dead in an abandoned mansion. If only I could lie back down and luxuriate in living, but there's no denying my stomach.

* * *

Now that I know Theodora's the Phantom, my plan for the masquerade ball is perfect, as long as she turns up. I invited her, assuming that she could be an Invisible, and she's already accepted the invitation. She'll most likely try to settle the score, perhaps trying to kill or kidnap me. What better time than when she's surrounded by alibis who'll swear she had no part in it?

What I'm counting on is that she doesn't know I also invited Inspector Wallace and his daughter, Rosana. It was a trick inviting such a prominent figure; in the end I used Father's connection to the Walker case to send the invitation. It's difficult to think of what to say to Rosana Wallace when I meet her. How will I explain my plan? I'll think of something. If not, Atlas will.

Mother won't allow me to go to circus practice until my arm is healed, so I won't see the Trinters until they come over for tea – eight whole days away! Reams of minutes. An infinity of seconds. I suppose I could just go over to 416 and ask to see Atlas, but Mr and Mrs Trinter must be getting word of my comings and goings somehow. They mustn't become suspicious of our activities.

* * *

ON MONDAY, Mother makes me try on the dress I'm to wear to the dance. It's really not too bad – the hemline reaches just below my ankles and pockets are hidden at my hips. It has cap sleeves, but, because of my arm, Mother insists they be extended, meaning there will be another fitting next week.

On Tuesday, I help Mother with the decorations. She bustles about the house, choosing between this or that. She asks my opinion only to go with her own anyway. Helping gives me a chance to determine extra escape routes for the ball. I have seventeen and a half planned out before dinner.

On my way to the dining room, I pass the door to Father's office, which is open. I stop midstep.

It's like seeing a ghost. The ghost of some long-dead friend: Father's telescope.

Once, when I was little, he bundled me up and let me see the full moon through it. I've wished so many times that I could remember what it looked like more clearly, but the impression of its beauty outlasts the moment. I do recall asking Father, kneeling next to me, if he would bring out his telescope the next night. He hesitated, his breath clouding in the cold air between us, the smile frozen on his face. "We'll see, darling," was all he gave for an answer.

Of course, the next night I waited through dinner for him to mention the telescope and stargazing, but the verdict of a case he'd been a part of had just come in and that was all he could talk about.

I eventually gave up waiting and asked. Father paused, as if trying to remember what telescope I was talking about. "No," he said quickly, once the memory came back to him. "I'm going to be busy and you saw the moon yesterday. Maybe some other time."

For the next few weeks I kept hoping to hear the racket of the tripod being adjusted, or Father asking me to join him on the balcony. I had my winter coat and a blanket for the two of us ready at the end of my bed. But eventually, I put the coat in the wardrobe and the blanket deep in the closet.

Father never mentioned the telescope again, and I haven't seen it since. I searched the attic for it a few years ago, but all I found were his old astronomy textbooks. He'd filled the margins with notes and clever jokes. For months, I pored over the books with only a lamp in the dark, and imagined Father was teaching me the constellations and their legends. But every morning I woke to see only the latest volume on my windowsill. After reading each, I put them back up in the attic. Partly to avoid being caught with them, but also because their presence eventually felt more like absence.

I think Father wanted to be an astronomer, but I can't be sure, because he's never told me so.

Standing in the hall, the sudden and overwhelming urge to show Father all that I've learned about his sky assails me.

"Father?"

"Yes?" He pokes his head into view. His hair is mussed.

"Is that your telescope?" A ridiculous question, but other words abandon me.

Childish light dances in his eyes. "Yes! Do you remember it? I showed you the full moon once." He laughs, shaking his head at the floor. "Probably a terrible idea. It must've been below freezing —"

"I remember."

Father catches something in my voice and looks up. I continue before he can ask the question that comes to his lips.

"Why have you brought it out?"

"Mr Trinter also studied astronomy and hasn't seen a telescope in some time. When I mentioned my reflector he expressed interest in seeing it." A thought suddenly strikes him. "Did you know he was studying to be a teacher! Mrs Trinter too, I believe."

"Atlas told me. Are you going to leave out the telescope?"

Father appraises me. "Yes, if you'd like." He turns to the brass body of the instrument, already pointed out the window. "Though, it's been so long it may take me some time to get reacquainted with adjusting it," he trails off.

"I could adjust it." The words are out of my mouth in a second. "I read your books. The ones in the attic." Why do I have to say such stupid things?

Father's expression falls into something akin to bewilderment. "My old books? The textbooks? You read them?"

"I'm sorry, but you weren't using them and they were just rotting up there and I fixed some of the covers that were falling apart - I'm sorry."

He walks to me, almost in a daze. "You liked them?"

I look from the buttons of his shirt to my hands. "Yes."

The seconds seem painfully long. I'm about to add to the pitiful description of the books' state when I found them when Father speaks.

"You may keep them if you enjoy them so much."

I meet his eyes: larkspur-blue like Olive's. "Really?"

He laughs, shaking something loose inside me. "I didn't realise you'd like them as much as I did. You could have asked about them. I have more in my office if you'd like to read them."

I gasp. "Really?" How have I not noticed them before? What are they about, exactly?

"I'll show you later. Come on, let's go down to dinner." Instead of moving, he peers quizzically at me a moment longer before saying, "You've gotten taller."

We walk together to the dining room.

* * *

"THEY'RE HERE! Phoebe, they're here!"

The balcony door slams closed. The sudden heat of my room compared to the spring chill presses down on me.

"They're here? Of course they're here. They're perfectly on time." She snaps closed the tiny pocket watch on her chatelain and rises to her feet with painful slowness.

"Yes, but it's taken *so long* for them to be on time."

After greetings have been passed around and Olive is introduced to the guests, Mrs Trinter holds up a new protective cylinder.

"These are the plans I want you to see. Is there a table I can lay them out on?"

Costumes that Mother hasn't seen yet? Atlas's unreadable look is completely useless.

"Of course. Indigo, why don't you and Olive show Atlas the grounds?"

What? She doesn't want me to see them? And we have to go with Olive? My sister folds her hands against her dress, fabric crinkling. She's trying to hide her disdain… or perhaps it's impatience. She's probably anxious to write Thomas Evans back.

"And Phoebe should go with you," Father adds hastily.

"I'll go ask her." I turn and take the steps two at a time.

"Indigo," Father says warningly.

I mount the last five steps one at a time.

When I'm hidden by the hallway wall, I sprint to Phoebe's door. She answers in only four seconds. Her knitting is still in her hand.

"Is anything wrong?"

"Nothing. Mother just wants you to accompany Olive, Atlas, and me to the gardens."

"Oh! Lovely. Did you leave Olive and Atlas downstairs?"

I glance down the hall. "I had to. Atlas should be fine, though."

Phoebe sets down her latest project and closes her door,

and we descend the stairs in a more stolid manner than I came up. Olive stands alone at the bottom of the stairway, drumming her fingers on the bannister, stopping only when we reach the bottom step.

Atlas pulls his blue jacket onto his shoulders as he comes through the doorway of the parlour, where the adults are. Once we're all together, I let Phoebe and Olive stride to the front. Phoebe, with a glimpse at Atlas and me, starts a conversation with Olive about her outing with Violet yesterday.

"Sorry, I didn't know *she* would be here," I whisper to my companion, inclining my head towards Olive.

"It's alright. Sorry Louise couldn't come…"

Olive opens the door and leads us outside. Sunlight looks down on the lawn, brushing it with gold. Carefree birds soar across the bright blue sky above, chirping spring melodies.

"I've never seen your house in this much light," Atlas says softly. His voice is cloaked by the sound of our feet on the gravel.

Even though some of their edges are crumbling, the bricks look rosy in the cherry sunlight. Forest-green moss and pale lichen poke between some of the slate roof tiles, before the decorative black railing marks the beginning of the flat roof. My balcony and ladder cast shadows on the windows below.

Gravel turns to a flagstone path. Our footsteps are no longer loud enough to cover a private conversation, so we pass the gazebo in silence, listening to Phoebe and Olive. The stately structure has a white painted frame topped with the same lichen and slate tiles as the house. Two trees spotted with pink blossoms stand on either side of the entry. Our "lake" – the size of a pond and only a few feet deep – lies beyond the little gazebo. A smooth stone wall about two feet high rings the perimeter. Playing by the lake was one of Olive's favourite things to do when we were younger. I pushed her in once. She was speechless with rage until I jumped in after her.

Following the path, we skirt the lake and come to the main part of the garden. Paths lead through the beds of flora. The opening flowers add verve to the various shades of green. My favourites are such a violent shade of blue they almost seem purple, but others are lacy yellow or fiery orange. Some already display their full glory: the white flowers with spots of yellow near their centres, and small bouquet-like blossoms that have pink and white petals. I hold out a hand and let it brush against the plants. The petals tickle my palm and wrist, there and gone in a second. A breeze – with a breath of colder weather – slips between the stalks and foliage, waltzing with the flowers.

At the centre of the garden reigns a tall fountain, over-flowing into a small pool. Waist-high hedges outline a paved circular walkway. The sound of the water must remind Olive she isn't making conversation, because she turns abruptly to Atlas.

"I understand that you have two siblings, is that right?"

"Yes. Louise should've been here, but had to stay home to practise her reading."

Olive presses on, "But your brother, he's older than you, isn't he?"

We pass through the white picket gate and enter the vegetable garden. Newly turned-up earth is marked with signs for cucumber, leek, and beetroot.

"Alexander is twenty…" Atlas squints; partly in thought and partly from the sun. "Twenty-three, I believe. He'll turn twenty-four in October."

Olive arranges the fall of her skirt, which is immediately ruined with her next step. "Do you see him much?"

Atlas shrugs, looking down at his shoes. "Not much anymore – he's off in France."

"Why?" Olive looks at Atlas from the corner of her eye. "Does he have a wife?"

I roll my eyes. Phoebe catches me and raises an eyebrow.

Atlas pretends not to notice. "No. He's studying to be a painter in Paris."

Olive nods slowly. "That's nice."

I suppose Thomas Evans will have to find some other hopeless romantic to send his poetry to. So sad. Maybe the heartbreak will inspire better verses than the ones he sent Olive.

Honeysuckle covers the fence protecting the vegetable garden. The plant has taken more and more of the white pickets with its twining fingers. Ahead lies the willow tree with the twin swings. Its ancient body stands even higher than the living walls of the maze.

There are two entrances to the maze. Both can lead you to the centre, but one is slightly faster. The walls are sanded wood with massive wisteria vines climbing all over. Already, some of the purple flowers drip down. Some vines are trying to cross over to the other side, but reach only into the walkway. Olive brushes these to the side contemptuously. To her credit, she never wavers, going through the maze just as deftly as we did years ago. We both know the fastest way to its heart, as well as its other secret spots. It's shadier in here, and I feel my brow relax.

"There's one more thing you need to see." Olive leads the way down the longest hall of the maze, to the very back. Looping around the wall and following it to another turn, we find ourselves at a shady dead end.

Olive's glove slips behind a knot of purple flowers and finds the iron handle. The door swings out easily, the vines still clinging to wood.

She strides out onto a small field. The trees on this part of the property remain untouched, sheltering what resides among them. We walk the length of the open field with Phoebe leading the discussion.

"Has your brother taught you any French?"

"A bit. I try to write to him in French, but sometimes I ask him how to say something."

"That's amazing," I say. "Mrs Wood tried to teach me, but she said my accent was so offensive it'd be better if I could honestly claim I didn't know a word." I laugh. "I've done my best to forget it all."

Phoebe and Atlas chuckle with me. Olive joins in, but scolds me with a look.

"You have gotten good at reading German, though. You can read that gymnastics book, can't you?" Phoebe probes.

"I find German much easier than French."

The brim of shade cast by the trees covers our party. Before us stands the outline of a raised platform, about twelve feet off the ground. Wide stone pillars lift it closer to the canopy of English oaks. The matte stone is weathered by years well beyond mine.

"We don't know why it was built, but Mother and Father sometimes have gatherings on it." I give Atlas a significant look. He nods. Our plan for the masquerade relies on this detail.

"They even thought about getting married up here," Phoebe adds wistfully. "They didn't, but it would've been so romantic."

Olive's mouth hardens. "It would have been highly irregular."

I run up the moss-covered stairs, calling over my shoulder, "Don't be so stiff, Olive."

Before she can tell me not to, I sweep away a patch of fallen leaves and sit on the edge of the raised floor. My feet dangle over the ground below. The pit in my stomach still drops a bit at the sight of the ground, but after jumping from a hammock, it's not so bad.

"Indigo…" Olive begins, but Atlas is already sitting beside me. She wouldn't dare chide him. I look over and he smiles conspiratorially. Olive waits a full thirteen seconds before suggesting we go back.

Instead of joining her, Atlas and I stay behind and convince Phoebe to try to find us in the maze. She starts counting back from thirty without warning.

I snatch Atlas's hand and we run across the sun-bathed field. The air rushing past my ears and cheeks has the same edge as earlier. My skirt tangles around my legs, but I don't slow down. Phoebe was being a bit cruel with thirty seconds; it's just barely enough.

Inside the maze, I lead Atlas to the corner farthest away from where Phoebe will enter. Knowing her, she'll take a methodical route, checking each nook before moving on. When we reach the corner, I let go of Atlas's hand and drop onto the bench.

"Let's go over what will need to be in place before the guests arrive. I'll put the ladder on the guest room balcony."

"How are you going to get it up?" Atlas interrupts. His shirt is untucked from running and his jacket hangs from his shoulders. A slight flush is receding into his collar.

I shrug. "Take it through the house, I guess. Don't forget to bring the chalk."

"I won't." He takes the seat next to me. "Has Theodora rescinded her acceptance of the invitation?"

"No. Not yet, at least. Do you think she will?"

Atlas props his elbow on the arm of the bench, resting his head on his knuckles. "I don't know, honestly. If it doesn't work then we'll try something else."

If it *completely* fails and one of us dies, then I suppose the other could still continue the case.

"Indigo, Atlas! Where are you?" Phoebe is closer now; only a few walls divide us.

I spring up and shout, "Come try to catch us." I sprint down the hall, waving a hand at Atlas. He races after me.

CHAPTER 18

Mother doesn't schedule any circus lessons this week on account of the ball. Something about being "properly prepared". It's probably because she doesn't want me to be sore or bruised. However, at my request, Mother and I have devised a surprise for Phoebe. I'm at least kept busy with that and the new astronomy books Father shared with me.

After an early dinner on the evening of the ball, I sneak downstairs while Phoebe is writing to her sister. Mother waits in the foyer with the secret bundle in her arms.

She speaks softly. "Make sure you don't wrinkle it."

"I won't." I run up the stairs on my toes.

"The envelope is wrapped inside," Mother whisper-shouts behind me.

After stowing the gift in my wardrobe, I knock at Phoebe's door.

"Yes?"

I lean down to the keyhole. Phoebe sits at her desk, one hand tilting the paper up while the other hovers a pencil over the next line.

"My dear Phoebe, we simply must start getting ready."

She sets her pencil down on the desk with a hollow tap. "What? You want to get ready now?" Her pocketwatch clicks open. "It's so early."

"Certainly finish your letter, but then we really should begin."

Phoebe stares confoundedly at the keyhole for a few seconds. "If you say so…" After a few blinks she picks up her pencil again, shaking her head. "I'll be done in a minute."

Back in my room, I take out my tin of hairpins and arrange the chair at the dressing table until it's just so. Skipping to the wardrobe, I unfold the bundle and dig out the envelope.

Phoebe walks into my room. "Indigo… What's going on? I know you have something —"

I spring to her and throw my hands up. "Close your eyes!"

She closes them and knits her brow. "What are you going to do?"

I take her hand in one of mine. "Take this." I lay the creamy envelope in her open palm.

"Can I open my eyes now?"

I step backwards. "Yes."

Her brown eyes widen at the sight of the supple paper. With a short intake of breath she lifts it up to gaze at the name in looping ink: *Phoebe J. Adgate.* Her little finger slides easily under the flap. The sound of paper against paper precedes a surprised gasp.

"Indigo…"

I run to the closet and lift out her costume. "Here! I wanted it to match your necklace."

She takes the dress gently, almost reverently, from my outstretched hands. As she does, it unfolds; the mask, tied to one of the buttons, drops to its full length. It's a gorgeous imitation of a luna moth. The white underskirt is layered with a pale green satin edged with burgundy. The green bodice is detailed with buttons to match the trim.

"What...?"

My fingers knot themselves together. "I had to steal one of your dresses temporarily to measure everything. But I put it back right away, exactly where it was!" I bite my lip. "You don't mind, do you?"

She lays the dress across the rocking chair, smoothing an errant wrinkle. "Mind?" A golden laugh tumbles out of her. "It's perfect. Thank you so much." She hugs me and I let out a breath. After a moment, she lets go to wipe her eyes with a hand. "I don't know what to say."

"Just have a fun evening."

Phoebe laughs again and rests her hand on her hip, looking down at me. Her scolding look fails to hide her smile. "Now, we have to get you dressed or you and I will have the devil to pay."

I will not allow it. After helping her dress I motion for her to sit at my dressing table. "Please be seated, Mademoiselle. It's no use arguing the point."

"Oh..." Phoebe frowns, but only with one corner of her mouth. "Alright." She situates herself before the mirror. "What are you thinking of?"

"A French plait, of course, twisted into a bun at the end." I separate three thin strands of her thick hair from the top of her crown.

"Oh! Ow!" Phoebe screws her face into an expression of agony, wringing her hands. "You're pulling my very scalp off. I have a sensitive skull, you know."

I drop the pieces of hair. "I'm so sorry! I'm sorry! I thought..."

Phoebe relaxes instantly into an impish grin. "I was teasing, Indigo. You always claim I'm rough when I do your hair. But I never pull hard, or even —"

"You startled me." My cheeks grow hot and I gather new strands of hair, twining them around each other. "I thought I was hurting you."

"You hardly touched my hair."

"Whatever you say, Mademoiselle. I just know that if I were doing someone's hair and they expressed intense pain, I would want to be extra careful."

"I am extra careful," she sighs. After a moment she taps the wood with a finger. "So, I heard that Atlas is coming tonight..." She blinks at me in the glass, a quirk to her lips.

"Yes." I pick up more hair, closer to the middle of her head. "I thought it was fitting." I look up, pausing my work. "Did I overstep?"

"No!" Phoebe shakes her head. My hand is pulled in her wake. "Not at all. I was just noticing."

"Hmm." I return to the plait.

If it was completely fitting, then why would she bring it up? Is she worried about him coming? She doesn't know about the case, so what could... Oh, no! What if she thinks he's a pyromaniac who's going to burn the house down? But she doesn't have anything to worry about. Atlas isn't a pyromaniac. He's far too cautious. Should I tell her that? Would that be odd? She might take my confidence as too quickly given and worry about me dying in the flames. Perhaps not specifically set by Atlas, but some other well-meaning pyromaniac. She can just imagine my crisped hand outstretched in a final bid for salvation... How tragic.

But Phoebe shouldn't worry about me. Not about me dying in a fire set by Atlas, anyway. I won't tell her, then. Who knows how she might picture things? Can't have her getting any preposterous ideas into her head.

I reach the nape of her neck; all the hair has been brought into the plait. "Hairpins?"

Phoebe pushes the tin to the edge of the dressing table. They rattle as I select one.

"Did you ever go to any dances, Phoebe?"

"One or two. They were usually just at one of my friends' houses." A distant smile touches her face. "I was always so tired the next day."

I thread the strings of the mask through her plait. "Try that."

She shakes her head to make sure it'll stay.

"But there was never anyone like Atlas." Phoebe's unreadable smile creeps over her face, as if she's trying to pry something from me.

It doesn't *seem* as though she thinks Atlas is a pyromaniac; but then what *does* she think?

"Anything else I should do?"

She shakes her head in the mirror. "Not a thing, thank you."

I give her a hug from behind. She squeezes my arm. The comforting effect is ruined by her suddenly serious look.

"Your turn."

* * *

No one, excluding Phoebe, will know I'm wearing my boots. Or another skirt with ties (already done up) and a shirt beneath my dress. Phoebe assumes it's because Leo, Poppy, Atlas, and I will escape for some fencing. I am to be the sky. The skirt and bodice of my dress are pale blue, with silver buttons down the front. The high collar and bishop-sleeve cuffs are white. The dress isn't too hot and it shouldn't be hard to change out of quickly. Phoebe plaits my hair around my head and adds a cloud-shaped silver hair comb at the back. My mask is painted blue with white clouds.

It's finally time for guests to begin arriving. I stay at the top of the stairs while Phoebe, the luna moth, gracefully floats down. She turns her head back up to me. "Aren't you coming?"

"I'm going to watch the others arrive."

Phoebe looks at the front door, then nods at me. "Alright."

Just as she reaches the bottom stair, a family arrives. A mediaeval king and queen accompany Marie Antoinette and an army general. The Luckfords! Marie Antoinette is a perfect fit for Violet. The mediaeval monarchs greet Phoebe kindly, but the general is the one who asks her questions as they disappear from view. Leo hasn't seen Phoebe in over a year. Such a long time, considering we used to see them so often.

Next arrives a trio – perhaps Poppy and her family? There's a rose, a lion, and someone from the turn of the century. Poppy must be the rose. How ironic. It isn't customary for children to be invited to a dance, but because I'm the one who suggested the idea, Mother was willing to acquiesce to my request.

The rose's hands flit from her face to her hair while the lion and perhaps one of Jane Austen's characters illustrate a point with their hands. When they pass, others, harder to recognise, file through the door: a woman in a glowing yellow dress, a man in a colonial costume, a couple with colourful garlands around their necks. I lean a shoulder against the wall. After a few more couples file past I prop my elbows on the railing. None of the guests think to look up to the top of the stairs.

Next comes a single person. A woman in a fitted black gown strides through the door. Her shattered black mask has been put together with something white, creating a spider web across her face. By her side is an elegantly carved walking stick with a heavy silver handle. I stiffen. What is she trying to be? She's wearing that mask to… What? Scare me? Challenge me?

I take a deep breath and walk down the stairs, lifting the front of my dress. I trail Theodora, losing sight of her only for a moment as she follows the guiding ribbons around a corner. When I come around, she turns her head just slightly to call back, "You can't hide from me in that costume." She shows her profile now. "Do you like my mask?"

A single vein of white by her eye is extra-wide. They must have been unable to find all the pieces. Is the piece I cut my bonds with back in that mask? I left it there, so perhaps.

I take longer strides to draw even with her. "I heard that you told everyone I knocked you out and broke your mask. My legend grows, I suppose."

The black glove resting on the cane grips it tighter. "I did what I had to."

We follow the gold ribbons that are strung up to guide the guests. Some of Theodora's natural composure returns.

"I would call you brave for inviting me into your home, but it's likely foolishness."

Before a retort comes to mind, we enter the parlour. Theodora breaks away and melds with the party, instantly invisible.

If I remember correctly, the refreshments table is just on the other side of the room. If I make my way there, and don't get distracted, Rosana will show herself in time. I thread my way between guests. As they notice me, I'm met with a few strange looks. On the invitations, Mother thought it best not to mention that youths would be attending. I agreed wholeheartedly. Theodora won't be expecting Rosana *or* Atlas to be here.

"Indigo!" Leo catches my arm.

"I thought you were the general. What a brilliant idea!"

His hand drifts toward his lapel to play with a black-and-red striped ribbon above a silver medal. "Thank you. Have you seen Poppy?"

"Yes, she's here somewhere. I saw her come in."

Over his shoulder, a couple decked out in red and another curious character stroll into the room. I don't immediately recognise them, but they head straight for me.

"Indigo, what a lovely costume!"

Mrs Trinter's pearl-coloured dress is embroidered with diamond-shaped red glass beads. Ropes of jewels lie across her shoulders and a crown of red diamond shapes is nestled into her hair. Mr Trinter's doublet is marked by the scarlet ornaments and by his side is a sword and scabbard inlaid with the same. Atlas's costume is blue and silver; his half-mask has points at the top, like inverted icicles, and white tips the ends of his dark hair. He must be Jack Frost.

"Thank you! You're all dressed marvellously! This is my friend, Leonard Luckford. Leo, this is Mr and Mrs Trinter, and their son Atlas."

"A pleasure," they all say.

The room now seethes with guests, more than I can give names to. But out of them all, I don't see who I am looking for. Wait, there! That must be Rosana and her father. "I must go greet the Wallaces, if you will excuse me."

Jack Frost tips his chin down in a nod.

The Wallaces start to move off, but I fall in behind them and catch up before they start talking to an older couple.

"Welcome, I am Indigo Taylor. And you are…"

They turn and I retract my hand.

The man and woman bow. "I am Andrew Leithe, and this is my wife, Bridget. A pleasure to meet you, Miss Indigo."

I curtsy. "The pleasure is all mine. If you will excuse me…"

I'll have to try again. Mr and Mrs Leithe move off, leaving me in the swarm.

Jack Frost comes up beside me, speaking under his breath. "How's your arm?"

I no longer have to keep bandages on, but I feel the raised edge of the scab underneath my sleeve. "It's fine. How about you?"

"I'll be fine if all goes to plan. I think I found Rosana. She's the one dressed as a Greek muse."

I can't see where he's looking through his mask. Atlas slightly inclines his head as a large Louis XIV moves through. Not ten feet away is Rosana. She is indeed wearing a linen dress trimmed with red, and a golden half-mask.

"How are you going to ask her?" He sounds curious, and perhaps even… anxious?

"I have something in mind."

Atlas purses his lips. "Will it work?"

"Possibly."

I lead the way to the Greek muse.

"Hello, Rosana. I'm Indigo Taylor. This is my friend, Atlas." Just in case this plan doesn't work *quite* as I imagine, it's best not to involve the Trinters' name.

"A pleasure to meet you both."

She curtsies deeply. Should I have done that? Rosana is the daughter of an important figure. I can't remember all the rules, but her gesture seems unnecessary.

Rosana smiles coyly at Atlas. "I… well." She titters lightly. "I suppose you already know my name."

I clear my throat loudly. "Rosana."

Her gaze snaps away from Atlas. She appraises me from head to toe with a neutral expression. No time for dealing with her personal opinions – this is too important.

"We're in great peril and we need your help."

I can't see Atlas's face clearly, but I *feel* his eyebrows go up. Rosana looks suspicious.

"What is it?" She takes off her mask to look at us directly, but her expression remains reserved. She has a dainty oval-shaped face and hazel eyes. The police outside of Walker's house must never have actually seen Rosana, because other than our dark hair and silhouette, there's very little in common about our appearance.

I steeple my fingers. "It's a rather long story. But before you answer you need to know that if you help us, you may be putting yourself in grave danger. I need you to keep this a secret, though. If you tell a soul, even whisper it to anyone, Atlas and I will probably be dead by morning."

Atlas's eyebrows go up further behind his mask.

Anger mixed with confusion clouds Rosana's face. "Why me?"

"That is also a long story, which we don't have time for. Before I can tell you more, you have to decide. Will you help us?"

She waits a moment, looking between us. She glares at Atlas as she opens her mouth and raises an accusatory finger. "I don't know what you two are playing at, but I am not interested. If you would like to have a *civilised* conversation, I'll gladly lend an ear." She turns wounded eyes away from Atlas.

Rosana sniffs and stalks off, putting her mask back on. I scoff.

Jack Frost tilts his head. "That was an interesting tactic. I would have gone about it a little differently."

I wave a hand in Rosana's direction. "I appealed to her bravery and selflessness." If someone had told me they needed my help or someone was going to *die*, I'd see what's to be done.

He hums. "That may not have been a good plan."

In the corner of my vision, Poppy hovers at the edge of the crowd, peering at the guests. She doesn't notice Leo sneaking up behind her. He covers her eyes and she throws up her hands. He moves away; they're both laughing.

Another awful scheme appears in my head, fully formed, as if it's been waiting for me to notice it.

"What is it, Indigo?"

I stomp and turn to Atlas. "You can do that even when I'm wearing a mask? It's nothing. I won't do it. Don't do that thing where you predict what I am thinking to make me loosen my tongue. It won't work. We both almost died last time."

"Well, Indigo, I need you to not keep this a secret. If you don't tell a soul, or even whisper it to anyone, you and I will probably be dead by morning." He copies my speech, even my tone.

I glare at him.

"Unless you can think of any other plans, I think we're going to have to go with whatever you just thought up. Rosana either thinks we're insane or playing with her."

"*If* we tell them, we'll have to explain *everything* before they make their decision."

"Why didn't you help Rosana understand?"

"I didn't want to say too much. She'd probably tell her father, who might try something early."

"I wondered if that was your reason."

"Oh, be quiet, you."

* * *

"So you've been leading a secret life all this time?" Poppy's eyes are wide.

"It is not a secret life… It's more like a second nature." I confess in the privacy of the library.

Leo steps forward, his hand resting on the hilt of his costume sword. "Well, whatever it is, count me in. Of course I'll help you."

Poppy stands next to Leo, taking his arm. "I will too. Why didn't you tell us sooner?"

"Well, I asked Rosana Wallace, but she refused to help." I say her name with a trace of bitterness.

"The Inspector's daughter?" Leo looks impressed.

"Yes. We look somewhat similar and are about the same height. She and I were going to leave the dancing just before the party heads outside."

Leo's brow furrows. "Outside?"

"Yes, it's already set up. It's all part of the plan." I nod in Atlas's direction. He took off his mask once we got to the library and I introduced him to Leo and Poppy.

"Do tell us this plan." Leo squares his shoulders.

Atlas and I explain the gambit, what the Invisibles will likely be wearing, and describe Theodora's mask.

"I can take Rosana's place," Poppy says hesitantly.

"Are you sure about this?"

Leo and Poppy nod.

* * *

As we walk back to the party, I go over the plan in my mind. Poppy, Leo, Atlas, and I will complete some mandatory dancing. I'll leave. Soon after, Mother and Father will announce that everyone is moving outside, Poppy will follow me. When we meet in my room, she'll put on my mask and dress. By this time, everyone will be on their way to the platform beyond the gardens.

This will be the most likely time for an ambush. Poppy will sit on my bed, while I hide underneath. They will either come from the hallway, the balcony, or one of the windows. When they do, Poppy will throw chalk in their eyes, run onto the balcony, and scream. I'll emerge and run for the guest room balcony, climb the ladder to the roof and kick it away. I might have a pursuer, but that's unlikely - Poppy will be wearing my dress. However, once on my balcony she'll be in view of the Inspector, thanks to Leo and Atlas. When the Inspector is done arresting the Invisibles, Atlas will come find me.

"Indigo... Indigo?" Poppy is worrying her lip and staring at me.

"Yes? Sorry, what is it?"

People have moved towards the centre of the room, and music has already begun.

"We should join the next dance."

I shake my head, clearing it. "Right. Of course. I was just thinking through the plan again."

Leo and Poppy both gawk at Atlas. He shrugs.

Poppy whirls around to me. "He told us you were thinking through the plan and wouldn't respond."

Atlas grins. An exasperated sigh escapes me as I select a shortbread square from a plate. The dance has already started, so the four of us hang back in the ring of spectators, conveniently next to the sweets. Leo and Poppy stand in front of me, whispering. Between their heads, I catch sight of Phoebe, dancing.

Phoebe deserves all the happiness I can give her. All the happiness in the world, really. Maybe someday that means that she'll have to leave… but I hope that won't be for a long, long time. I let another shortbread square dissolve on my tongue.

Jack Frost steps up next to me. He takes a dainty but doesn't ferry it to his mouth, instead using it to point out the tall woman on the outskirts of the room.

"Mrs Thwite has an interesting costume." Atlas's tone wouldn't be out of place at an afternoon garden party.

Theodora isn't dancing, choosing instead to chat with Mr Leithe.

"I don't like it much."

"The cane looks heavy. And the handle is made to be held differently."

I follow his look. The collar is extra long, and the derby handle is barely wide enough for her fingers.

I swallow. "She could be injured?"

He shakes his head. "It is hard to tell, but I think it's part of her costume." The last words are coated with extra emphasis.

"Hmm. I see what you mean."

Atlas still doesn't eat the sweet.

"Are you going to eat that?"

He contemplates the biscuit. "No."

I pinch it from between his fingers, a few crumbs falling to the floor. I push them under the tablecloth with the toe of my boot.

"Mother doesn't like them, so we never have any in the house."

"How can you eat now?"

"This is either going to work, or it isn't." I hold up the stolen biscuit. "So I'm going to enjoy this while I can." It'd be easy for Theodora to slip some of Walker's "creation" into my glass, which is why I'm not drinking anything.

Below his mask, the corner of Atlas's mouth turns up. "Don't forget this."

From his pocket he takes the fist-sized jar of chalk. I pop the biscuit into my mouth and dust off my hands. The blue glass is warm. Inside is a fine, snow-like powder. I tilt it, sending an infant avalanche towards the lid.

"Perfect. Thanks, Atlas."

"You're welcome."

The glass fits neatly in my pocket; the skirt hides the jar well. All the pieces are coming together. Not long now.

"So I suppose you and I will be dancing together?"

Atlas looks almost surprised. "Unless you'd prefer not to?"

"Who else would I dance with?" I say dismissively. "Besides, I very much doubt you want to partner with Rosana."

The sound of polite clapping marks the end of the dance. The first strains of a cotillion sound as Leo, Poppy, Atlas, and I step out onto the floor.

The tune is fast-paced, but the turns will allow us to observe the entire room without looking suspicious. Four couples stand in a square. Pairs on opposite sides meet in the middle briefly before going back to their original places. Leo, Poppy, Atlas and I repeat this, before we all turn outward to the people ringing the floor. The motions come so naturally that I hardly have to think about them. Instead, I turn my energy to searching for Theodora in the crowd. Andrew Leithe is easier to spot; he's in another group of four couples with his wife Bridget.

Atlas and I are split apart and a short woman comes between us in time with the music. I follow the steps and am beside one of Father's friends. He just has time to recognise me and furrow his brow in confusion before I'm back with Atlas. His eyes flick away, pointing to something.

As we turn, I look over his shoulder. Theodora is talking to the Inspector. A bold choice. She's probably trying to secure him as an alibi. She must have gathered by now that we have a plan and might be trying to see what the Inspector knows about it. Luckily, he and Rosana are totally uninformed. Theodora can't wheedle any information out of him or his daughter, making it impossible for her to use our scheme against us.

Atlas leaves my side and Leo takes his place, only for a second. As the music ends, I'm hit with the feeling that I wish the dance had been longer, that I could have had a moment more. Atlas bows and I curtsy. The four of us cluster at the dessert table. Violet Antoinette glares over a golden-brown pastry from across the table.

"Remember the plan?"

Everyone nods. I pull my shoulders back and march around the perimeter of the room. Few notice me as I pass them, and those who do return to their conversations in a moment. In the doorway to the hall, I turn back. Leo and Poppy talk with heads together, shadows falling over their tilted faces. Atlas stands with his arms by his side, watching me. For a moment my view is blocked by a young couple. When they move on, I see him again. He nods once.

I lift a hand and turn away.

Mother and Father – or Queen Vic and Albert – tap champagne flutes with spoons, capturing the room's attention.

* * *

THE UPSTAIRS HALL is dark and quiet. A faint spine of light emanates from under Phoebe's door, but there isn't a note of movement to disturb the stillness. The scrape of my door's latch is like a shout in the empty hall. Before it can retract all the way, clicking in its housing, I press the wood inward. The visible wedge of my room is as I left it. Every object remains in its place. The balcony doors and windows are still locked. Not much protection, but good to know all the same.

I lock the door to my room behind me. I start on the buttons at my neck. They're so petite and smooth, it's hard to loose them. My fingernails slip a third time. I blow out a breath between my lips. Calm down.

I snatch the buttonhook from a drawer in the dressing table and finish the job. Peeling off the dress, I lay it on my bed. Just as the buttonhook is thrust into my pocket, knuckles tap lightly at the door. *Knock... Knock, knock... Knock, knock.*

Poppy is paler than usual. I pull her over the threshold and lock the door behind her.

"Are they starting to leave?"

She speaks in a hushed, breathless tone. "Yes. Leo and Atlas have begun talking to the Inspector."

She turns her back to me and I start on her buttons. Seventeen seconds later, they're undone. Poppy takes my dress and shimmies it up her waist. When I'm done with the buttons, I hand her my mask. The light from outside is enough to see her features dimly; most striking is the terror in her eyes.

I take her hand. "Poppy. You need to relax. It's going to be over soon. You'll be fine."

She bounces her head up and down. "Do you think the switch will work?" Her voice trembles.

"I'm sure it will. With chalk in their eyes they won't be able to make out our faces. The jar is in your pocket. Do you think you can make it down the ladder in my skirt?"

Poppy looks down at her feet. "It shouldn't be a problem."

"The boys will have the Inspector waiting for you outside."

I lift the bedskirt and climb under. The bed creaks slightly as Poppy sits. I settle in for the wait. I count two minutes and thirty-two seconds. Still silence. Three minutes. Four minutes. What if there isn't going to be an attack? What if the Invisibles decide to take the Inspector hostage? What if it wasn't Theodora behind that mask? No, that was definitely her voice. What if she does something unexpectedly... expected, and simply enjoys the evening?

A tap sounds at my window. My pulse thumps inside my ears. Ticking comes from the hall door: the sound of a lock being picked. The bed groans, and I see Poppy's shoes on the floor. She's shaking. As the soft metallic sound continues, her red slippers advance to the door. The lid of the jar scrapes open.

Click. The door handle turns slowly. All the muscles in my body are tense as I hold my breath. A bead of sweat runs down my neck.

A howl and a cough.

"You little —"

What?

"You —" More coughing. "How dare y—"

Poppy screams and her feet dash across the rug to the balcony door. A small, metal object clatters. Poppy's breathing is panicked now, inhale and exhale barely separated. The key! Its tiny body lies prone on the floorboards, glinting in the last light of the sun.

The blue cloud dress flares out around Poppy as she drops

to her knees and gropes for the object. Boots stride across my rug. Despite their size, they make hardly any sound. I reach out, take the ankle in my hand, and pull. The man's body crashes to the floor, the back of his head connecting first. I'm out from under the bed and take the key from the floor. I thread it into the keyhole and twist.

The wardrobe begins to open.

The wardrobe! An Invisible was in here since the very beginning? They've heard everything!

A dark-grey wolf mask leers between the ever-growing opening. Poppy's hand plunges into the jar and an arc of white trails her fist. The powder lands squarely in the open eyeholes of the mask.

"Out. Now!" I push Poppy out the balcony door. She stumbles, catching herself against the railing. The fallen assassin, wearing a mask made of newspapers, regains his feet just as I fly past him.

"No, don't! They're bringing the Insp—"

The shout is unheeded, and the balcony door slams.

The Invisible from the wardrobe stumbles after me into the hallway, trying to dispel the dust without taking off his lupine mask. If I go for the ladder, he'll catch me before I can get up. Guess I'll have to use one of the other routes. I duck into the linen closet. Climbing the walls, I reach the top shelf. A few sheets fall to the floor with a *whump*. The door is flung open. I pull myself up through the hole with my hands first, then push off the timber with my elbows.

The Invisible catches my bootlace. I kick with the other foot. My toes connect with nothing but a shelf. Still, the lace slips through his gloved fingers. An unholy snarl comes from the man. My knees find purchase and I scramble up. I'm sure he'd follow if he could, but even I can barely fit through.

There's enough space for me to walk in the attic if I'm crouching, but none to spare. My head bangs against a low beam but I hardly feel it. One foot in front of the other. How long do I have until he finds the other way up into the attic? It's more likely he'll find me here than think to climb the ladder to the roof. I can get to the roof, but it's risky.

The west-facing windows let in shafts of the fading sunset. All that's left now are pink-and-purple clouds. I pull the catch and tug the glass circle towards me. It's about one-and-a-half feet wide. It swings in with a shriek. Turning my back to the window, I use an underhanded grip to pull myself up and sit in the curve. I extract my legs from the small opening to stand on the flair of the roof.

A balcony is below, but after that… only the ground. I bury my head in the crook of my arm while my left hand grips the coping. I can do this. I skirt the edge of the dormer, lean forward and scramble up the sloped tiles to reach the decorative railing that rims the flat of the roof. I hoist myself up and over.

Exhaustion forces me to sit for a moment. My hip is bruised badly, and a lump is rising on my head, a few tresses of my hair are aged with chalk. Small price to pay.

The lights of the party shine across the field and through the oaks. Wind orchestrates the branches of the trees. The pastel clouds are fading to blue-grey. The stars will be out soon and the moon is already up.

Relief washes over me at the sound of footsteps on the roof. They're coming from the direction of the ladder. Atlas! Clearing my head, I stand to greet him. "How did it go —"

Theodora strides forward. She now wears trousers and a black frock coat. Her cracked black mask looks somehow livid as she draws a slender sword from her cane. The silver blade is inlaid with a single line of black.

I wish I could draw a sword, perhaps an all-silver one, with strands of metal spiralling out for a guard. All I can find in my pocket is the buttonhook.

"Interesting choice. Did you not think to bring a sword?" She takes off her mask, stowing it in a pocket.

"No, I thought I'd give you a fighting chance." Why *didn't* I bring a sword? That would have been a good idea… aside from the fact that I don't own a *real* one and it would have made my climb thrice as difficult.

Theodora gives a bemused smile. "How very considerate."

"Why are you here? Don't you want to secure your alibi among the partygoers?"

"I would, but my companions are indisposed."

"Shall we have a real match, then?" I wave my weapon. "You give me your sword, and you can have this?"

"No, I think not."

Well, that was a bit of a stretch.

She advances slowly, step by step. In a flash, she lunges, trying a stop-hit, stop-cut, but she times it badly and I step out of range. She attempts a flèche. I duck out of the way. I execute a point-in-line with my buttonhook, but she's not playing by any rules. She attacks. I'm forced to parry with my hook, which isn't much better than a knitting needle. I disengage, and my feet pound across the roof.

She chases. I turn and stop in time to counter. Her parries are more like attacks, making them difficult to combat. I try a balestra, but go to the side instead; her blade catches the buttonhook. She spins, bringing her sword around. I drop to my knees to duck the blow, pain hammering up my thigh. I hear the swish of her next cut above my head.

I stand and bring my "sword" around, catching Theodora's blade. The metal of her weapon slides down mine. The tip is only inches from my face. The central ridge of her blade flashes the light of the sky above. I step back and let her sword swing out. This leaves her open. I hit her shoulder where it meets the collarbone with the handle of the buttonhook. She screeches, retaliating by roughly swinging her sword in a large arc. The abused shaft of the buttonhook clashes with the edge of her blade as it comes back. The force of the impact vibrates up my wrist.

I switch hands. Theodora makes another attempt, forcing me to back up again. The roof behind me is quickly running out. I try to duck her next attack, but her swing is lower than expected. I roll to the side. The solid roof beneath my spine is unforgiving. When I'm older, I'll have a straw roof, just in case I need to duel with any murderers again.

When I'm up and standing in the en garde position, Theodora rushes in a frenzy. I go under her arm and come around, hitting her in the back of the head. She falls to the roof limply, her head striking slate with a loud *crack*. Blood oozes from under her hair.

The trickle of wine-dark liquid forms a widening pool.

I didn't kill her, did I?

As much as I don't like Theodora Thwite, I don't want to kill her. Kneeling, I put two fingers to her wrist. Nothing. I move them inward.

Erratic beats pulse, too fast to count.

Theodora catches my wrist. Before I can blink, my arm is twisted behind me and I hear my buttonhook clatter away. Theodora flips me over, planting her heel in the soft spot below my sternum. What little air is inside my lungs comes out in a pained cry.

In slow motion, Theodora raises the blade above her head.

I've never seen anyone look so tormented. It's as if she's lost everything in the world, like she is all that's left. Her anger burns unshielded, and it hurts to look at. I can't tell whether her fury is directed at me or herself.

The dying light gilds the blade as it starts its slow descent. From here, it just appears as a slit in the sky. A line almost overlooked. How could so small an imperfection end everything?

I wonder what my family will think when I am dead. Phoebe will miss me, won't she? My poor family. They'll have to hire someone to clean all the blood from the roof. I certainly wouldn't want to do that. Maybe my head will roll into the shrubs and they'll go searching for it. It doesn't really matter, I suppose, where my body ends up after I am dead.

I am onto the next great adventure.

CHAPTER 19

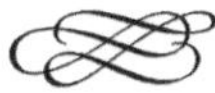

"Oho there! Stop that! I am an Inspector of the Royal Crown. Drop your sword, this instant!"

Stepping over the roof is a man in an Inverness cape and deerstalker hat, a pipe dangling from the side of his mouth. Cuffs are already clinking in his hands. I don't think I'll ever be happier to see Inspector Wallace.

"That's it. Now, slowly turn and face me. I'm placing you under arrest, Theodora Thwite."

All the fight has drained out of her. She looks dazed.

"Give me your hands, madam."

She obeys immediately, like a child afraid of being scolded. Inspector Wallace slips the manacles over her wrists and I hear them lock.

He peers down sideways at me. "You are alright, aren't you? Very good. Do you have a place to hold four people while I send for my associates?"

"Four?"

"Yes, four. Do you have a root cellar, or outbuilding?"

A moment passes before the answer comes to me. "We have a cellar."

He shifts the unlit pipe to the other corner of his mouth. "That'll do nicely."

"Where's Poppy? What about Atlas and Leo?"

Theodora's eyes blaze like a cat who's just caught an elusive bird.

I mentioned his name. Now she knows that the boy with me was either Leo or Atlas, and she can easily figure it out from there. Why did I have to ask? How could I be so careless?

"Hmm? Oh, yes. They're fine. The girl is in some shock, but the lads are seeing that she calms down. Come along, now."

* * *

"I'M SORRY, Indigo, I am so, so, so sorry. You almost… It would have been all my fault." The tears that have been filling her eyes finally spill over. I haven't seen Poppy cry in years.

Atlas and Leo are talking to the Inspector, so I lead Poppy to the kitchen. Atlas made sure I was warm when I was in shock, so I can't think of a better place to take her. The cooks leave after one glance.

"It would not have been *your* fault. But while I was up on the roof, I had a thought." I wrap my arms around Poppy and she clutches my neck. I speak in a very calm, soothing tone. "When I die, which may be sooner than I think, I need you or someone else to sprinkle dried rose petals over my coffin – some of the ones from the abandoned mansion." I pat her back, like Phoebe used to when I had a nightmare. "You may want to start drying them now."

Poppy bursts into a new onslaught of tears. But why? What could be more assuring than the fact that I've come face to face with mortality and have placed my few simple requests with a loving friend? What else could I say?

Atlas and Leo peek into the room with worried looks. I hold up a finger. They disappear from the doorway.

Poppy steps away and wipes her eyes. I put a hand to her back and guide her to the sink, where she splashes her face. When she's done I hand her a towel and she delicately pats it dry.

Atlas and Leo reappear on opposite sides of the doorway. I wave them in.

"Are you both alright?" Leo walks over to Poppy. She's putting on a brave face now. It looks more convincing without tears.

"I think I am alright, just… just had a scare, that's all." She looks apologetically at me.

Atlas lightly touches my arm where blood had seeped through my sleeve. "Opened your wound, did you?" He smiles weakly.

"I had to."

Poppy looks shocked. "Wound? From what?"

I wave my hand. "It was nothing, really."

"She got shot," Atlas deadpans.

"Indigo!" Leo and Poppy both shout.

"What? I'm clearly fine."

"You have to tell us these kinds of things!" Leo scolds.

Poppy flinches, turning slowly to Leo. He doesn't look away from me. I shake my head, but Poppy doesn't pay attention. "Then now may be a good time to mention that the Inspector told me Indigo almost got beheaded."

She snitched on me! How could she! Poppy looks at the ceiling, blinking rapidly.

"Indigo, is that true?" Atlas steps forward, fear frozen on his face.

"I knew it might be a possibility if we tried this plan. I'm just lucky that the Inspector showed up when he did. Thank you all."

Atlas pulls out a chair and sits down heavily. Poppy and Leo take seats as well. I climb on the countertop to reach a tray of raspberry danishes that Mother thinks I don't know about. I set the plate on the table.

The Inspector marches past, then circles back and lifts one of the pastries. "How are you all faring?" He sinks his teeth into a colossal portion of the sweet. "Any terrible injuries? Shall I call a doctor?"

A speck of half-chewed something lands on my sleeve. I flick it off with my forefinger. Before I can assure him that everything is in order, besides Poppy's emotional shock, Atlas speaks up. "Yes, Indigo needs a bandage for her arm. Probably some compresses for bruises as well."

Him too?

"I will call immediately. For now, wash the wound, and if you have ice, put some on it. I think you can help her." The Inspector nods to Atlas and wipes the crumbs from his coat.

When he is gone, I roll up my sleeve. The entire left side of the scab has come off, but the blood is clotting nicely. Poppy groans and lays her head on the table. Leo looks as if he has just seen a ghost. The soap stings, but it's not like washing it the first time. I grab a bit of ice and wrap it in a clean red dishcloth. The cold feels pleasant, alleviating some of the pain I've been ignoring. By the time I sit back down, a third of the pastries are gone.

I look around the table. "The Inspector mentioned that there were four Invisibles, including Theodora. I only saw two others. Where was the third one?"

Poppy shudders. Leo puts a hand on her back. "Under your balcony."

"Very clever. How'd the Inspector catch the two that were in my room?"

"They were on their way down the stairs as the Inspector was going up. They surrendered themselves immediately."

Leo nods, adding to Atlas's answer: "We told him you'd be

on the roof. And that you got there because of the ladder. He must've found it."

"Yes." I pull the ice away from my arm for a moment. "Theodora found it too. That's how she got up. I should've tucked it closer to the wall."

Father charges in, Mother on his heels. I can hardly pick out who is saying what.

"Indigo, the Inspector told us all about it!"

"I am so sorry, dearest!"

"We should never have invited that woman!"

"Indigo, you're bleeding!" Mother pulls away the ice to look at the gash.

"I'm fine."

Mother embraces me rather forcefully.

"Please don't squeeze my arm. Yes, that's better. I love you. You don't have to be worried about me."

Father takes me from Mother, crushing me against him. "Yes we do, dear. You almost died!"

Mother cuts short a wail, drawing her eyebrows together. "Are those my tarts?"

She reaches over and plucks one from the plate, eating it quickly. Father doesn't even appear to notice the raspberry bleeding into his glove as he eats one as well.

Phoebe runs in, one hand hiking her skirt up to an indecent height. She grips my shoulders. Her eyes are immediately drawn to the blood on my arm.

"Indigo! Oh, Indigo!"

"I'm fine, just reopened my scratch."

Her eyes flick to mine. "You scared the living daylight out of me, Indigo. Don't…"

"I will try not to scare you like this again," I recite. I will *try*, but I can't help but feel I won't be very successful. What child doesn't scare their loved ones from time to time?

"Tonight has been quite a shock." Phoebe lifts a hand to her brow. "I need – are those danishes?" She pops a whole one in her mouth.

Atlas, Leo, *and* Poppy's parents all sprint in. They rush to me, but when I nearly shout that I'm fine, they cradle their respective children. By the time they take their tarts, the plate is empty.

* * *

I WAKE UP SLOWLY, still cold. I kicked all my covers off in my sleep and am only in my nightdress. The clouds are gold and yellow, while the sky is just lightening to blue. It must be early – somewhere around seven o'clock. There's enough light to read by, so I retrive *Emma* and my blankets.

Phoebe opens the door softly and slips in.

"Good morning, Phoebe."

She whirls around, hands to her bosom. "Indigo, you're awake!"

Her voice is too high-pitched – something must be wrong. The floor is cold under my feet as I walk to the wardrobe and ask, "What is it?"

"Inspector Wallace would like to see you. He's here to take a statement."

"I'm surprised he didn't last night, to be honest." I shake my hair out of its plait.

Phoebe puts a hand on my shoulder, turning me to her. "Indigo, it'll be alright. You don't have to worry anymore."

Along with her concern is a note of triumph. The Phantom is captured, and will soon reveal her secrets. But somehow, I think… Well, it doesn't matter what I think.

"I hope so."

* * *

INSPECTOR WALLACE HAS TAKEN the house by storm with his curly moustache, choosing the drawing room for the interrogation.

"Ah, Miss Indigo, won't you sit down?" He gestures to a chair in front of him.

Mother and Father sit behind me so I cannot see their faces.

"I have a few questions, and I need you to answer them truthfully. Do you understand?"

"Yes."

He clears his throat. From his pocket, he draws a small leatherbound book. "Did you, prior to last night, have any acquaintance with the woman by the name of Theodora Ember Florence Thwite?"

Starting with the easy ones, are we?

"I didn't know she also carried the name Florence."

"That's her maiden name." His eyebrows tick up. "Answer the question, please."

"The first time I met her was at a party on the tenth of May. We were at the Luckfords'."

He scribbles something down before continuing. "What was your impression of her at that time?"

"That she was smart, yet sorrowful." I sound like an automaton, but the Inspector doesn't look up from his notebook, fingers still piloting the pencil.

"Why, then, did you invite her to this party?"

"I invited her to our party in the hopes that we could have another chat about women's rights. And she seemed so devastated by the death of her husband that I wanted to cheer her up."

The Inspector's eyebrows rise at the mention of women's rights, but he clears his throat and keeps at it. "Why would you care so much about the happiness of this stranger?"

"I felt sorry for her plight."

He lifts the pencil tip and his gaze. "And what would that be, in your own words, please?"

"That she lost her husband. I cannot imagine losing anyone so close to me. Can you, Inspector?"

"When you're in my line of work, you must consider all possibilities." The Inspector looks at the wall for a second, curling his coiffed moustache with his finger, hardly blinking. "Never mind – it is not something you'd understand. How did you get on that roof in the first place? And why did you go up there?"

"I took the ladder you came up to get away from the masked man chasing me."

He notes something and continues. "And how did Mrs Thwite get up there?"

"She came up the ladder as well."

The Inspector grunts to himself, graphite still scratching the paper. "What happened next?"

How to finish the story?

"Then she seemed to say something and came towards me, drawing a sword from her cane."

He finishes the line on the paper and stares at it. Finally, he shakes his head and looks up. "Do you believe she intended you harm?"

"I'm sure of it."

The Inspector sits back in his seat, sighing heavily.

"What's wrong, Inspector?"

He rubs his chin. "I fear we may not have enough evidence to convict her of attempted murder. Mrs Thwite claims that you were having a pretend duel, and that it only *looked* like she was going to decapitate you. Do you have any proof she had malicious intent?"

I laugh. "Only that she was about to murder me in cold blood! How did she explain the weapons she had stowed on her person? Or the three uninvited guests?"

He cocks his head to one side. "There were no other weapons on Mrs Thwite or the others. Mrs Thwite's sword wasn't even sharpened – the edge was dull as an old butter knife."

What? Why would they come without weapons? Wouldn't they have needed them to take me? Hmm. I suppose they didn't think so. And they were probably right. Theodora had me well enough by the end. They could have just pushed me off the roof or slung me over one of their shoulders.

"As to the uninvited guests..." The Inspector flips back a few pages. "Mrs Thwite said *she* invited them."

"I was never given any notice —" Mother starts.

The Inspector holds up a hand. "I am questioning your daughter, Mrs Taylor."

I jump in before he can ask another question. "What other evidence do you need?" I narrow my eyes. "Specifically."

He looks down, frowning. I must tread carefully.

"*Anything* more substantial." With a groan, the Inspector gets to his feet. "I'll likely have more questions for you at a later date, and you may be asked to come to the hearing of Mrs Thwite. I will do my best to keep you updated on the proceedings of the case."

"I'd appreciate it if you would."

"Miss Indigo, Mr and Mrs Taylor, I wish you the best in the coming weeks. Mr Taylor, I'll see you on the eighteenth. Until then."

He gathers his things and Father shows him out the door. And just like that, the next moves begin planning themselves out in my mind.

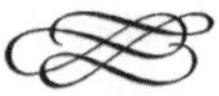

"Not enough evidence?" Atlas runs a hand through his hair, letting out a controlled breath. "Where do we go from here? If they can't convict her, and if she won't tell the authorities anything... How do we find more evidence?"

I tap my fingers against each other. "I have some ideas."

Worry weighs down Atlas's expression. "When should we form a plan?"

"On our breaks, I suppose. Do you know what I'll be practising today?"

"Cicely will be teaching you some things on the floor."

I'll be taught by Cicely? What a pleasant surprise! Atlas ducks back into the schoolroom, and I catch a fleeting glimpse of Louise and a few other children sitting at their desks.

I open the door to the glass room. The awe hasn't worn off, and after the masquerade, I feel a special fondness for it. The smell, the light, the glass and iron, the mats; all of it seems like walking into a dream.

Cicely waits in the middle of the floor, rolling out her ankles.

"Good morning, Cicely!"

She smiles, but it doesn't quite reach her eyes. "Good morning, Indigo. It's good to see you."

Is something wrong? Have I done anything I shouldn't have?

She strides up to me and takes my hands in hers. "Are you alright, Indigo? I heard about Saturday."

Oh! She's just worried about me.

"I'm fine. I just got a few cuts and bruises."

She shakes her head gently, her dark brown eyes staring into mine. "No, what I meant was: are *you* alright?"

Psychological damage. I suppose I *should* have some... Perhaps I'll notice it in my old age. My greying hair will be a monstrous tangle, while my eyes will be rimmed with the colour of sleepless nights. I'll stow a knife in my boot and a pistol in my corset, perhaps even have a brutal dog by my side. My family will think I'm stranger than my grandmother.

I shrug. "I'm fine. Practice will be good for me."

The wrinkle between her brows lessens. "In that case, let's begin."

Cicely's careful not to do anything that could even remotely hurt my arm, so mostly I practise splits. It isn't terrible. Cicely warms me up so thoroughly that it hurts much less than I expected. Still, I have about eight inches between the peak of my split and the floor, while Cicely slides easily into hers.

At some point during centre splits, the sound of Mother's laughter startles me into falling over. She and Mrs Trinter take their seats on the bench. I lend an ear as I relax into each position.

At first they talk about wallpaper and costumes, and then what Mrs Trinter wore to the ball. (Apparently, her dress is from their show Playing Games: the costume of the Queen of Diamonds.) From there, Mother brings up the subject of my almost-execution. Immediately, she's choking back a sob.

Cicely freezes in her front split, letting it go extra long. Twin tears slip down Mother's cheeks. She wipes them away with her thumb. Mrs Trinter wraps Mother in an embrace, comforting her with the notion that it's all over and Theodora can no longer hurt me.

But what's to stop Theodora from sending someone else to get the job done? The fact that she's in jail? What is that to the Phantom? She may not even need to issue the order; the Invisibles may act on their own.

Mother pulls away and changes the subject as she dabs around her eyes. After some time, Cicely takes my wandering attention for hunger pangs, which are certainly part of it. She sends me to the kitchen.

The other children are out of class by now, and Atlas, Abbott, and Nora are at the table. A bowl of fruit sits between them.

"Hello, Indigo." Nora smiles kindly at me, some of her shyness gone.

"Hello, Nora. How was class today?"

She shrugs. "It was good. What did Cicely teach you?"

I pick a rosy apple from the bowl. "Splits."

Nora nods slowly, pretending to know how difficult those are.

Abbott stands. "Nice to see you again, Indigo. I trust you are well?"

Everyone must know about Saturday. "I think breathing certainly counts as 'well' in this case." At their blanching, I amend, "Yes. I'm fine. I wasn't really hurt."

Abbott glances at Atlas. "That's good. Sorry to rush off, but Nora and I have schoolwork to catch up on, so we must be going."

Nora stands too. "It was nice talking to you. Goodbye." She and Abbott walk from the room, heads together, whispering.

"What was that about?" I ask.

Atlas follows their path out the door, then looks at me. "It's not that they don't want to talk to you. I'm sure they'd love to hear your version of the story, but I told them you might still be sensitive." He heaves a breath. "We need to talk."

I raise my eyebrows and take a bite of my apple.

"What happened while you… After you and Poppy split up? I'll know if you leave anything out." Atlas crosses his arms, but he looks almost afraid I'll answer his question.

My bite of apple decides to lodge itself in my throat. After a brief coughing fit, it slides down whole. I go in for another bite.

"Indigo…"

This time I chew and swallow. "When you left, almost everything went to plan."

"Then why did you almost die on the roof? Was that part of the plan?"

"It was a possible outcome." He should have known that.

"In the future, we need to make better plans. But for now, Indigo, I want to know what

happened."

I set my apple on the table and take a seat. I try to talk quickly; soon Cicely will be looking for me. When I'm done, Atlas looks somewhere between horrified and relieved. His arms are still crossed, but now rest on the table.

Atlas drags a hand through his hair. "Why do you think Theodora's blade was dull?"

I scrub the skin of my remaining half-apple. "It makes for a good alibi, and if she wanted to murder me, she could've shoved me off the roof and gone back to the party. Or they could've dealt with me elsewhere, or used me to get to you." I hold my breath. "Also… I might have accidentally told Theodora your name."

I look up at him. He hesitates.

"Are you sure?" He doesn't sound angry.

"When the Inspector came up on the roof and got

Theodora, I asked if you three were alright. Now she only has two possible names: Leo and Atlas. It won't be hard from there to figure it out." I bite my lip. "I'm sorry."

Atlas's fingers tap against his arm. "I'm sure she was getting close. The party was always going to narrow it down. She would have cross-referenced it and gotten the answer soon enough. It's not your fault, Indigo."

"But…"

"You almost died. I'm sure you weren't completely yourself." His shoulders relax, and the corners of his mouth twitch. He smiles to himself, then starts to laugh.

"What's so funny?"

His shoulders shake with a new fit of mirth. "Did you really tell Poppy she should start drying rose petals to put over your casket while she was in shock?"

How could that be funny? "It was a comforting thing to say."

This only makes him laugh harder.

"*I* would find it comforting," I say in my defence.

"I'm sure you would." He does not expand on this.

I straighten my spine. We must keep to the important things. "What should we do about the evidence?"

It's like throwing water on a fire; Atlas sobers immediately. I almost wish I hadn't said it.

"I don't know. I haven't been able to think of anything. We've given them all the information about the trapdoor and Theodora, along with three other Invisibles. Short of coming clean, what can we do?"

"I'll be back here in a few days, I think. By then, one of us will certainly have thought of something."

The feet of his chair scrape backward as he stands.

"I hope so. I have to work on an assignment, but I'll probably see you before you go."

* * *

I SHOULDN'T HAVE WORRIED about Cicely; she's lost track of time on the trapeze. In fact, it was probably a relief for her to do something more exciting than leading me through conditioning exercises. Mrs Trinter, now dressed in a leotard, a skirt, and her trapeze boots, has introduced another woman to Mother. They chat on the bench. When I come in, Mrs Trinter excuses herself from the conversation and crosses the mats to me.

"I told Cicely that I would work with you. I hope you don't mind."

"No, of course not! What will we do?"

Mrs Trinter beams. "Ever tried tightrope?" She opens the closet by the door without pausing. "I think you'll like it."

After a moment of thought, she pulls a box down from a shelf, blowing a film of dust into the air. Inside are… boots?

"I think these should fit, but it's been so long since anyone's needed them I might have overestimated the length."

I take the long black box and sit. The boots have a thin sole of leather and the inside is lined with a soft fabric. I give the black laces a tug. The shoe is tight heel-to-toe – not enough to be uncomfortable, but still noticeable.

Mrs Trinter *tsks*. "Hmm… So I did. Still, they'll help more than hurt."

She offers me her hand and helps me up. The shoes – if they can be called that – are strange. They feel almost like stockings, but the laces are so like my boots it's hard to think of them as anything less. When I turn, Mrs Trinter has already mounted the step of the low-strung tightrope. She raises her arms out to either side.

"Try not to hold your arms in a line," she says. "Keep them in front, slightly." She brings her arms forward and steps onto the twisted cord. "I find it's easier when I don't look at my feet. Instead, I look ahead and just a bit down." She steps again, her balance only marginally wavering. "Lead with your toe, so you never lose the rope."

Mrs Trinter turns her head for just a moment to look at me. "The posture is a bit like fencing. Always know where your weight is…" She begins to tip to one side and snaps back forward, her eyes dropping a few degrees. "And where it's going." She adjusts her arms and bends her knees slightly. The rope beneath her stills, and so does she. "That's the most important thing."

She takes a few more steps before bending her knees deeply and setting her left foot on the ground. Her hands fall to her sides and the sharp focus of her gaze softens.

"Try it."

The blond rope waits stiff and still, daring me to step on it. I draw in a breath and feel my lungs press against my ribcage. The sole of my shoe grips the step; I feel it slowly let go of the wood as I put one foot on the rope, toe first. It wobbles as I ease my weight onto it. The next foot follows. For a second I'm still, then the rope trembles. My hands fly out to the sides before I think about it.

Mrs Trinter takes my fingers in hers. "Back straight. Take a breath." Her chest expands with her own inhale. I straighten my spine. "Good! Take another step. I've still got your hand if you need me for balance."

Following the rope with my toe, I turn my foot out marginally.

"Good leading with your toe, but keep your foot straight. Another step."

Mrs Trinter's light hold on my hand steadies me even as I lilt to the left. She places her other hand against my shoulder blades. The tip of my boot slides along the line in front of me. My shoulders slowly cave, but Mrs Trinter's hand catches the impulse.

"Pick a spot on the wall to look at instead of your feet. It's tempting, I know."

The tip of an iron leaf becomes the only thing I see. My toe leads me to the centre of the rope. With my next step in the air, before my foot can rest on the rope again, my balance wavers. My foot hovers, finding steadiness again, before slowly inching to the line. Only a few more steps and then I'll be across. At least I'm not high off the ground.

I take a longer step than before, which means I must keep my next step in the air for another second. Mrs Trinter's hand saves me from the floor.

"Steady on." She pats my back once. "You'll get there."

I nod once to the wrought iron leaf, heat high in my cheeks. With two more steps, I reach the opposite platform. My arms come down slowly as I adjust my balance.

"That was very good, Indigo. This time, try not to stop moving. Momentum will actually help you stay centred."

The second time my foot leads, and I keep my arms just where I can see them in my peripheral vision. However, when my back foot arcs around my first too widely, my balance comes into check. I stop, my arms windmilling. Mrs Trinter's hand falls away. Panicking, I crouch.

"That was perfect, Indigo. If ever you feel yourself losing control, get closer to the rope. If you're high up, you can always pull yourself across. That's what I did my first time on the high ropes." She looks up to the higher tightrope with a light sigh. "Come on. Let's try again, shall we?"

After going many more times, Mrs Trinter claims it's time for me to change.

"Are you sure? Can I try just one more time? I think I can do it without your hand now."

Mother comes up behind me, stroking my hair. "No, I am afraid we must go. We'll be back on Friday. Thank you so much, Helen, for teaching Indigo. I have never seen her posture so straight!"

Mrs Trinter nods. I look up at Mother; her hand is still on my hair.

"We? You're coming with me again?" How... strangely touching.

A shadow crosses her face. "I'm not ready to let you go anywhere without me yet, dear."

That will be a problem.

An odd glint appears in Mrs Trinter's eye. "I'd like to meet with your mother again soon. For now, though, you must go home. I'll meet you by the front door in ten minutes to see you off?"

"That should be more than enough. Thank you, Helen, for everything." Mother dips

her head and shows herself out of the room.

* * *

ON MY WAY to the front door after changing, Atlas joins me in a rush.

"Did Mama tell you what she's planning?"

"No. She's planning something? You wouldn't happen to know anything about it, would you?"

He shakes his head. "I am as curious as you are. I assumed she'd tell you something about it. Mother and Father never keep things from me. Well, except the costume designs. It's all very strange. I think I'll go stark raving mad." He shoves his hands deep into his pockets.

I shake my head at him. "What a shame. I thought you could read minds."

"Not quite. I'll try to figure it out while you're gone."

The hallway opens to the foyer and Atlas stops. "See you soon, I guess."

"Goodbye."

* * *

AT HOME, light rain begins to dance on the roof. Perfect weather for thinking. My casebook is spread across my knees. The watery light aids me as I sketch out Theodora's mask.

What can we do now? Going back to the mansion is too dangerous. Or they might have abandoned it entirely. We'll be caught long before we can break into Walker's house. What more would we find there anyway? And if so, would it really connect Theodora to anything? Unlikely. If her own word can be believed, she has only recently come to power among the Invisibles.

I erase the curve of the mask and run my pencil along the paper again. Those eyeless pits stare back at me. I shade them in with the edge of my pencil, the tip against the paper making the faintest music.

* * *

AFTER A BATH and a quick change into my nightclothes, I fall into bed, hoping dawn will find me before the night terrors. Luck, it seems, has other plans, and the black tendrils of a dream pull me under.

I look out a thickly paned window towards the seaside. White-frothed waves lap at the shore, tossing pebbles violently into the air with their crashes. I've been to the beach once in my life, and I wasn't allowed to go more than ten feet into the water because of the steep drop-off. I was terrified of it. The rocky shore and turbulent waves were utterly foreign to me. I regret that fear, now.

I find my way out of the house and walk onto the sand. The sky is grey and the sea is heather. The horizon is only a distant

229

haze between the hues. I sit at the edge of the water, my toes just touching the highest reaches of the frigid waves.

There's something in the ocean. It lodges on the shore. As the wave retreats I scoop the object up. It feels almost glassy in my hand. I retreat from the salty water to take a closer look.

It's the mask. It's so clear: glazed black porcelain with a spiderweb of white. The mask breaks into a grin, ivory lines buckling. She whispers to me, "Indigo. You have forgotten something."

I smash the mask to the stony shore. Pieces of black fly everywhere, falling in with the other pebbles. I start running down the beach as fast as my legs will carry me. The rocks and midnight shards split my skin. Theodora's voice follows, as if she's close enough to catch my hand.

"You have forgotten it's all only a dream."

Her mocking laugh echoes in my head.

CHAPTER 21

Phoebe flings open the curtains. I wipe my brow and trail a hand against my dress. My feet brush the cold floor as I sit at the edge of my bed.

"What's wrong, Indigo?"

"Nothing."

"Another dream?"

My head bobs. I get dressed in a grey blouse, a green skirt, and my boots.

After a half-day of school, Mrs Wood lets me go early, something she rarely does. It's becoming more and more apparent that I'm reaching the end of what Mrs Wood can teach me. My parents will soon have to send me to finishing school. Poppy will be there... But so will Rosana. As long as Poppy is there it shouldn't be so *terrible*. Should it?

It will be torture. How can I do anything so... so... suffocating? Stifling? I don't really know the right word. But there are more important things at hand. The mask from my dream whispers in my ear. I push the voice away, but it still haunts me.

I snatch my casebook and a hand towel and stow them

in my bag, climbing down my ladder and walking in the direction of the maze. It rained shortly before lunch, and the green grass still jealously hoards water. The earth squelches beneath my every step and my boots are wet to the ankle before I find my refuge: a black bench standing out against the wood walls draped with wisteria. The towel soaks up most of the water left on the bench. Once I'm settled, I pull out my notebook and it falls open to the page from yesterday. My drawing of Theodora's mask stares up at me.

Something about it tickles the back of my mind. Masks… I trace its contours with a fingernail; all the broken shards stitched together again.

Abruptly, I stop.

Masks.

* * *

I ENTER the circus room without my uniform on, as per Arlo's instructions. He also stated that Mrs Trinter was finishing a meeting and would be down soon. Mother follows behind me, more timidly than when she's with Mrs Trinter.

Atlas appears from behind the door, supporting a well-maintained penny-farthing bicycle. The bike has an attractive red frame with handles that dip artistically at the end, but the most prominent thing about its appearance is the enormous front tyre.

"Oh, no."

Atlas cocks his head teasingly. "It's just a bike."

"It is not just a bike, and I'm afraid for *you*. You'll have to teach me how to ride it."

"It's not that difficult."

I raise an eyebrow.

Atlas sighs. "Relatively." He rubs a handlebar with his

thumb. "Wonderful to see you again, Mrs Taylor. I trust every-thing has been quiet lately?"

Mother straightens. "Perfectly fine. Thank you for your concern." She clears her throat lightly. "Are you… going to teach Indigo to ride that?"

"Yes, Mrs Taylor." His dark eyelashes frame innocent eyes.

She scrutinises Atlas, then the contraption beside him. "Where? You can't possibly do it here."

"No, but just outside —"

"Who will supervise?"

Atlas blinks. "Everyone else is busy or out. I assure you, the street is quite safe."

Mother raises a hand. "Be that as it may, I'd like to have an adult keeping watch on my daughter while she's outside. Until one is available, I shall do it myself."

"I completely understand," Atlas replies in a chipper voice. "If you'll follow me."

We take the bicycle through the front door. Outside, I fall in step next to him. He looks at me sideways with raised eyebrows. I dip my chin ever so slightly.

I have a plan, I mouth soundlessly.

Atlas narrows his eyes in confusion. I mouth the words again. This time he forms a silent *Oh.*

Mother, Atlas, the contraption, and I pass through the gate. Atlas sets the bike on the pavement. Father has a penny-farthing. It's black and taller than this one. When I was very little, he set me on the seat, holding the frame steady. I'd never been so high off the ground without someone holding me, so I started to cry until he brought me back down. I've avoided them ever since, despite Phoebe's encouragement.

"The hardest part is getting on," Atlas assures. "It's fun once you're up. You'll see."

Walking with it for a few steps, he uses the peg on the back-bone of the frame to hoist himself onto the seat.

"It's a bit difficult to turn. You've got to go to the corner."

Hard to get on and turn? Wonderful.

At the corner Atlas steers the massive front tyre just enough to clear the road and turn around. Any more and his balance would have been thrown off.

"At least it has brakes," he remarks casually as he rides back. Before he coasts all the way to Mother and me, he dismounts the same way he got up. "Just try to ride on the step the first few times, then get off to turn."

The heel of my boot fits well around the peg, and I push off once, twice, with my right foot. The curved handlebars are so far away that I'm forced to bend over the colossal front wheel to reach them. The hem of my skirt drapes just shy of the spokes. At the corner, I touch my right foot on the pavement. To guide the bike a hundred and eighty degrees, I reach a few inches above my shoulder to grip the bars and turn the thing to the left. That wasn't so hard. On the way back, I forget to hide my giddy smile, and Atlas catches me. I can't bring myself to regret it, though.

"See, it's fun."

"Oh, alright." I step off the peg and walk the last few feet. "It's fun. I'd still choose a safety bike over this to do anything more complicated."

Atlas concedes the point.

The door to the house opens, and Mrs Trinter peeks her head out, blonde hair curled into a high bun. "Oh, there you are!" She steps out into the cooler afternoon air, a knitted shawl draped over the shoulders of her straightforward dress. "So good to see you again, Mrs Taylor."

While Mother turns to greet her, I make a fuss of testing my foot against the peg while I whisper to Atlas, "We can find the maker of the masks."

His eyes become questioning, but I continue.

"We'll have to use the one you borrowed from the mansion, but I think it'll work."

Atlas glances briefly over my shoulder. He angles his face down, speaking quickly. "There are two porcelain makers: Crow and Son, and Jackaby. That's only in this city; they could have taken their order elsewhere."

"Well…" It is possible. We don't even know that the Invisibles are an isolated society. There could be chapters in other cities.

"Indigo!" Mrs Trinter makes her way down the short path to me. "How's the cycling?" Her hazel eyes are unusually bright and excitement makes her face glow.

"I made it to the corner and back alright, but I was just coasting."

She blinks curiously. "Have you never ridden one before?"

"No. I've been rather afraid of them."

Mrs Trinter smiles. "They can be intimidating, especially when you're accustomed to safety bikes. Keep on, you'll get used to it. Your balance is already refined from fencing." She squeezes my hand and then starts back towards Mother.

A smile teases Atlas's lips. "I think your mother will tell you Mama's idea tonight." Something about his tone is different than it was two days ago.

"You know what it is now!" It's more an exclamation than a question.

"Mother and Father told me about it and asked me what I thought."

"What did you say?"

He shrugs, but the motion isn't natural. "I think it's a good idea." His smile looks a bit like his mother's, only more mischievous.

"Will you tell me what it is?"

"No. Mama wants your Mother to tell you. I agree with her."

I rest my chin on the arm that still steadies the bike. "Can you give me a hint? Please, Atlas."

He purses his lips, then bends to whisper in my ear, "She wants to learn how to pilot a dirigible."

I jerk back. "That can't be it."

He inclines his head, a guilty grin across his face. "No, it's not. But it is true."

I huff. "You're no help at all."

"You'll find out soon. Your mother's watching us now."

I sigh and start pushing the bike with my foot. After a few more rides back and forth, it's time to try actually sitting on the thing. Atlas demonstrates.

"The pedals are directly attached to the wheel, so every time you push, the front tyre shifts slightly."

My dress is a problem. Because I need both my hands on the bars, I can't hold it up, nor can I ride with it down. "Don't tell Mother," I say, tucking some of the fabric of my skirt into the waist, pulling it up high enough so my ankles would show if it weren't for my boots. While I'm at it, I tuck in the ends of my laces. That should do the trick.

On the bike again, I get into the seat. My back straightens on its own and my hands rest casually on the bars. The cycle rides smoothly and the turn poses little challenge. Arriving back in front of 416, I dismount. Landing solidly on both feet, I blow a coil of hair out of my eyes. "How was that?"

Secret happiness teases Mrs Trinter's lips. "An excellent ride to end on."

Atlas and I manoeuvre the penny-farthing back through the double doors and walk it down the hall. Mother and Mrs Trinter walk behind.

"I've been thinking. The number of masks needed would be too much for an amateur. What if we asked the two shops to make more masks, just like the one you have? If they mention something about another order, or anything else suspicious, then we've found the contact."

Atlas still looks unconvinced. "But which one do we try first?"

I look at the colossal wheel spinning between us. "Do you know where they both are?"

He nods falteringly.

"Do you have a map of the city?"

"Yes, but how are we going to find the maker by using a map?"

"Deduction and reasoning."

"Indigo?" Mrs Trinter calls. We've walked quicker than the two women, and now there's quite a gap between us. "How would you like to try fencing on the balance beam today?"

Fencing? On a beam? What a wonderful idea!

* * *

"HA!" The square tip of my foil touches the chest of Atlas's fencing jacket. "That's fifteen for me."

He takes off his mask and bites back a grin. "And I was so close. Damn."

"Atlas," his mother says warningly, "Louise should be down soon. Don't let her hear you say that."

"Yes, Mother."

The world loses its grid as I take off my mask and sit on the low balance beam. Between breaths, I ask, "Where is Louise?"

"With a teacher from a nearby school. We think he may be able to help Louise with her reading," Mrs Trinter replies. "She's been having some trouble." She looks between Atlas and me. "Go to the kitchen and drink some water. When you come back, Indigo, let's try something new. You two can return the equipment to the closet."

* * *

Atlas rolls a map across his desk, and I place books at its edges.

He points to a rectangle of space that was empty when this map was made. "This is Jackaby's shop." The porcelain maker is near the outside of the city by the river, but on the opposite side from the abandoned mansion. "And here's Crow and Son." The name is in plain black ink, situated in the industrial district of town.

"It is difficult to transport porcelain, so the maker should be close to the abandoned mansion." I draw a circle around the name *Crow and Son*.

"Unless," Atlas says, holding up a finger, "each member had to get their own mask. That would eliminate the problem of distance."

"Not *entirely*. It isn't likely that every member would retrieve their mask if it's three hours away."

He numbers the constraints on his fingers. "So the maker would have to be close and established enough to fire, say, a hundred masks, depending on how often they break. Anything else? Both of these makers fit the description?"

I worry my lip. "The masks are also in different colours – white, grey, and black, at least."

"Both of these makers could do that."

"I can't think of anything else. Do you have any ideas?"

Atlas stares at the name *Crow and Son*, lost in thought. Slowly his eyes focus, eventually coming to rest on another space on the map.

"What if we don't need the location of where the potter *makes* the masks, but where he keeps or sells them? For one of our shows a long time ago we needed fifteen masks of varying shades of green. Father went to pick them up, but instead of going to the workshop, he and I went to the *warehouse*. I still might remember where it was. We ordered from Crow and Son; the warehouse was... here. I remember it being near Louise's orphanage."

Atlas taps a spot on the map only a few streets away from the abandoned mansion.

"That's it. It's got to be. What do we do now?" He looks up. "I suppose you already have a mostly-thought-out plan?"

"I wouldn't call it *mostly* thought out. It's at least halfway, though. That's really all we need – the rest can be made up as we go."

He looks reluctant, but I lay out the plan I've been thinking of. Atlas nods.

"It's more than half a plan, but we can't do it today. We'll be missed."

"I can get away tomorrow."

He rubs the back of his neck. "I can try. It'll be easiest to leave at nine. I can be at the warehouse by nine-thirty and get bread on my way back. They'll assume I just stopped to chat with Mr Perkins. Do you think we can be back in two hours?"

"Certainly."

"Should we meet at the warehouse?"

"That'll work."

* * *

WE PRACTISE tightrope for the next hour until Mother tells me it's time to go. She leaves, but I hang back.

"I don't know what you did to my mother, but thank you, Mrs Trinter."

Her gaze follows Mother out of the room. She looks down, "You're welcome, but I haven't done anything amazing. I'm simply being a friend."

"You are planning something, though." Perhaps her reaction will give me insight.

Her concern is set aside as Mrs Trinter gives a sly smile. What does that mean? I bet Atlas could tell what his mother's thinking. And how she feels about it. And who else she told and when. One day I'll be able to tell what colour socks he is wearing on any given morning from the twitch of his left eyebrow. One day.

"I see what you're trying to do. Atlas's bad habits are rubbing off on you. Or perhaps you're just like him." Her smile broadens, but then falters, turning into something more bittersweet.

"What's wrong?"

Mrs Trinter wipes her eyes. "Oh, nothing is wrong. In fact, something is quite right. It's just – never mind. Run along, now."

What is it? All I can see is that she's trying not to cry. I walk to the door, looking back to see Mrs Trinter standing by the glass wall, her back to me.

It is a difficult ride home. I try asking Mother questions, but she is so preoccupied with her own thoughts I can't get anything from her.

At home I tell Phoebe about the day. She listens intently, sometimes asking questions. She assures me that it's not likely anything's wrong. I try to listen to her, but the thought of what I'm to learn at dinner – or during the conversations after – sends my mind in discouraging directions. And yet, like a soldier off to battle, I suit up and head into the fray.

* * *

MOTHER SETS her fork on her plate with a reverberating *clink*. Her lips are pursed tightly and lines mar her forehead. Father gently touches her shoulder and tries to catch her glance. She clears her throat.

"Indigo, why don't you join your father and me in the drawing room after dinner? I am afraid I cannot eat anymore."

I slide my plate away. "Why don't we go now? I'm not very hungry." That's because I practically inhaled my food, and why wait for the news?

Olive looks at the three of us, fork halfway to her mouth. Father seems to agree. He, too, pushes his plate away.

"Let's go, dear. The drawing room, you say?"

Mother nods.

I flip some of the new switches, and light fills the room with a soft glow. Mother sits heavily on the couch, Father by her side. I take a chair across from them, managing my impatience by counting the seconds before Mother speaks.

"Indigo, before I begin, I believe you are worried that it's something terrible. It isn't. It will just be a hard decision for us – all of us, I believe – to make. Mrs Trinter has proposed that if you wished… then you could go live with them, as a sort of boarding school arrangement. You would go in lieu of finishing school if you decided to."

Mother glances at Father, who nods tightly for her to go on.

"She's had the idea of taking on a gifted student for some time, but wanted someone she knew would be up to the task. Mrs Trinter would give you lessons; Mr Trinter too, I believe. You would learn academics in the morning and the circus arts in the afternoons." Mother pauses, glancing at the ceiling. "And she also offered you a position in their upcoming show."

Oh, Mrs Trinter! And I'm sure Mr Trinter had something to do with it too. Oh, yes, yes, yes. Still, I would have to leave Mother, Father, Olive… and Phoebe.

"We could visit you anytime we wanted, and you could come home on the weekends and holidays. Mrs Trinter was a teacher before she met Mr Trinter, so she knows how to handle a classroom." Mother pauses, then begins anew. "Indigo, we don't want you to leave. We love you, but after the masquerade…" Clearing her throat forcefully, she continues. "You may be safer living elsewhere. And at 416, you'd only be a short drive away. Even so, I will miss you sneaking out of parties, or trying to put extra pepper in Olive's soup…"

"I haven't done that in years!"

Father's eyes spark. "Ah, but you did add a bit of cayenne to her dinner when that Frederik boy was here. That was only a few months ago."

I smile. It was as good as any opera – better, actually – to see Olive, nose running and eyes watering in front of Frederick, trying to hide it behind a napkin. "Oh, yes. I do remember now. Did you enjoy that?"

Mother and Father share a glance, lips pursed into suppressed smiles. None of us had liked Frederik. Father clears his throat, giving me a hard stare. Well, trying to. "No, that was very wrong. You shouldn't do that again." He has to look away to maintain his disapproving visage.

"Would you miss me if I added some extra cayenne to your dishes?"

Now they laugh. Mother wipes tears from her eyes.

"Not *especially* at that moment. But, yes, of course we will miss you," Father says. "*If* we let you go, we would visit often and drag you home on the weekends."

"How long would I go for?"

"It would be for a few months at first, as a trial run," Mother says. "But if, after that, you should want to continue, we could talk about it. Your father and I will think about it. If we decide you can go, you can move in as soon as you wrap up your studies with Mrs Wood. You wouldn't *have* to go so quickly, that's just the earliest —"

"Would Phoebe come with me?"

Mother shakes her head, slowly. She'd been expecting my question. "We need her here, especially with Olive's debut coming."

It's the truth I've been ignoring for years. Phoebe never would have gone with me to finishing school. I suppose I should've been more prepared, especially with the threat of Mrs Moring's, but the impending reality catches me off guard.

"Did Mrs Trinter say anything else? Like who I'd share a room with or what I should bring?"

"I believe she did mention a few names, but I've forgotten them. She assured me that you'll get along very nicely. You don't need a packing list yet. You have plenty of time for that later. For now, you should try to get some sleep."

"I will."

That's my best lie yet.

CHAPTER 22

I wake up slowly, a small beam of light striking my face. I can't remember exactly when I fell asleep. I was telling Phoebe about Mrs Trinter's news and then my body felt full of sand. I don't remember any dreams, either. This, for some reason, unnerves me.

The clock reads eight twenty-seven. I can eat and make it to the warehouse in plenty of time.

* * *

I LEAVE Quest a few streets away from the warehouse and walk until I see my destination. *Crow and Son* is painted in large, theatrical letters on the side of the building. Above the letters are hundreds of panes of green glass, sending blinding morning light in different directions. The brickwork is artful around the curved ground-level windows and door.

I left the house, saying I was going to read in the maze, at eight fifty-two. It took me thirty-one minutes and fifty-seven seconds to get here.

"Morning."

I whirl around to see Atlas. His hands are tucked into the pockets of his unbuttoned coat and he's left off the flat cap.

"Morning. Manage to get away alright?"

"It was easier than expected. Did you hear about Mother's idea?"

"Yes! My parents seemed hesitant, but I think they'll agree. I'm so excited! I was this close" – I put an inch between my thumb and finger – "to going to Mrs Moring's Finishing School. Now we can finish the case, and practise circus, and play hide-and-seek, and I can see Louise practise trapeze… and…" All the possibilities are overwhelming. So many things to try, so many moments to live.

Atlas is beaming. "Louise will be thrilled to hear it."

A horse and cart trundles past loudly. The driver manoeuvres around the back of Crow and Son.

"We'll get back to this later. Shall we?" Atlas inclines his head in the direction of the building.

I nod and we cross the street, into the sunlight. Massive cracks split the way around the back of the imposing construction. Atlas puts out a hand to stop me before peeking around the corner. Already, I can hear loud grunts and shouts of "Careful with that!" or "Steady, steady. Keep her even, boys!" clamouring for attention.

Atlas brings his head back from the edge. "I think we should go in through the front. There are too many people back here. I can hold the clerk's attention while you sneak in to have a look around. If I can't find a way to join you, I'll be waiting with the horses."

"Sounds like an excellent plan."

After walking back, I wait outside while Atlas pushes the door open. On my toes at the window, I see a young man sitting at a small wooden desk, scribbling something into a ledger. Atlas asks a question and the clerk looks up eagerly, nodding.

After a few more words, Atlas points to the book the clerk had been writing in. The man shakes his head but gestures to one side. My companion nods gratefully, and the shopkeeper jumps to his feet to disappear behind a door.

I take my chance and push the door open. Atlas turns.

"Good luck. Be careful," he says under his breath.

"I will."

The room opens into the main part of the warehouse. Out of sight of the desk, I stop to take a breath behind a large tower of boxes. Huge beams line the room, supporting the ceiling, which is dotted with electric lights. Wooden crates fill the space, wide aisles between them.

Keeping to the wall, I make my way around the perimeter. As I suspected, the office rooms sit in a row on the far side. They're conveniently labelled for me. I knock on the door labelled "Records" and wait for a response. This trick is one I learned long ago. If the knock is answered, I learn who, if anyone, is inside. If the conditions aren't right, I walk away, and let the person inside think they're going mad.

After I'm sure no one is inside, I quietly open the door and walk in. The room is free of people, but in case of an emergency, there's a glass-fronted display case situated in the corner with just enough space to crawl behind. The drawers of the enormous desk are unlocked. I go through the contents, looking for a book or ledger that would have the receipts in it. After searching the whole desk and finding nothing of interest besides a peculiar specimen of dust bunny, I reach for a filing cabinet behind the door. It, too, opens at my tug. I search the "T" section of invoices, but none bear the name Thwite. Shame.

I turn back to the door, but something under a desk in the corner catches my eye: a small crate. It's locked and *DO NOT OPEN* is stamped on the side. It might as well read *I'M SUSPI-CIOUS, PLEASE OPEN ME.* And... locked? Wouldn't crates normally be nailed shut?

I retrieve my lockpicks and the job is done in thirty-two seconds. I set the padlock in my lap and lift the lid. Hay decorates the inside. I brush it away, and my palm touches something matte. The contents stare up at me. Bone-white masks, rough and unglazed, lie inside. Exactly the same masks the Invisibles wear. My heart raps against my ribs. "One, two, three…"

I lift the mask in the corner. Just to disrupt the image that comes so easily to my mind, I poke my fingers through one of the eyes. How can anyone wish to put this on? It's so frightening. I spread the hay over the remaining masks and let the lid down. After a moment, the lock clicks shut again. Crawling from under the table, I slide the mask into my pocket. Nothing else in the room looks amiss.

I slip back out and retreat back toward the entry. I cannot spot the clerk. Now that I think of it, all I remember about him was that he was of average height and average build, had an average look, and was writing in what had to be an account book. As I think of the book, something pricks my memory. What could it be? The book was leatherbound, with numerous pages and small script.

Stalking back into the shadows, I follow the trail until the light is at the wrong angle and I have to step out into the sun. I hear a man speaking in the next room; even his voice is unremarkable.

"Well, it should be here. I am sorry, this may take a moment."

"That is alright, take your time."

That has to be Atlas. Perfect – the plan is still working. Or it will be if the clerk could find what he's looking for.

I scout the room first: Atlas is at the front desk and the man is flipping through the book, agitation written on his face. I casually walk behind some old cabinets. Atlas notices me. I signal to the book, and he looks away, pretending to be admiring the architecture, nodding his approval.

"How old is this building, Mr Ackroyd? It's beautiful."

"About thirty years old, sir."

Sir? Atlas met this man not ten minutes ago, and he's already attained the title of "sir"?

"Do you know who built it?"

The man, who had been intently scanning pages, looks up in thought. "I don't rightly know. Perhaps I shall ask Mr Brighton about it later."

"That's alright, just an odd curiosity. I am an amateur architect when I am not at my horse races. I hate to be a bother, but would you mind showing me around the warehouse?"

The clerk perks up. "Why, certainly! It is not often that anyone comes in here and wants to appreciate the beauty of our warehouse." Leaving the book behind, he walks out from behind his desk, Atlas following in his wake.

The ledger lies on the counter, open to the middle. I scan the first page. There's a rough table of contents. Turning the pages quietly, I find nothing suspicious. Next, I check for any code language that could be used. I'm met with disappointment. Fanning the leaves, I look for any that seem to be pasted together; there are none. I check the leather cover itself, hoping for a miracle.

There's a seam in the binding. I push my fingernail into the hairline crack, widening it just enough to fish out three wafer-thin papers. They're so delicate that I accidentally tear one of the edges. As I gently set them down on the desk, they almost float to the wood.

The first one is an order for some sort of wine press; the next is for a gun partly made from porcelain, though on this one there's a note written in red ink: "Failed experiment". The last is what I'm looking for. Drawings and numbers for the masks, along with colours written on the side. At the bottom there are three signatures along with three totals: the first is only for thirty, dated ten years ago, with the initials J.B.; the next is for fifty masks, six years ago, signed with O.Q.T.; and the last is for only three masks last week, all in black, signed with T.F.T. The last one has a strong possibility of being Theodora's handwriting. Though the wobbly letters look like a child's hand, and the slants lean to the right, rather than the left... Theodora must have substituted her left hand for her right. And why would she leave off her middle name?

I hear Atlas talking, rather loudly, about the intricacies of the brickwork a short distance away. Gently sliding the papers back into the book – sans the one for the masks – I push the seam closed and hurriedly position the book as it was when the man left it. Quickly folding the paper and easing it into my pocket, I dash out the door.

I count to fifteen and re-enter the building. Atlas is in front of the clerk again, but he turns to me. "Has Mother sent for me?"

What? This is the story he's come up with? "Yes, she wants you to come home immediately."

Atlas sighs, turning back to the man. "I'm sorry to have caused you so much trouble. Thank you for showing me around and answering my questions. I should have an order ready within a week."

"No trouble at all." The clerk looks between us. "Beg pardon, but are you two siblings?"

"Yes," we both reply.

The man doesn't look convinced.

"I'm adopted," we say in unison.

I glance at Atlas. In an effort to avoid switching claims, I repeat my statement. The only trouble is that Atlas has the same thought, and we are in an even worse predicament.

Atlas puts on a look of surprise and says, "Mother told me *I* was adopted."

"Wait, she told me the same thing – do you think… Could we both…"

The clerk clears his throat uncomfortably. "Well, you two have a nice day."

I give him a distracted nod, still aiming to look as if my whole life has been a lie. Atlas gives a final goodbye and we hurriedly leave the building.

* * *

"So you're saying we send the mask and the paper to the Inspector," my companion confirms as we ride side by side down a street toward the thick of the city.

"Then he should be able to connect the masks Theodora and the other three were wearing to the ones made by Crow and Son, most recently ordered by someone with Theodora's partial initials."

Atlas shakes his head. "But that won't be enough to convict Theodora of Walker's murder. Smith will still be in danger."

"Yes, but this is a start." I pat my pocket. "Maybe Inspector Wallace *will* be able to connect this handwriting with her signature. He has to have something she's signed on record."

Atlas waits eleven seconds before answering. "Did she reply in writing to the masquerade ball?"

"No, she typed it."

He frowns. "Will you send the Inspector the package today?"

"I'll have to find some way to keep the mask from breaking, but I'll think of something. I can do it before the last post is taken."

"Maybe this will be enough to keep Theodora in jail until we can find conclusive evidence," Atlas says, almost to himself.

* * *

I BLOW on the typewriter ink. This time my letter reads:

DEAR INSPECTOR,

I HAVE RECENTLY COME into possession of some compromising evidence against Theodora Thwite. I understand that you found, in the room under the floor at Walker's house, evidence of a secret society. The society in question call themselves the Invisibles, and I happen to know that the leader of this group is referred to as "the Phantom". Mrs Thwite is this Phantom.

IF YOU ARE willing to help, I can prove it.

I HAVE ATTACHED a receipt showing the purchase of the masks worn by the group and manufactured by Crow and Son. I believe the last signature was made by the right hand of Mrs Thwite.

I KNOW this is not enough to prove her guilty of any crime, but it may aid a future line of inquiry.

FAITHFULLY

I SNEAK from Father's office to go wrap my gift for the Inspector.

* * *

As I TAKE my seat at the dinner table, Father recounts the meeting he had with one of his associates – the outing that gave me my chance to sneak into his office this afternoon. The parcel to the Inspector is on its way, thanks to Eliza and the Corner Shop.

After the story ends anticlimactically, with Father saying it was a very fruitful rendezvous, we all eat in silence. In the quiet, the tapping of silverware against plates is excruciating. I take a sip of water and look at my family over the rim of the glass. Olive scoops another spoonful of peas, raising an eyebrow at my scrutiny.

Mother finally speaks. "Indigo, has your opinion about going to live with the Trinters changed at all?"

"It hasn't. I believe I will learn so much from them. I'm excited for this marvellous opportunity."

Olive sets her spoon in her bowl with a sharp *clack*. "Indigo is leaving?"

Mother and Father didn't tell her?

"Not immediately. The Trinters have offered to take her on as a student in academics and the circus arts. We'll allow her to go if she wishes," Father affirms. The phrase "circus arts" still sounds wooden on his lips.

Olive snaps her head to me, looking betrayed. "Why didn't you tell me, Indigo? How long will you be gone?"

"I didn't tell you because I wasn't sure if I was going – I only heard about it last night. It'll only be a few months at first, and I won't be far away. I'll visit often." I fold my hands under the table, averting my eyes. "And I didn't think it would affect you all that much."

"How could you think that?" She stares at me. "I will miss you, Indigo."

She will… miss me? How… odd. Some old part of my heart, one that I've long since forced to stop caring for my sister, starts beating faintly again.

"I'm sorry, Olive. I only found out about it yesterday, but I suppose I should have told you."

Olive nods tightly. "I forgive you. Sorry I interrupted, Mother and Father. Forgive me."

Mother turns back to me and I'm surprised to see her eyes brimming with tears. She smiles warmly at me as she wipes them gently with a napkin, gesturing for Father to go on.

"Indigo will complete her lessons with Mrs Wood in the coming weeks, and then she will move to 416 for the summer to see how it fares."

Father speaks so calmly about it, but how? How can he think of logistics when the very idea of living – living! – at 416 was as distant a possibility as touching a star? If I can finish my studies with Mrs Wood early, there may be the chance that I won't have to wait so terribly long. I can't wait to wake up and see Louise put ribbons in her hair, solve arithmetic problems in the schoolroom, and learn to stand on my hands like Alice!

CHAPTER 23

No dreams plague me, except an odd one about sailing in a parasol with a carrier pigeon on my shoulder. I won't mention the mess he made on my dress.

Upon waking, I brush my nightgown to make sure it was all a dream and pull the curtains open. The sunny weather from yesterday has gone; instead, fuming clouds roll across the sky. No matter. The sun will show itself again.

Phoebe rushes into the room, throwing the morning's edition of the newspaper at me. It sails into my lap.

"What's this?" The headline is almost the same as yesterday's.

Phoebe's arms are crossed tightly to her chest. She hasn't looked this worried since the night of the masquerade. "Turn a few pages."

The paper crinkles as I flip through, looking for... I don't know what. But then I freeze, page hanging in mid-air. I found it.

Theodora E. Thwite, recent widow, wrongfully apprehended by police for attempted murder. Set to be released tomorrow...

Oh, heaven help me.

"Are you alright, Indigo?"

I walk to my wardrobe, accidentally stubbing a toe. "I'm fine."

How could this happen so quickly? Or at all? Do the Invisibles have someone on the inside? What am I going to do? Did the Inspector even receive the mask and receipt? He must have. Perhaps the order had already been sent. More likely, Theodora had already bribed or threatened her way out.

Phoebe wraps her arms around me before I can reach for the wardrobe handle. "I'm so sorry. But she won't hurt you anymore." An edge comes into her tone. "We'll make sure of that."

Oh, Phoebe. I put my hands on hers.

"I know."

* * *

IN THE AFTERNOON, Phoebe finds me at my desk and kneels down. I loop my last letter for Mrs Wood's homework and finally set the pen down. The exercise did not help me think of a way to find Theodora's handwriting.

"Indigo… are you alright?" Phoebe looks up at me, clearly aching to resolve my anxiety.

"It's just… Mother and I aren't going to 416 until tomorrow, so…"

"Is that all?" The burden on her shoulders seems to lessen. "Your mother just told me that the Trinters have invited you and your family to dinner tonight."

"What?"

"Your parents wrote that you're open to the idea of living with them, and the Trinters thought it would be proper to introduce your family to the other residents. Their invitation came just a few minutes ago."

I skip into the air, my chair toppling and ink spilling over my freshly completed sheets of lettering. I grab a handkerchief, already stained from other mishaps, to soak up the worst of the spill.

"That's perfect!" I squeeze the rag over a funnel I keep for situations like this and all the rescued ink goes back into the bottle.

"Try not to stain your hands too badly. What are you going to wear?"

Lid spun back into place, I pluck the auxiliary napkin from the side of my desk to clean my pen. "I don't know. Does it matter?"

Phoebe looks fit to burst. "Of course it does! What kind of a question is that?"

"I suppose you have some ideas?"

"Maybe a few."

* * *

I WEAR the awful dress that debuted at the Luckfords'. I don't understand why – just two days ago I could wear any old thing I wanted, and tonight it's completely different. And why dress up to eat, anyway? All my debating got me nowhere with Phoebe, though, and repeating my arguments in my head now is just to distract me from my nerves.

"This is our stop," I chirp. The top of my hair just clears the ceiling as I open the carriage door and step out. Olive exhales a long-suffering sigh behind me. She's upset because she had to decline Violet's dinner invitation.

At the door, Arlo leads us to the old theatre room, which has been transformed. When Atlas brought me here for hide-and-seek, the stark shadows gave the room a dramatic but lonely ambience. Now, a vibrant glow fills the space. The light makes the gold on the stage curtain blaze against the green. But it's the people who change the room the most. They are so bright themselves. I've seen most of these faces in the training room over the course of my classes, but it's different to see them dressed for dinner.

Mr Trinter greets us. Father soon starts asking him about the races, so Olive, Mother, and I excuse ourselves.

From behind us a voice hails, "Indigo!" Alice appears from the entry hall. "How have you been? I haven't seen you since you hurt your arm. Is it feeling better?" Her hazel eyes are wide with concern.

"Yes, it's feeling much better, though I'm afraid that I'll be unable to practise handstands for a bit."

Alice looks genuinely disheartened.

"Indigo, who is this?" Mother looks Alice over.

"This is my friend, Alice. Alice, this is my mother and my sister, Olive."

Alice inclines her head. "A pleasure to meet you both."

Mother puts on a reserved smile. "Do you live here?"

"Yes."

"Has Mrs Trinter explained her plans?"

Alice nods vigorously. "Yes! I think it'd be great fun if Indigo would come and live with us."

"Who else is in your room?"

Alice answers immediately, "Everly, Nora, Louise, and me." Her entire expression falls and then rights itself so quickly, I might have missed the change if I'd blinked. "Well, actually, I have my own room now."

Olive turns wary. "Why do you have your own room?"

"Olive!" Mother chides.

Alice's shoulders cave slightly. "No, it's alright. I have my own room because I have night terrors on occasion. I was frightening Louise, so I left."

Oh, Alice! I feel terrible for not having known, even though that makes little sense. Perhaps we can swap nightmares later.

Mother puts a hand to her heart. "I am sorry to hear that."

"One day they'll cease to bother me, I'm sure." Alice rounds back on me. "I should introduce you to Everly! She'll be in your room."

As we walk to the small party of other children, I apologise for Olive's interrogation.

"Oh, she just wants to make sure you don't bunk with anyone…" Alice waggles her eyebrows. "*Disturbed.*" She lowers her voice to a conspiratorial whisper. "Atlas has been waiting for you all day."

She seems to want a reaction from me, but why? Does she know about our plans? Or Theodora? How could she have found out? Atlas wouldn't tell.

"Has he?" is all I say. He must have seen the news as well.

We stop at the edge of the circle, and Alice studies my face for two seconds more, then taps a girl on the shoulder.

"Everly, meet Indigo."

The girl reminds me of Cicely, with perfect dark skin, ebony hair, and regal features.

"Lovely to finally meet you! Welcome to room three."

"Thank you. And it's nice to meet you as well."

A clear sound, like a toy bell, rings out, causing all my peers to start towards the table. My second of hesitation separates me from Alice and Everly, but I find Atlas by my side.

"Did you see the paper?" I ask.

"Yes," Atlas says under his breath. "After dinner we're going to play games; we can talk more freely then."

* * *

WHEN ALL ARE SEATED, Mr and Mrs Trinter introduce my family. Thankfully, it's over quickly. The food is delicious, but I don't give it the attention it deserves. I'm kept busy answering questions and thinking about the trouble of handwriting.

After dinner, the adults disappear into the drawing room

while Cicely leads the youths to the circus room. In a matter of moments, there are groups playing cards, halma, chess, checkers, and backgammon at tables set up around the room. I stand surveying it all as Cicely leads Olive to a table. She must have opted to stay with me instead of joining the grown-ups.

As she sits, my sister looks around at the people at her table – particularly a tall boy of about seventeen across from her. She straightens the sleeves of her dress while somehow managing to smile and take her hand of cards at the same time. So she didn't stay for me. I should have known.

"His name is Daniel."

I flinch. "Don't do that."

Atlas smiles crookedly. "I wasn't trying to scare you."

An idea suddenly forms in my head. "Daniel, you say. Well, it seems that he's pleased to meet my sister. I seem to remember Edgar saying you have a talent for practical jokes – do you think we could…"

Atlas shakes his head, clucking his tongue playfully. "Now, Indigo. That's not the most important thing we could be doing. Besides, Daniel is my friend and roommate. What are we going to do about Theodora?"

Filing the idea away for later, I refocus my attention. "I don't know, and I'm having second thoughts about my handwriting approach."

"Why? What's the problem?"

"The invoice at Crow and Son was clearly signed by her off hand. Even with her dominant hand, Theodora might have two different styles of handwriting. Oh, don't look at me like that; it's not like I *often* use my second handwriting."

"How long did it take you to learn?"

"I'm still refining it."

He blinks in utter puzzlement. "Why?"

I shrug. "I wondered how easy it would be, or if I could even do it. And it is handy sometimes."

"When? Never mind, you can tell me later. So are you saying that we have to collect multiple samples of her handwriting? Do you have any ideas where to find them? I can only think of one, and I really don't like it."

"Then we must be thinking of the same one."

He grimaces.

"Atlas, Theodora will probably try to flee the city as soon as possible. Maybe even the country. She may already be gone! And even if there's not a sample of her handwriting at her house, I'm sure there will be something else."

"It's too dangerous."

"Clearly, the Inspector couldn't find enough evidence to keep her in prison. So we'll have to do it ourselves. And we have to do it soon." I pause. "Father prosecutes Edmond Smith in less than two weeks. I have to find some evidence strong enough to make his case fail."

"Your father is prosecuting Smith?" Atlas smacks his forehead. "Of course! How did I not see it?" He takes his hand down and looks at me anew. "That's why you started looking into this case. That's why you want to make sure it's solved."

I shift uncomfortably. "Well, yes. That's part of it, I suppo—"

He tilts his head. "Why did you never say anything?"

"It doesn't change anything about the case. This still needs to be solved, and we're the ones to do it."

Atlas purses his lips. Eventually, he nods. "Alright. But we have to be careful."

"When will we enact the plan?"

"Tomorrow?" Atlas offers. "Can you meet me here with the address?"

"Certainly. How about three o'clock?"

He nods. "It's settled."

I let out a relieved sigh and look out over the tables.

"I bet you can't beat me in draw poker," he grins.

* * *

I CANNOT BEAT Atlas in draw poker, no matter how many times I try. My consolation is that no one else can either.

Marc, Atlas's other roommate, throws down his cards. "Really, Atlas?"

"What? You're the one who decided not to drop." Atlas takes the chips from the centre of the table.

Alice counts her remaining chips. "You're sure you're not cheating? Not even a bit?"

Atlas sighs as he stacks each marker into its colour pile. "I only knew you had the jack because you looked shocked when Marc mentioned it. It's not cheating."

Alice whirls on me. "Did I look shocked?"

I shrug. "I didn't notice."

Mr Trinter comes in, clapping his hands. "Alright, everyone, thank you for a lovely evening. It's time for my students to get ready for bed. It's a school day tomorrow."

Atlas pushes his share of the chips – the lion's share – into a drawstring bag, then passes it to me. My share falls into the bag with a single clink. I did manage to hang onto one chip.

"Goodnight, everyone."

"Bye, Indigo!" Alice waves cheerily. Marc mimics her, eliciting a groan.

When they're gone, Mr Trinter says, "Olive, Indigo, your parents would like you both to join them in the drawing room."

"Thank you, Mr Trinter," Olive replies demurely. She's still flushed from her encounter with Daniel.

* * *

OLIVE AND I enter the drawing room, where the electric lights cast an amber glow. Mother and Father are sitting opposite Mrs Trinter, who's telling a story. I've never seen them so enraptured. It takes me sitting down for Father to notice my presence.

"Helen, I'm so sorry to interrupt, but would you mind starting the story over again so my girls can hear it?"

"It would be better to show you as I tell it."

Mr and Mrs Trinter lead our little party to a beautifully painted door, black with red and pink flowers around the edge.

"This room was painted by our first adopted son, Alexander. He was orphaned at a very young age. He'd had a hard go of it when we found him. When we brought him here, this house still needed work – entire rooms were yet to be touched. This was one of those rooms. One night I found Alexander painting a blank wall with some colours he'd taken. He didn't notice when I came in, he was so intent on his work. For a long time, I just stood watching him. Eventually I tapped him on the shoulder, startling him. He spun around, clutching his brush to his chest, getting paint all over the apron he'd apparently borrowed that morning. He said we could paint over it, that he just wanted to try it. He was so sorry to take things without asking. He would wash the apron and put back the rest of the paint. He was terrified I'd drag him from the room and shout at him." Mrs Trinter's voice breaks.

"So what did you do?" Mother's words barely come out, they're so quiet.

Mrs Trinter clears her throat thickly. "I sat him down and told him that he didn't need to steal things, and that he could have just asked. And I said that we would not paint over the wall." She squeezes her husband's arm, on the verge of tears.

Mr Trinter inclines his head toward the door. "Would you like to see?"

"Yes, please," Father says, quietly.

Mr Trinter holds the door open for us.

Every wall in the room is painted black, but over that are bursts of flowers in every colour imaginable: red, magenta, royal blue, canary yellow, all working together to form a massive painting. It travels over the door and even onto the ceiling in places. In the centre of the door, over the top of a camellia, is the outline of a boy painting it, in black, almost like a shadow.

Mrs Trinter has recovered enough to continue the story. "Alexander painted his shadow the night I found him, and had begun on the first flower. Now, he's grown up and is off in Paris, studying at an art school there." Her brow furrows as she turns to Mr Trinter. "He is joining us at the exposition next year, isn't he?"

"Yes, he said he'll meet us at the docks. I can hardly wait." Mr Trinter speaks softly, so as not to disturb our examination of the walls.

Mother must not have heard. She is still vacillating between awe and discomfort at the art. "How old was he when he painted this?"

Mr and Mrs Trinter both answer, "Fourteen."

Mother soundlessly repeats the word; she has decided to be awed.

"Well, he started when he was fourteen. He continued working on the room and only stopped two years ago. That's when he left for France."

Quiet reigns as we absorb the room. Mr Trinter is the first to break the silence, saying that he must go see that the children are all settled in for the night. Unfortunately, this reminds my parents that we must get home as well.

Mother, Father, and Olive chat about the evening on our drive, but I can't bring myself to join. I am consumed with my own thoughts about tonight… and tomorrow.

* * *

FLOWERS REACH above my head like trees, towards the starless sky above me. The thick grass beneath me remembers my shape as I sit up from where I was lying.

I am alone, with only the breeze to console me.

The stems of the flowers leave space enough for me to navigate a winding path through them. An invisible compass needle points me past the last flower – a boldly coloured camellia – to a dark lake. The missing stars reflect on the smooth surface of the water. Taking off my boots, I wade in. Ripples rearrange the stars into the shape of a door just as I reach it. My hand disappears below the fathomless surface, celestial light illuminating its silhouette as I take the handle.

Instead of the door pulling outwards, I am pulled under.

Pavement is a shock to my shoeless feet. I'm in the city, across from what I assume is Theodora's house. It's rotting, like the abandoned mansion, but impossibly it manages to not seem out of place between newly constructed neighbours.

As the water from the black lake drips into an inky puddle at my feet, a mask peers out at me from a broken window. It's Atlas, I know, but he shouldn't be in the house alone. The plan might not work without me, or at least another person. Did Atlas find someone else to search the house with?

A pale hand appears on his shoulder, wrenching him away from the window. He's replaced by Theodora's leering face, taunting me.

Before I can think about what I'm doing, I charge up the steps and throw open the door to the house. I hear sounds of a scuffle and shouting, but I can't find either of them anywhere. It always sounds like they're in the next room.

When I can't run any more, my legs collapse beneath me, and I feel myself dying.

"You will never find me, Indigo. I am Invisible."

CHAPTER 24

Mrs Wood is especially boring today. The most captivating thing about her is that she forgot to pin down a strand of hair. I watch it bob up and down as she drones on about the importance of memorising and understanding poetry. To ensure that my grasp of the slippery art is comprehensive, I must write my own poem. I've already got it mostly down, but as Mrs Wood will find, I am no poet.

Theodora could, at this very moment, be planning to murder Atlas and me in our sleep, or escape to some faraway country. Why does the world make me go to school at a time such as this? How could lives hang in the balance of a poetry lesson? It's ridiculous! Absurd!

Mrs Wood closes the poetry book with a thump. "Indigo, pay attention, please. And do stop scowling. It's frightening."

"Sorry, Mrs Wood."

* * *

WHEN I ARRIVE AT 416, Atlas has already saddled Emil, and they're waiting for me.

"Got the address?"

"Yes. Ready?"

He looks down the street. There's a note of hesitation in his voice as he says, "Yes. I'm ready."

* * *

I HOLD up the paper and double-check the number. "This is it."

There's not much to see: unpainted brick, a white door, windows with uncomplicated locks, and very little yard to speak of. It's just the same as every other house on the row.

"For some reason, I was expecting something more… striking, or intimidating, or just something *else.*" Atlas's voice is rough from not speaking in some time.

"That's why she's good at what she does. She hides in plain sight, and makes others believe her. She's practically invisible to them." The dream from last night is still as frightening as it was while I slept.

A man walks his dog, calling good morning to an old woman watering a rose bush. They have no idea they live on the same lane as a murderer. We ride to a tearoom we passed to leave the horses and return on foot.

Back at the house, we find our entry: a window, partially open, just above the dirt of a flower bed. Atlas eases it up and tries the gap first. The window is above a sink that might not be strong enough to support our weight, so instead of stepping on it, he drops to the floor. I copy him. It's not as hard as it looks.

"Should we close the window?"

"Probably best if we don't. What if we need a quick way out?"

He has a good point.

We've gotten ourselves into a washing room. Below the brick walls, the floor is laid with creamy tiles, sloping to a central drain. A silver washtub occupies the corner to our left. Next to it stands a drying rack, on which is a maid's frock. One glance shows it's much too large for me. Lines cross the length of the room with damp sheets slung over them. They twitch in the breeze that's snaking its way in through the open window. To someone with any sense, they would just seem like sheets drying. But, still, I hesitate to pass them. Atlas motions for us to go around the edge of the room, avoiding them.

The hard soles of my boots make it difficult to traverse the tiles silently, and try as I might, every step is accented. Before we make it ten paces, a conversation halts us. They're coming our way.

We fold ourselves into a closet a few feet ahead. The double doors have slats angling down, just far enough apart to see through. At my height I only have a view of the tiled floor. However, the closet is tall enough for me to climb on Atlas's back – with some effort – to the height where I can now view half of the intruders and the washtub. Well, technically *we* are the intruders, but no matter.

"…she's glad that Victoria and Emillia were here."

"Of course. We're all lucky."

"I wouldn't say that."

Both women wear black-and-white livery matching the one on the rack. The first turns on the water that flows into the basins. The other maid, who is smaller, dumps a red rag into the basin, turning the water a rusty colour.

Blood? It has to be even more than what I lost from my brush with the Invisible's bullet. My thoughts start to cloud over. How can someone lose that much blood and still… Never mind.

While the water splashes loudly into the basin, the taller one slams the window shut. Our way out. I didn't realise how comforting that little open window was.

"Are you saying that if the house'd burned, you'd – what? Be glad?"

"No. That's not it at all," the taller maid says defensively. "I'm not heartless."

The maid doing the accusing turns off the water and opens a tin of laundry soap. She scrubs the fabric rigorously against a washboard.

"You know, I was wonderin' when they'd try this. They don't know how much Theodora's helped us. She's only done what 'ad to."

"But now she's got to pay for it. We all do." The taller maid seems despondent as she moves into place by the other's side, taking up another washboard.

The shorter whirls back on her. "Sure, but don't be ungrateful. Where were *you* before she brought you in?"

"I'm just saying, all this might have been avoided if she'd simply kept her head. No need to get so upset about it."

The smaller maid sighs, wringing out the fabric. "I just don't like all this talk flyin' around. Puts me on edge."

They work in strained silence for long minutes.

Eventually the taller maid speaks. "I don't want you to think I'm not —"

"It's fine." The shorter interrupts, her voice is quieter and I almost miss it. "It's not you I'm worried 'bout."

She sets her washing to dry, and the tall maid follows suit. In a moment they exit.

Cautiously, Atlas cracks open the door. Between the hanging sheets, the coast is clear. We tiptoe down the hallway in our stockings, shoes in hand. Every time our steps make a noise, I wince.

The hallways are a peacock blue, without any pattern. Crowning the ceiling is an intricate black trim. The floors are old wood, occasionally covered by a rug, a brief respite from the slight creaking noises of our steps.

As we turn a corner, I almost walk directly into sight of the maids at the end of the hallway. Their white caps are bent toward one another in rapid whispers as they stand poised to go through a door. I silently press a hand to my mouth to keep my startled cry inside. Atlas pulls me back behind the corner. I lean against the wall for a second, gathering my wits.

Atlas peeks around the corner. After a moment he waves his hand and we are down the hallway again. We pass a drawing room, kitchen, dining room, and water closet. When we come back to the door the maids went through, I turn its copper handle to find a staircase. Just as expected.

We hurry up the stairs, not wanting to get caught halfway. On the next floor, I gesture to a room that's empty apart from an old chandelier and a few pieces of fine furniture. The ceiling is a blue sky with scattered clouds in the style of a Renaissance painting, while the walls are lemon yellow.

"In the washroom, the maids were cleaning bloody rags. I think it might have something to do with what happened." I whisper.

Atlas hides his shock well. "Then why would they only be cleaning it up now?"

"I don't know. It could have been last night."

He rubs his chin. "Do you think the maids know about Theodora?"

That would make sense. Why wouldn't they? If I were a duchess of crime, I'd either be completely anonymous or surround myself with allies I'd never fully trust. Theodora seems to have opted for both.

"That means we'll have to be even more careful."

"We should find what we came here for and get out. Where do you think her office is?"

A tiny trickle of surety runs through me. "It must be on this floor."

I lead the way into the hall and lean down to look through

the first keyhole. In the middle of the room is a massive bed crowned with four posts and rich curtains patterned in forest green. The bed is unmade, as if someone threw off the covers not one minute ago. A necklace of purple gems is strewn on a table beside a man's pocket watch.

I stop. Atlas notices my reaction and points at the door, silently asking the question. I don't answer; I enter and set my boots on the floor.

Directly opposite the bed are two wardrobes. The one on the right is filled with men's clothes. They're pristinely arranged, though imperfectly set on hangers. On the floor are three pairs of shoes, all shined tastefully. The doors close with a slight bump as I go to the next wardrobe.

When I open it, I can't help a small gasp. I've only ever seen Theodora in black, but here are her old clothes. They can only have been hers: a silver evening gown, a floral house dress, slim skirts, and formal shirts embroidered in an array of shades. Narrow shoes and a garish hat box are set on the floor.

There was a time before her mourning. The image of Theodora laughing merrily at a party, wrapped in satin with gemstones at her throat, comes so easily to my mind. It catches me off guard. I close the doors a little more quickly this time.

"What was it?" Atlas turns from his post guarding the hallway.

My hands still rest on the carved handles. "Just clothes."

I move on to the dressing table, brushing a fingernail across the unadorned shell of the timepiece. I slide my fingers under the watch and cradle it in my palm. Texture presses into my skin. Turning it over, I see expertly crafted lines of precious metal stringing together to outline the initials T.E.F. and O.Q.T. I stare at the letters, the cold circle lying in my hand without a heartbeat. The smooth chain slips through my fingers as I flip it over and click the top open.

Dark Roman numerals are laid in a creamy face: the three

inky hands tell nine twenty-three with five seconds to twenty-four. I've never liked how you can tell the exact moment a timepiece stopped. It's as if the springs and gears are saying, "You left me alone to die."

"Is that Theodora?" Atlas appears at my elbow. His finger lightly pulls down the front of the timepiece and my attention is directed to a small photograph set on the opposite side.

A young couple stand on a bridge over a river. Instead of looking at the camera, they look at each other. It's just possible to see their hands entwined.

"That must be her husband, Owen Thwite." Atlas hovers his little finger over the man.

"Her late husband."

It isn't easy to make out any features on him, but the woman is clearly a younger version of Theodora. Her hair is wound up in a bun with strands curling at the base of her neck. In heels, she's as tall as her husband.

"We have to keep moving," Atlas says gently.

I snap the watch closed and replace it precisely. "Right."

At the end of the hall, we turn a corner. It's a dead end except for a pair of double doors – black with ornate bronze handles shaped like thorns, spreading across the breadth. From inside comes the sound of papers being shuffled. Theodora must be in there. If we open that door now, we'll practically be calling on our dear friend.

I pivot to my accomplice and mouth, *The attic?*

We find our way back to the stairs and head up, but instead of a dark, dusty space, we find a bedroom, apparently Theodora's. The ceiling is slanted, victim of the roofline, and left as unfinished wood. The bed is clothed in black sheets and multiple quilts, which seem unusually cheerful compared with the rest of the room. The top one bears a pattern of yellow flowers bordered with blue cotton. A single pillow presides at the top of the unmade bed.

The windows at either end of the room are covered by sheer curtains. Under the window seat is a shelf stocked with a few old volumes and a diary. I snatch the small book. Inside the front cover is the name *Theodora Ember Florence*. Underneath is written *Theodora Ember Florence Thwite* with a date beside it. The first few pages reveal a light, elegant hand. This is certainly hers.

"Atlas! Look at this." I hold out the book to him, but as it passes from my hand to his, a letter slips from between the pages. I sit on my haunches to retrieve it. The return addressee is someone by the name of Gabriel Florence. It's already been opened. I slide the sheet out and look up at Atlas.

"This is in French. Do you mind reading it?"

"Hold on a minute." He flips to the last pages of the diary, his eyes scanning quickly. When he reaches a certain point he stops and shakes his head. "This ends just after she learns that her husband died. There's nothing about Walker or becoming the Phantom. We have to get into her office."

Atlas walks over to an empty patch of floor, putting his ear to the ground right over where Theodora's office likely is. "There are at least three people in there."

I stow the letter in my pocket. "Do you think we should create a distraction?"

After much whispered debate, it's decided that I will be the distraction. I'll go downstairs, make a racket, and escape as dramatically as possible. Hopefully they'll chase after me, giving Atlas time to have a look around before meeting me at the teashop.

Just as I turn to start back downstairs, Atlas takes my hand. Have I forgotten anything?

He searches my face as if I might have the words he needs. His fingers slip through mine before he decides on, "Be careful."

Surely he doesn't think I'm going to *recklessly* draw all Theodora's murderous attention?

"I will."

I make my way silently down to the ground floor, shoes in hand. Having learned from my mistake last time, I check the corners before going around them. I find myself constantly looking behind, almost expecting an ambush.

Just outside the washroom door, the tip of my foot catches on the edge of the hallway rug. The floor rises towards my face, and instinctively my hands reach forward to break my fall. I don't hit the floor with my entire body, so I haven't created too much of a disturbance. But my boots tumbled out of my grip with twin thumps. I slowly let out a breath that's clawing to be set free.

"'Ello, Indigo."

I look up to see a maid – the short one – leaning against the doorframe to my left, her arms crossed. I see now that she has a pale, washed-out face, light blue eyes, and thin hair tucked into a bun. She's not the kind of person someone would usually notice. She seems…

"Theodora told me 'bout you. You're the one who broke into the office."

Bile-like panic rises inside me. Office? I haven't broken into her office yet! What does she know? Could she mean at the abandoned mansion? That's got to be it. Personally, I'd call it "my lair". But how could she know that?

"She told me to look out for you – that you're crafty."

I push myself up to a kneeling position and use the distraction to take the edge of the rug in my hand. "Crafty? That's high praise coming from her."

"She also said that you could be quite troublesome."

"Well, everyone has their faults." My heart rate is becoming dangerously fast, and what seems like gallons of adrenaline cause me to shake slightly. "So I suppose you are an Invisible, then?"

"I think you already knew that. I am surprised you don't recognise me." She tucks her knuckles under her chin. "I suppose I was wearing a mask."

Suddenly, I do recognise her. Not her face, but her body type and stance. Her toes always seem to be pointing straight ahead, and her shoulders cave stiffly. "You were the one who led me to Theodora. You…"

The woman unlocks her arms, standing on her own power. "Theodora also told me to contain you. She usually just tells me to kill intruders, so you should count yourself lucky."

My shoeless foot slips across the floor into position. "I like to think it's because of my charm."

She frowns and rolls back the cuff of her sleeve, revealing something that looks much like the arm guard Leo wears while practising archery. She guides a smooth black metal spike from the fabric.

Before the projectile can leave her hand, I lift the rug in front of me like a shield and move behind it. The sudden lack of target means the spike leaves only an inconsequential tear in my dress. The maid begins walking toward me, no doubt readying another spike. When her weight pulls on the rug, I stand and yank it from under her feet. I have about two seconds before she's back up; I use them to dash down the hall.

I vaguely register the sound of my pursuer whistling, but I don't have much time to realise the implications. Turning a corner, I startle another maid. In a split second she rips back her cuff and chases me. Depending on how I think of this predicament, it could be favourable. Hopefully, Atlas is getting the documents and escaping.

Another maid barrels down the stairs just behind me. "What the…?" She stops at the bottom, taking in the scene.

"Get her!" the blonde maid screams.

If the maid wasn't lying, they aren't allowed to *kill* me, though they seem content to pierce me with their bizarre weapons. The corner is my saving grace. The front door should be just around it. As long as I can get out into the street, I might be able to escape this madhouse.

My breath comes in quick rasps, and my chest is heaving as I reach the corner.

A dead end.

Not an empty dead end where I might bravely make a last stand or dash out the front door just steps away. No, I run straight into the waiting arms of Theodora.

"Hello, dear," she says. "I was wondering when you would come to see me."

<h1 style="text-align:center">CHAPTER 25</h1>

I collapse into Theodora with my full weight, throwing her off balance. We both hit the floor: she on her hip and I on my shoulder. Before she can catch me, I get to my feet and try the front door handle. It's locked and there's no key. I fly to the window, throwing my body into the catch to force it open. It doesn't budge. Why won't it open? The latch is undone —

"I painted them shut. You won't be able to open it."

Why hadn't I realised earlier that the windows are painted shut? Years of paint; coats and coats of the stuff. I guess we got lucky with the washroom window. They must need that one to open for drying laundry.

I turn to face Theodora. She regains her feet and glares at me coolly. "Why are you here?"

If I tell her a convincing lie immediately, she won't believe me.

"I wanted to see you. I thought you'd be getting lonely."

It sounds annoying, even to my own ears. Theodora's face flashes with something so briefly that I almost miss it. I imme-

276

diately try to recall her expression, but the moment passes like a bolt of lightning.

She balls her hands into fists. "Lucy, will you help Indigo stand still?"

"Theodora, I know my limits."

"You also know that you can surpass those limits in a heartbeat if you know someone needs your help."

No, no, no, this is going all wrong. "Who? I mean, really, who needs my help?" My voice has risen an octave or two.

Theodora's face hardens. "Let's not pretend, Indigo. Where's Atlas?"

"Atlas? He isn't here." I'm still a bad liar.

Theodora massages the spot between her eyes. "Now, really, Indigo. Stop wasting my time."

Understanding floods her expression. She looks up from the floor and takes her hand slowly from her head.

"You were the distraction." Furious colour rises in her cheeks. "Charlotte, watch the hallways. Victoria and Emillia, with me to my office. Lucy, stay with Indigo."

Only one for me? I may yet escape. But what about Atlas?

In under five seconds, every maid has left the room except Lucy. She is the guard I'm already acquainted with. With a final look, Theodora stalks from the room with a swish of her dress.

After four seconds, Lucy purses her lips and takes off her cap to stow loose blonde wisps of hair. She has no reason to be on edge. She guards the only plausible exit, which is down a hall that goes past the staircase leading to Theodora and the rest of the maids. I would have to first pass Lucy, then outrun her – and the maids she'd call – to get out the washroom window. I'll never make it.

I fill my lungs slowly through my nose to quiet the electric hum in my head. There's no other sound, aside from Lucy's breathing and my own. I watch the door. Soon, my eyes sting from keeping them open. Perhaps Atlas got away already? If he

found the evidence quickly, he could've gone out the window…
No, the paint. He might have found a letter opener and scraped
it away? Please, please…

Something shifts uncomfortably in my hair, caught in my
curls. I reach up as if to scratch my head, and my fingers press
against a cold, smooth surface. One of the maids' throwing
spikes – it was caught in the hair at the back of my neck!

Slowly sliding out the prize, I put my hands behind my
back, tapping my foot as if I am impatient. If I'm lucky, the
tapping sound will mask the scratching of metal against paint.

"Don't worry, it'll be over soon enough." The Invisible wrig-
gles her cap into place, pulling it down with a final tug.

This window will never work with Lucy standing in front
of me, but perhaps in the chaos that will inevitably ensue, I
may find an opportunity. I tap my foot even harder and just
manage to manufacture a convincing whimper.

Because the spike has no sharpened edge, I have to use the
tip to perforate the dried paint. If I could turn to the window, it
might not be so bad, but in this position my wrist is bent at an
awkward angle.

Lucy pushes up the fabric of her sleeve and wraps a hand
around her spike-cuff with a grunt. I move slightly to the left. I
must be nearing the end of the sill. It can't be much wider. The
point of the spike strikes the edge of the window frame and I
accidentally drop it. The side of it collides with my foot,
muffling the sound.

"I really don't want to die." I say the words loud enough to
mask my error.

She looks up from her wrist for just a second. "Everyone's
gotta go sometime, love. You should feel lucky you made it this
far."

Paint presses under my nail as I widen the rifts with my
thumb. I bend down to retrieve the fallen spike from the floor,
slipping it into my pocket.

"Ey, what are you doing?" Lucy takes menacing steps towards me and thrusts her hand into my pocket. She pinches a scarf, and as she draws it out, the spike falls deeper inside.

"What did you think you'd do with this?" For a moment she stares down at the scarf. Then she crumples it between her hands and pulls it apart again. "What's this for?"

"I'll give you a guess."

"You'll tell me," she practically growls.

"It is part of a disguise I was going to put on as soon as I escaped."

"Why is it red?"

"If you were looking for me out there and saw a woman in a red scarf, would you think it was me?"

She aims a finger at me and opens her mouth. After a second, she seals it and lowers her finger. "I see your point."

There's a thunderous battering noise upstairs, followed by Theodora screaming. A cry of pain turns over something deep inside me. I try to casually walk to the doorframe, but Lucy snatches my arm.

"I just want to see —"

"They're bringing 'im down 'ere."

Something comes crashing down the stairs. That couldn't have been Atlas, could it? Twelve seconds later, a large herd of people stomp back into the foyer, with Atlas in the grip of the Phantom. A cut by his right eye is letting blood drip down his face like unnatural tears. He's limping slightly, favouring his left leg. Behind him, Theodora is watching my reaction.

"You liar." She spits the words between clenched teeth.

I have to keep myself from laughing. "I'm sorry, did you just call *me* a liar?"

"Never mind. Charlotte! Lucy! Take Indigo and Atlas down to the cellar. I'll be down in a moment."

We're pushed into a large, dank room. They leave a lit candle.

"We will be guarding the only way out. Don't try anything." The woman named Charlotte slams and bolts the door. The sound is unnecessarily loud, drilling deep into my ears.

Atlas hobbles over to the far side of the room to rest against the wall. He holds his face in a tight expression until he sits with his legs straight out in front on the dirt floor. Pulling his sleeve over his hand, he dabs at his eye.

"How was the distraction?" He looks at me over the crimson stain on his shirt.

"Oh, it went rather well. How'd things go with you?"

He nods. "You were right, she does have different handwriting styles. I found one that matched the paper she signed at Crow and Son, so there'll be no mistaking it. And there was another letter dated today from a contact within one of the newspaper companies, alluding to a longstanding bribe. I assume it was for supporting Smith as the murderer."

"That's amazing! Do you have them now?"

"No. I'd just found the document I needed when I heard them on the stairs."

I collapse to the floor. Not again. We were so close. How could we get this close and still let her get away?

Atlas continues, smiling. "While they were trying to force the door I folded the evidence into paper birds and threw them into the yard. Had to cut some paint off the windows with a letter opener, but they're safe. If we can get out of here and send them to the Inspector, we could finish this."

Dread drains out of me, and I shuffle across the floor to sit next to him. I don't feel tired or hurt at all anymore, though I must have several bruises and have probably stubbed all my toes by now.

"Why didn't you just say that? Now, waiting is so much easier." I prop my back against the wall, and look at the red line by his eye. "What fell down the stairs? You could probably hear that throughout the neighbourhood."

Atlas winces. "That was me."

"You? That's why you're limping?"

"Theodora pushed me down the stairs. I managed to fall without getting hurt too badly. I think I just bruised my back and knees and elbow and… Well, never mind. I'll be fine."

"How did you cut your eye?"

"After they forced the door open, they started throwing metal spikes."

"That was close! One got stuck in my hair and I used it to cut the paint that was sealing the window by the front door. If we get the chance, we can go through that."

Atlas presses his hands into the floor to move closer. "Do you still have it? The spike?"

I extract the thing and pass it to him. He handles it carefully, turning it over. I stare at the candle. The outline of the flame sears into my vision.

"Atlas, the light is moving. Do you think the air flow from the trapdoor to the house would be enough to cause the draught?" The door isn't airtight by any means, but another source could be our passage out.

"There must be holes in the door, or – oh, I see what you're getting at."

I take the candle and search the cellar. In a corner, short steps lead to an exterior hatch. I force it up. A seam of daylight widens for a brief second, and then chains rattle and my progress is halted.

"It's locked from the outside." I release the door, letting it fall back into its frame, and the candle gutters out.

"Indigo." Atlas's tone is forced calm. "You didn't happen to *blow* out that candle?"

"No, it went out when I let go of the door."

Atlas sighs, and I picture him running a hand through his hair. My heart gallops. I crawl back to where he should be.

"What do we do now?" His voice draws nearer.

"Should we try to make a hole in the trapdoor? You still have the spike."

If they hear us scraping at the door, what will they do? Open it and take the spike? March us to Theodora? Then we'll have another chance at escaping.

"Yes. Let's try it."

It takes a few moments to relocate the exterior door. My shins find the stone steps first. "Found it," I say through clenched teeth.

Atlas follows the sound of my voice and we're soon taking turns chipping away. After a few minutes of scratching, a barked order echoes upstairs. Footsteps pound on the floorboards above our heads. More shouts, short and direct. It goes on like this for three minutes and twenty seconds and then everything goes silent.

"What do you think that was?" My voice is small after the cacophony.

"Haven't the faintest. Should we keep going?"

We continue, but the smooth spike is difficult to hold and I soon tire of gripping it so tightly. My sweaty hand cramps up after shorter and shorter turns as Atlas and I pass it back and forth. After another minute, the sound of calls – distant, but growing more clamorous – reaches us. Heavy boots clump up and down stairs above our heads. Doors slam closed.

We halt our work again to hear what they're saying. It gradually becomes clearer, indistinct mumbling evolving into men's voices. Atlas and I must come to the same conclusion, because we both say, "The police!"

It takes a few moments to find the inside hatch. "In the cellar," I shout. "We're down here!"

In eighteen seconds the bolt is thrown back. Light blinds us, and calloused hands lift us out of the cellar.

"Are you alright? Do you need assistance? Is anything broken?"

When my eyes adjust to the light, the curled moustache of Absalom Wallace is the first thing I notice. The Inspector crouches down and puts his hands on our shoulders, then does a double take.

"You two? What the devil are you doing here?"

"We're fine. But did you catch her? Did you catch Theodora?"

Inspector Wallace wrinkles his brow. "There's someone else in the house?"

"We didn't lock ourselves in the cellar, now did we?" My voice rises with each word.

The Inspector ruffles at my comment. "I am perfectly aware of that," he sugar-coats his voice and speaks slowly, "but there's no one else in this house besides you and us."

"How could she have known you were coming?" Atlas breathes, shocked.

I jump up, Atlas behind me. We sprint out of the tiny room. The hallways are empty. The rooms are empty. Theodora's study is populated only by the blank paper and pens found in any office. It's as if no one has been here for a week; the only evidence of any recent activity is wet laundry hanging in the washroom. They've disappeared.

Inspector Wallace orders his men to pursue. "They can't have gone far… I mean, it isn't as if they have turned invisible."

No, that is exactly what they've done – just not the way he thinks.

CHAPTER 26

"We've had our experts read over these documents and they do agree that they are written by the same hand," the man at the desk drones on from behind a stack of papers. "We have now issued a warrant for the arrest of the woman in question, if and when she is found. Currently, we are looking into Richard Banks, of the Daily Call newspaper, and his correspondence with Mrs Thwite. We will keep you informed."

This man doesn't know how important this is. He doesn't understand what Theodora can do. Or any of the Invisibles. And here he is —

"Indigo, it's time to go." Atlas jars me from my thoughts. He's clearly as upset as I am, but our mothers are walking towards the exit.

It's raining as we hurry into the dry interior of our ride. Mrs Trinter sighs, looking out the window, her shoulders slumped. It hasn't been easy these past few weeks. Theodora escaped and remains missing despite all the efforts of the police. With her went any incriminating papers, except the ones Atlas flew out the window.

The reason the Inspector was at Theodora's house at all was because he was sent an anonymous note that read, "Thwite residence, 4:30 p.m." Atlas confessed to me that he'd sent the note as a precaution. I can't believe he didn't just tell me! I would've had no objections with the idea of arranging some backup. I'm not *unreasonable*. Did he think I'd try to stop him?

"It's out of your hands now," the police say. "You have no reason to worry."

They're lying to a child. Or perhaps they believe it. I don't know anymore. Theodora got away and the rest of the Invisibles remain anonymous. This is my fault. I stuck my foot into something I didn't know the extent of, and now it could take months to find them. Or they may never be caught.

No, I can't think like that. This isn't over. I'll track the Invisibles wherever they hide, even if it takes me years.

Our official story is that I was kidnapped from my house, and Atlas was taken from the streets by The Empty Tray. It was a bit tricky to explain how Atlas decided to fold important documents into the shape of birds and fly them into the yard, but he managed. He claims he'd been trying to signal some neighbours with the paper, but was caught and thrown into the cellar with me.

Everyone believes us except Officer Laurier, who vehemently argues that we are in league, somehow, with Theodora. He's been to see us quite a few times, and each time I liked him less. Now I loathe him. I haven't seen him in a week, though. I suppose it's still too much to hope that he was fired, but I would settle for a demotion.

Mustn't dwell on fantasies. My comfort is that Mr Smith is safe for now. The evidence against him being the murderer is too much to deny. Despite the public outcry, the trial has been postponed until further evidence can be unearthed. So I've done what I set out to accomplish, I suppose – but that's little consolation now.

Soon Theodora will become restless, and I must be ready. If I am not paying close attention, I may miss my chance, but for now, I can enjoy this time. I can enjoy the show.

The hackney rolls to a stop, and we all sway in our seats.

Mother takes my hand. "Goodbye, Helen, Atlas. See you tomorrow."

Mrs Trinter smiles. *Tomorrow.* What a wonderful word. *Tomorrow* is the day I move into 416 Old Twinings Road.

"Tomorrow. Good day, Amethyst. Goodbye, Indigo."

I haven't heard Mother's first name in such a long time. It's odd to hear someone outside our family say it. Grandmother is not an ordinary woman, and she never pretends to be. She wanted to give her only daughter a name that was unique and beautiful. Often, Mother only goes by Mrs Taylor, reserving her first name for those she's truly friends with. I am glad she trusted Mrs Trinter with it.

"Goodbye," is all I can say before Mother drags me out into the rain. Then I'm running for the shelter of the portico. Mother doesn't scold me, only looking on deep in thought. Phoebe waits just inside the door to open it for us.

"How was it, Indigo?" She doesn't take her eyes from my face as I shrug off my coat.

"As expected."

"I'll be up in a minute to help you finish packing," Mother says as she runs a hand along her hair. "I'm going to see about some warm tea."

* * *

"I can't need *all* of this."

I stand in the midst of boxes, bags, trunks, and a random assortment of anything *remotely* related to daily life. I'll never even use half of it, and it won't fit under my bed at 416. Mother is hidden behind a checklist, marking off things that've been packed. Phoebe and I share a nod. We'll leave most of it behind.

"What did you say, dear?" Mother doesn't look up.

"Nothing. I can pack my bags into the hackney tomorrow."

She nods distractedly. "That's wonderful."

We stop for dinner, and I eat everything on my plate and more. After folding her napkin and replacing it on the table, Mother says that she must get some sleep and won't be able to help me pack any further.

Phoebe and I chat while sifting through my belongings. In the end, I fit everything for my regular life – if there is such a thing – into one trunk: books, notebooks, clothes, shoes, and toiletries. The other trunk is for my disguises. Finally done, I slump onto my bed and fall into a deep sleep.

I WEAR a dress made entirely of white rose petals as I lug my trunks into a hackney. Mother must have packed, as there seems to be an *endless* amount of baggage to arrange. When every trunk is secured, they stick out the windows and sit precariously on the roof. I even have one in my lap as I ride.

At the docks, I find my boat, which turns out to be a white parasol with the words *HMS Shade* embroidered in vibrant green on the side. After all my things have been stowed in the parasol, I set sail.

WHEN I WAKE in the morning, Father orchestrates the loading. Before long, he's kissed me goodbye and we're on our way to 416. I try to content myself with looking out the window, but when we pass Madame Resselin's, I suck in a sudden breath.

"I did pack the black veil, didn't I?"

Phoebe smiles reassuringly. "Yes, Indigo."

"And Mother's old gloves?"

She nods. "They're in your trunk."

"And everything from the secret drawer?"

"There was nothing left when you checked this morning. You can always go back tomorrow if you forgot something, but I don't think you did." Phoebe puts a hand on my knee. "There's no reason to be nervous, Indigo."

"Nervous! I'm not nervous. Why should I be nervous?" I can't look at Phoebe and instead return my gaze out the window.

"It's perfectly alright. I'm sure your mother was anxious when she first left for boarding school. And your father, too, for that matter."

"I don't understand why I would be. Nervous, I mean." I turn back to her. Phoebe's eyes have a knowing kindness.

"You're moving away from the only home you have ever known. Away from your parents. And even though you know it's what you want, maybe you're afraid it won't be what you imagined. And maybe..." She pauses. "Maybe you're afraid that things won't ever be the same with your family."

"So..." My fingers play with the fabric of my dress. "What do I do?"

Phoebe lets out a dramatic sigh, as if I missed the entire point of her monologue. "Nothing is ever the same, so just enjoy whatever it is you have now."

"But what if —"

The carriage stops and Phoebe raises a hand.

"No more 'what if's." She takes my hand for a second. "I won't be far, and your parents and Olive are coming to dinner. It isn't as if you'll never see us again. Let's go." Phoebe pulls me to my feet and out into the morning air.

Mr and Mrs Trinter are already waiting outside the bright green doors. The background pairs well with Mrs Trinter's blue-grey skirt and Mr Trinter's dark hair. A raindrop falls on my hand and trickles down my fingers. The sky's been dark all morning, but now rain begins to dot the ground. Immediately, everyone springs into action.

"Morning, Indigo." Mr Trinter unties the trunk from the roof and I reach up for it, taking it into my arms and setting it on the ground. The second trunk is handed down after.

In the house, Louise, Alice, Nora, and Everly come running towards us, laughing and cheering. The older girls insist on carrying my luggage, so Louise takes my hand and talks all the way. I still haven't seen my room; they wanted to keep it a surprise. I rebelled against this and even tried to sneak in (multiple times), but was thwarted.

As Louise opens the door, I gasp.

The room has two large windows, with early morning light cascading in. Beneath the windows are two canopy beds with their footboards touching. A little ragdoll – the one Louise had with her in the park the day we first met – lies against her pillow. To either side of the door are two more canopy beds. All the beds have drawers beneath and white curtains that close for privacy. Light blue damask wallpaper contrasts nicely with the matching yellow-gold flower pattern on the sheets. The walls between the beds are decorated with a few pictures. On the other side of the room is a black handle that looks randomly placed in the wall.

"That's your bed." Louise points to the right of the door before clambering onto her own bed. The trunks are set gently onto my mattress, each one making a light *humph*.

"Do you want any help organising?" Alice asks.

"That's alright, I can manage it. Thank you so much for all your help already."

Louise waves away my appreciation. "It was nothing."

Everly titters. "That's because you didn't carry anything!"

Turning to me, she continues, "You're welcome, we're happy to help. Do you want to know where the closet is?"

"Is it this?" Upon further examination, the mysterious handle looks like a starling bird in mid-flight, just like the front door.

Alice laughs. "We were going to surprise you, but oh well. Go ahead and open it."

As I pull the handle, part of the papered wall opens, revealing a deep and orderly cupboard with two racks on either side and a tall bookshelf in between. A few editions are already in places of honour: *Heidi*, *Gulliver's Travels*, *Little Women*, *An Old-Fashioned Girl*, and, to my surprise, *Treasure Island*. I read that one when Leo snuck it to me, as Mother would never approve of it. I loved it. I haven't read any of the American books. I must ask Nora her opinion of them.

"Lovely!"

Nora tilts her head and says, rather quietly, "Did you bring any books? There's plenty of space on the shelves."

"Yes. Just a few."

As I unpack, the conversation continues, often interrupted by laughter. Each girl sits on her own bed, except Alice, who is cross-legged on the floor. I can just see her head over the edge of my covers. After I finish stocking the bookshelf and start on my disguise case, there's a knock at the door.

"Come in," we all say in unison. This causes another round of giggles as Cicely pokes her head in.

"I was just coming to see how it was going."

I report my progress, and Cicely puts on a falsely suspicious look.

"I hope none of these young girls are distracting you with conversation?"

I put a hand to my heart. "What? No not at all."

"Just checking. Everly is a toss-up… Never know with her."

Everly arches a finger towards herself. "Me?" Cicely wraps her in a hug.

"Are you two sisters?" I ask. As if on cue, they glance at each other, then put their faces side by side.

"I don't know, are we?"

Indeed, even their expressions look nearly identical."I knew it!"

The pair pretend to look startled. "Oh, no, is it that obvious?" Everly laments. They laugh, and we all join in.

Cicely stands. "Alright, I'm going to help with lunch. Don't have any fun without me."

We all promise that we won't, and she's off.

Thirty minutes later, I'm finished putting everything away and we all head down to eat. If I'd had to come down by myself, having unpacked alone all morning, I would have felt very apprehensive. Since quite the opposite is true, lunch slips past quickly.

Afterward, Mr and Mrs Trinter take the girls from room three, along with Marc, Atlas, and Abbott, to the park across the street. The day has cleared up and the puddles reflect the blue sky. Alice brought a jump rope, so we decide to hold a tournament. Marc's time is the shortest, which he attributes to the rope being "too short", despite the fact that he's only an inch taller than Abbott, who wins. We enjoy the park until Mr and Mrs Trinter say we must go back.

* * *

MOTHER, Father, and Olive join us for a delicious dinner and just before they leave, they remind me of the rules.

"Brush your teeth *every* night," Father begins.

"I already d—"

"Bathe often, and don't neglect your hair." Mother emphasises the latter half of the statement. "Don't look at me like that, Indigo."

Father tucks his hat under his arm. "Listen to Mr and Mrs Trinter."

"And don't be nosy," Olive gets in.

I don't think that one counts. So far I'm alright, though keeping up with my hair can be trouble.

"Don't do anything dangerous," Father finishes.

Mother narrows her eyes and searches my face. "What is it? Indigo, you just had your guilty look. I know you too well for this."

I laugh, trying not to look guilty. Think… Think… What could… Oh!

"But isn't trapeze dangerous?"

Father shakes his head and gives me a last hug. "Oh, not like that. Of course, be careful on the trapeze. I meant don't do any ill-advised things."

There are plenty of loopholes with that rule. "I won't."

* * *

AFTER BATHING, brushing my teeth, *and* combing my hair, I change into my nightgown. Everly and Louise have drawn their curtains and fallen asleep, Nora is reading a book in her bed, and Alice has gone to her own room. It's peaceful.

"Do you have a pocket watch?" I whisper to Nora.

Her head snaps up from her book. She nods and passes me a silver watch on a chain. The time reads ten-thirteen.

"Thank you."

Nora smiles and goes back to her book. With a quick glance at my new schedule, I see I have another seventeen minutes before lights out, and I know just the thing to put me to sleep.

Padding over to the closet, I snatch *Emma* from the shelf. Now, where was I… Yes, Mr Elton has just sent Harriet and Emma that ridiculous charade. It only takes me one pass to figure out the answer. How much longer is this book? I pinch both the pages I have read and what I have yet to read. Ugh. Not even halfway.

A few pages later, my eyelids start to droop, so I put away the book and turn off my lamp.

Only a second after that, it seems, Louise flings my curtains open, letting early morning light blind me.

"Morning, Indigo!"

"Louise?"

"Yes!"

"What time is it?"

"Seven."

"Ahh. Good morning."

She puts one of her small hands on my shoulder. "Do you need help waking up? Everly always takes off my covers and sings to me." Her hand inches toward my warm sheets. I clutch them to me.

"No, no, I don't need any help! You go get dressed."

She skips off. I pull out my trusty charcoal dress with the flowers I embroidered. I'm just doing up buttons when someone knocks at the door.

"Come on, Indigo!" Alice calls. "Why are you moving so slowly?"

I open the door. "Sorry, I didn't know I was being slow. Why is everyone in such a hurry? Breakfast isn't until eight."

Her eyes widen to the size of saucers. "The costumes arrive today! Mrs Helen is probably setting them up in the circus room right now!"

At the word "costumes", my brain starts working, and by the time she says "right now", I'm plaiting my hair as fast as my fingers will go. We trip over each other on the way to the circus room, only to be rewarded with a locked door. We're not the only students waiting. Everly, Louise, Nora, Abbott, Marc, Daniel, and Cicely are already there.

Just as we're starting another game of Oranges and Lemons, Mr and Mrs Trinter slip out of the room. All heads turn, but just as we rush the door Mr Trinter throws up his hands, laughing.

"I think you all know the rules, but just in case you forgot, here they are: no pushing or shoving to get inside, do not destroy the tag with your name on it, and no wearing costumes until Helen or I call you into the dressing room. Understand?"

A sea of bobbing heads assures him the rules are as clear as crystal. He turns to his wife, grinning. "Should we let them in?"

She considers for a second. "I think so." With a flourish, she opens the doors. As I pass through, Mrs Trinter gives me a secret smile, but quickly looks away to remind Marc not to shove.

The mats have been placed against the walls, racks of clothing taking their place. Handwritten signs note the age groups of the costumes. I pick out the rack where my ensemble will be, and standing beside it is —

"Mother!"

She gives me a hug. I knew she'd been working on the costume designs, but I didn't know she'd be here!

"Do you want to see yours?" she asks.

I find my tag dangling from the neck of the hanger. My costume looks fit for a Shadow Knight. There's a black fencing jacket and balloon trousers, smoky, knee-length boots, grey fencing gloves, a black scarf, and a sabre.

"What's this?" I hold up the scarf. Mother puts it up to her eyes: holes have been cut in the centre so it becomes a thin mask.

Throughout the rest of the room, others are holding up ensembles. Not everyone is in the upcoming show, but all are curious about the costumes. I've never seen so many incredible disguises in one place and I feel a giddy tingle in my fingers.

Atlas opens the door of the training room, yawning. Taking his time, he makes his way to our rack.

"Morning, Indigo. Morning, Mrs Taylor."

"How were you not up earlier? Everyone came down here to see the costumes!"

He raises his eyebrow. "Not everyone. I managed to go back to sleep for another precious thirty minutes and didn't have to wait by a locked door. Costume days are one of the few days you can sleep in. The only other way is to be sick." He leans in. "I tried it once, pretending I was sick. Mother gave me the most disgusting medicine." Faint lines appear between his eyes. "Come to think of it, she probably knew I was pretending. I bet it wasn't medicine at all."

And to think! I could have gotten thirty minutes' more sleep *and* avoided waiting!

Atlas reads my thoughts. "Well, now you know for the next show." He lifts down a hanger. "Oh, it seems I'll be a clown."

I blink. "The next show?"

"Oh, yes. I suppose you don't *have* to be in them if you don't want to." Atlas holds his costume at arm's length: a white shirt with a large black bow, some fencing trousers with a pattern of black-and-white triangles, and a half-mask.

Marc claps Atlas on the shoulder. "Don't forget the shoes!" He points to a pair of shoes in the same black-and-white triangular pattern as the trousers, complete with a giant puff-ball on the toe. Before Atlas can say anything, Marc snatches his own hanger from the rack and bounds off.

While I've been examining Atlas's clothes, he's been looking at mine. He snaps his fingers.

"I know who you are! I knew they were going to choose you for the Knight."

Mother wags a finger at Atlas. "Don't tell her anything – not yet."

Atlas nods and slips his feet into his clown shoes.

* * *

Two months pass quickly, and 416 is almost never still. Apart from a bit of summer schoolwork, there's also show practice, chores, costumes to adjust, sets to paint and build, and the usual hubbub. Finally, after some blood (from a misplaced hammer during set building), sweat, and tears (also from the hammer incident), the morning of the show's debut arrives.

I'm up before Louise… and most everyone else. I steal downstairs to find Mr and Mrs Trinter preparing the kitchen for breakfast duty with Daniel.

"Good morning, Daniel – oh, it's you, Indigo! What brings you down this early?" Mrs Trinter scrubs a bar of soap against her hands in the sink while Mr Trinter cuts a loaf of bread.

"I was just going to practise my fencing for tonight."

Mrs Trinter turns off the water. "Indigo, are you feeling well?"

"I'm fine."

Truth be told, my stomach is all in knots. I've never been on stage, or even had to present to anyone besides Mrs Wood, Phoebe, or my parents.

"Are you nervous?"

"Why should I be?" Why indeed? I was more confident sneaking into the abandoned mansion.

"Stage fright is natural. And nothing to be ashamed of." Mr Trinter severs the last chunk of bread into two.

"You can practise some, but be careful not to tire yourself out too much," Mrs Trinter says. "I'd rather there be someone with you, but no one else is up."

* * *

I'VE NEVER SEEN the training room empty, but it feels like a cathedral: quiet and still. I take a sabre from the closet and test the weight; assembling images around me in my mind until I've painted the Cirque du la Reine stage.

"En garde. Go."

As my whisper dissipates, I go in for a lunge and aim for my opponent's waist. I have taken advantage, so he tries to make me fall short. He goes for my chest, I parry, and he fails his riposte. I score a point on his mask. We start again, going in at the same time, but he gains advantage. He attacks, swiping his sabre up to meet my wrist, but I block just in time. I try again, this time for his shoulder. He moves to parry, leaving his wrist unguarded. I lunge forward to tap it, but before I score the point, he guides his sword to my torso, taking the tally.

I go on like this, fighting against an invisible opponent. This is natural to me. It feels familiar.

Just as I make a riposte on my adversary, a real sword catches mine. The focus I had is broken, and my surroundings return.

Atlas stands there, sabre in hand. "It's time for breakfast."

So soon?

"You've been in here for over an hour. You'll be bone-tired before tonight." He lowers his weapon and offers to take mine. I hand it over.

"Sorry. I didn't realise so much time had passed. Does Louise think I've been spirited away?"

He puts the swords back into the depths of the closet. "Just about. What got you up so early?"

"Wanted to seize the day, I suppose."

He chuckles, looking back at me. "Everyone gets stage fright, Indigo. You can just tell me."

"That's exactly what your father said," I mumble.

Atlas closes the door and we start towards the kitchen, stopping in the changing room so I can wipe away the worst of the sweat.

"He's right, you know."

I appraise Atlas's demeanour. "Are *you* nervous?"

"It went well during practice, so, not much." He shrugs. "Still a bit, I guess. Don't worry about it now; if you do, it will only build up and be worse later. What you need is a distraction. Do you want to play a game of Killer Killer after breakfast?"

* * *

BREAKFAST IS ESPECIALLY CLAMOROUS. Everyone's buzzing about the show. Louise guesses there'll be over five hundred people on opening night and then polishes off the last of her porridge. I guess not everyone's nervous.

Because Mr and Mrs Trinter don't want anyone to be exhausted before the show, we're encouraged to rest for the day. All afternoon we play Killer Killer, Oranges and Lemons, and Here Comes an Old Soldier from Botany Bay.

I get away with not eating anything at lunch, but dinner is another story. Nora encourages me to eat, as does nearly everyone else. I try, and I do eat some. It should be enough to get me through the show. I ease my fork down onto the table.

Mrs Trinter rounds on me. "Indigo, you have to eat more. You'll be ravenous halfway through the show."

With a heavy sigh, I pick up my fork.

CHAPTER 27

I'm relieved when Mr Trinter dismisses us to go. We've each been given a number that corresponds to the adult who will escort us to the theatre. I'm to travel with the second group; Mr Trinter is our chaperone.

Before long, we're on the tram, the dimming city sliding past our windows.

"Do you want to play a game?" Nora says as she flourishes a string fit for Cat's Cradle.

"I haven't played in years. Will you remind me of the basic tricks?"

It wouldn't have mattered if I'd spent a century studying the game; Nora would know more formations anyway. She loops and unloops the string, making it look effortless. We play the entire ride, stopping only when we arrive outside the theatre. We quickly file through the grand building's backstage entrance.

It's a medium-sized space, crowded with all the things one would need onstage: swords, dust packets, pitchers of water, hand chalk, and so many other things. The low light might almost be comforting if I didn't know what – or rather who – waits beyond these walls.

Changing into my costume is quick, and after putting on the basic amount of powder, I'm ready. I distract myself by helping others. Alice is to be a shadow, so all her hair must be stuffed into a hood, which is easier said than done.

Next, I help Everly – a canary – paint bright yellow feathers from her eyes and forehead down to her shoulder blades. It's a difficult business, but when we tried using actual feathers two weeks ago, they all ended up bent or broken on the floor.

By this time, backstage is bustling with people as Mother and another woman adjust costumes; two others I've never met arrive to get cosmetics done. One of them calls Everly over to draw her feathers, but is shocked to find that they're already painted on.

"Who did this?" His voice is somewhere between fury and awe.

Everly points to me. "Indigo."

The next position in Cat's Cradle flies from my mind. I can't think of anything else to do besides wave. If he doesn't like the feathers, he can take them off.

"Did you do these?" He gestures to the golden-yellow on Everly's face.

"I did."

His hard countenance softens, and he nods once. I hear him mumble something and call Cicely over.

After Alice and Atlas are done, they huddle around our game of Cat's Cradle.

"I don't understand how you know all the transitions," Alice says to me. "I always get stuck in the first five minutes."

"Indigo's learning the positions as I do them. I do it once and she remembers." Nora magically pulls one corner and the shape changes.

"Really?" Atlas looks from the string to my face. "How?"

"I don't know. I just… do it."

"You there."

All our heads snap up.

"The one who did the feathers." The man who was doing Cicely's cosmetics is pointing at me.

"Yes?"

"Come over here and let me show you something."

Slipping my hands from the string, I walk to the mirror. Arlo sits patiently in a chair while the cosmetic artist, Jacque, stands behind him.

"None of the clowns need any face paint besides the King. He is to be completely changed. He'll be entirely powdered, with black lips and black around the eyes, one side curving up, the other down." He looks at me, as if examining a pearl to see if it is genuine. "Do you think you can assist me?" Before that has time to sink in he adds quickly, "It goes faster with two and it's always good to have someone with fresh eyes."

The ink-coloured flourishes are by far the most problematic; each side has to be equidistant from Arlo's eyes with the same thickness and curvature.

Just as Arlo gets up, Mrs Trinter comes in to make sure everyone is ready. She starts when she sees Arlo. "Well, that certainly has the right effect."

When Arlo tells her that I helped, she comes over to me.

"You assisted Jacque with Arlo's face paint?"

"Yes, it was a bit difficult, and I think one of the sides is slightly off…"

She shushes me by taking one of my hands. "I think it looks wonderful, Indigo." She sees something in me. Some hesitation. "How are you feeling?"

"Keeping busy helps."

She gifts me one of her angelic smiles. "You'll do fine. We open the doors in a few minutes; try to relax. I'll be in the first row if there's an emergency. Your mother and Edgar will be back here the entire time." And then she's gone.

I struggle to take a deep breath, something seems to be squeezing my lungs. Nora taps my shoulder, holding up her string. We sit down. Atlas joins in. After what feels like only a few minutes, but is nearly half an hour, Mrs Trinter comes backstage again, announcing that the show will begin after Mr Trinter welcomes the guests. My stomach flips uncomfortably.

Nora rests a gentle hand on my shoulder. "It'll be fine."

My hands start shaking, so I grip the handle of my sabre. Even counting the passing seconds doesn't help.

"Don't let them frighten you." Atlas hasn't put on his mask, so I can still clearly see his eyes. "It's not as if Theodora's in the audience."

My smile is a contortion.

* * *

CICELY, a few others, and I move into the stage left passage as the curtain rises. A general gasp erupts from the audience, and I can't help smiling a bit.

The show I saw looked like a village, but this set is an enchanted forest. Enormous silk flowers hang upside down from the ceiling in gauzy shades of green, blue, red, pink, and purple. The occasional flower has a lightbulb in it, casting a mystical glow on the stage below. Directly in the centre stage is a heavy wooden banquet table set with plaster food, except one pie that's real. In front of the long table is a magnificently decorated arbour.

The background is made up of layers. The farthest one the audience can see is a large forest, painted by none other than Mr Trinter, with some help from his son Alexander. The painting is massive. Mr Trinter claims it took him twenty years to paint it (since the time he and Mrs Trinter came up with the idea for this show), and that it'll take another twenty for his hand to recover.

There are mushrooms as tall as me, made from layers of tea-coloured netting and wire, their stalks wrapped in muslin. Trees with clouds of trailing Spanish moss stand sentry by the waves of background. Flowers – modelled after poppies, though not quite the same – spread out across the front of the stage, a few with small lights inside.

The orchestra starts and Ms Martha, Alice's mother, dances out onto the stage. She's dressed as an elf, wearing a white tunic embroidered with dark green thread, and flat shoes embroidered with the same green. Her wig is silver, fashioned into a wide fishbone plait spun up into a bun on top of her head. Even though her hair is silver, her face is youthful, and I can picture her smiling at the forest around her.

Martha carries a massive book, weathered and bristling with ribbons. She takes her place under the arbour. Reaching down, she pulls a tiny loop, raising a podium made of twisted pipes painted to look like branches with vines encircling them. As if she didn't hear the audience's surprise, she places her book on the newly raised podium and flicks her hand to the orchestra, who abruptly change their music. This is the signal for the Sun King to come from stage right with his entourage. I was disappointed when I learned that Daniel was the Sun, as this would only encourage Olive, but he does fit the part rather well.

The Sun and his court are dressed in grandiose costumes. The King himself is fitted in a red brocade frock coat with gold ropes over the arm, a one-shoulder cape, and a crown with spikes rising from his head like the rays of the sun. His attendants are similarly dressed, but without crowns. His committee includes a personal guard, Marc, and a few members of his court. There are about ten in all, made up of the extras who typically work in Cirque du la Reine performances. They parade around for a bit as the crowd claps. Then Martha holds up her hand for silence, and gestures to the orchestra again.

The music becomes slower and more melodic. It's our turn. I wish Cicely would stall, that something would prevent us from going onto the stage, but when I look to my right she's calmly waiting for her cue.

Habit, ingrained by a thousand repetitions, pushes me to walk by Cicely's side as we step onto the stage. I am the Lunar Queen's personal guard, Cicely being the moon herself. She's arrayed in a dress with a bodice of black-and-silver brocade, long sleeves, and a full skirt topped by layers of sheer black-and-silver silk. A silver diadem disappears beneath her upswept hair. While Daniel looks like a young man in a brilliant costume, Cicely looks like a queen.

Because I'm dressed in all black, I'm a bit different from the rest of the court, who are wearing variations of Cicely's attire. Almost at once, we're halfway across the stage; Sun and Moon courts now stand opposite each other. The Elf, who is the marriage officiant, calls up the Sun and the Moon. Each takes their personal guard to stand by the edge of the arbour.

I try not to look at the hoard of people whose eyes are probably boring into me at this very moment. Why did I want this? Why did this seem so exciting?

Marc and I stand by our respective monarchs. The Elf looks to the Sun expectantly. He signals to a member of his court, who wheels out a giant birdcage. Inside is Everly in her canary costume. She slouches on a lyra hoop. The feathers on her face stand out beautifully, perfectly matching her leotard: bright yellow with fluttering imitation feathers. This is just the sort of gift the Sun would give.

Reaching into the cage, Daniel pretends to wind up the bird. After the third turn Everly straightens, beginning to mechanically perform on the hoop. It's incredible, even to me, someone who's seen it a thousand times. When she's finished, she sits in the centre of the hoop and droops once again. The audience claps uproariously.

The Elf holds out a hand to the Moon. Cicely whistles. Alice enters, walking on her hands. Black tights lead to a black leotard with a high neck and hood. She makes it to the centre of the stage, where she rolls out of the handstand and pops back up. To demonstrate what Alice is, the Queen summons another figure; this time it's Nora. Mr and Mrs Trinter chose Alice and Nora because of their almost-identical stature.

The second Alice sees Nora emerge, the Shadow positions herself beside the figure opposite the sun. Nora looks behind her shoulder, trying to see what stalks her. When she moves, Alice mirrors her. Nora curls over into a backbend. Her mimic does the same thing. After precisely three seconds the figure and her shadow stand in unison. But, in a flash, both the girl and the Shadow bend backward and kick over, rounding off by bouncing into a flip. I cross my fingers for them. This is one of the more difficult acts, and they've been practising relentlessly.

Nora and her Shadow cartwheel three times. On the fourth time they both stop midway in a handstand. Slowly, Alice is only a tiny bit faster than Nora, they curl their legs over and touch their toes to their heads.

They move through increasingly difficult stunts in perfect synchronicity until Nora gives up and spins around. Alice startles and flees to hide behind the Moon. The Queen gently pries the Shadow's hands away and bends to whisper in her ear. Alice jumps to attention and bows to the Sun.

With gifts exchanged, the wordless vows between the Sun and Moon begin. As the music morphs into a wedding theme, Louise and Thomas, the young son of one of the seasonal performers, bring the rings. Louise is dressed as part of the Sun's company, Thomas the Moon's. The rings are about to be exchanged when the stage lights flicker and go out. I hold my breath and count the seconds.

The audience murmurs and shuffles in the darkness. When the lights come back on a few seconds later, clowns are spread in a semicircle around the two courts and the Elf. They are fifteen in all. As part of my role, I push Thomas behind me and draw my sword in front of my Queen. Marc does the same for the Sun. The clowns stand in their half-masks, leering at us.

The lights keep flickering out, and each time, the clowns move closer. I brandish my weapon at them. Finally, under the cover of darkness, they draw black-and-white daggers. Marc and I rush forward to engage the enemy. The clowns begin to fight us back. Both courts draw swords and sprint into the fray. Out of the corner of my eye I see the Elf hand the book to the Shadow, who sprints off.

As the courtiers rally against their enemy, two clowns push over the arbour, pinning the Elf and catching one ambassador on the head. Using the distraction, the clowns press their advantage. Meanwhile, another villain, who slipped in after the battle started, opens the canary cage and carries out the bird. The King and Queen are herded into the empty cage. The twin courts rush the clowns as they attempt to cart off the monarchs. Some of the enemy fall, incapacitated by imaginary wounds, while others engage the courtiers.

The clown who snuck in from the side and opened the cage – and is now trying to take it away – is Atlas. I confront him as he unsheathes a sword. We exchange a few quick blows; he backs me up into the centre of the stage. I manage to parry his strikes. Just as he returns, I launch a riposte. He pushes back with a flurry of strikes. I am forced to take the higher ground on top of the banquet table. Atlas and I topple the counterfeit food everywhere with each lunge and parry.

My adversary eventually finds the *real* pie and flings it at my face. Even though it's planned, I still have some difficulty getting the pie to hit me just so. But as all the tips and instructions flash through my head, the pie lands squarely in my face.

The audience cheers and gasps. As I wipe cream and purple filling from my eyes, Atlas steps in and raises his sword to my throat. I stomp on his foot (not really, of course) and he hops off the table in agony. When his injured foot hits the floor, he returns to nursing it. I leap off, successfully completing a middle split in the air. On the floor we return to exchanging blows, Atlas hobbling slightly.

Meanwhile, the courtiers have been fending off the clowns, felling more and more of them. The Elf draws herself up from beneath the arbour and reaches into her tunic to throw a voluminous cloud of dust into the air. A thin, translucent curtain falls between us and the audience. For this brief moment, we are obscured from view. Atlas and I switch places. Inside my gloves, I flex my fingers, waiting for this strange interlude to pass.

When the dust finally settles, the curtain is drawn back up. Many of the clowns are disoriented, some lying on the floor, "dead". Those courtiers still standing stare dazedly at the battleground. All the fighting has stopped.

To the horror of the audience, the Clown King now descends between the upside-down flowers hanging from the rafters, sword at the ready. Before the Elf can turn to defend herself, she is cut down in one motion. Martha collapses to the ground, her body hidden by the arbour. After an initial gasp, the audience is silent. Arlo really does look frightening now that I'm not judging the curve of the face paint or a smudge in the powder. He summons all the remaining clowns. It takes a moment for the order to make it through the lingering effects of the dust, but slowly the clowns form a small crescent around their King.

Atlas, who was back-to-back with me in the confusion, whirls to place his sword against my neck. The crowned clown stalks over to the cage where Cicely and Daniel are still trapped. He tears open the door of the cage, causing the prisoners to flinch. Two clowns step in and haul out the monarchs.

The evil King forces them to kneel at the edge of the stage among the flowers. He holds his sword aloft. All eyes are drawn to the royals, so the shadow slipping from behind a mushroom goes unnoticed. Alice runs across the stage until she's right behind the Clown King. She raises the heavy tome that was clutched to her chest and strikes him in the head.

Atlas starts forward, but I thrust the pommel of my sabre just behind his ear. He crumples to his knees and then the floor.

The Clown King, hardly phased, turns on Alice. She raises the book in front of her face in a vain effort to deflect the blow she knows is coming. Sure enough, the tyrant raises his hand to strike her, but at the same time Marc lunges forward to cut the bonds of the Sun and Moon. Taking his vassal's sword, the Sun charges the Clown King, who has just enough time to parry.

As their swords meet, the lights inside the flowers in the air and on the stage grow brighter, inciting exclamations from the audience. Seeing their King fighting back gives the courtiers new courage and the clowns are pushed back. I glance around to see who's left. The rest of the clowns are either in confrontations or being pressed into the birdcage.

The Moon starts towards the two Kings. Before she can get far, I step into her path, kneeling to present my sword. The metal reflects the brightening lights among the petals above. Cicely lifts its lightweight frame from my hands and advances. The Clown King notices her just before she strikes and wheels to meet her sword with his. When their edges connect, all the flower lights go dark.

The evil King is now forced to take on two opponents from opposite sides. While he swings his blade out towards the Queen, sensing her the weaker of the two, the Sun jabs him in the back. Arlo arches in pain and lunges for the Sun, leaving Cicely a chance to strike the fatal blow. The tip of her sword disappears into his back and this time he looks down at his wound, stumbling into the table before collapsing, dead.

The remaining clowns throw down their knives and raise their hands, or flee into the trees and mushrooms. Ambassadors from each court lift the fallen usurper and carry him offstage. The others march their caged adversaries and dead bodies away as the Sun and Moon help to fashion a stretcher from the Sun's conveniently large cape. We gently lift the Elf onto the contraption.

A courtier has opened part of the ground – a trapdoor – with a shovel hidden behind a tree. We lower Ms Martha into the hole. The orchestra suddenly rests, creating a perfect moment of silence. Even the audience sits in hushed reverence. A single violin begins to play a haunting melody as the lights in the trees and the flowers overhead slowly brighten, casting a blazing light. This is one of my favourite parts, as it's an effect that's *more* wondrous from the stage. The lights look like fireflies gathering in the trees. Their glow paints the faces of everyone onstage.

Marc and I stand the arbour again as Alice presents a member of the Sun's court with the ancient book. The wedding theme returns, slower than before, as the Sun and Moon gather beneath the arch, hands clasped and heads bowed. The marriage is a solemn occasion instead of the joyous one it was supposed to be.

After a pause, Louise turns to Thomas and curtsies deeply, spreading out her skirt. He bows in turn and the orchestra launches into an ancient folk dance melody. At first only Louise and Thomas have the heart to dance, but then Marc and I join them. After a few more bars, the courtiers pair up and we all dance beneath the trees. As we change partners, the velvet curtains draw to a close.

The roar of the audience is deafening. Was it this loud at the show I attended?

As the curtain opens again, each court files to its respective side, the clowns in the middle, and all performers thank the audience with many bows. Louise was far off with her guess of five hundred. It must be well over a thousand.

It is a relief to have it over.

And I can't wait to do it again tomorrow.

* * *

BACKSTAGE, Nora helps me find a sink and washcloth to wipe away the cosmetics. The poor scrap of fabric is mottled with powder when I'm done. Closing the door behind me, I wind my way back to the others. Before I come around the last turn I hear the unmistakable melody of Leo and Poppy talking over each other.

"I'm Leo. What's your name?"

"You were amazing! Weren't you scared to do all those tricks?"

"Especially that flip. How did you learn to do that?"

"Is it difficult?"

"No. Well, yes. I..."

Poor Nora is fidgeting with the dark blue cuffs of her costume while Leo and Poppy wait expectantly for her answer.

I rescue her, "Poppy! Leo!"

At the sound of my voice, their heads turn. "Indigo!" they chorus, rushing toward me.

"How did you get back here?"

"Oh, Mrs Trinter told us where to go!" Poppy's eyes look even brighter than usual.

Leo appraises the sword at my hip. "That was incredible! You had excellent form on the table. I suppose you were using a sabre?"

I take it out and pry the tip back and forth. "Yes, but it's a bit more flexible than our usual kit – harder to get used to than I thought."

"We should fence again soon. Perhaps you'll have something to teach me."

I snort. "Don't be ridiculous."

Leo starts to refute me, but notices someone over my shoulder. "Atlas!"

"Leo? Poppy?" Atlas peels off his half-mask, spreading his hands wide. "What did you think of the show?"

"What did we think? What *could* we think? It was incredible!"

"Indigo, who's this?" Alice steps up, now changed into a blue dress. Over her arm rests a similar garment.

"Alice, this is Poppy and Leo. My friends."

She bobs her head. "I'm Alice."

"Pleasure to meet you. Who were you?" Poppy blinks, hearing how it must sound. "In the show?"

"I'm the Shadow."

Poppy gasps, giving Alice a start. "That was one of my favourite things! You were perfect!"

Alice puts a hand to her chest. "I'm glad you think so! I could have stuck a few of those landings better, but I'm glad it didn't show. Where's Nora?"

Leo frowns a bit guiltily. "I think we scared her by asking a lot of questions."

Alice looks around. "I do it all the time. I have her dress, I need to give it to her."

"She went off down that hallway." Atlas points to the direction of the female dressing rooms.

Alice sighs. "I have to go find her. It was nice meeting you Poppy and Leo."

"Nice to make your acquaintance," they both return.

Leo can't decide whether to look at Atlas or me. "I heard about Mrs Thwite's house…"

"Ah." I look at Atlas.

"Pretty much everyone's heard by now." Poppy shivers. "Did she really just disappear?"

Atlas's brows draw slightly together. "Looks that way."

Arlo walks by, getting the last of the black face paint off. Leo waits until he's passed to say, "Have you thought of trying to search her house again?"

I don't have to look at Atlas to guess his expression.

"Only about a million times," I huff.

Atlas throws his hands up. "I can hardly get her to stop talking about it."

"I don't talk about it *all* the time."

He nods with eyes closed. "You're right. Only the vast majority."

I turn on the heel of my boot. "We did it with Walker's house. We can do it again."

"We'll get caught if we do it now. Wait a few months and things will quiet down. At Walker's house we were unrecognisable. Now, as Poppy pointed out, everyone knows what happened. If we go anywhere near that house, we'll be spotted. And then we'll have to wait even longer."

Poppy is trying to find some place to look without appearing to be escaping the conversation, while Leo watches our debate intently. "I think he's right, Indigo."

One corner of my mouth pulls down. Of course Atlas is right. We can't lose our only chance to try it, but why, oh why, does time have to take so long to pass? At least the show will take my mind off things for a bit.

"Indigo?" Mother leads Father through the backstage door.

I step away from the group. "I'm here."

Mother wraps me in her arms, kissing my brow. "Excellent job, Indigo!"

"Very well done," Father echoes, laying a hand on my shoulder.

I scour his expression for any of the disapproval he expressed at my wearing pants, or his general hesitance about having me on stage at all, but I find no trace.

"I'm so proud of you," he says, just loud enough for me to hear.

"Th-thank you." I give him a sudden hug. He steps back from the force of it. After a few seconds he gently pats my shoulder and extricates himself from my embrace.

"Phoebe's here as well," he steps aside.

Sure enough, there, in her best dress, is Phoebe. She's ready for my embrace when it comes.

"You didn't think I would miss your debut performance, did you?" She laughs richly, the sound rolling from her.

"Well, no…"

She tucks my head under her chin. "Good. You were incredible, Indigo."

"Thanks."

"I love you."

"I love you too."

* * *

AFTER GETTING BACK TO 416, bathing, and changing back into my charcoal dress, I go to look out a window in the drawing room. The quiet is nice after so much noise, so much nervous energy. The moon is bright and I watch it for a while.

Soon a voice comes from behind me. "Incredible show tonight. Do you see now why you don't have to be nervous?"

"I think I do. Excellent pie-throwing."

"Why, thank you!"

Atlas joins me at the window. The view is dark, except for

the ever-present glow of the streetlamps. It makes me think of the night we infiltrated the abandoned mansion.

Atlas moves a few inches closer, looking at me. "We are going to find her."

"I know, I know," I sigh. "Do you want to reread the letter from Gabriel in the morning?"

"No!" The dark brings out his eyes as they widen. "I'm sure you've already memorised it. And don't forget we have another show tomorrow."

"Another time, then."

We stand there, staring out over our city in silence. Our next steps are clear.

Theodora won't hide long. She's running out of time.

EPILOGUE

Theodora sits in her plush seat, refusing to clap. It was a good show, one of the best she's seen, but she won't clap. She watches as Indigo steps forward to bow. She's next to a boy who isn't Atlas. She can't pick *him* out, but she's sure he's there – perhaps one of the clowns? Theodora's hands clench the playbill. The paper is crushed between her fists, tearing in two.

She takes a shaky breath, letting the pamphlet fall to the floor. She hopes never to see Indigo and Atlas again. But that's a foolish wish. This is not the end. And they're running out of time before her plan is set into motion.

She stands abruptly and sweeps down a flight of stairs towards the exit. A man in a red-and-teal suit holds out her mantle. "Thank you for joining us tonight, Ms Lizborn."

She nods, giving a gracious smile and wrapping the folds of the garment tightly around her. With only a few more steps, Theodora walks out the ornate double doors, disappearing into the night.

THE END

ACKNOWLEDGMENTS

The book you just finished took a winding route to get here, but it began very simply. I've always had trouble falling asleep. One night, while staring at the dark ceiling, the idea came to me, "One of my favorite authors should write a murder mystery with circus, featuring a character like the one in my head."

My next thought was, "That's never going to happen."

Then, a small voice piped up from the back of my mind, "Why don't I write it?"

The next day, December fourteenth of 2019, I started *The Second Nature of Indigo*. I didn't talk about my book for days. I told myself it'd be my secret project; destined to grow dusty beneath my bed.

After the first few chapters (I didn't write the prologue until after the first draft) the under-the-bed idea was beginning to seem untenable, my excitement was overflowing. When I asked my family if they wanted to read it they were enthusiastic. For the next three months, I spent blissful hours each day typing as fast as my fingers would go (which was NOT fast at the time). At night, I'd read the day's efforts to my family.

I made up the story pretty much as I wrote it, with few exceptions. This led to an unbelievable amount of plot holes and, because I rarely went back over my writing, even more typos.

And still, my family cheered me on. So, the first people I'd like to thank are them: Mom, Dad, Hank, and Ella.

I spent three months writing that first draft of seventy

thousand words. The next two years were spent reshaping, ripping apart, revising, adding to, and polishing.

Some amazing people helped with this process. Firstly, Mike Roy and Eileen Chevalier who helped with plot, writing style and a million things in between. I was also fortunate to have Roisin Heycock as my developmental editor, and the fabulous Claire Bradshaw as my line editor. I loved working with both of them. They understood my characters, the time period, and setting, providing their insight and knowledge. I could never neglect my cover artists, Eileen Chevalier and Mike Roy. Really, everyone at Knight King Press made me feel like family and that made all the difference when slogging through edits.

Alas, there are a few people I haven't thanked yet; Jack and all the beta readers, whose feedback was super helpful. And finally thank *you* for reading. It's an incredible privilege to share this with you. Indigo and Atlas's story is far from over, and hopefully you love them just as much as I do.

Until next time,

    —Æ